"An honest, compelling page-turner...a thought provoking read from an author with an experienced hand and an incredible depth of understanding for what women can experience in a man's world."

—Stella Harvey, Author of *Finding Callidora* and Founder of Whistler Writers Festival

"With vivid prose and a heroine to root for, *Brooklyn Thomas Isn't Here* is a clever take on the ways women change shape to fit into society. Part existential study and part feminist rally cry, Alli Vail's incisive debut is a reminder that it is never too late for a second chance at life."

—Holly James, Author of *Nothing but the Truth*

"In *Brooklyn Thomas Isn't Here*, the unreal becomes real and the surreal works in a donut shop. This thought-provoking story about a woman who exhibits key signs of being dead while she struggles to find whatever it is that makes life worth living is a twisted tale about fitting in, speaking up, grief, love and obsession. Alli Vail is definitely here, and she's a fiercely imaginative new voice in Canadian fiction."

—Katherine Fawcett, Author of *The Swan Suit* and *The Little Washer of Sorrows*

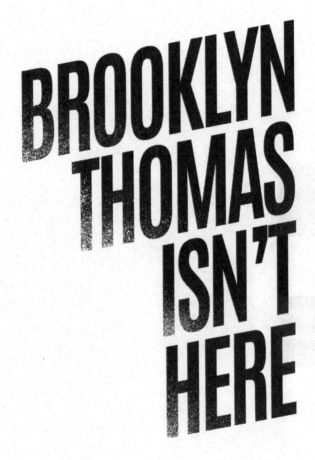

ALLI VAIL

BROOKLYN THOMAS ISN'T HERE

A NOVEL

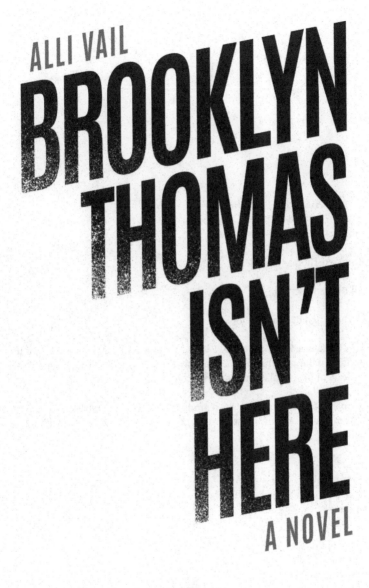

POST HILL
PRESS

A POST HILL PRESS BOOK
ISBN: 979-8-88845-289-9
ISBN (eBook): 979-8-88845-290-5

Brooklyn Thomas Isn't Here
© 2024 by Alli Vail
All Rights Reserved

Cover design by Jim Villaflores

Post Hill Press
New York • Nashville
posthillpress.com

Published in the United States of America
1 2 3 4 5 6 7 8 9 10

For Crystal, the most resilient and bright-hearted woman I know.

JUNE

PROLOGUE

If there were warning signs, I missed them. I didn't notice my heart becoming sluggish, didn't realize that, from its cozy spot beneath my left ribs, it was only tepidly thump-thumping. Maybe it slowed to stillness over days or weeks or months. Years. The exact progression is speculation. I wasn't paying attention. There's a reason we slowly turn up the heat on the proverbial frog in the pot. Same logic applies, I guess, to a heart.

Before it stuttered and stopped, I would have confidently said there was no way I could hear or feel my heart beating inside. I probably could have rattled off a litany of medical facts pulled from social media and quasi-scientific TED Talks about the impossibility of sensing the daily functions of one's own heart.

But when it's not beating? That's a whole other thing. On the first day of summer, I woke up to complete silence. The faint echo where the pillow cupped my ear like a seashell and captured the throb of my beating heart was gone.

Nothing moved inside my chest. Still half-dreaming and groggy, I pressed my fingertips against my wrist. Zip. I woke up in a frantic instant. I checked. Checked again. I flew out of bed and dug a heart-rate monitor—last used eight months ago when I still ran obsessively—from a desk drawer. Once I was outside, my body remembered hill sprint patterns even though it lacked the required fitness to finish them. The fitness watch stayed at zero while I threw up from exertion on my neighbor's lawn.

I was sure I was dead.

No one else noticed. Not then. Not later. Not my mother, who assumes with a mother's single-mindedness that she sees and hears everything. Not my father, who's concerned with the structural integrity of bridges, not people. Not my coworkers, who only notice adorable customers in the latest jeans carrying books or guitars. Not my friends, because they've moved on in the big, wide world.

The morning I woke up and realized my heartbeat was gone, I did what anyone would do. I went to work.

JULY

CHAPTER 1

Cute Lil' Doughnuterie's front door is swollen shut. Again. The wood, covered in a chipping, municipal government–approved heritage paint color, swells, sweats, and sticks to the door frame anytime the temperature jumps over eighty-two degrees Fahrenheit. I jam my key into the lock, wiggle it, and then use both hands and my shoulder to drive the protesting door inward as I twist the antique metal doorknob. Two good hits usually does it.

I've been complaining about the door to Matt, and he's been ignoring me, since he hired me back in April. I think he knows, on some deeply buried level, that I'm not the glowing twenty-two I said I was to get this job. At twenty-nine, I'm well over his threshold for attention. We're too close in age. Still, I've been trusted with a key to this fucking front door and the accompanying opening shift. I like it; before 7 a.m., there's no one to keep me company except the odd neighborhood resident rattling by with a shopping cart filled with all his worldly goods.

This morning, thanks to the humidity, I'm forced to shoulder-check the door a third time. It squeals. I prop it open with a rock painted to resemble a doughnut. We have Matt's ex to thank for the kindergarten-level quality art. The ex-girlfriend before the most recent ex-girlfriend.

I neatly tuck the cash into the till drawer, stock the display counter with doughnuts that were delivered from the baking location sometime earlier this morning, and flick the neon sign against the window to "Open." The sign is locally made by one of Matt's buddies, this one an "artisanal sign-maker," and it's also the shape of a doughnut.

I make two espressos and neglect to note them on the staff meal sheet. I pour one into a paper cup loaded with sugar and milk and grab a bag of day-olds from the fridge. Keeping the door to the shop in view, I cross the street and leave the snack outside a ratty, faded blue tent sitting at the edge of a park. I've never seen the person in the tent—the angle of the sun into the doughnut shop or the crowds lined up outside the window normally hides the view of the park. The coffee cup and doughnut bag are always gone, along with the tent, by the time my shift ends.

Back inside, I reflexively press my fingertips into my neck, a nervous habit I've managed to craft and perfect in only a few days. I've had time to get used to the idea that my heartbeat is absent—gotten used to falling asleep not sure I'll wake up. But I do. It surprises me every time, although surprise is turning into the more familiar feeling of ambivalence. It's been over a week. Canada Day has come and gone, along with all the red-frosted strawberry-banana-flavored doughnuts decorated with white vanilla bean stripes.

Nothing. Stillness. My prying hands fall back into my lap. I wait. This location, outside of Vancouver's main commercial and financial areas, means we don't get a crowd until people start heading into their offices, several Skytrain stops away. With no orders for pick-up to prep, I feel entitled to sit.

I flick through headlines on my phone, avoiding local news and focusing on overseas coverage from Syria. The news isn't good—activists killed, bombs dropped, people starving, the country fed by violence and political posturing. Even the past is being wiped away, ancient structures gone in a burst of light and sound. I wish my own past could be erased so quickly, as much as it distresses me to see the destruction of history a world away.

Syria. It's where Penny Parker, my best friend, vanished. She was—is—an international aid worker. Syria swallowed her one night last August and hasn't given her back.

I read the headlines every day, searching for the one I want to see more than I've ever wanted anything, the one that reads "Missing Canadian Nurse Found Alive After 11 Months." I refuse to believe she won't come back. Penny, who saves lives while I unload day-olds onto a squatter in the park.

Outside, the sky brightens to cerulean, and out of the corner of my eye I see a short woman with blonde hair flit briskly past the front window. I paste on a semblance of a smile and wait for my first customer, but the front doorway remains empty. Minutes later, Kailey bounces in.

"Brooklyn! I had the best class this morning. Come to yoga with me this week. No more excuses." It's quarter after eight, early for her, even considering her shift started at 8 a.m.

"You know me. I don't do yoga." Or jog, or do Pilates, or hike, or loiter on bar patios on sunny Vancouver evenings. Not anymore. Not for months. I was exhausted, emotionally and physically run down about Penny—about life—even before I noticed that my heart quit on me. Now I can barely muster the energy to drag myself to work and fling carbohydrates at customers.

Kailey is only a few inches shorter than me, but leggy and almost naturally red-haired, although she denies her stylist has anything to do with the color. She stands like she's balancing a yoga block on her head. Sometimes, I imagine there's an actual divot between her shoulder blades where her lime-green yoga mat snaps into place. I've never seen her coming or going without it.

She dumps her stuff in the back, talking the whole time. It's easier to let her. She doesn't seem to notice my silence. She asks me a question, and I jam a new doughnut flavor in my mouth so I don't have to answer. Peachy Keen. Sickly sweet, filled with peach compote and drenched in iced tea–flavored frosting. The tourists are going to die. By die, I mean line up out the door for more than an hour's wait just to taste it. Some weekends, the line wraps around the block, forcing the tourists and foodies with fancy phones to compete for sidewalk space with the unhoused people who live and sleep outside. There haven't been any quiet weekends since some Portland food blogger raved about the place online. Her post led to an article in the *New York Times* food column, which led to mayhem for those of us stuck behind the counter. Everyone who works at Cute Lil' has had to learn how to kindly crush the dreams of wannabe Insta-famous food connoisseurs because we usually run out of new flavors well before closing. Matt believes that scarcity will improve demand. He's not around to deal with the fallout and has never been yelled at by someone who drove in from the suburbs—or Seattle—to try the hottest new treat only to be told it wasn't available.

"There's a note for you," Kailey says as she bounds over to the front counter, holding a piece of paper between two long fingers. "From Matt."

"Brooklyn," she reads theatrically, "Can you edit the press release about our summer flavors and then send it to your contacts? The cool online pubs, social media influencers. No newspapers."

He signed the note with an oversized *M* with a slash underneath it.

"He could have asked nicely," Kailey says. "You have a fucking PR degree."

"Bachelor of communications," I correct automatically, used to clarifying my education for people. Used to explaining to clients at the expensive, boutique marketing firm I previously worked at that yes, I have the experience to do my job and that no, I'm not the boss's assistant.

"Come on, Kailey. Why would he ask nicely? He's got those amazing abs. They mean he doesn't have to ask for anything."

"Consent joke. Funny." She rolls her eyes.

Kailey is the only other employee who is not in love with Matt. Everyone who works here is female, thin, or curvy in the "right" way, and under twenty-two. Except me. I stew about this blatant display of sexism, about Matt's conviction that only pretty young women can sell doughnuts, and welcome a hot rush of anger. The heat is invigorating after a constant state of listlessness.

But what can I do about Matt's hiring practices? Nothing, I realize, my anger dissipating and leaving me deflated. Matt is incapable of being serious, except about doughnuts and his hair. And his abs.

"Do I look okay to you?" I ask, needing reassurance from someone, anyone, that I'm perfectly healthy. That despite evidence to the contrary, I'm not actually dead. This morning in the mirror I was pale, and a little blurry around the edges. Expensive eye drops swiped from my mother's medicine cabinet hadn't cleared up my reflection.

Kailey looks at me critically. "You look the same as you always do. I don't know why you always wear a white T-shirt and that black skirt, though. Washes you out. You could try some color. But you do you. Or whatever."

"I don't look sick?"

"Why? You got your period? I think I've got some painkillers. Heavy duty ones. Or you want something stronger? It's a bit early but..."

"No. Definitely no. Forget it."

Kailey is sweet and outgoing—not someone to confide in. She's a perky stranger, despite our mutual culinary prison. Our conversations are as fluffy as the doughnuts we serve. Besides, I've never been good at sharing with anyone except Penny, and even Penny and I had our limits. I'd always been envious of close, tell-all friendships between women. It looked so easy on television, the way besties were knit together with each other's secrets.

"Oh my God." Kailey's fingers wrap around my wrist and her royal-blue gel nails bite sharply into my skin. "Guess who?"

Henry Cavill walks in the door. At least, a close enough approximation of the actor. A thinner, less meaty version. Right down to the slight dimple in his chin. We'd already started calling him Henry Cavill when we found out his name is, in fact, Henry. "Besotted" is the fancy, BA-in-communications word I'd use to describe how I feel about him. It's ridiculous. I know nothing about this handsome man, except that he likes his coffee with a splash of milk and he will order whatever doughnut we recommend. He always looks happy to see us. Not me. Us, I remind myself. His smile is real and his eyes crinkle in the corners.

"Brooklyn, Kailey. Good weekend?" He remembers all our names.

"Super good," I lie. I spent the entire time I wasn't at work alternating between lying on the floor hyperventilating about my missing heartbeat and watching Netflix on my laptop. I was too afraid of what I'd find out if I Googled my heart issues and stuck with familiar reruns of *This High-School Life*, which I'd watched compulsively as a preteen. I have nothing to add to Henry's inquiry, so Kailey jumps in with an anecdote about a friend who fell into a nearby lake and was pulled out by his dog. She even takes out her phone and pulls up a video of the incident, while I mutely look anywhere except directly at Henry. Kailey has tried to befriend Henry on my behalf since she saw me drop a Blueberry Crumble Chai doughnut on the floor the first time he came in. Half a cup of coffee joined the doughnut. She'd harassed me for days to admit that he was adorable, but so far I've resisted the urge to fawn over the way his nose crinkles when he grins. Out loud, anyway.

My crush is real, even if it isn't followed by an increase in heart rate. The rest of the symptoms are there—the urge to fidget and to giggle hysterically at the ordinary, unfunny words coming out of Henry's mouth. I've never devolved quite so much over a man before.

I'm also never more aware of my job status and how it's deteriorated than when Henry comes in, sharply dressed and friendly. I used to have invites to exclusive events, big international brands as clients, a discretionary budget for expenses, a travel allowance, staff to delegate to, stylish clothes, and a professional aura validated by high-quality business cards and a fancy job title. Marketing and communications director. The title barely fit on the card.

When Henry stops by, I mentally make excuses for this new unmotivated and unimproved Brooklyn, who's wearing scuffed runners, a T-shirt, and a dour expression. I long for my designer dresses, my flat iron–crafted beachy waves, my three-inch high heels, my pre–doughnut consumption body weight, and the confidence borne from success. When Henry isn't around, I don't have the enthusiasm to care about those things. But his presence is a reminder of who I used to be.

That Brooklyn and Henry would have had something in common. Here, I put a doughnut in a tiny paper bag and a coffee in a compostable cup and he goes off to do whatever it is he does downtown, in an office building with an ocean or mountain view. At least, that's what I assume. I have no idea where Henry works, having never gotten past asking him what doughnut he wants and gaping at him silently. Given my nonverbal performance around him, it's mystifying to think I used to get paid to say exactly the right thing when six- or seven-figure budgets were on the line. I can't fathom the amount of liveliness that Brooklyn had.

"Busy morning?" Henry asks, while waiting for his coffee. Kailey is dragging her feet. I catch her spilling an Americano back into the waste tray.

"Pretty quiet. It'll pick up later, when the cruise ships come in. The Gastown location will send overflow this way."

Could I be more pedantic?

He grins at me, apparently comfortable making benign chit-chat while I cringe inwardly.

He snaps his fingers. "I just remembered. I need a dozen for pick-up next week. It's our accountant's birthday, and this is her favorite doughnut place. I can't believe I almost forgot. Heads would have rolled. Probably mine." He crinkles at me again.

"Sure," I mumble, pulling the order pad off a shelf under the till. "What do you want?"

"You pick," he says, leaning toward me conspiratorially, his eyes practically sparkling. I draw a sharp breath. He smells like laundry detergent and a freshly peeled orange. "Make them all different. Nothing powdered. Sugar everywhere. No one eats those."

"We don't do powdered," I say. I try to smile charmingly. I try to be cute. My lips stretch with the effort.

"Perfect," he says, flashing his white teeth and deepening his dimples. Somehow, he's not affronted by the fact that my lips are tight against my teeth like the grimacing emoji.

He picks up his coffee and doughnut, says goodbye, and steps out into the beautiful, gleaming morning. Then, he walks past the storefront window and is gone.

"You're terrible at this," Kailey says, interrupting my ruminations, which have followed Henry down the street in some vague fantasy of him cooking dinner for me while I curl up with a glass of wine and a book.

"At what?"

"Talking to Henry," she says.

"Why would he want to talk to me? He wants his doughnut and his coffee. I'm office furniture. Doughnut shop furniture," I amend.

"He wants to talk to you because you're cute. You have this whole smart-and-sassy vibe when you're not grumpy, which, admittedly is most of the time. And you have sexy eyebrows and big, blue cartoon eyes. And a nice ass." She reaches over and slaps it firmly enough that I jump.

"You're wrong," I say.

"He came in on Friday and made a quick retreat when he realized you weren't here. When you're not working, he doesn't hang around," Kailey says. "Barely says a word. He talks to you. He's trying to get you to talk back."

I shoot her a skeptical look. "I'm sure he's just being nice. He seems…nice." He seems perfect. His dimples certainly are.

"You're ridiculous. Go for it. Go for him."

"You don't understand," I mumble. No heartbeat. No interesting career prospects. No friends. No hobbies. No ability to function like a responsible adult. I had to move back in with my parents for God's sake. I'm an emotional disaster. My hermitting skills, however, are razor sharp.

"I do understand. You think you're above all this doughnut shit because you had a *real job*." Kailey uses air quotes. "You always act like working here is beneath you, or like we're all a little worthless. Watch it, or Matt is going to fire your ass for acting all superior. You think he can't tell that you hate him? That you hate all of us?"

"I don't hate you," I say, because it's the truth. Whatever I feel is complicated and messy and tinged with jealousy, yes. But it's not hate.

"You're lucky no one else wants the morning shift, or you'd be done," Kailey says, flicking her loose hair over her shoulder. She's the only one who refuses to wear the mandatory high ponytail. Matt doesn't care. He's blinded by her fiery glow.

We've had this conversation before. She always gets over it. I wouldn't. I'd be disgusted with myself and my bad attitude and my snide remarks. I would write me off as hostile. But by the end of our shift, she'll have her arm around me and be trying to convince me to come to yoga with her. Kailey would feel bad for even thinking I'm hostile.

Mostly, our interactions make me feel like I'm missing some necessary piece of programming that connects me with other women, especially women like Kailey who are genuinely kind and caring. Kailey is twenty-one, almost certified to be a yoga instructor, and in September she's going to university for a BA, followed by an art therapy diploma. Kailey has a plan. I can't plan tomorrow. My plans have shattered around my Puma sneakers and I have no idea how to put them back together. I don't even know if I want to.

Kailey handles the customers, directing goodwill toward them and irritation toward me, while I pull shots of espresso.

"Fine," I say, after working in silence and tired of Kailey boring holes into the back of my head. "You're right. Henry is adorable. I think he is a sexy, gorgeous man with excellent taste in dress shirts and if things were different"—*if I were different*—"I'd go for him. Whatever that means." All true, except the part about going for him, and she doesn't need to know that. I cross my arms over my chest and glare at her.

"Knew it!" Kailey crows, fist pumping. "Yes you do!"

Of course she knew. Last time, during Henry's coffee pickup, I'd stood there holding a tub of lemon custard frosting, the tips of my fingers dipped into the cold, clammy lemonyness while staring in the direction he'd left for an uncomfortably long time. I'd gone to throw out the contaminated filling, and Kailey had pried it out of my hands before I could. She'd methodically scraped the top two inches off, her shoulders shaking with laughter, before putting the container back in the fridge.

In between waves of sugar-starved workers, I plug away at Matt's press release on the laptop he keeps in the tiny staff room at the back of the store. The press release is filled with adverbs and adjectives. I cut them out, knowing he's going to put them back in the second he reads my changes. I send it off to a few publications, influencers, and bloggers who I still have good relationships with. I send it to Matt too, because I know he wants to make sure I did what he asked.

"Some help?" Kailey calls. I close the laptop and stuff it under a pile receipts Matt keeps for this purpose. He says the mess will distract would-be thieves. No safe, just crumpled paper to protect the computer.

"Coming!" I yell back. Given the rumble at the front of the shop, it's once again packed. I sigh outwardly and loudly. Sure, a busy day makes it go faster, but it means talking. So much talking. I rub my chest and sigh again. At this point, there's no reason to think my heart is suddenly going to start revving again.

Then things get worse. So much worse that there is a roaring in my ears and my fingers start to tingle. Within seconds the tingle spreads up my arms.

Kyle hasn't changed. I spot him three customers back in the line that spills out the doorway. His face hasn't changed from age or weight gain, although his hair is shorter and his clothes fit better. I wish I was unrecognizable, buried in years or plastic surgery. But no. I still look like me, even though I feel less me than ever.

"No," I whisper. "Anyone else." Panicked, I scan the room for an exit, or someone, anyone, who can help. Kailey catches my eye and whatever's on my face causes her mouth to tighten, but her hands are full of Coconut-Maraschino Cherry Dumpling doughnuts, and even if they weren't, there's nothing she could do.

Kyle is the last person I'd ever want to see me working behind the counter of a doughnut shop, no matter how trendy it is. It's devastating, worse than when Henry comes in because Henry is a stranger, one whose only hold on me is his overall hotness. I numbly help serve a customer at one till while Kailey handles the other.

"Brookie," Kyle says, smiling, when he's standing in front of me. The smile doesn't reach his hazel eyes, which captured my attention and my wrath in university. He couldn't have known I worked here. This must be an accident. Please. An accident.

"Kyle." I try and fail to sound friendly and nonchalant, as if I'm thrilled to be standing behind a counter ready to serve him a tequila sunrise in gluten form.

"I heard you were at Lawrence Communications," he says, craning his neck to look past me, as if there's some sort of explanation at the coffee station that would explain my presence in this blazingly hot café. He refocuses on me, looking for some weakness that allowed him to surpass me without any effort on his part.

"I was."

He raises his eyebrows and a corner of his mouth. Something strange—maybe the way his mouth asks a question without him saying a word—tricks people into answering when they intend to remain silent.

"I quit," I blurt.

"Why?"

"Long story." I don't want to say anything else.

"A doughnut shop?"

"For now." I seal my lips firmly.

"You'll find something else."

"Of course."

Fraught silence builds between us while the lineup grumbles. I haven't seen Kyle since I cut off all contact, right after graduation. I despise how we slip right back into our speech patterns. We were never good at talking. We were incredible at arguing.

"I'm working at a PR agency that does crisis management," he says. He tells me the name and I promptly forget it. I'm sweaty and anxious and stupid.

"That's great," I say, trying to blot my forehead with the back of my hand without him noticing.

"Brookie. This is crazy. I can't believe you're working here. What happened to you?" He wears faux concern like a mask—as if I haven't seen it before, used against someone else before he went in for the kill. As if it didn't used to thrill me, the way he could find someone's exposed belly and gut them before they ever realized he was close.

"It didn't work out."

"You cracked, huh?"

I cracked.

"I didn't crack. I needed a break."

"Sure." He looks at me for a long time. My entire being is screaming at him to leave, but I can't find the words to ask him to. I could. I should. People are waiting, crankily. I can ask him to leave. The words stick in my mouth. He leans on the counter and seems to hear the muffled discontent behind him.

"I'll take a Lemon Cup Custard Frosting," he says, and I almost bark with laughter, remembering my fingers in the container. Instead, I dutifully collect his order.

"You know, now that I think about it, I did hear something about you leaving Lawrence Communications while I was at an awards dinner. I didn't believe it, of course. The Brooklyn I know wouldn't just quit, not when she worked so hard to claw her way to the top."

Fuck. Kyle had known I was here. He'd come looking. After all this time, he hadn't gotten over the fact I got a job first. Or that I'd graduated at the top of our class, him trailing behind me. Or that I'd walked away from him without a second thought. I'm not sure who was more surprised that I'd managed to shake off his thrall.

"Somebody mentioned you wrecked some big accounts and got fired."

"Not true," I grind out. I need Kailey to rescue me, but despite her frenetic activity to my left, the line isn't getting any shorter. I catch her eye again and she shrugs helplessly before turning an icy gaze on Kyle, which he breezily ignores.

Kyle's proximity is making my stomach roil. He's not a big guy—only a few inches taller than me, and slim. Nonetheless, I shift away from the counter, sinking my weight into my heels for the few extra inches it will put between us. It's hard to breathe; my lungs are flat and airless. *Threat*, my body screams.

A slow grin creeps onto Kyle's face and he casually crosses his arms. This is his moment of triumph, which he doesn't deserve and which I can't fathom being needed after all this time.

"The guy seemed pretty confident. You should've reached out. I would have been happy to help find you another job."

"I'm good. Thanks, though."

I step around the counter and hand Kyle his order, stretching my arm as far as possible to keep space between us. But he closes the gap and puts his arm around me to squeeze my shoulders.

I'm trapped against his chest. My flesh crawls under the weight of his limb and my knees quake. There's something on Kyle's face, something dark and familiar.

"Things will get better," he says. Smugness oozes from his Gucci loafers to collar of his mint-green Lacoste polo.

He leaves and my lungs fill with air and relief. Somehow, I manage to help Kailey with the remaining customers even though the tingling in my hands has spread up my arms, and from my toes up to my knees.

"Who was that?" Kailey asks when the last customer has drifted away from the counter. She hovers next to me, her hand outstretched like she wants to put it on my shoulder but isn't sure she should.

Moisture beads on my forehead, and if I could get my hands to function normally, instead of being locked into claws, I would blot it with a napkin. I settle for swiping at my face with my forearm.

Answering feels impossible. That's Kyle. We went to university together. We dated.

But that's not the question she's asking.

She wants to know who made me sweaty, shaky, and desperate for her help.

I inhale and open my mouth. Close it again.

"He seemed like an asshole."

"Yes," I spit out.

She frowns harder.

"Old…boyfriend," I manage to say, rubbing my hands together, trying to get the tingling to dissipate and my hands to flatten out from their T. rex curl.

"You? And that guy? Can't see it. He's a creep."

I try to swallow but don't have any saliva, and my throat sticks closed.

"Oh Brooklyn," she says, gently, so kindly, as if she heard every word I didn't say.

As if she'd heard that I'd slept with him, and kept sleeping with him, even when he sabotaged my projects or trash-talked one of our classmates. How I'd given back as good as I got. How one time I'd shredded his paper so it would be late and I would get a higher mark. How on the rare occasions I bested him, he would be furious but impressed, like I was a good little protégée. Our behavior had escalated in our efforts to outperform each other and I'd *let* it, because it made me feel strong and in control, even though now it's clear we were out of control. I was high on being unafraid for the first time in my life. Now, though, I'm ashamed of who I was with Kyle.

Back then, Penny had let me have it. Told me I was acting like a narcissistic maniac, that I was going to hurt myself or someone else. After she did, all I could think was how I didn't want to be like Kyle. Or someone worse.

Kailey keeps staring.

"Bad breakup?"

"The breakup was fine," I say. "The relationship was… problematic."

I'm gripped with the urge to blurt out everything that's gone wrong in my life. Penny. My career. My family. My heartbeat—or lack thereof. I bite my lip so I don't spew anything that will make me seem more bonkers. Telling the truth did nothing in the past. There's no reason to think it will make a difference now. Instead, I stagger to the counter and reach for an empty glass from the shelf. I fill it from the tap and drink it in one go. The cold water steadies me and I stuff the memories down.

Kailey seems to be waiting for more, but I hold my silence.

"We all date the wrong guy at some point," she says after a long pause.

"It was a long time ago," I say. "I learned my lesson. No more assholes." I try to smile, but my lips stick on my teeth and my mouth is still dry despite the water I just downed.

"Which is why Henry is perfect for you." She stretches the vowels and grins like a cherub.

Later that morning, Becca comes into Cute Lil' Doughnuterie wearing a red and black long-sleeved flannel, sleeves rolled up, tucked into a ratty blue denim miniskirt with buttons in a row down the front. She's topped with a commercially produced knitted beret pulled so far up her head a slight summer breeze would send it tumbling.

"Seriously Becca? It's nearly ninety degrees out," Kailey says.

"I'm freezing," objects Becca.

I believe her. She's skin stretched over bone. She doesn't eat anything in the shop. She doesn't eat—period. Meanwhile, I spend every day at work mechanically consuming doughnuts, even when I'm not hungry. Sugar is the only thing that gives me a jolt these days. Aside from Henry, who is so none of my business.

When I worked in marketing, I barely ate. Who had time? I made excuses, like I needed my clothes to fit, or that hunger gave me an edge, forced me to keep moving, forced me to drink water to fill the gaping hole in my stomach. I was trying to take up less space, or fit in the one that had been carved for me by the mostly male colleagues at the firm. The resulting thinness didn't make me any happier, or make life any easier. I was just hungrier. Is it ever our idea, that thinness is essential? Becca had gotten the message, no matter the source.

"Is Matt in?" Becca asks, craning her neck to see down the hallway that leads to the microscopic staff room.

"Later, maybe," Kailey says. "Why do you care anyway?" She chucks an apron at Becca.

Becca says nothing, but she wraps the apron around her teeny waist and wears a tiny, secret smile.

Matt doesn't care how we dress as long as we wear our aprons, which of course no one does unless they know he's going to make an appearance. My apron is stuffed behind the stacks of extra coffee mugs.

Becca perches on a stool behind the counter and flicks through her phone while I dig the store laptop out from under the papers in the office and carry it to the storefront so I can help with the inevitable afternoon rush. As expected, Matt has already heavily reedited the release with indecipherable tracked comments in the margins of the Word doc.

"What do you think 'communicate flavor' means?" I ask Kailey. She peers over my shoulder and her chest rises and falls against my back. There's a heartbeat underneath it. It seems to thunder through me.

Great. Now I'm envious of Kailey's bodily functions, on top of her career plans.

"It says the flavor right there. Maple sugar with anise, or whatever." She touches the screen and leaves a smear of pink icing behind. I wipe at it.

"I know what it says. What does he mean?"

"It means you need to, like, make people taste it. Show not tell." This insightful comment comes from Becca, who will be starting year one of a two-year marketing program at one of the local colleges in September.

"It's a press release, Becca," I say. "Not a short story. Most pubs will cut most of this out and just run the facts. People aren't going to read paragraphs about a doughnut." I sound like a bitch. Becca's frostiness doesn't bring out any of my better qualities, and I don't have the will to muster them on my own. The only reason Kailey and I get along at all is because she's so effervescent. I have nothing to do with it.

Becca shrugs. "Well, that's what his comment means. He talked to me about it right before I got here. I said when you finally finished it, I'd put info on my Instagram. I have ten thousand followers."

"That's great, Becca," Kailey says. "Why don't you rewrite the press release so people can really taste the doughnut? Then, reach out to your vast network of media contacts."

Becca shoots her middle finger at Kailey, hops off her stool, and goes to the back counter to load the dishwasher.

Matt turning to Becca for marketing advice isn't a good sign. As much as I grouse about the extra work, it feels good to string words together, turning and twisting them to get them just right. I have enough competitive spirit left to not want to be replaced by Becca. The idea forces me to suck it up and give Matt what he wants in the release. Or, an improved version of what he wants. I'm not writing "awesomely innovative flavor synergy." I have limits.

Matt does whatever he can to get services for free. The neon signage from his bro, the loaner artwork on the walls from a never-ending rotation of local creators. There's a reason Kailey leads the yoga practice at the company's spring "retreat"—Matt feels he doesn't have to pay her because she already works for him. It's the same reason he gets me to fix up his attempts at marketing. No professional service fees. Instead, I write his shit while serving doughnuts for minimum wage.

"You're pretty good at this writing thing," Kailey says as she reads my edits.

"Really?" I say. "My high school guidance counsellor told me to get into nursing or teaching."

Kailey cries with laughter. "You would be terrible at both those things. You can barely hand customers a cup of coffee without throwing it at them. Could you imagine handling teenagers? Or being nice to sick people?"

"My best friend's a nurse. And my mom's a nurse," I say, as if that somehow proves I'm not completely without empathetic social and genetic qualifications. My stomach flips. Penny. Where is Penny?

"So, Mom would have loved it if you followed in her footsteps?" Kailey says, wiping tears from her cheeks, unaware that I've drifted.

"She got something better than a nurse," I say, absently. "My brother is in med school."

Shit.

"Wait. You have a brother?" She stops laughing and pins me with a stare.

Interest piqued, Becca wanders over from where she's been digging in the half fridge where we keep our milk and milk-like products. This is a neighborhood that loves soy and almond milk. Or mylk, or whatever it is that marketers are branding the nondairy replacements with after a series of lawsuits from the dairy lobby.

"Spencer." Who lives in the corner of my brain labelled "things to avoid." I didn't pay attention for one second and he slipped out.

"You've never mentioned him. Is he hot? I could date a guy in med school." Kailey bumps Becca conspiratorially with her shoulder.

"Too serious," Becca says, dismissively. "Insane student loans. No money. Not for years."

"We're not close, Kailey." My voice comes out strangled and higher pitched than usual. My fingers stray to an old scar, four inches long, on my forearm.

"I'm kidding," she says. "You need to relax. You should come to yoga with me. You practically can't stand up straight your shoulders are so tight."

"Right. Because contorting myself into uncomfortable positions with a bunch of people sweating in stretchy fabric is super relaxing."

"You'll love it."

"About as much as I love working here."

She opens her mouth, but we're interrupted by customers and I focus on plunking pastel blobs of yeast and sugar onto plates and into boxes that cost more to print than the doughnuts do to produce. Spencer retreats into the closed-off corner of my mind as I deal with an onslaught of people and paste a toothy, customer service–approved smile on my face.

I help restock the display cabinet and wipe down tables before packaging a Peachy Keen for my dad and saying goodbye. Becca ignores me.

Kailey grins and hip checks me out the door and into the afternoon sun. There's laughter from the groups of people drinking poorly concealed beers and playing Frisbee in the park across the street. A tiny flame of envy flickers in my stomach and my hand strays to my neck, where I dig for a pulse. *I'm fine*, I tell myself. *I'm fine.*

I turn away and pause on the sidewalk in front of the shop's window to convert my ponytail into a bun. My outline is sharp in the lightly tinted glass. Inside the shop, Becca has put down her phone and is chattering away. Huh. Maybe it's just me she doesn't like.

As I adjust my hair, my reflection fades in the glass. Skin first, then ropey red muscle and tissue, gone. Bones are left stacked, neatly and precariously, in a human shape. Then, they vanish too. There's an empty spot where I once stood. I blink and rub my eyes, still able to feel the heat of my skin and the soft texture of my eyelashes.

But the spot where I was just seconds ago reflected in the window is empty. I wave my hands around and there's no corresponding movement in the glass. Kailey and Becca jump to work as a group of teenagers enters the store. None of them look at me, even though I'm less than a meter away.

Panic surges in my chest. This can't be happening. This can't be real. I reach out to tap the window, softly, with a fingertip. The glass is hot and solid. I bang on it with a fist. No one inside the shop spares a glance my way. I howl a feral, frenzied shriek before stuttering to a shocked hush. Behind me, activity in the park goes on, uninterrupted by my scene. I stare at nothing in the window, gasping in viscous summer air. Then I bolt down the sidewalk.

CHAPTER 2

I make it three blocks before I realize A: I'm sweating and gasping for air, and B: my reflection reappeared during my desperate dash to find a cab to take me to a hospital. I sag against a brick storefront that mercifully has an awning shading me from the worst of the afternoon sun. Across the street, my watery reflection in the window of a boutique selling handmade soaps and wicker baskets follows my movements as I put my hands on my knees and inhale deeply. I straighten and discard the idea of going to the ER.

"It was a trick of the light," I say to reassure myself. It's the only logical explanation.

A woman walking past with a stroller shoots me a worried look and pushes her baby as close to the edge of the sidewalk as she can.

"Oh, sure, now people can hear me," I say. The woman picks up her pace and slips around the corner.

At least I'm scaring other people instead of myself for once.

What would I say at the ER? Any explanation I could give would result in me peeing in a cup and being sent for a mental health evaluation. My mother would find out. I shudder. Nurses somehow always know when another nurse's kid comes into a hospital.

I walk home and the twenty-five-minute jaunt zaps the last of my strength. Even my underwear is soaked with sweat.

"Gross," I complain as I wriggle my damp feet out of my socks. My toes are shrivelled and pink. I flop on my unmade bed in the basement suite of my parents' house and drag my laptop toward me. The urge to confide in someone about the weird day, about vanishing, about my heartbeat, swamps me. There's no one to tell. I take a deep breath and shove the feelings away.

Reality is overrated. Television can fill most gaps in life. I press play on an old favorite. I'm asleep in seconds.

— — —

My body stretches and recoils like an elastic band released from fingertips and I jerk awake. Whatever I was dreaming about rapidly retreats into some inaccessible corner of my brain, leaving behind a frazzled feeling. The laptop is still open next to me, the dark screen communicating that the battery is dead and that I've been asleep for hours.

I'm not alone in my room.

"Hey!" A woman on the edge of my bed cheerfully greets me.

"Who the fuck are you?" I yell, scrambling backwards, searching for a weapon. My fingers collide with the metal of my laptop and I grasp it with both hands, prepared to swing.

The woman watches me jerk around my bed and tangle my feet in the blankets as I struggle to put distance between us. She's petite, blonde, familiar—and wearing athletic tights and my pastel pink sneakers, paired with a gray, chunky cable-knit sweater that looks exactly like one I know is buried in my closet. Her outfit looks great. I wish I'd thought of it.

The woman stands and briskly straightens her—my—clothing before flicking on the overhead light. She looks like the teenage nerd from *This High-School Life*. The actor won an Emmy when her character sustained an injury to her legs that meant she could no longer walk, after one of her fictional television friends drove drunk and ran her over. At age fourteen, I'd bawled through the forty-five-minute story arc. I'd also been in love with her onscreen basketball captain boyfriend. Their romance was a real "will they or won't they?" for six seasons.

I manage to stop flailing. "Emily Porter? What are you doing in my bedroom?" My hands, still holding the laptop, drop.

"I thought you'd be grateful for my company," she says, rolling her eyes. "Or do you have an amazing social life I'm not aware of?" She's got the same sass as Ella, her teenage brainiac character. "I'm famous. People usually like that."

Dreaming. I'm dreaming.

"Wake up, Brookie," I mutter, slapping my face lightly. "It's time to wake up." I'd fallen asleep watching *This High-School Life*, and Emily's character was my favorite. When I was an awkward thirteen-year-old, did I wish for Ella and I to become BFFs so hard that I was sure it would come true? Yes. We'd meet by accident in the mall and have an epic conversation, and then she'd take me back to *This High-School Life* with her and I'd become just as beautiful and famous. I imagined every detail down to my outfit and begged my mom to take me to the mall every weekend. Each trip was a crushing disappointment. I'd been so *sure*.

Ella was smart, outspoken, and unafraid of her mean, bullying classmates. She'd reminded me of Penny. Or Veronica Mars. I'd wanted to be like her. God. I probably still do.

Emily reaches over and pinches me. I yelp. Her hot-pink acrylic nails are sharp and get a stronger grip on the inside of my bare thigh than my own chewed digits ever could. I grab her bird-like wrist. It's bony and warm.

"No offense, but you stink," she says, her full brows drawing together over her hazel eyes as she snatches her hand back. There's a bruise blooming where her fingers twisted my skin.

I catch a whiff of perspiration, stale coffee, and deep-fried sugar. When was the last time I washed this shirt?

Emily bounces next to me on the bed, followed by a waft of lemons and lavender. Hallucination, dream, or not, she used the soap in my bathroom. She settles in, her shoulder brushing mine.

"Anyway, I'm here now. What's new?" She folds her slender legs under her. "I've got time for a chat." She smiles—the smile that made her famous. Year ago, in a *Seventeen Magazine* article, a writer gushed that Emily Porter's smile would rival Helen of Troy's. It was a regrettable hyperbole, but her smile does make you feel like she's your best friend and will always have your back. The wattage she's beaming at me makes me feel duller, blander, and more washed-up, and so tired that I barely think about the next words out of my mouth.

"My heart isn't beating," I blurt. It sounds ridiculous out loud, even if it's only in a dream. It's a relief when Emily doesn't laugh or roll her eyes or call me bananas.

"That happened to me once. Flatlined on the table. The doctors said I was a goner. Dead."

I grab her arm. "But you're alive? Fine? How? Tell me!"

Emily flushes and leaps off the bed. "Actually, it was in a scene from a straight-to-DVD film, early in my career," she clarifies, scuffing the toe of my pink sneaker into the carpet and staring at the ground. She looks up apologetically. "The character decided she had to live for the man who loved her. She wasn't ready to leave him."

Disappointment crashes through me.

"The writers couldn't come up with a more compelling reason than a man?"

"Literal much?" Emily scrunches her nose. "It was a metaphor. Or an analogy maybe? The point was that she had something to live for." She sighs. "It was a terrible movie. Lower your expectations. I guess it's not quite the same thing."

"Not helpful." I wrinkle my forehead, then run my fingers over the Klingon-like lines on my head, trying to smooth them out. The beginnings of a migraine are brewing. "It's too much. It's all too much. You're not real. I'm asleep and I'm going to wake up and be alone."

"I hate being alone," Emily groans. "I do everything humanly possible to avoid it. I hang out in coffee shops, or go to movies and sit next to a stranger, or talk to my neighbor about her plants and that woman has a lot to say about the optimal soil composition for prizewinning tomatoes."

I glance up at her between my fingers. "I'm used to it. My best friend travels a lot for work." There's a sharp pain in my gut at Penny's absence. I'm used to the dull ache, but every now and then I remember and it pierces: she's not just gone. She's missing.

"I'm here," Emily objects.

"I'm not sure you count."

"Better than nothing." Emily pulls my sneakers off her feet and places them next to the bed, before she stretches her toes and bounces on the balls of her feet. "Is there anyone besides Penny who can drag you out of your sad little room? I think you should engage with the world a little bit." She gestures wildly. "I always feel better when I do."

Spoken like a true extrovert.

"Get out there. Think about it, at least."

I groan and drop my head into my hands. Hallucinations giving advice. Just what I need. Through the ceiling, there's the usual loud thump as my dad gets out of bed.

When I look up, Emily is gone. My room is devoid of life, except me and a shrivelled, browning spider plant by the window. My cable-knit sweater is draped over a chair. I haven't taken that top out of the drawer in months. I stuff it as far back into the closet as I can and shake off the bizarre conversation. Hallucination. Nightmare. Dream. Whatever. My incoming headache left with the picturesque blonde. The digital clock next to the bed reads 6 a.m. It's Saturday. When I worked in marketing I'd already be up, on my way into the office and thrilled to be there to deal with overnight emergencies instead of the pile of dishes in my tiny studio apartment. The more I worked, the more I convinced myself I was succeeding, escaping the past, becoming someone.

I drag myself into the shower and through the motions of getting ready for the day. I dig a lipstick out of the bathroom vanity's bottom drawer and stuff it in my purse. Maybe I'll put it on at work tomorrow. Maybe Henry will notice.

"You might as well go out. You're up anyway. Listen to your Emily Porter–shaped subconscious. Do something. Get it together," I mutter to myself in the mirror, relieved that my reflection is clear and mouthing the words back to me. I wave at myself, and immediately feel like an idiot.

Clothes are flung around the room. My current activities don't require much variety, and my wardrobe requirements have shrunk accordingly. I have interchangeable black pants, skirts, and white T-shirts scattered on the floor, on the foot of my bed, and piled on my unused desk. My pink sneakers are the only spot of color on the floor.

"Hike. I'll go for a hike." My voice comes out a whisper. I clear my throat and try again. It's nothing but a scratchy murmur. I try to speak again. Muteness. I'm full out Little Mermaid-ing after she meets the sea witch. I grab a pillow off my bed and scream into it until my throat is raw and I'm panting with the effort. Nothing louder than a croak.

The enormity of how unnatural my existence has gotten bowls me over, and I collapse on the bed. No heartbeat, no reflection, Emily Porter, and now no voice. I curl into the fetal position and clutch a pillow to my chest. *How did I get here?*

Then, quivering with the effort, I sit up.

I don't need a voice to drive my car and walk outside. I nurse a small but growing hope that the exertion from a steep climb will kick-start my heart. That's what I've been doing wrong—sitting around, giving into exhaustion. A serious shock to my system, that's what I need. Running used to clear my head. Maybe exercise will clear my body too. Hiking is perfect. If you go up, you must come down. I'll have to finish what I've started instead of giving up and coming home by the time I reach the corner of the block, which is as far as I've made it during a handful of pathetic attempts to take up running again.

I unearth a pair of capri leggings and a tank top, pick up my pink runners from where Emily—it must have been me, in a fugue state—left them, and head upstairs to find snacks.

My dad is already up, sitting at the kitchen table with a cup of coffee and whole-wheat toast smeared with raspberry jam. This man has eaten the same breakfast for twenty years. Once, my mother bought strawberry jam by accident. On his way home from work the same day, my dad swung by the store and picked up the "correct" jam. The strawberry spread ended up in thumb-print cookies Penny and I made. We ate the whole batch, much to my mother's annoyance.

I risk a "Hi, Dad." The words come out. Weak, but audible.

"Morning, Brookie. Where you off to?" He doesn't notice the frailty of my voice. I clear my throat. Dad doesn't hear that either. If I was a miscalculated equation relating to the efficacy of a bridge deck, he would spot it in a second. People and their dis-organized illogical selves are harder for him. He can't quite retire from being a structural engineer, so he consults part-time. He says it relaxes him, but reserved is his default setting.

"Hiking. Up the Chief."

"You going alone?"

I fill my travel mug with coffee before answering. My father may or may not listen to my answer depending on the headlines he's reading on his iPad. He'll offer concern about going alone while simultaneously holding the belief that I'll be totally safe. He'll only speak up if he finds the risks untenable.

"There will be loads of people there." Loads of people. Take that, Emily. "It's probably safer than jogging on the seawall in Stanley Park."

The park sits on the outside edge of downtown and gets so clogged with tourists, walkers, joggers, and cyclists the traffic on the seawall virtually comes to standstill.

"A girl got attacked running there two weeks ago," my dad says, frowning at his iPad. Sunlight bounces off the shiny white laminate tabletop and into his eyes. He blinks and looks at me. "Even in peak summer, it's nearly deserted in the early morning. No one saw anything."

"I'll be fine," I say as I pull a granola bar and a nearly empty bag of trail mix out of the cupboard above the sink. "It's summer. I'm starting late. The climb will be packed with tourists and church groups."

"That's true. Have fun." Risk assessed, deemed allowable.

"Text your mother on your way home so she doesn't worry," Dad says. "You know how she is, especially because of Penny."

"Sure." I press a kiss to his forehead on my way out of the warm kitchen. "I'll be careful."

Before I get in the car, I do what I do every morning: I call Penny's parents.

"It's Brooklyn," I say to the voicemail. "Just checking in. Seeing if there's any news."

They never answer, and they never call back.

– – –

Squamish is a sixty-minute drive north of the city. It doesn't take long before the traffic thins out and the glistening skyscrapers disappear behind twists in the roadway. The highway runs above and alongside the coast. Far to the north ahead of me, the mountains are still topped with snow and their distance makes them look like children's drawings: soft, lumpy blue suggestions of mountains. In the fall and winter, small waterfalls flow down the craggy cliff side next to the inside lane. Now though, the trees and bushes along the highway's edge are crispy with drought. It hasn't rained in ninety-one days. I know this because at least two customers per shift tell me how long the city has gone without rain. Vancouverites and their weather stories.

I park in the gravel lot at the base of the Stawamus Chief Trail and avoid the area where the rock climbers congregate. They sleep in their vans and stay for days at a time, using the low-tech outhouses and cold-water taps. The climbers—the serious ones who stick around for a few days, or weeks, to scale the Chief's craggy walls—clump together. They're their own tribe, smelly and insular. They look down on the day hikers, the ones who by climber standards come up unprepared with nothing but runners and a small backpack stuffed with water and snacks to hike the more welcoming backside of the cliff face. For their part, the hikers judge the tourists wearing high heels and sandals who didn't do their research before showing up.

The sign at the base of the hike says: "This is not a walk in the park." The climb goes up and up and up, and if you're short, you need to stretch your legs over stairs formed out of boulders. The first forty-five minutes are the worst, a nearly vertical march over knee-high rocks and up flights of wooden steps.

I get the tourists' denial, though. It's easy to think that the rocky path will smooth out at any moment and become easy and picturesque—social media ready. I envy their optimism.

I tighten my laces at the bottom of the climb. A local, based on his well-worn boots, prepares to head up with an infant strapped to his chest. A leggy brown dog pants eagerly against the man's leg, yelps, and takes off when the man gives it a command. The stranger nods at me and gestures for me to go ahead as he ensures the baby is tucked safely into its carrier.

The climb starts immediately. My body is heavy and sluggish, courtesy of a diet of doughnuts and cheese slices from my parents' fridge. For the first few minutes, my thighs burn in protest and I suck in gulps of cool pine- and earth-tinged air. It feels good to move. But as I climb, the tiny flicker of hope I'd held onto fades. Despite the steep, rugged steps and the never-ending staircases, my heart rate stays at zero. By now, my heart should be bursting of my chest, and I should be gasping and regretting whatever impulse led me up here. I should be suffering from more than burning quads.

I stop halfway up a set of rock stairs and press my palm over my heart. Pressure builds behind my eyes and my skin burns. Oxygen flees my lungs and I inhale deep, useless gulps. My fingers and toes tingle. I recognize the symptoms of a panic attack, but they're alien without the racing heart. It still feels like I'm going to die. My legs wobble and I collapse on a flat rock just off the trail with a heavy thud. The man with the baby passes me without comment as I noisily suck in air. His eyes are focused on the path and he makes soothing, warm noises to the infant.

I start to call out, to make sure he can see me and that I haven't disintegrated like I did yesterday in the window. He's around a corner and hidden by trees before I can open my mouth. I close my eyes and press my palms into the rock. Bits of dirt and pebbles dig into the soft tissue. After a few more deep breaths, I use a nearby tree to pull myself to my feet. I drag myself forward and up for another forty minutes, and as I move, the anxiety dissipates. Finally, I scramble up the last set of rusting metal ladders, over the flat, smoother rock on the summit, and stagger across the gray expanse. Collapsing onto its stony surface, I splay my legs in front of me and let the sun, which had been hidden by the tree canopy, warm my limbs.

The sunlight glints off the ocean, which spreads out and 2,297 feet below me, interrupted only by blips of land and toy-sized boats leaving behind white wakes. Far below, cars move along the highway and into the town of Squamish. There's a small group of hikers to my right talking among themselves, but the breeze snatches their words. It's quieting, being up here, above the world. Why had I avoided coming back for so long? I haven't felt this unburdened in months.

You know why. You know.

Be quiet, my brain snaps back, too late. A memory presses against my skull—of sitting in almost this exact spot with Penny, Spencer, who'd tagged along, and a handful of high school friends. Of Spencer's elbow—too vigorous to be accidental—shoving me off the trail and toward a steep slope covered in boulders and spiky trees when we were out of sight of the others. Of being afraid of careening headfirst into a rock as I tumbled, but being more terrified of rejoining my brother. I remember wiping blood off my knees and arms while mumbling about tripping over a hidden root, and Spencer, laughing loudly about his uncoordinated big sister. Penny asking what happened, her face concerned.

I said, "I tripped. I'm fine."

She said, "You sure?"

I said, "Yes. Forget about it. I said *I'm fine.*"

CHAPTER 3

Descending the Chief is faster, slipperier, and more perilous than the ascent. I make good time by scrambling down ladders and jumping between wedges of rocks. July is peak hiking season, and big groups of high school kids from summer camps and churches are on their way up the narrow trail. Some wait more patiently than others for the descending hikers to get out of their way so they can race up the huge steps, impressing their peers, trying to prove something.

I don't find them irritating today. They look fresh and eager, like puppies who think you're going to give them a treat or a belly rub. Plus, the sun, when it makes it through the tree canopy, is warm and dapples everything in a soft yellow light. Nothing bad can happen on a day like this.

The moment this crosses my mind, the universe goes for broke. I slip on a patch of loose dirt and dry pine needles and my body careens wildly. My right ankle can't decide which way to go, so it bends to the left and the right before giving out and sending me shoulder first into the side of a boulder.

My stomach heaves, and I'm drenched in a cold sweat. My ankle is screaming, and I know intuitively that it has started swelling. Black spots block my vision and from very far away, a voice calls my name.

When I come to, I'm on my back and staring into Henry Cavill's face. Henry's face. Just Henry. *Please be a dream.*

No such luck. I've fallen at his feet like a damsel in distress. How basic.

One of Henry's hands is on my shoulder and the other hovers near my waist. He eases me upright and helps me sit with my back against the rock I collided with.

"Henry." He points at himself. "I come into the doughnut shop."

I think I nod. "I know." The words are thin and scratchy.

"That's good. You remember me. Fingers crossed that means you didn't hit your head." His face is close to mine, looking at my head for evidence of a cut. He smells appealingly of fresh air and clean laundry. "What happened? I came around the corner and you were laying here."

"Ankle."

"Ah." Henry says something over his shoulder. There are three guys with him, all of them fit and tanned and wearing Nike shorts with sturdy hiking boots. One of them kneels next to Henry at my feet. He turns my foot gently left and right. Fire shoots through my foot and a whimper escapes my lips before I can claw it back. The black spots from earlier reappear, along with a roaring in my ears. The ache quells any reservation I'd ordinarily have about being touched by a stranger. Cold sweat covers my face and drips down my back. There's a sensation in my stomach that I know from experience usually leads to puking or dry heaves. I don't want to do either of those things in front of Henry. Falling was bad enough.

"He's a firefighter," Henry says about the man prodding my ankle. "Has paramedic training." Henry looks at me with a worried and bemused expression, as if he can't quite place me out here in the wilderness. He doesn't seem to know what to do with his hands either. One is braced against a rock, supporting him while he's crouching, but the other hovers uselessly in the air above me, looking for somewhere to land.

His eyes are hazel. I hadn't noticed before.

The guy manhandling my foot isn't as tall as Henry, but he is more muscular. "You're screwed," he announces. "It's sprained. Can't tell how bad, but it's more than a little roll. Maybe a torn ligament. You'll need an X-ray and maybe a CT scan. Best to keep your shoe on tight until you're at the bottom, then ice it immediately. Not much else you can do up here."

"Fuck," I say. There are about thirty minutes left in my descent. Thirty minutes if I'd been able to move on my own two feet. "I don't want to be on the evening news as one of those dummies who came up here unprepared and needed to be heli-lifted out."

"You came up here alone?" Henry asks.

"Not smart," the firefighter says.

"I do the hike ten times a year," I say, figuring a little lie won't matter at this point. "Never slipped before."

The firefighter snorts, clearly disgusted with my life choices. He has no idea. This decision is so marginally catastrophic in the scheme of things it barely counts.

Henry opens his well-worn navy backpack and hands me some dried pineapple rings.

"You're white as a sheet. Probably shock. Sugar will help."

I accept the slices and they settle the worst of my roiling stomach. I surreptitiously wipe some of the moisture off my face with the hem of my shirt. The back of my tank is drenched through. Henry is conferring with his buddies, who manage to look at me, the idiot, sympathetically. Embarrassment washes over me. Finally, he comes back.

"I'm going to get you get home," he says. "The guys will finish their hike. You won't be able to drive even if you manage to get off the mountain."

"I can't let you do that," I object. "It'll ruin your day."

"Leaving you on the side of a trail will ruin my day," Henry says, grinning wryly. "It would be a mean thing to do to someone who threw an extra doughnut in my box last week. I don't mind. Honest."

Kailey had told me to add the extra doughnut. Bless her. Henry says goodbye to his friends as I try to breathe through the agony. My field of vision has narrowed to the white-hot twist in my foot. I'm barely aware of anything around me. If I don't let Henry assist me, I'm not getting back to my car unless I crawl. I'm out of choices.

"How are we going get down?" I ask when Henry returns. If he suggests carrying me, I will throw myself off the mountain.

Henry rubs his jaw, which has a shadow of stubble, something I've never seen on a weekday. It makes him look less like Henry Cavill, and more like himself.

"I'm not sure," he says. "How stable are you?"

Besides my heart condition, hallucinating a famous woman from my childhood hanging out in my room, losing my voice, and fading from mirrors? Totally stable.

I stand up cautiously, keeping my weight on my left foot. The black spots swim in my vision, but the cold sweat doesn't resume.

I can't put any pressure on the right without squealing. Surely being dead, kinda, should give me a pass on having to deal with this. I grimace. Henry is watching me closely and his arms look poised to catch me if I start to topple.

"You're not getting out under your own power," he points out. He doesn't accuse me of faking it to get his attention. This wayward thought points out my own insecurity. Why wouldn't a girl fake an injury to get a man's attention? In my isolation, I've been reading too many '80s and '90s women's magazines from the box I found in storage in the basement. I resolve to recycle them the second I get home.

We make slow progress down.

"I'm fine," I keep repeating when Henry asks how I'm doing. Otherwise, we're silent as I take one step with my good foot, lean into Henry's side, and scoot my bad foot forward while he bears most of my weight. With every step, I'm sure I'm going to vomit. However, I don't want to ruin Henry's day entirely by collapsing in a dejected heap, so I push forward. My body seems to know it has no choice but to keep moving.

When we reach a flight of stairs, Henry acts like a crutch. I sling one arm around him and brace the other on the handrail so I can hop down on my good foot. People passing us on the way up look at me sympathetically or with annoyance for taking up too much space on the path. One man asks Henry if his girlfriend is okay. He doesn't correct the man, just smiles, nods, and says we're doing just great. By the time we get to the bottom, I'm trembling from effort. The world is foggy. Henry lowers me onto a park bench near the trail entrance. Years have passed since I started the hike.

"You made it. Without complaining. Everyone I know, including myself, would have whined the whole way," Henry says, as he crouches in front of me. He pats my knee.

I look at him blankly. I'd almost forgotten he was there, I'd been so lost in my pain cave.

"You look queasy."

If this was a movie, I'd look adorable. Perfect makeup and a bouncy ponytail.

"I'm going to carry you," Henry says.

"You can't." I smell and I'm filthy from falling. "If we both sprain our ankles, we'll never get out of here."

He laughs. "Come on. Piggyback. Dignity be damned."

I shake my head and see stars again.

"It'll be faster," he wheedles. "I promise not to drop you."

My ankle taunts me. How long will it take to get back to the car if I hobble? Thirty minutes? Longer?

"Only if you don't drop me," I say.

"Fair." Henry crouches in front of me. I climb onto his back ungracefully. My arms go around his warm, soft neck, which is slightly sticky from sweat. My right foot is swelling out of my shoe like overproofed sourdough. I wouldn't have made it much farther. Henry strides toward the trail head that leads to the parking lot. He seems surprisingly jovial, under the circumstances.

The sun is hot on my back and makes me sleepy. Or maybe it's the heat radiating off Henry's head, bringing with it a soft smell of coconut shampoo. I cross my fingers that he doesn't realize my heart isn't pounding against his back. At the car, I slide down his back and land on my good foot. Henry finds my keys in a backpack pocket and eases me into the passenger side. He buckles me in so I don't need to twist while looking for the shoulder belt, then props up my injured ankle with our bags.

"See? No problem," he says.

"Have you carried women off mountains before?"

"Never." He dimples. And winks. My heart would have stopped. In a way, being delirious with pain is helpful. I'm suffering too much to giggle.

My soupy brain recognizes that getting into a car with someone who's basically a stranger is a bad idea. I could have called my dad, once I made it to the car. Who knows what kind of guy Henry is, outside of his doughnut choices? He could be a serial killer. But a guy who occasionally orders a chocolate butterscotch dip can't be that bad.

Henry lets himself into the driver's side, moves the seat back, and adjusts all the mirrors. I drift in and out as he takes off down the highway, until he stops at a gas station and gets a bag of ice, which he drapes over my ankle.

"You gonna make it?" He grins as he asks the question. "You look like you're not totally with me."

"Just a sprained ankle, right?" I say. "No big."

"Couple days, ice, and some tape to keep the swelling down, and you'll be good as new."

Henry talks at me during the drive and doesn't seem to expect me to say anything coherent back. Despite his superhero good looks, he's got a run-of-the-mill job as an urban planner for the city.

"I get to work with all sorts of people, from architects to residents who are pissed when we densify their neighborhoods. I learn new things all the time. I love it."

"Building codes and zoning practices are super interesting," I say, forcing myself to pay attention. After today's performance, the chances I'll get to chat with Henry outside work again are slim to none and I'm dying to learn more about him while I can. "Who doesn't want to keep up to date on the latest in mixed-use planning?"

"I'll let you make fun of me, in deference to your sprained ankle," he says.

"As you should."

He laughs. I made him laugh. My mouth twitches upwards.

"Must be nice. Loving your job."

"You work in a doughnut shop. That's pretty great."

Sure. If you're nineteen and have the metabolism of a fourteen-year-old-boy.

"It's temporary," I say.

"You don't like it?"

"Heck no."

"At least you seem like you know what you're doing. Everyone else burns the coffee."

It's nothing to be proud of, but I'll take it.

"I used to work for a high-profile marketing and communications agency, but I decided to look for another job. I'm taking the summer to check out firms and networking events to find a good fit."

I've done none of these things. I haven't even updated my resume. Whenever I open my computer to work on it, I fall asleep.

"Why doughnuts?"

"I couldn't afford the rent for my tiny apartment anymore, and my mom told me if I wanted to live in her basement suite for free, I had to get a job. I think she meant a 'real' job. But since she wasn't specific, I applied at the doughnut shop." I muster a grin.

I'd been aimlessly walking the city, lost in a mental conflagration about Penny's disappearance and my own failures, and saw the help wanted sign. I walked in without a job, and walked out with one. Done. Effortless. All I could manage.

Henry laughs again. "There are worse summer jobs. What kind of clients did you have at your marketing job?" He keeps his eyes on the curving road.

"The agency represented a lot of television shows. Influencers. Brands with big budgets. It was fun. It's a flexible industry. Lots of options. Opportunities."

All those things are accurate. But I'd only gotten into marketing because my parents were willing to foot the postsecondary school bill for it. I'd wanted a history degree, capped with a creative writing minor.

My mother said, "You need to do something more practical. Like Penny and Spencer."

I said, "I'm not getting into medicine. History."

My mother said: "We'll pay for a communications degree. You can do marketing or whatever it is people like that do for museums and art galleries."

I accepted her decree. In a way, my mother had done me a favor. My first job paid well enough I could move out of my parents' house and get away from Spencer, who lived at home for four more years. Four years of peace and safety felt worth giving up the history degree for.

"Anyway, marketing is just about good communication," I say. It sounds vacuous, said out loud in front of Henry and without any enthusiasm. "It's mostly about finding ways to make things informative or interesting enough to get people to act the way you want them to."

"When you put it like that..." Henry starts.

"It sounds bad, I know," I say.

"Actually, you helped me out on a project recently." Henry beams at me and my body warms. For a second, I forget everything: Penny, my missing heartbeat, my aching ankle. I blink hard. Being beamed at is dizzying.

"What? How?"

"I overheard you at Cute Lil'. You said people don't question their physical environments, cultures, or societal structures because they're used to them. They assume there's a good reason for things being the way they are. But then you said something even more brilliant. You said most people forget that the world has evolved, and the reason something was designed a specific way might not exist anymore. You said we need to frame everything in today's context, not dated rationale, or because it's always been that way."

Why do I talk like that? No wonder everyone at works thinks I'm a snob.

"I was ranting. One of the girls at work was talking about marrying her high school boyfriend, which sounded crazy. I was explaining that women used to have to marry to improve their financial situation, but now women can make their own money, so we should redefine what a marriage is and what its role in society is."

Henry laughs. God, even his laugh is cozy and comforting.

"Anyway, I started applying that sort of thinking at work because cities, just like people, get stuck in old patterns. And let's face it, a lot of the old guys on the team are just riding it out until their retirement. No risks, nothing new. But I started obsessing about how everything, from road widths to street layouts, everything, is based on old paradigms. Some of our city planning docs were written in the '70s and we still use them. Think about parks, for one thing. So many single-family homes have been knocked down and replaced with huge apartment buildings since some of our park plans were developed. We need more creative ways of adding green space because fewer people have homes with yards. I used your argument to present an idea for revitalizing a heritage block with aerial gardens. It's going to come up at city council."

He's lightly tapping on the steering wheel with his fingers and his face is animated as he talks about his work. I want to reach out and touch his arm, like the besotted creep I am. Except, it hurts to move.

Henry glances at me. "I'm probably boring you to death."

"No! I think it's great you care about your job. Do I get some sort of plaque or city bench if your project is approved?"

"Nope. You only get those if you turn over some cold, hard cash."

I laugh, but the motion jars my ankle and I brace myself as daggers slice up my leg. The rest of my body is starting to ache and stiffen from the fall.

Henry glimpses my expression and winces on my behalf. "Bad?"

I nod, careful not to move anything below my collarbone.

"We're getting close to city limits now." The mountains are behind us, and we're descending to sea level.

"We've all had jobs we don't like," he says. "You know what my first real job was?" He scrunches his nose and offers me a sheepish twist of his mouth.

"Pizza restaurant mascot?"

"I was an adventure tour guide up north," he snorts. "I thought it would be cool. I'd get paid to be outside all day and meet loads of girls."

"And was it everything you dreamed?"

"Not even close. I sweated all summer and froze my ass off in the winter. The money was shit, and it turned out the women I was into were 100 percent not into outdoor adventuring. I lived in a cabin with four other guys who were not big on showering. I thought I was going to be this big adventure guy. I barely lasted a year and a half."

"What made you quit?"

"Too much booze, too much weed, not enough sleep. My body was falling apart. I was sick all the time. I'd gone to school part-time for urban planning, and my mom was nagging me to come back and finish my education. I caved, moved in with some buddies, and went back to school full-time."

"How'd you know that you were meant for a desk job as an urban planner instead?"

"I didn't. It worked out though. Sure, I'm stuck indoors, but I get to think about the outdoors and how people use it. And cities are pretty interesting."

"You changed your whole life, just like that? And it worked out?"

"Best decision I ever made."

"You make it sound easy. To veer in another direction after all that effort."

"I felt bad that I couldn't hack it as an outdoor guide, especially because I talked a big game about how great it was going to be," Henry says. "But change was necessary."

"I couldn't do it," I say.

"You just climbed down a mountain with a sprained ankle," he says, and glances at me. My cheeks heat under his gaze. "I think you could do whatever you need to."

I avert my eyes first.

"Want to stop at a hospital?" Henry asks as we hit civilization.

"Mom's a nurse. You don't go to the ER unless you are legit dying. Her rules."

Dying. Damn. Does not having a heartbeat count?

"Your place then?" Henry asks, and flushes slightly. I let it pass and instead give him vague instructions to my parents' house, which is in a quiet residential area, several blocks away from a busy street. The trees lining the sidewalk are too thick to put my arms around. Most people have lived in this neighborhood for decades. It's why my parents will never move. They know everybody and everybody knows them.

"I'll walk you in," Henry says, unbuckling his seatbelt.

"I can do it. Call an Uber or something to get home. I'll e-transfer you the amount."

"I don't think so. You're as white as a ghost, and I heard you whimpering when we went over the speedbumps. Stay put."

He comes around to the passenger side of the car, opens it, and reaches in to pick me up. I let him—any motion I make on my own causes my vision to swim. The afternoon sun beats on my shoulders as I point Henry toward the back of the house, where we can go into the ground-level basement suite.

"Wow," he says, as we round the corner. "Nice yard."

"My mother's pride and joy. Next to my brother, the almost doctor."

Tall Douglas firs, their lower branches strung with white fairy lights, invisible in the daylight, grow along the back of the yard. High tree branches extend toward the oblong deck my dad made one summer, which has a gas fire pit. There are other trees too, including a pine we decorate at Christmas. Nothing with leaves, as to avoid raking. Most of the yard is landscaped with pebbled rocks and elevated planters to keep the water bill down. A small vegetable patch is planted next to a flower garden with a rose trellis. There's only a small patch of grass, enough for a beach blanket or a couple of chairs.

"Your brother is a med student, huh?" Henry says. "Some parents really have a thing about their children becoming doctors."

Henry lightly sets me down on my good foot and uses my keys to unlock the door. I prop myself against the wall and maneuver myself to face him. The afternoon sun glints off his nearly black hair and forms a halo around his head.

"You can come in," I blurt. Yes, I'd fucked up my ankle, but I hadn't been lonely the entire time I'd been with Henry. "Only if you want. You've more than done your good deed for today and if you want to take off, I totally understand." *Stop babbling, Brooklyn.*

He holds up the bag of ice. "Let's get you sorted out."

Thank God, the bedroom is the only place that has totally succumbed to my messiness and that I closed the door this morning to keep my mother out. Habit.

Henry follows me through the entrance. "You got a bucket?"

I point at a closet by the stairs that holds the household cleaning supplies. He finds a blue plastic bucket and rinses it out in the small kitchen sink while I hop to the living room area and gingerly lower myself onto the couch. I groan as I take off my sneakers and socks. Henry dumps the remaining ice into the bucket of water and places the whole concoction on the floor, next to my foot. The chill from the bucket creeps along the laminate.

"Sorry about this. You're going to need to put your foot in there."

I look at him warily. "No."

"It'll be worse if you don't. It's going to suck. But you can do it."

I yelp when my heel touches the water.

"Serves you right, hiking the Chief in unsupportive footwear. By yourself." He plunks himself next to me. He's left his sensible boots by the door. "I'll go with you next time, assuming eventually you can wear shoes again." He winks.

My stomach flips and I will my ankle to heal.

The ice water creeps into my veins and my teeth start to chatter, but at least I can't feel my ankle anymore. Henry reaches behind me and pulls the wool blanket that's draped on the back of the couch onto my shoulders. I snuggle into it. Henry doesn't seem in a hurry to leave—he asks me where the remote for the Apple TV is, turns on the screen my dad mounted on the wall but never watches, and digs through Netflix.

"Hard pass on horror," I say. "Unless there are vampires. That's an acceptable compromise."

"Food documentaries?" he suggests.

"Only if there are snacks. I can't watch food shows unless I'm eating too. We don't have snacks."

He fishes a package of trail mix from his backpack and two squished granola bars out of mine.

"These shouldn't count," he says.

My stomach growls. "Give it," I say, and snatch the bag of trail mix. I give him both bars.

"Fantasy shows?" I ask, picking up our television talk. "Dragons? Tales of vengeance?"

He grimaces. "Heck no. Classic movies?"

"Only musicals," I say around a mouthful of almonds and cashews.

"We clearly don't have any shows in common," he says. Then he narrows his eyes and taps is chin, thinking hard.

"Got it," he says, scrolling again. "Real life unsolved murder investigations, but," at this he holds up a finger and turns to look at me, "with a paranormal twist."

"Sold." I toss him the trail mix.

"I thought it would come down to rock, paper, scissors. I would have had an advantage due to your preexisting condition."

I laugh and gesture for the trail mix, which he hands over after scooping some out.

He puts on the show and we sit in silence for a few minutes, but one question leads to another and we stop paying attention—although I make a mental note to rewatch later. I'm stuck in my very own paranormal special. Maybe the show will have explanations, something I can use to get out of this mess.

Henry tells me stories about the mayor, who won't sit next to the city manager in meetings because he hates the sound of her breathing.

I tell Henry about the time a customer threw a doughnut at Becca's head because she'd mixed up his order. "He legit turned purple. I thought he was going to have a heart attack, right there, when she gave him a Pecan Crunch instead of Maple Sugar for Lunch."

"Being behind a counter shouldn't make someone fair game for verbal abuse."

"Well, you're always very nice," I blurt—and he blushes. I flush in response and clutch my blanket tighter.

He gestures to my foot, and it seems like we're both glad to turn our attention elsewhere. "RICE. Rest, ice, compression, elevation for that swollen monstrosity."

"Mom's a nurse, remember? How do you know so much? All that outdoor adventure training?" I tease, unable to resist because of his pious expression.

"Girlfriend. She's in med school," he says. He looks me right in the eye a beat too late.

"She taught you well," I say, managing to sound unbothered. I swallow around a lump that has suddenly grown in my throat. "You were highly prepared for a klutz in the wilderness."

"Speaking of doctors, do you have someone to take you to one? Because you should see a doctor. A real doctor, not your brother." He pokes me in the ribs, lightly, with his elbow.

The movement brings him closer, and we're nearly hip to hip on the couch. His presence doesn't feel as loaded now that his girl-friend is in the room with us. I'm in the friend zone. Acquaintance zone, if that. He'll probably meet up with his pals and laugh about the ridiculous, clingy girl he rescued off the mountain and never come into Cute Lil' again. The best I can hope for is that Henry never picked up on my stupid, stupid crush.

"My dad can take me," I say around my tight throat. "He's mostly retired. I'm surprised he's not home."

Henry looks at phone, which has sat untouched on the side table.

"I should head out. Marvin, my cat, gets lonely." Henry pats my shoulder and I wave from the couch as he leaves and pulls the door shut behind him.

A girlfriend. Of course. She's a med student. Of course.

CHAPTER 4

While I wait for my errant father, and try to distract myself from the fact that Henry carried me off a mountain, practically saving my life, I rewatch *Dracula: Winter of the Vampyre*, a modernized, musical adaptation of the venerated novel. The feminist-slanted miniseries and the book have very little in common, except the characters' names and the existence of Dracula himself. I've watched it four times already, mesmerized by the performance of the petite actress in the role of Mina. She sings her heart out through a crying fit brought on by horror and exhaustion as she tries to avoid the menacing Count Dracula while mourning her dead friend Lucy, and I end up bawling along with her every time.

"This was one of my better parts," a wry voice says next to me.

I blink awake and rear up. My wounded ankle prevents me from scurrying away.

Emaleigh Taylor's gray eyes, framed by thick black lashes, are inches from my face. She's leaning over me, her hands on her knees, wearing my favorite pink T-shirt dress. "Don't you think? I should've won an Emmy for my performance as Mina. Everyone said so. I *was* her."

I rub my face but she's still standing there, waiting for me to say something. This, I can write off as a figment of my imagination, brought on by exhaustion and the emotional and physical trauma of my accident on the Chief. The thought is comforting.

Emaleigh's head is shaved, which draws attention to her sharp cheekbones. I'd watched an interview on YouTube where she mentioned that she buzzed her hair for a slasher miniseries and sobbed when the first thick, black curls hit the salon floor. But after the shock, she decided it suited her.

"What happened to you?" she asks. She gestures to the bucket and the condensation puddle surrounding it. We both look at my ankle, which has already begun turning purple. I can tell it's going to eventually turn black, followed by a putrid green and yellow. I have specialized knowledge in bruising.

"Accident?"

"I fell."

"Fell? You sure you fell?" She looks skeptical, but her voice is kind.

"I was hiking. Tripped."

"Really?"

I understand why she's suspicious. According to one of my mom's *People* magazines, Emaleigh's boyfriend beat her up. She hadn't hesitated. He'd hit her; she'd walked into a police station and reported him. He got arrested. I almost cried when I read the article, I was so proud of her. I'd gotten attached, after all my viewings of *Winter of the Vampyre*. I'd even watched her questionable horror series.

"How'd you get home?" She still looks dubious. Her arms are folded across her chest and she's pinning me with the same stare she used on Dracula to get him to talk about who else he'd victimized.

"A friend helped me."

"Male friend? Helped?" she practically spits.

"Yes, male, yes, helped." I roll my eyes, but feel touched by her concern. At least the figments of my imagination are sympathetic. It's a novel experience after the real world.

"Alright then." She looks mollified but yanks my blanket away. "Just checking. You have a lot of scars on your legs and arms."

I self-consciously pull it back. She's stronger than me, but finally releases it and I jerk back into the couch. "I played a lot of sports in high school. Intramurals in university."

"Sure you did," Emaleigh says.

I gesture to the far wall, which is covered in trophies, medals, and awards. "Soccer, volleyball, track."

Emaleigh furrows her brow and taps her front teeth with a blood-red nail, which is filed to an aggressive point. Her fingers look like weapons. "I wonder" is all she says.

"He's not the problem. I've dated problems," I say, as Kyle unwelcomely flits through my mind. The handful of men I'd dated since Kyle hadn't been much more than human-shaped fillers on the rare occasion I couldn't bring work home with me. I never got too close. They all carried a whiff of threat. Henry though…With Henry, I didn't feel the urge to cautiously back away. Meanwhile, he beat a quick retreat. I try to resign myself to never seeing him again.

"How did you do it?" It's the question I've had since I read Emaleigh's story in that magazine.

"I rehearsed my ass off," she says, scrubbing a hand over her dark fuzz. "And it still wasn't good enough. Fuck the Emmy committee and their old white dude bullshit."

"Not your performance. How did you—" I clear my throat, which has closed over the words trying to escape. "How did you find the guts to report your boyfriend?"

"Oh. That 'it.' I was terrified. And furious, mostly at myself for letting it happen in the first place." She sees the look on my face. "I know it wasn't my fault," she hurries to add. "But knowing isn't the same as believing."

"Everyone found out what happened when you went to the police."

"The whole damn world. I got hate messages on social media from strangers. His friends and his mother called me a liar on national television. It didn't help that he was white and more famous than me. All his ex-girlfriends came out of the woodwork. 'He never hit me,'" she mimics.

"I believed you."

"Lots of women did. Strangers. Old women on the street. Teenage girls." She nods. "That's how I endured the threats, the victim shaming."

I stare at my swollen foot and press a hand against my heart. I will it to beat. For a breathless second, I swear it's going to. Stillness greets me, and my hand drops lifelessly into my lap.

"Was it worth it?" I ask.

"My friends and some coworkers stood by me. Held me up when I couldn't stand on my own. They spoke the truth over and over when others defamed me."

"What if you don't have anyone to do that? What if you're alone?"

"You should still tell someone," Emaleigh says as she wraps her fingers around my wrist. She squeezes gently. "Even if it's hard." Emaleigh cocks an eyebrow, waiting, while words wobble in my throat. Upstairs, the cuckoo clock chimes four times. Emaleigh releases my wrist.

"I need to meet some friends downtown. Do something about that thing." She flicks a red talon in the direction of my ankle.

With that, she marches toward the door, but spins around on her heel. She's wearing hiking boots. "For what it's worth, I'm here," she says.

"Sure, you are," I say, as she slips outside. Still wearing my dress. Wonderful. My hallucinations, dreams, whatever, are prone to theft.

I pause *Winter of the Vampyre*, which had been playing in the background. It's near the end: Emaleigh's terror-filled face is frozen on the screen. Dracula looms above her, his arms outstretched, reaching, always reaching. His curved claws nearly reach her throat. Emaleigh's—Mina's—fear fills the scene.

I suppress a shiver. Between the cold basement and the bucket of ice water, my extremities are turning purple. I spend nearly twenty minutes crawling up the stairs from the basement to the landing by the front door, and up the next flight to the living room. It's warmer upstairs and sometimes my parents forget I live in the basement and I don't see them for days. The chances of them coming downstairs while I'm stuck there with a swollen ankle are slim. I might starve to death.

Upstairs, in the brightness of an early summer evening, I shake off Emaleigh's appearance and convince myself it didn't happen. I imagined it. I had Emaleigh on the brain and had a bad shock only a few hours earlier, plus the crushing disappointment about doubtlessly never seeing Henry again. My brain is doing a thing, a weird, wonky thing. That's all.

"Your brain, your heart, your body," I mumble to myself. "Get it together."

I arrange myself on the upstairs couch so I can see my parents when they come up the stairs. I've just settled in when I hear keys in the lock and feet on the stairs.

I clear my throat when they appear at the top and gesture dramatically at my grotesque foot. "Ta-da!"

"Brooklyn! What have you done now?" My mother, ever sympathetic. "You need to be more careful. You're always injuring yourself."

"Can someone drive me to the clinic? I think it's open for another hour or so."

My dad pulls his keys out of a pocket on his cargo shorts.

"We can call Spencer," my mother interjects, always looking for an excuse to get in touch with Spencer. She's a nurse for God's sake. She knows what to do about a sprained ankle, although mine is bad enough to warrant a trip to the doctor, in case I tore a ligament or tendon.

"No," I say, sharply. "I'd much rather see a real doctor."

"He's almost a real doctor." My mother rolls her eyes and starts searching her purse for her cell phone. Last year, my parents caved to common sense and dumped their landline in exchange for two cell phones. Now, I get incoherent emoji messages from mom. My father, as far as I know, has never used his phone except to take the occasional incoming work call.

I do not want my brother anywhere near my ankle. Just the thought causes acid reflux. "I need an X-ray. Or a CT scan. Or an MRI. He can't requisition those. Neither can you."

"I suppose," my mother says. I can tell she wants to call Spencer anyway. He hasn't been around in over a month, and she's mentioned how she's dying to hear how his summer classes are going.

"I'll take her. It's no problem." My dad stares at my foot as if he's not sure how I'm going to drag it down the stairs. It's twice its usual size, and it's once again hot to the touch. The one thing it isn't doing is throbbing—since I don't have a pulse.

"I don't think your father has ever taken you to the doctor before," my mom says, putting her hand on her hip and grinning. "Look at us bucking gender roles."

"Right, Mom. When was the last time you mowed the lawn or took out the trash?"

She's been taking a gender studies class at the behest of a friend who's teaching it. It has not made her more insightful, nor has it lessened her parental pride in her sweet boy, the almost doctor, or her disappointment in me, the unemployed, almost-broke daughter.

I let my dad support me until I get to the stairs, which I slide down on my ass. Maybe I should have gone down the Chief on my own. It would have been less embarrassing.

At the clinic, we wait. The air conditioning has failed and the sound of wet coughing makes me squirm on the plastic seat, grateful I'm still wearing my leggings. The idea of my bare legs sticking to the chair makes me want to gag. Who knows who was sweating in this seat before me. The sun beats through the windows facing the street and the room gets hotter the longer we wait.

"I wish you'd been more careful," Dad says, a thick line appearing on his forehead. The groove has always been there. It's just deeper, longer, than it was when I was a kid. My parents are getting older, and Dad has always been older than the other kids' parents. He and my mother met and fell in love later than their peers, and my dad had been married once before. My mom's parents weren't impressed. She married him anyway. Years together have made them more alike. It's my dad, now, who goes to nurseries and picks out the plants that my mother puts into the ground. My mother, on the other hand, has developed an apathy about shopping that matches his. I drag her out twice a year and force her to buy clothes for both of them. Spencer always tells Mom how nice she looks.

"It was an accident, Dad."

"How'd you drive with that foot?"

"I met a friend who was on his way up. He took me home."

"That was nice of him," my dad says. He picks up an office copy of *Country Gardens*, and is lost to the latest in koi pond design. I pick at my nails, which still have dirt embedded under them. *Lovely, Brooklyn. Henry must have been overjoyed to spend the day with you instead of outside in the fresh air.*

The doctor pokes and prods my foot when it's finally my turn. She prints off a requisition for a CT scan, repeats everything Henry said about compression and elevation, tells me to buy a brace from a drugstore, and to stay off the ankle for at least three days.

"Looks bad," she says. "Can't know for sure without imaging. Depending on what we get back from the CT scan, I'll put you on the list for an MRI."

She looks at me expectantly, and then at the door.

"Can you check my blood pressure?" I ask.

She looks at the door again.

"Please."

She rolls her eyes, but does it. The cuff wheezes as it tightens on my arm. Then she frowns and shakes the electronic device.

"That's funny. My sphygmomanometer isn't working. I just used this." She shakes it again, tightens the cuff, and tries to get a new reading. The cuff crushes my bicep, but the results screen stays gray. No flashing numbers.

"Is it the battery?" She grumbles to herself as she pulls the device off my arm. "I'll have to borrow one from a colleague. I'll be right back."

Another sphygmomanometer isn't going to do a damn thing.

She marches out of the treatment room complaining about cutbacks to healthcare and faulty equipment. As her footsteps vanish down the hall, I rush—as much as someone with a sprained ankle can—to leave the room. There's no sign of the doctor in the hallway and I manage to hobble back to the waiting room and hustle Dad outside without being seen by anyone, including the receptionist. No one questions my ungainly flight from the clinic. My father is still pondering koi ponds and water foliage. I can tell by the tilt of his head and the faraway look in his blue eyes, which are the same color as mine.

"Good?" he asks.

"Just fine."

"You always are, Brookie."

CHAPTER 5

I cancel my next three shifts, as per the doctor's orders, via email.

"Not great for me, but I'll get Kailey to sort it out," Matt emails back. "Maybe you can write some social posts for next week. You're laid up anyway."

Hard pass, I tell myself, but end up writing fluff about doughnuts anyway. For the forty-five minutes it takes me, I'm not obsessing about Henry, his perfect and very much alive girlfriend, or my heartbeat. Every now and then, I pick up my phone to text Kailey and ask if Henry has been in, but manage not to hit send.

One unpleasant task done, I force myself to do a second. I Google "how do I know if I'm dead?"

Hot topic. More than one person has written a listicle with titles like "Indications You Are Already Dead."

Basic symptoms include: no reflection, no tan, seeing glitches, immobility, trouble sleeping, difficulty making decisions, no forward motion, feeling punished, spotting the same crow repeatedly, and hearing dead chickens clucking.

Alright, so I'm symptomatic. At least I haven't heard any dead chickens.

"I can make decisions if I want to," I mutter. "And I haven't seen any creepy crows."

According to Dr. Google, which I consider a more reliable source of information than my brother, I've contracted four different catastrophic illnesses and am simultaneously a medical mystery. Internet doctors and hypochondriacs alike tell me I could have Parkinson's, or schizophrenia, or some form of dementia. Or a brain tumor.

I spend two days reading articles about death and hallucinations, certain that Emily Porter and Emaleigh Taylor are the result of a quirk in my brain or body chemistry. Hallucinations are harbingers of nothing good: drug use, high fever, severe physical illness, sleep deprivation, mental illness. I rule out drug use and high fever. Sleep deprivation too—I sleep to pass the time. I've never slept so much and still felt so unrested. I've been sleeping since Penny vanished somewhere into the desert landscape of Syria. There's no way to remember while I'm asleep.

It's rare for people to experience auditory and visual hallucinations at the same time, and they can't typically interact with what they're seeing or hearing.

Unless they're dying.

Which fits. Mostly.

I devour firsthand accounts from emergency room doctors and palliative care or hospice nurses whose deathbed patients saw and spoke to loved ones who'd already passed on before they too slipped away. Shouldn't I be seeing Auntie Karen or the grandmothers I never met?

The comments under all the posts and articles go on for pages. By day three, I'm way, way down the rabbit hole. Username isalldark14 writes that we're all caught in the same hallucination, but some people *know* it's not real. He has proof, but if he tells anyone, a super-secret government agency will cut off his head and burn his body, and he won't be able to save the world. I find myself sympathizing.

"Okaaaay, that's probably enough Reddit," I say, and thrust the computer away.

Imposed exile forces me to realize how dependent I've become on my crappy job for human contact. Even my parents are absent: My mother goes to work, and my father is handling a small project for an engineering company. Kailey sends a handful of texts bitching about customers. Henry doesn't have my phone number. I vacillate between whether that makes it easier or harder. At least I can pretend that's the only reason he hasn't checked up on me.

Henry has a girlfriend, I remind myself. *Nice guy, saving a hapless hiker. Would have done it for anyone.* I have no claims on his attention, no right to it.

The closest thing to social interaction I have in three days are the messages I leave on Penny's parents' voicemail.

"Hi, it's me, I mean, it's Brooklyn. I just wanted to check in and see if there are any updates about Penny. Please let me know. Please. Bye."

I leave the same message almost every day. Their lack of response is sharp as a knife into my ribcage. Soon, it will bury itself into my heart. Will I even be able to feel the cold tip as it penetrates?

A world without Penny is unfathomable. Penny is alive—misplaced, lost, but alive. I believe it. How could she, a wisp of a woman containing more energy than a nuclear reactor, vanish silently and without a trace into an unfamiliar landscape nearly seven thousand miles and a complicated plane journey away from my doorstep?

I was used to Penny's absence even before Syria. It'd been years since we'd been in the same time zone for more than a week—even longer since we shared secrets in the intense, confidential way teenage girls pour their hearts out. Despite that closeness, some secrets never spilled out over stolen coconut rum and peach-flavored coolers as we sat cross-legged on the floor in her attic, giggly and heartfelt. My secrets were too big to share.

What did we bond over in kindergarten when we first met and realized we'd stick together? Our shared hatred of pink crayons? What we have in common now is tenuous, based almost entirely on a shared past. She saves lives; she provides medical treatment to people who've left their homes with almost nothing while members of her team look for landmines or give out food and water. I serve doughnuts to hipsters who are younger than me and in art school, or studying literature or economics or software engineering. I could have done more than I'm doing now. Whatever *more* means is elusive—I can't do what Penny does. I'm not a highly educated nurse who speaks English, French, and Mandarin, trained to handle public health crises. I can barely handle a family crisis, or a personal one. I should be able to. It's not like I haven't had practice.

On day four of my ankle recovery, I go back into Cute Lil'. White T-shirt, black skirt. I wear flip-flops because I can't get my ankle, wrapped in medical tape and a bandage, into anything else. Footwear safety be damned. My father drives me, and Kailey meets me at the shop so I don't have to do opening duties by myself. She body slams the swollen door, and I thank her profusely because she had to give up a yoga class to help me out.

"It's not the end of the world," she says. "The Wednesday morning instructor is super into chanting and it's impossible to focus while he's going on and on."

She does most of the work to open the store. All I can do is the twenty-three online orders, because putting doughnuts in boxes requires minimal hobbling.

"Why are there so many?" I ask, sure there's been a mistake.

"It's National Junk Food Day," Kailey says.

"Food-themed days only exist because a bunch of marketing people decided they wanted to shove more product into consumers' shopping carts," I say. "That's how cheese became such a big deal in America. And milk. Bacon too. All of it was surplus, and food producers needed to sell it, so a bunch of marketers and food lobbyists spun some stories and aspirational bullshit and everyone went for it and look where we are now. High cholesterol and dairy allergies."

"You're too much. And who cares?" Kailey says, plucking a Raspberry-Almond-Bacon doughnut out of the box I just put it in. "It's all delicious."

I sigh and replace the doughnut she swiped. I've devoured my fair share of Cute Lil's offerings and I keep wearing my black skirt because it's the only one that still fits. Despite the revolutionary flavors Cute Lil' claims to offer, nearly every doughnut tastes basically like white sugar. I look at the racks of dough blobs distastefully. Today, they seem oily and indigestible and I can't imagine eating one. I keep packing the orders neatly into boxes with one eye on the clock above the door. If Henry was going to pop by on his way to work, he would have done so already.

He has his girlfriend, a career, a life. I force myself to stop looking up every time the sensor above the door dings.

"What are you looking at?" Kailey says, after I spend fifteen minutes glowering at the infuriatingly empty sidewalk. She pauses as she restocks the sugar packets next to the counter where we keep the cream and fake milk.

"No one."

"That's not what I asked."

I ignore her and lumber over to restack the magazines on the ledge along the front window. I pause over a familiar face. Emily Porter.

Wait.

"Emily Porter is dead!" I yell. "When did that happen?" I check the date on the magazine. It's two weeks old.

"Who's dead?" Kailey asks.

"Emily Porter."

"Who?"

"She was in a bunch of great shows," I say. "*This High-School Life*. Bunch of movies."

Kailey shrugs. "Never heard of her."

Right. Age gap. *This High-School Life* was already a couple of seasons in when my mother decided I was old enough to watch it. Kailey would have missed it entirely.

"Never mind." I flip through the magazine until I find the article. Emily Porter was forty-three when she died. There's a recent picture of her holding a grinning, blonde-haired toddler. The woman in my room was nowhere near this old. I skim the article. According to her live-in boyfriend, Jeffery Theodore Shipman, he'd found her collapsed at the bottom of a flight of stairs after he returned from a three-day business trip. Her son had been staying at Grandma's house. The coroner had not yet released the cause of death, but was investigating.

Easy. The boyfriend did it.

I stare at Emily Porter's picture and feel…grief. For Emily, for the little boy in her arms. And for myself. I'd grown up with Emily, and who she'd played on television. Aside from Penny, I didn't make friends easily. There was too much risk. Risk they'd hurt me. Risk they'd find out something they shouldn't. Risk they'd get hurt. *This High-School Life* was safe. Ella, Emily's character, was there for me. And now she's gone. But I just saw her. She was right there, in my bedroom, years younger. Not dead. My mind flashes back to my Reddit spiral. Was I like those patients on their deathbed, communing with their loved ones who'd already passed? What did that say about me, that who I connected with on a postdeath level was someone I'd never met? Something so lonely and lost I can't look directly at it. I press back tears with the palms of my hands.

This feels more real, somehow, than the day last August when I found out Penny was missing. I'd been at work. Vancouver was on day nine of a heatwave, and the office air conditioning had crapped out. Everyone at work was cranky and melting, and the air was thick with more than just tension. That morning, my boss's boss and heir apparent, Lawrence Junior, had shut me out of a meeting and reassigned one of my clients to a new strategist. I was thrilled to be rid of the client; he hated everything our copywriter, a woman, wrote and told anyone who would listen that a man would understand his business better, but Lawrence Junior had asked me pointed questions about why I hadn't been able to satisfy the client.

He said, "You should have assigned Dave to handle the web content."

I said, "You told me to assign the best writer we've got. Specifically, you said 'Not Dave.'"

It wasn't the first time Lawrence Junior had given me contradictory instructions.

I'd fled the building with visions of iced coffees dancing in my head. Heat bounced off the sidewalks and the city was cloaked in a potent combination of urine and tangy garbage. I came to an abrupt stop when I noticed my dad's ancient but immaculate silver Honda wedged between a white Escalade and a tiny BMW from a car share. He stared out the windshield, not moving, his hands at ten and two. I knocked on the window three times before he noticed and turned his sweating face to mine. He unlocked the passenger side, and I slid in.

"What are you doing here?" I asked as I rolled down my window. "How long have you been waiting? It's a bazillion degrees in here."

"I wasn't sure when you'd be done," he said. He looked dazed. "Brookie. Brookie..." He stalled out. He looked at me, his eyes wide, wet, and bloodshot. My stoic father was on the edge of tears.

"Is it Mom?" I demanded. Whatever my father—who rarely displayed any emotion except mild interest—was going to say would destroy me. I knew by the pallor in his face.

"Helen's fine. It's Penny."

"Penny," I rasped. "What about Penny?" White stars shot across my vision and my whole body started to tremble.

My father put his hand on my shoulder and then snatched it back. We're not the kind of family that resorts to physical comfort. We're comfortable being uncomfortable and untouching. Separate. It cost me then. I'd wanted to dig my hands into someone warm and real. I'd wanted to grasp their bones.

"I don't know much," he said. "She didn't come back from a remote clinic. Helen talked to Lane and Robert Parker and told me to come get you."

"When did Mom tell you to come get me?" I opened the car door and dry heaved into the gutter. Nothing came up. I hadn't eaten more than a banana and half a granola bar all day.

"Around 3 p.m."

"Fuck, Dad! It's almost 6 p.m.! Why didn't you come in and get me?"

"It is? I forgot my phone. I just kept thinking: What if it was you? Didn't realize the time. Shit. Helen is going to be mad."

Swearing and worried about Mom while Penny was in trouble. Unbelievable.

"Why. Didn't. You. Come. In."

"Because, Brookie. Because I wanted you to be as happy as you could be for as long as you could be."

This was how my father showed his love. He gave me a few extra hours of obliviousness.

My hands quake over the magazines, but I manage to stack them all into a haphazard pile, covering Emily's face. Before long, the line is out the door and chaotically spewed onto the street—thanks to a fresh wave of food blog posts on the West Coast, as one woman emphatically tells me. My shift ends, but I keep working, even when Becca comes in to take over. I can barely hear people's orders and twice serve Lemon Soda Pop instead of Cinnamon and Chocolate Hot to unwitting customers. Earlier, Becca had broken a full coffee carafe and the floor is slick and dirty beneath my flip-flops. There hasn't been time to mop. The shop heats to boiling from the afternoon sun coming through the front window. Everyone is grumpy, wilting, and hangry. My ankle twinges every time I forget about it and step casually.

"Fucking heritage building. No air conditioning," Becca gripes, as she pushes her wet bangs off her forehead. She has abandoned her beanie.

A customer yells over the din at Kailey about getting the wrong doughnut. I slap the right one on a plate and shove it down the counter. Kailey manages a grin, but it's too toothy. Her hair is lank and her whole body is drooping. I've only seen her lose her cool once before, and it's clear she needs a break. The line is still swelling and bulging like a just-fed snake. But Kailey is going to lose it in front of witnesses and be embarrassed about it later. She lives to be Zen.

"Go," I yell over the noise and point toward the back of the shop. She shakes her head and stamps her foot stubbornly.

Becca neatly hip checks Kailey away from the counter and pastes on an enormous, customer-eating smile. Kailey flees, too exhausted and angry to mask her relief. A surly tourist lectures me about the importance of service when I inform him we're out of Honeycomb-Vanilla Twists. He settles for Maple-Walnut Cookie Crumble, but lets me know he's dissatisfied by loudly announcing he'll never come back. The teenage girls behind him aren't impressed with his performance. They side-eye him so fiercely I'm amazed he doesn't disintegrate under their combined loathing. I comp them an extra doughnut.

Becca boxes doughnuts wearing an expression that suggests there is nothing she'd rather be doing than serving boxes of sugar and carbohydrates to ecstatic Millennials and overwrought suburbanites whose tempers are frayed by traffic, heat, and the fact that a dozen doughnuts is thirty-seven dollars.

Into this madness, when I least expect him, walks Henry. I don't spot him until he's just inside the door. He could stop hearts with the smile he sends in my direction. I'm safe from that, at least. I grin at my own joke while my brain mimics hyperventilating and creates a word vomit mashup of *ohmygodineedtonotlookstupidhelpsocutepleasedontbestupid.*

When our eyes collide, he waves his fingers at me. Then, he gestures to the crush in the store and mouths, "What is going on?"

I shrug and mouth back, "People are crazy."

He laughs and lifts his palms resignedly.

Henry has stayed in the heaving line for God knows how long. Surely not for a doughnut, which he can pop by for anytime. Me. He came for me. Maybe?

I allow myself a fragment of anticipation and sneak glances at him as the line inches forward. He has his phone out, but I can feel him watching me.

"How's the ankle?" he says, when there's finally no one between us.

I ignore the other customers and limp around the counter, waving one hand theatrically in the direction of my still-swollen foot, which had miraculously felt better the second I spotted him.

"Nice wrapping job," Henry says. "Doc say you're going to live?"

"She did." Not sure she can be trusted, though. She didn't realize I don't have a pulse.

"Probably no more hiking for you this summer?"

"I think I've learned my lesson about hiking in general. Maybe I'll stick to yoga." I shoot Kailey—who has recovered enough to make drinks—a conspiratorial, chummy look. She stares at me incredulously as hot water from the coffee machine overruns the to-go mug she's filling.

Henry and I beam at each other like maniacs.

"I was camping," he blurts. "With some friends. No reception. Super last minute." Then he flushes, as if he realized I hadn't asked, that he's disclosing more than he should about his absence to a woman he doesn't need to explain himself to.

"It's my first day back."

Becca veers around me and shoves an elbow in my ribs before she turns to Henry and sweetly asks to take his order.

Henry looks startled, as if he hadn't realized there was anyone else working.

"Honey Apple Bacon," he says. "Please."

"Coming right up." She plops his doughnut into a perfectly-sized paper bag and hands it over.

"Thank you so much," he says.

"My treat," I say.

"No," he objects.

"Please. For getting me off the mountain. It's the absolute least I can do."

"It was a pleasure." The mass behind him shifts anxiously as he lingers. People move out of line to identify the holdup.

"I have to…" I gesture at the crowd.

"Not a good time for a break."

I shake my head, aware of the growing tide of discontent from the line and the fact I'll be subjected to speculation from my coworkers about my interaction with Henry the second they get a free moment. Gossip is a spendable currency. Becca steps on my uninjured foot to hurry me along.

"I'll call you," Henry says, brightening, as if this has just occurred to him.

I nod. He melts into the mob, and we manage to serve the crowd with no more major mishaps or broken glassware. Finally, the rush slows to a trickle before stopping entirely. The store is deserted; the sun has dropped and is casting long shadows outside. Kailey, Becca, and I collapse around a table and exhale as one. Kailey puts her forehead down on the crumb-ridden Arborite.

"I can't wait to never serve another doughnut," she breathes.

"People were pissed when we ran out of Cotton Candy-Candy Corn," Becca marvels. "People could be starving to death. Legit starving. With no food anywhere. No clean water. And they're screaming at us because we're out of a doughnut? Get over yourselves." She snorts disgustedly.

She sounds so much like Penny I almost like her for a moment. It feels like we've done battle together.

"We've got nothing left," Kailey says, wearily taking in the empty shelves and display. "I'll call Matt. We'll close early or get a delivery from the other location."

"Please, doughnut gods, let us close early," Becca says, her palms clasped in the prayer position.

Kailey returns from the back of the shop with the news that Matt wants us to close. Scarcity is his jam. Plus, we've moved thousands of dollars of product. We're legal drug dealers. Sugar, carbs, and caffeine. It's probably been our best day all year.

We block the doorway with a stool, turn the open sign off, and passive aggressively ignore customers who peer into the store while we wipe every sticky surface with cleaner.

The three of us slog through closing tasks as indie pop plays in the background and makes us nostalgic for experiences we've never had. Becca mops the floor and doesn't complain for once. Every now and then she stops to answer a text message. Her phone never stops buzzing.

"I don't get it," Kailey says, as she restocks and wipes down the soda fridge.

"Get what?" I say from the stool where I'm counting receipts. I eye her warily.

"Last week you could barely look at Henry. This week he's saying he's going to call you and you're chatting like old friends."

I provide the shortest rendition I can manage about my ill-fated hike and Henry's appearance. She squeals. Becca looks bored, but she doesn't mop out of earshot.

"Well, I guess if you had to ruin the rest of your summer due to a wrecked ankle, that was the best way to do it," Kailey says. "You gonna sleep with him?"

"That's a pretty big leap. He's got a girlfriend and I barely know him."

She rolls her eyes. "You're such an old lady."

"Millennials have less sex than previous generations," I say. I worked on a campaign aimed at twenty-two- to thirty-four-year-olds for a condom company that encouraged young people to have more sex. Another stellar example of the difference between Penny's contribution to the world and mine. Who knew you'd have to convince people to have sex?

"If he's got a girlfriend, why did he look so excited to see you?" Kailey asks.

The words "did he?" spring to my tongue, but I bite them back and shrug nonchalantly. It's too much to want and too much wanting is a hunger that all the doughnuts in the world won't satisfy.

"He's not going to call."

"How do you know?" Becca says, pausing the swooshing motion her arms make as they drag the mop back and forth.

"He doesn't have my phone number."

She rolls her eyes. "Everyone is findable on social media."

My accounts are dead and deleted. Looking at other people's shiny and bright lives was exhausting. I had nothing to contribute to the glossy streams of content.

"You should sleep with Henry," Kailey decides. "He's hot. He looks fit. When was the last time you even went on a date?"

Before Penny went missing last August. Before, before, before. "I date. Have dated."

Men, whose lives outside of their online dating profiles were ordinary and bland. I'd been less interested in the men themselves than their confidence, their quick wit, their casual disregard for planning, and their ability to brush off embarrassment or hurt. I wanted their ability to avoid problems with distractions like a soccer game or a well-thrown punch. I studied their easy success and wondered how they just *knew* their lives would work out. I didn't want to date them so much as find a way to subsume their lives.

"When?" Kailey demands.

I wag my fingers noncommittally. Kyle. Another boy in college, Marshall. I whinge inwardly. Neither of them was my best moment.

"That's what I thought. Too bad about the girlfriend, though." Her tone is casual and light. "Good thing you don't care if he calls."

"Bitch."

She swats me with a wet kitchen towel. It snaps against my hip and stings. "You love me."

I will give Kailey this—she's the closest thing to a friend I've got right now. It's not her fault I put distance between us. I don't know how not to. After we lock up, she helps me into an Uber. I clutch my phone and wish that Henry had my number.

CHAPTER 6

At home, I wrap an ice pack around my ankle and curl into my faded pink comforter to ward against the chill, which creeps up my calf. The temperature doesn't improve when my mother sticks her head into the basement's living area.

"Good, you're home already. Family dinner. Spencer is coming."

"How'd you wrangle that?" Spencer usually gets out of dinner by offering polished excuses complete with science terminology and long-winded tangential logic.

"I didn't 'wrangle.' He said he wanted to pop by."

"Played the mom card, huh? 'Doesn't he care about his poor, poor mother?'"

"He needs a good meal. He doesn't eat like a bird like you do, Brookie." She starts peeling away the blanket and the ice pack. "Your ankle isn't looking quite as swollen. Seems to be healing."

Spencer was probably worried she'd cut off the funding he puts toward bottles of nice wine. He lives on sandwiches and frozen foods. Those frozen meals, according to a television heart health campaign, contain enough salt in one serving for four people. Salt leads to hypertension. My brother, the doctor. Wild applause for his choices.

"I have plans," I say, desperate to avoid dinner, which never goes as well as my mother dreams it will.

"No, you don't. You never leave this basement and it's been worse since…" She trails off, but I can hear the name she swallowed. Penny. We don't talk about Penny. One, or both of us, ends up crying. Me, mostly, because she's missing, because my mother can't get it through her head that the only thing that matters is that Penny isn't here. That I don't have the energy for anything but her absence. Mom wants me to be whoever I was before.

Once, she'd started to say, "Penny wouldn't want you to…"

I cut her off so sharply we'd both been shocked by the fury in my voice.

I said, "You don't get to say what Penny would want."

Her mouth snapped shut. Penny has gone unmentioned ever since. Mom doesn't know I call the Parkers every morning.

I exhale as loudly as I can manage and my mom helps me to my feet.

"It's not going to be that bad," she says, her hand hovering under my elbow as we ease up the stairs. "Spencer's been so busy with summer electives; we haven't seen him in months."

I hate how happy she sounds.

I'm in the living room, nearly hidden by the front window curtains, when Spencer arrives. My mother hugs him as if he's been away at war and she wasn't sure he was ever coming back. My father escapes onto the upstairs deck to check on the barbecue, waving at my brother as he exits the sliding door.

"Brooklyn," Spencer says, folding his long frame onto my mother's modernist faux leather couch. He smirks at me and shakes his head.

"What?" I say. He's been here ten seconds and already I'm defensive and prepared for a verbal fight, which will result in Mother rushing to protect him.

Last Thanksgiving, after a couple glasses of wine, I'd pointed out that when she talks about his medical school achievements to her friends, his grades improve with each retelling.

"You've always been jealous of your brother," my mother said, "because he's in med school and you only did that communications program. We would have paid for you to go med school too. Or law school. Or accounting. I hear that's a growing field."

"I'm bad at math," I said.

"Your brother is such a good student. You'd have done better, if you'd applied yourself a little more."

At that point in the conversation, I'd stormed out and locked myself in the bathroom. My final grades weren't as impressive as my brother's top-of-class finish, but I'd been first in most of my university courses. Sure, I'd gotten in more trouble than Spencer did in high school—for cutting class or inciting rebellion and protests with Penny, or getting caught with booze during a volleyball trip. I may have convinced the senior soccer team to vandalize our rival school's field, but we didn't do any lasting damage.

The only thing I didn't do was apply to med school. Or law school. Or study something my mother covets the way some people covet Kim Kardashian's booty. Her obsession is almost lustful.

She was thrilled when she'd found out Penny wanted to get into nursing and needed help with college applications and internships. She had a son considering medical school and a pseudodaughter following her around the hospital during practicums.

Her real daughter was going to study marketing and communications. "Two out of three isn't bad," I heard her say once, jokingly, to my dad.

My dad said, "That's not funny."

Now I'm stuck sitting on a rocking chair that my mother used for feeding us when we were babies and doesn't have the heart to get rid of, even though it's uncomfortable, and my brother is stretched out on the new couch, chatting to my mother about how well he's doing at school and how he's looking at residency programs in Toronto and Montreal.

"Who knows," he's saying. "I can probably go wherever I want."

I hope he goes. Far away, across the country, and doesn't come back. My mother would be heartbroken and I would feel relief. I wouldn't cry with her at the airport, and she'd take it as another sign of my disdain and jealousy toward my brother. Hell, I won't go the airport. If I had people to invite, I'd throw a thank-you-for-leaving party.

"There are lots of good opportunities around here," my mother objects. "It's expensive to move, and to go back and forth. What about holidays? What if something happens to me or your dad?"

Mom is nuts if she thinks Spencer is going to take care of them when they're old. Older. Spencer distracts her with a story about a professor who gave him 83 percent on a paper. Can she believe it? He spent four weeks on that paper.

My mother makes clucking noises and shakes her head. She looks like a chicken, waggling her aging neck, her hair loosening from its bun and falling in her eyes.

Don't be an asshole, Brooklyn. They let you live in the basement for free.

Well, Dad lets me live in the basement for free. I overheard Mom tell him they should charge rent.

My mother said, "It will encourage her to go back to work. Get a real job."

My father said, "Penny's situation has been hard on her. We don't need to make things more difficult. We pay Spencer's rent. We can't charge Brookie for living in our basement."

My quiet, uninvolved father had actively done something parental, and my mother had dropped the subject of rent. Out of the three of us, I'm not sure who was the most astonished.

From the kitchen, Dad hollers at us to come eat. Dutifully, we traipse into the dining room and find the spots we've always sat at. There are teeth marks on my side of the table from where I gnawed on it as a kid. Spencer's side has a burn from when he'd slammed a hot cast-iron pan down. Mom's side still bears evidence of hot-pink glitter nail polish, which I'd spilled when I was fourteen. We pile our plates with teriyaki chicken and steak rubbed with Montreal seasoning, which my dad swears is tastier than anything on the market. He has no idea what's on the market. He hasn't entered a grocery store since the strawberry jam incident.

We eat in silence, beautiful silence, until the asshole breaks it.

"I hear you're hanging out with Henry Martin," Spencer says.

"Henry's last name is Martin?"

Spencer's eyes narrow. Shit. With Spencer, it's best not to engage or respond. He uses what he learns against me—now, later, eventually.

"Not hanging out," I correct, too late to deny any knowledge. "He's a customer. Comes in every now and then."

"That's not what Kashvi, his girlfriend, said. We've got some electives together."

This city is too damn small. I didn't know her name before Spencer said it. I really know nothing at all about Henry.

"I ran into Henry while hiking," I say. Another mistake. Word diarrhea. "I sprained my ankle and he drove me home."

"I should look at that." Spencer starts to stand, shoving his chair back with a squeal on the linoleum.

"No thanks. I went to the clinic. Doctor said it's sprained."

Skepticism rolls off him. Since we were kids, he's always implied I do and say everything for attention. I'm not sure how he's always managed to turn the tables on me; I'm older by eighteen months. I should be able to crush him. I blame Mother's voice in my head: *Be nice to your little brother.*

"Why not get a second opinion?" my mother says. She reaches across the table to pat Spencer's arm.

"He's not a doctor yet," I say.

"My opinion is more valid than yours," Spencer says. "Since I don't work in fast food."

"It's an artisanal doughnut shop." Why am I defending it? Cute Lil' is not the hill to die on. I'm mortified to be working there, with my education, at my age, no matter how often I deny it to Kailey. I do think I'm better than the fucking doughnut shop. But I'm worse than my coworkers, who have dreams and plans and friends.

"You were always falling down when we were kids," Spencer says. "You were a walking disaster. Covered in bruises and cuts. Didn't you break your arm two summers in a row?"

"Honestly, Brookie, I was constantly bandaging you up," Mom says, spooning more potatoes onto Spencer's plate.

"Remember?" Spencer says.

I remember. My hand trod upon by soccer cleats; car doors closing on my foot; a teeter totter grazing my cheek; a locker door slamming on my fingers; my chin colliding with a metal water-fountain spout; a basketball bouncing off my skull; a sudden jostle and a slip down a flight of stairs. Spencer, looming nearby, guiltlessly out of reach.

"I played a lot of sports," I object, as a small tremor of rage goes through me. "Girls are vicious. They aren't the only ones."

The words slip out of my mouth, unbidden. The second they do, a dark look crosses Spencer's face and his foot comes down on mine, hidden by the tabletop. I yelp as it connects to my sprained ankle.

"Sorry, sis," he says, moving his limbs away. "Didn't realize your foot was right there."

I stare at my plate, over-dressed salad, meat, potato, and corn swimming in my blurry vision. My mother hands Spencer a dinner roll. He's always been the baby in the family. He'd been unplanned and almost died as an infant after he contracted a virus in the hospital. Our mother had been told she couldn't have any more children after me; she was too old. She called him her miracle boy. Surviving the virus made him twice a miracle.

"Mom says you don't talk to anyone these days. And you're putting on weight," Spencer says, his voice rich with concern and empathy. I'm the only one who hears it ring false. "You need to pull yourself together. Who would possibly be interested in you?" He points at me with this fork. His words are too pointed, too close to the ones I tell myself, for me to build any defense.

Blood roars in my ears and my cheeks burn. My brother leers. He's won. He knows it. I imagine picking up my baked potato, luxuriant with butter, sour cream, and salt, and chucking it right in his face. I wouldn't miss—all those volleyball and basketball trophies aren't for show. I picture the potato sliding down the front of his face, coating his eye and his left cheek in thick, rich fats. My hands twitch toward my plate.

"Asshole," I hiss. Then, I remember what a bad idea speaking is. My jaw snaps shut. I sit. I quiet. I fold inward.

Spencer rattles the tableware and shoves back his chair with a screech as he stands up. I shrink into my seat.

"You're so hostile," he says. "All the time, even as kids. And now you're back here, mooching off Mom and Dad."

My mother nods frantically. She lives for this shit. Spencer frames himself in the best possible light while ensuring I can be written off as belligerent or the cause of the problem to begin with. Mom laps it up—the attention, the drama, the way her boy looks out for her.

"That's enough." My father intercedes, placidly, less affected by the drama, which has played out over dinner for years. Usually, he just lets us snipe at each other before he flees to his office to read Asimov, or Dick, or Le Guin. "I just want to have one family dinner that doesn't end in you two children squabbling and upsetting your mother. I've had enough of your nonsense. Both of you." And with that, he leaves the table, taking his plate with him in the direction of the kitchen.

My mother wrings her hands. I eat mechanically. Everything on my plate tastes the same.

"I need to get going anyway," Spencer says, as he blasts me with a glare.

"You have homework to get to, I'm sure," Mom says. "I'll pack you a Tupperware." She stands and clears off the table.

"Are you kidding me?" I say. "You're going to make him a dinner to go? He's an adult. He can feed himself."

"Brooklyn, he's a student." My mother inhales deeply, as if she's trying to suck her feelings up inside her. She straightens her back and marches out after Dad.

"Why do you do this?" I whisper.

"Do what?" he says. "Look out for my friends? Kashvi is amazing. Smart. Beautiful. She doesn't deserve to have her life messed up by someone like you going after her boyfriend. She's going to be a surgeon. You couldn't even handle a marketing job, and now you work in a doughnut shop." His face is twisted into something ugly.

"It's none of your business." I shouldn't defend myself. Retreating is the only way to get out of Spencer's line of fire.

"You probably flung yourself at him. You're nothing."

I rear up, accidently overturning my plate onto the table. Salad dressing seeps into the lace tablecloth. Spencer has always known how to find the soft tissue and cut into it. He's used his skills against me, again and again, since we were children. How well he's turned my weaknesses around to protect his own. The tears that have been pressing into the back of my eyes spill out. To my horror, I start to cry. Big, wet gulping sobs.

"You're disgusting," he says softly, so my parents, who are still in the kitchen, don't hear. He rounds the table and looms over me. We're a tall family, but at 6'3" Spencer towers over all of us. The whisper of his breath crosses my cheek, and my breathing constricts as his hand reaches toward the squishy, tender flesh on the back of my arm. Sweat blooms on my forehead and my intestines cramp. The clatter of dishes in the other room stops, and my mother's footsteps get louder. Spencer steps away from me.

I take the opportunity to bolt. I practically fall down the stairs to the basement, not being at all mindful of my ankle, and fling myself on the old couch. It was relegated here after my mom got her dream IKEA sofa upstairs.

I hate myself for letting Spencer get a reaction out of me. Knowing who he is doesn't change the fact that I still expect him to miraculously evolve into a good brother, the past erased, or forgotten, after a tearful apology. From him, obviously. That, or I'll morph into someone he doesn't want to harm anymore. Someone impermeable. I dry my cheeks on the bottom of my shirt and will away a fresh bout of crying. Tears are an ineffective problem-solving technique.

My mother bustles into the room and sits, primly, on the piano bench across from the couch. The beat-up piano hasn't been played in years. None of us took to it, but my mother harbors the fantasy that one day one of us will turn out to be a virtuoso.

"I've cleared the table off," she says. "I'd appreciate it if you'd vacuum the floor and wipe down any sticky spots because you made such a mess on my nice tablecloth."

"Spencer started it," I say, reverting to childhood patterns even though that excuse never flew.

A muscle jumps in her jaw and her knuckles turn white. Her wedding band sits loosely on her finger, held in place by a diamond engagement ring. I've never seen her without these two pieces.

"He shouldn't have said anything about your weight. That was cruel. But you're both adults and you're the oldest. Going after each other like that at dinner is unacceptable. I shouldn't have to tell you this."

"Did you tell Spencer his behavior was unacceptable?"

She frowns at me. "You called him an asshole. He's worried about you. He thinks you're depressed. That you should see somebody."

"I'm not depressed."

"I think he's right," my mother barrels on.

"So, his behavior is excusable because he's pretending to be worried about me? Who's going to pay for therapy? I make minimum wage."

She sighs. "We'll pay, if you want it. I just wish"—she exhales again, so heavily her shoulders deflate—"that you two kids would get along for once. He says you avoid him, and that when you bumped into him a few months ago at a coffee shop, you practically ran out the door when he waved. His feelings were hurt."

I grope for the words that will strip away whatever spell my brother has cast over my otherwise smart mother. It might not be a spell at all. It might be that he's a male child in medical school. My mother doesn't believe in gender bias, no matter how many articles I send her from *The New Yorker*, or how many articles I cut out of women's magazines, or how many stories I tell her about things my female coworkers and I have experienced at work or while walking to work. I think she took that class on gender studies so she could argue with other students.

It's why I won't tell her why I quit my fancy, decent-paying job in an industry I worked my ass off to get into. I stick to what she understands: I'm lazy; I'm bored; I need a change; I'm indecisive. I take the words she's used for years to describe me and return them to her. She accepts them, satisfied with her own assessments. Happy that she's been right about me. Happy that I've confirmed her worldview. I want her to change. I don't know if she can.

"I know you love Spencer," I say. "But he doesn't always tell the truth."

She shakes her head. "He's a good man. Immature sometimes, but he's becoming a doctor to make a difference. Like…" She hesitates, and pushes on, "Like Penny."

I bite back a string of expletives. "He's becoming a doctor because you're paying for it. And because he wants us all to call him Dr. Thomas."

My mother rolls her eyes at me. I roll mine right back. She already calls him Dr. Thomas. She calls me *her daughter*. Like she owns me.

CHAPTER 7

Exhaustion settles in after my mom goes upstairs. I stagger to my bed and start to drift, but am snapped awake by a voice.

"Don't you have more important things to do than sleep? Like date? There are apps for that, you know."

Strands of thick brown hair dangle in my face and tickle my nose. An angular, beautiful woman with green eyes hovers over me. I scramble backward on my mattress, only to smack my head on the wall behind me.

Though half-dazed, I recognize the face. Emmalee Jones, dragon slayer. Or at least she'd played one in a television show called *Dragonslayer*. In it, dragons are freed from their underground lairs thanks to a crack in the northern permafrost and make their way south, ravaging American cities where the human population has already been decimated by a deadly flu caused by released gases and bacteria from the melting north. It ran for four seasons before being cancelled. Even a fan uproar couldn't save it. Lawrence Communications had been hired for the original marketing campaign when the show launched. I'd watched *Dragonslayer* out of duty, but became one of the outraged fans. There was something else, some other reason she'd been in the news recently, that I can't quite remember. I rub the back of my head.

"Ouch."

"Baby." Emmalee's wearing a pair of skintight leggings and a white camisole I know came from my closet. Her biceps are defined, and she's more menacing than someone five feet tall and 110 pounds should be. She looks like the women from the CrossFit gym next to Cute Lil' who come in on their cheat days. Seeing the definition in her legs makes me miss the strength I'd had when I'd been running daily. I never huffed and puffed up the stairs.

"Why are you cooped up in this disgusting room? Is that a dead plant? And an empty doughnut box? It smells in here."

"Ankle." Alone, friendless, sulking, bored, beyond tired. Beyond furious. No heartbeat. No Penny.

"Looks bad. But honestly, it's just a sprain. That's nothing. I broke my collarbone once. Want to talk about how much that hurts? Jesus. They shot me up with snake venom or some shit just so I could lift my arm again."

"What?"

"Snake venom."

"Snake venom."

"Yes. It was brutal. So painful."

There's something wrong with this, something I can't remember. She shouldn't be here. Should she? Something about Emily. Something about Emmalee.

"You should go on a date," Emmalee carries on. "I work too much to date, and people are still remarkably judgy about who celebrities date. But you're nobody. You should be out there!"

"Nope."

"Why not?" Emmalee stares at me with the same expression she used while considering the best way to overcome some insurmountable, dragon-related apocalypse before snatching a solution out of thin air. The resolution typically involved an enchanted sword.

"Why not?" she repeats.

"It's too much. It's draining."

"Life's exhausting. You still need to live it," Emmalee says, matter of fact.

"Am I even alive? No heartbeat."

She purses her full, glossy lips. "You look a little tired." She snaps her fingers. "Exercise. That might work. Elevate your endorphins and all that."

"Last time I exercised, I sprained my ankle."

"Right. Dating it is." She writhes suggestively. "Should be no problem. You're adorbs."

"Adorbs isn't enough," I say, staring at my hands, which are suddenly disintegrating and rebuilding like a bad special effect in a 1980s horror movie. My skin melts like wax, blending and dissolving into my tissue and muscle to reveal the white of my bones. I should be freaking out, but I'm resigned. My body, and for once my brain, has nothing to say about the weirdness I've been experiencing. All I can do is hope I'll eventually solidify into some Brooklynlike shape. Or not.

"You're...smart." Emmalee says this dubiously as she takes in the piles of '90s era romance novels and old magazines scattered around the room.

"It's not enough," I say again. The apps. The swiping of men's faces. The bars. The chitchat. The stories meant to sound the way Instagram posts look: perfect sound bites shouted over a house band or painstakingly typed into the profile boxes online. My skin crawls at the effort it requires.

"It's not like you have anything else to do. Given the state of your social life. When was the last time you went on a date?"

God, she's practically Kailey, only shorter and scarier. And something else. Something not right.

"One date, last year," I say, trying to think. My head is aching and I'm massively underreacting to this absolutely bananas situation. I should be screaming. Instead, I feel like I'm underwater and my lungs are compressing and running out of oxygen. Any air I suck in can't travel further than my upper chest. My tissue and skin slowly reform over my bones. I hear flies buzzing for a few seconds before the sound is gone.

"I dated. In college. Marshall."

Marshall and I had been nearly the same height—okay, I was taller—and he had floppy hair and soft hands. He'd been committed to his causes: the student newspaper, photography, and the power of public transit. He lacked presence; if I needed to, I could overpower him. I was strong then from years of sports and the associated weight training. On our second date, he reached out to hold my hand, leaving ample time for me to say no. He came home with me for dinner once. After he left—having eaten little due to a recent conversion to veganism—my mother said: "He's not as smart as you."

I'd snorted. My mother had made it clear, many times, I wasn't the smart one in the family.

She said: "He's morose. You're so energetic. And pretty. Really Brooklyn, you could find someone more suitable."

Her compliment was so shocking, I'd opened my mouth to agree. But she followed up with a soliloquy about the lovely, brilliant, and exceptional budding scientist Spencer was dating. To punish her, I dated Marshall for three more tedious months.

"Oh, and I dated a real dirtbag named Kyle," I say, warming to the subject matter. I'd kept him far away from my parents, although I suspect my mother would have loved him. She's not that discerning.

Emmalee's eyebrows shoot up under her bangs. "I didn't say date an asshole," she says. "Not everything needs to be done to the extreme."

"It was a pretty destructive relationship all round," I say. "I wanted to destroy something. Someone."

"Did you?"

I shake my head.

Sure, Kyle and I cut a swath through each other in one-upmanship taken to unhealthy levels. But it hadn't been Kyle I'd wanted to cut down, he was just easier to reach than my actual target. He was vulnerable in ways Spencer wasn't.

Emmalee prowls around my room, displacing stacked books and clothing. "Maybe dating will get things going." She gestures to her heart, then unearths a ten-pound dumbbell from under a chair in the corner and hefts it effortlessly over her head. Her mouth counts off reps silently.

Emmalee is too energetic. She's doing squats now, her perfect butt nearly skimming the floor.

And then it hits me.

"You're dead," I blurt.

Emmalee Jones died in a motorcycle accident after her show was cancelled. Hit-and-run. I remember. I'd read it on Twitter, but I'd been buried in work and deadlines and angry clients and passive-aggressive bosses and it hadn't registered. It was just another horrible headline in a year filled with bad news. It had seemed far away, a thing that had happened to a stranger with a familiar face.

"Are you threatening me?" she says.

I try again. "No, I mean, you...died. Not 'I'm going to kill you.'"

Shit. Should I be telling this to her? Does she know? Does it matter, since I'm the one with hallucinations and some serious issues with my brain chemistry?

She rolls her eyes at me and keeps counting. Twenty squats. Twenty-one! Who does that? Me, before I had a desk job. I'd be lucky to knock off five squats these days.

"Shouldn't you be taking the form of some beloved dead relative?" I snap, irritated by her vitality. "A grandparent or something, if you're a hallucination I'm seeing while I'm on death's door? Maybe Aunt Karen? Shouldn't I be seeing dead loved ones?"

"Would you prefer chatting with some old dead relative?" Emmalee asks, pausing midsquat. "Or my badass self?"

I mentally catalogue the people I know who've died. Two grandparents I never met and two whom I never got along with. Aunt Karen when I was six. A girl from elementary school with cancer. A boy from my high school hit by a drunk driver.

And now I feel it: a dark, suffocating wave of fear, Penny somewhere on its crest. It crashes over me, leaving me reeling and disoriented.

"You, I guess," I gasp.

Emmalee crouches next to me. "Maybe I'm all you've got right now." She frowns. "You alright? I didn't think you could be any paler, but you just..." She gestures at my face. "All the color went *whoosh*."

I try to breathe. I don't let the idea of Penny, dead, gain any purchase. I don't let the idea of anything gain any purchase. Every thought that could surface I push down until there's nothing in my mind but a void.

Emmalee's hand settles on my shoulder. It burns against my skin, and the chill I haven't been able to shake since I got home from work starts to slip away.

"Breathe. You need to breathe."

This time, when I inhale, the air settles deeper in my lungs.

"Panic attack," Emmalee says, matter-of-factly. "Had them every day on set for four years."

"Why?

"I was exhausted and couldn't sleep because the director spent half the day screaming at me and someone was leaving super inappropriate notes about my ass in my trailer. I felt under attack—all the time."

Sounds familiar.

"I get plenty of sleep."

Emmalee pets my arm. "If you say so."

"I sleep all the time," I object. But have I ever slept well in this house, while Spencer has keys and carte blanche to come and go?

"Sleep now," Emmalee says. "I'll sit. I'll keep watch."

"You'll what?"

"Just sleep, Brooklyn."

As if I'll be able to sleep after the scene with Spencer upstairs.

But when I wake up it's morning, light is seeping through the blinds, and the dumbbell is sitting on its flat edge in the middle of the room like a sentinel.

CHAPTER 8

I eye the dumbbell skeptically while I root around in my room for something remotely clean to wear. I try the pants Emmalee was wearing, but they're too snug. Giving up, I scoop everything up and start the laundry. I leave my message for Penny's parents. Then, I Google "Emaleigh Taylor." Two dead Emilys can't be a coincidence.

"What the actual fuck."

She died too. She'd been to her doctor complaining of severe pain in her arm. He'd told her she was having anxiety and gastric reflux and sent her home. The next day, she collapsed on set and was rushed to the ER. The doctor there couldn't decide if she was having some sort of inflammation attack or shingles, and told her to slow down a bit and try meditation for stress relief. A third doctor finally did an angiogram after Emaleigh's father, who'd had a heart attack three years earlier, demanded it. That doctor rushed her into surgery—she'd been having a type of heart attack called a spontaneous coronary artery dissection. For three days! And not a single doctor had taken her concerns seriously. By the time she was on the operating table, it was too late. Her heart was damaged and couldn't pump properly. There was nothing they could do.

"It's not fair," I say. "You fought so hard. It's bullshit. They should have listened to you."

I wipe the tears off my cheeks.

None of this makes any sense—why these talented, amazing, strong women are gone, or why I can see them. None of them deserved what happened. They'd been there through my childhood onwards, through bad days at work, through the mundane daily banality of life. They'd all been there, on television, right when I needed them the most.

I stay in bed all day worrying. About me. About Penny, tough and smart and missing. Penny who'd drifted away from me so slowly I barely noticed until the first time she packed her bags and headed off on a deployment.

I should have spotted the changes in her sooner, but I was stuck in the loop of my own needs. The signs that things were evolving had been there. When we were sixteen, Penny told our elderly history teacher to fuck off after he remarked that without the Second World War, women probably wouldn't have entered the workforce in droves. He'd also made the argument that without women working, we'd have a stronger economy. After the same teacher refused to acknowledge Canada's early human rights violations (he'd called the internment of Japanese Canadians during the same war "justified," and the Chinese Head Tax from 1885 to 1923 "necessary for progress"), Penny took her complaints to the school board. That old, racist immigration policy wasn't an abstract, dry fact from a textbook to Penny. It was personal. She and Lane had ancestors who labored for years to pay off the crushing fee the tax inflicted on them when they came to Canada to build a new life.

I'd gone with Penny to the school board meeting, a silent, shaking witness in the face of the authority of the people who ran the city's education system.

"We have little control over the teachers' union," the chairwoman had said. "We can't fire people. We can request an investigation."

"You have a fucking teacher who marginalizes women. And minorities," Penny said, crossing her arms, seeming much taller than five feet.

I'd written Penny's speech, and I'd winced at her use of fucking.

The school board said they'd think about it.

Penny led a protest. Hundreds of students turned out. Someone's mother worked for the local paper, so a photographer and a reporter came out. I still have the picture of Penny that appeared on Page A12—her fist is raised toward the sky, her mouth is open in a triumphant shout, the other students railing behind her. I'm standing next to her, watching her with an amazed expression on my face.

The teacher kept his job. Penny got expelled for a week.

Her parents marched into the principal's office and hollered at him about legal precedents and the right to protest and demonstrate peacefully. Penny and I waited for them on the uncomfortable chairs by the secretary's desk. Penny was trying to eavesdrop while I attempted to figure out who could drive me home if Penny wasn't in class or around to walk home with after school. If I was alone, I might bump into Spencer and catch him at a bad moment.

When her parents eventually came out of the office, Robert was trying not to smile. He shook the principal's hand.

"It's the right choice. You know how teenage girls are. You offend one, you offend them all. You can't imagine Brooklyn Thomas is going to let Penny be unjustly expelled from school for a whole week without causing further disruptions herself. She'd probably end up protesting Penny's suspension."

Robert gave me more credit than I deserved.

"Verdict?" Penny asked, jumping to her feet.

"Expulsion is suspended," Robert said.

"We explained there wasn't any property damage and that protest is lawful and educational," Lane added.

That was all they said. They went back to work. We went back to class. And Penny's purpose in life crystalized. She would fight to make a difference in the world, wherever and however she could. She slowly pulled away from me until one day she was physically gone too.

— — —

"This is not going well," I groan to Kailey after two—count 'em, two—children smeared salted dulce de leche filling across the front window. And up my leg. Their mothers pretended not to notice.

"Full moon? Harmonic convergence? Is Mercury in retrograde? Is it Friday the thirteenth? Did you see the guy who looked me in the eye and then poured his full cup of coffee on the floor in front of the garbage station?"

"I missed that while I was cleaning up the smashed plates from those teenage boys."

"When did that happen?" Kailey asks. "And how are there still two hours left in my shift? I hate the evening shift. People are animals."

"All I want to do is go home, collapse on my bed, and never move again."

I did that all day yesterday, but it hasn't lost its appeal. Boredom begets boredom.

Kailey's head snaps up. "Whose phone is buzzing? Is it yours? I've *never* heard your phone go off."

"But I have such a thrilling social life," I say as I reach for my phone, which I'd left on the counter behind the till while I cleaned up the disaster zone at the front of the restaurant. Not actually a disaster zone, I amend to myself. Those are where Penny goes.

I scramble to see the display. Is it the Parkers? Penny? For a breathless moment, I'm flooded with certainty. It has to be Penny. No one else would be calling me.

But the number is local and unfamiliar. I hit mute and drop the phone back down, optimism crashing back to Earth with it. Hope deferred. It's worse to feel it brush against me before being snatched away than to not have it at all.

"You should answer it," Kailey says with a mischievous glint in her eye.

"Telemarketer," I say, rubbing my chest, which has tightened painfully. There's a rock in my throat I can barely swallow around, and I want to bawl.

"You sure?" Kailey asks, just as my phone buzzes again.

Text message. Same number. Trying to dislodge the lump, I pick up the phone again.

Tiki tonight? Bunch of us going for drinks. Will be fun.

A second message comes in while I'm reading.

Oops. This is Henry BTW. Pls come, if you're not busy. Everyone will be nice.

I take my phone and my apron and go out the back door of the shop. I let it slam shut behind me before silently screaming into the bundle of cloth.

My phone goes off again, and I nearly drop it in the filthy laneway.

Castaway's Volcano, 9 p.m. Henry uses a pleading face emoji.

Before I can rationalize my way out if it, which I most definitely should because of the many reasons not to get more entangled with Henry—Kashvi and my "health" issues among them—I text, *Fun! See you then!*

I don't agonize over what emoji to use. Grinning face, thumbs up, tropical drink, hit send. Refuse to second guess myself. Try not to read anything into the invitation. Breathe. I'm acting like a teenage girl who just got asked to the winter dance by a super cute guitar player. Emmalee would be so proud that I took her advice.

"Kailey," I ask, after I take what's left of my dignity and return to the store, "how did Henry get my phone number?"

She bats her eyelashes at me. "Easy-peasy. I found him on Instagram and private messaged it to him."

"You did what now?"

"Relax. All I said was 'Brooklyn's #' and a smiley face." She shows me the message. I'm not sure if I should hug her or shake her.

"Ballsy," I say, weakly.

"He texted you, didn't he? I knew he was into you." She slaps my ass and grins ferociously. "Wear something nicer than your work outfit when you go out. Unlike me, you have boobs. Use them."

"Girlfriend," I remind her.

"Where's she at?" she snarks back. "I've never seen her."

To manage my expectations, I decide Kashvi will be there and that I'm one of many random people Henry texted on a Friday night. Best case scenario, I'll like Kashvi so much that I'll be able to be happy for her and Henry and snuff out my growing infatuation. Maybe Kashvi and I can be friends, and she'll have a sexy, not-doctor acquaintance that I'll meet at a dinner party and fall madly in love with. It could happen.

I arrive at the tiki bar late, because it's surprisingly difficult to get dried dulce de leche off one's skin. I'd resorted to stealing my mother's hundred-dollar, two-ounce bottle of microderm-abrasion age-defying exfoliator. She's going to be pissed when she finds the bottle in the downstairs bathroom. Plus, I couldn't find anything to wear until I dug out the camisole Emmalee had been wearing and paired it with a cute flowing skirt I forgot I had.

The bar is lit with hurricane lamps modified to use colored lightbulbs instead of kerosene and white mini lights draped across the ceiling. I peer through the gloom, which has been exacerbated by a smoke machine, to find a familiar face. Chairs are packed close together, and based on the volume and the smell, people are more than a few drinks in. The entire room vibrates with voices and laughter. Someone's hand brushes my butt as I navigate narrow spaces between tables and chairs. The servers, on point with retro hair twists and wearing bright patterns, look harried and their pinched mouths belay their chipper greetings. I know exactly how they feel.

Henry spots me as I approach a booth at the back of the bar, close to the kitchen entrance, and waves me over. Everyone scoots over enough for me to squeeze in. The booth is cramped and my outside leg dangles off the side of the bench. Henry shouts something I can't hear. I angle my head closer to his mouth.

"You made it!" he says in my ear.

I glance around the table, trying to determine which stranger is Kashvi. The two men next to Henry are the same ones he was hiking with. Next to them is another man with a woman half in his lap and whispering in his ear, and next to them, right across from me, are two women who are eating nachos off the same plate and eyeing me speculatively.

"Kashvi couldn't make it. Study group decided to meet," Henry says. His breath stirs my hair, which I've left down and in loose curls. The outsides of our quads are pressed together, and the heat from his leg passes through the thin fabric of my skirt. I try to keep my smile polite sized, not, "Thank God, I didn't actually want to meet your girlfriend or for her to be here" sized. I'm in way too deep. I know it.

The petite, black-haired woman seated across the table grins and hands me a laminated drink menu.

"You been here before?" she asks. Not waiting for my answer, which is no, she points at herself and yells. "Grace! I work with Henry!"

"Brooklyn," I holler back. She makes a face like she didn't quite hear me. Flustered by the awkward exchange and the feel of Henry's body against mine, I open the menu to distract myself. And to make sure I don't melt against him. I'm faced with twelve pages of drinks filled with three ounces of rum or less. Henry tilts toward me and I smell vanilla and cinnamon on his breath as he shouts.

"Gin is on the last page. Most of the front pages are rum or tequila."

"We have a Coffee-Rum doughnut coming out next week." I wince. I've been at Cute Lil' long enough to start sliding it into conversation, using it as filler. I used to stuff the gaps with amusing stories about clients who made absurd demands. Like the time the client said they liked the cat in the logo for their new cat hotel, but could it be a dog—because dogs look friendlier—instead? Or the one who said the blue wasn't blue enough.

I don't want to talk about doughnuts. When I close my eyes at night, doughnuts dance in front of my eyelids. Except when my sleep is interrupted by diminutive, famous women.

"What'll it be?" the server asks, her face falling as she takes in the table. My arrival has shuffled the order in which people are sitting and now she'll need to remember who ordered what by face instead of seat.

I order a Mai Tai. At the bar, a man in a garish shirt lights a cocktail on fire, and the people sitting in front of him laugh loudly above the din. There's no way to focus on anything or anyone because of the noise. The room swirls in sound and color, and smells sweet and sticky from fruit juice and rum. I'm out of place and out of touch. I should say something, but can't catch a break in the conversations churning around me. Underneath my discomfort, there's something else. Guilt. I shouldn't be here, out, acting normal while Penny is who knows where. She'd probably mock the bar's décor and half the people at the table, but for a moment I miss her so much I nearly sink under the table to have a good cry.

I'm relieved when the Mai Tai appears and I have something to occupy myself with. Open mouth, insert straw.

"Good, right?" Grace yells. She leans forward, and I stretch my upper body toward her over the table. Henry is talking to one of the hikers.

"How do you know Henry?" she asks.

"He comes into where I work sometimes. And he helped me when I sprained my ankle hiking."

"You're Brooklyn!" Grace says, clapping delightedly. "That Brooklyn! How's your foot?"

That Brooklyn. Are there other Brooklyns? Henry's mentioned me? I glance at him just as he looks at me, and I quickly avert my attention back to Grace. He hasn't moved his leg away from mine, so I stay put. If I shift, I'll topple out of the booth anyway.

Grace and I chatter about injuries. She dislocated a shoulder once after being hit by a car. She'd rolled over the hood of a Civic and landed on the asphalt, jam-side down. It was how she met her girlfriend, Alisha, who'd been biking past and had rushed to her aid, like in a cute '90s rom-com. Alisha called an ambulance and stayed with her the rest of the day. They've been dating for two years.

"You never get bored of that story," Alisha says. "We need to get you new material."

Grace and I get up to use the bathroom at the same time. There are three stalls in the tiny, dimly lit room. Inside the hallowed four walls for gossipy women everywhere, Grace turns to me, squinting.

"It's great that Henry ran into you hiking. Have you met Kashvi? Henry picks up an awful lot of doughnuts, don't you think?"

I can barely keep up with the conversational detours.

"Not yet. I thought she'd be here." I try to sound disappointed. Grace raises an eyebrow. Okay, Henry aside, I probably won't be Kashvi's biggest fan because she seems friendly with my brother. "He must really like doughnuts," I say.

"He likes something. Our office is two blocks away from the shop," Grace says as she gives me a coolly assessing look. "So, what about you? You have a thing for him?"

Boundaries. Not a concern for Grace, apparently. Can I have a thing if my heart isn't functioning and the rest of my body is behaving in ways I can't anticipate? I'm not even sweating in the humid bathroom, while Grace's forehead is dusted with perspiration.

"Henry helped me with the sprained ankle, and he's super sweet to me and all the girls at work. But he was really clear he has a girlfriend."

"Was he?" Grace says. "He buys an awful lot of doughnuts for a guy who barely eats carbs."

"He told me about her. In passing. Once."

"Kashvi studies a lot," Grace says, as she pushes her long black hair away from her face and checks her dark purple lipstick in the full-length mirror. "Med school. You know. Busy-busy." She says this in a sarcastic voice, like she's heard it before, probably from Kashvi herself. "She's never around. Henry is on autopilot where she's concerned. But he's loyal. To a fault, really."

She watches me in the mirror's reflection. Thankfully, I don't disappear. That's something I don't want to explain.

"And yet, here you are," she muses.

I press my fingers into my dry forehead. "That's not...I'm not..." I splutter uselessly, trying to pick up the threads Grace is laying out while fighting a foggy brain from booze and Henry and God knows what else. No blood flow, probably.

Shut up, Brooklyn, I tell myself, and regain control. I put the pieces of what Grace isn't saying together, inhale, and say, "Kashvi seems very smart and talented, and it's too bad she's not here."

Grace laughs. "She is those things, but it's not an excuse to ignore the people you love or take them for granted. I wouldn't feel bad if Henry was looking at someone else. Neither should you."

"Grace," I say, the rum making me candid. "I'm twenty-nine, I work in a doughnut shop, I live with my parents, I eat my feelings, and I'm failing at life. I can't imagine there's any appeal. For Henry. For anyone."

Grace slings her arm around my waist and turns us to face the mirror. She has a beautiful smile and dark eyes that carry laughter. She barely comes up to my shoulder—I'm a giant next to her. My cheeks are pink from a heavy hand with a blush brush and I look unexpectedly flushed and healthy.

"You might be surprised," she says.

She drags me from the bathroom, and as the night stretches the liquor loosens me up. Henry regales the group with an overly dramatic rendition of what he starts calling "the ankle incident." Three drinks in, I hit the same groove as everyone else, and my sense of otherness fades. Booze: the great equalizer.

At the table, Grace is loud and excessive. She's unrestrained in a way I can't imagine being. She ploughs her way through a second plate of nachos and bets someone whose name I missed that she can outdrink him, which she does. His body droops and he keeps nodding off. Grace tells hilarious story after hilarious story. She touches everything: her girlfriend's hair, Henry's arm, my hand, a man's T-shirt, the creepy dried swordfish mounted on the wall. She doesn't notice my cool skin, even when she trips and grabs onto my shoulder for support on another bathroom trip. Everyone but me is sweating a little, which is unusual, but not as bizarre as having no heartbeat and vanishing from mirrors. Thankfully, at least no familiar, perky actors materialize.

"What do you do, for work?" I yell, realizing after a few hours I have no idea what Grace does all day with all that energy.

"I'm an accountant for the city," she shouts.

"No way! I pictured you as the gregarious award-winning bartender at a place way classier than this!"

She throws her head back and bellows gleefully. "I like her," she says to Henry. He grins and winks at me, and I grin back. Someone taps on his arm to get his attention and he turns away, but throughout the night I feel his eyes on me, the brush of his arm against mine. When his leg bumps mine under the table, he doesn't move it away. It's heady.

The next time I get up to pee, there's a lineup in the narrow hallway. I'm stuck standing next to Henry. I shift from foot to foot and pick at my nail polish to avoid uncomfortable eye contact, but Henry leans against me and I greedily absorb his weight and smell.

"Thanks for inviting me. I didn't know if..." I trail off.

I want to say, *I didn't know if you'd want to see me again.*

That sounds too much like a thing a girl you're dating would say. Or a stage-five clinger.

Henry saves me. "I knew you'd get along with Grace and Alisha. They're the best."

"They really are."

The line shifts by one person, but Henry makes no move to create space between us.

"It's great you came," he says. "How's your ankle?"

"Recovering. Still can't wear heels."

He grins at me and it crinkles the corner of his eyes. His eyes are brown and flecked with green. Not like Henry Cavill's at all. That's the thing about knowing people. It changes them. Or your idea of them. You're forced to see them.

In a miraculous first, the women's bathroom line dissipates first. I ease past Henry, the top of my head grazing his chin. He inhales sharply when our bodies brush, even though they've been touching most of the night. He looks startled. A jolt of electricity buzzes down my spine. I escape into the bathroom and try to breathe.

I'm starting to feel tired and drunk instead of pleasantly intoxicated, and any capacity I have to make good decisions has evaporated. I don't want to be that girl, the one who falls for an inappropriate guy and ends up with her heart broken because he can't leave his doctor girlfriend. Sounds like the basis of every country song on the radio. Sounds like a bad melodrama that Emily Porter starred in. It sounds like my life, at the moment.

Collectively, our drinking capacity tapers off. Our table is strewn with paper umbrellas, orange slices, and swizzle sticks. The bills stick to the table as everyone races to grab them. The server has done a rare and beautiful thing—separated the tabs. Alisha takes hers and hands mine to Henry.

"It's the least you can do," she says. "She put up with drunk work talk for hours and laughed at Grace's jokes."

"I'm funny," Grace says, elbowing Alisha. She throws an arm around her neck and presses a kiss into her cheek. Grace is wiggly and limp from the heat and alcohol.

"You're wasted. It's time to go," Alisha says, pulling her out of the booth. Grace scoots out and giggles as she wraps herself around Alisha, who's even taller than me.

I hold out my hand for my bill. "I'll take it."

"No," says Henry. "Alisha is right."

"Seriously," I say. Henry rolls his eyes and playfully pushes me out of the booth. I tamp down on the thrill the physical contact provides. He pays both bills at the till, despite my ongoing objections. I give up. I make minimum wage. Even living with my parents doesn't counteract the negative consequences of that decision, and my bank account regularly spirals downward.

We say goodbye to one of Henry's friends, who's sitting at the bar next to a girl resting her hand on his thigh. He stands to hug Henry in that macho, one-armed way that men in their thirties do. It's a hug, a greeting, an "I love you, man," and a goodbye all at once.

Outside, the sidewalk radiates heat but the air is comfortable instead of heavy and warm. Cabs rip by, and a group smoking outside a bar across the street laughs raucously. A cloud of tobacco and weed drifts over us. There's a slight ringing in my ears from the music and yelling inside Castaway's Volcano. I'm ready to be at home, in the quiet and dark. I've been hollowed out from noise, and liquor, and trying to keep some sort of emotional distance from Henry. My resolve is wavering.

"I'll walk you," Henry says. He scrapes a hand through his hair and doesn't quite look at me, as if he's aware that there is a line here, one between Kashvi and me, that he's about to cross. But then he smiles and I smile back, unable to stop myself.

"It's not far," I say, gesturing down the street. "I can make it."

"I'd feel better if I knew you were home safely."

I chew my lip and get a mouthful of lip gloss. We aren't in the best neighborhood. A few months ago, a man broke into a house, stabbed a woman, and cut off her index finger. My ankle still aches if I move too fast, so I won't be running away if someone comes at me. It's a good story. Apparently, I can rationalize time with Henry even though I know better.

"I'll allow it," I say, and Henry snorts as if I've made an excellent joke. Apparently, Grace is not the only one who's a little drunk.

Henry's forearm brushes against the bend of my elbow every few steps. The air is electric and full between us. I long for the moment his arm slides against mine and agonize that he'll suddenly realize he's casually touching me and stop. He doesn't. We pause in front of the path to my parents' front door.

"It was nice to see you without the smell of stale coffee and yeast in the air," he says. "And without a new injury."

"Lucky you. You didn't even need to carry me home this time," I say, and his body shakes with silent laughter.

He hugs me goodbye, and I can feel his heart thundering against my silent chest. I breathe in deeply, unwilling to step away, but aware one of us needs to. The air thickens, fragrant with honeysuckle, and Henry's hand cups the back of my neck. I ease away, unwilling to risk whatever is in the message of Henry's pounding heart.

His thumb grazes my collarbone before he steps back. "You're just so…"

"Charming? Witty? Brilliant? Tall?" I joke, swaying back toward him.

"Yes. All those things." He slowly blinks and puts his hands on my upper arms to hold me still.

"Oh," I say, breathless.

"'Oh' is right," Henry says, suddenly looking more sober. "It's a problem."

He sighs and gives his head a tiny shake. He lets go, and I realize for the first time all night that I'm freezing. My skin goose pimples and I cross my arms and rub my palms against my cold flesh.

"Well," Henry says, brightly and easily, as if I hadn't just felt his heart racing against me, as if I hadn't been pressed against him wondering if his mouth would touch mine. "Goodnight, Brooklyn."

He walks to the corner, where he turns and waves at me. I'm rooted to the sidewalk, regret and relief warring in my chest. He didn't try to kiss me. I might have let him. But I think I want something that's entirely mine.

CHAPTER 9

I t's official. I'm being haunted by petite famous women.

"Not again," I groan. I'd startled awake, my brain jerking my body into action, somehow knowing I was no longer alone. There's a gentle *tsk tsking* from the edge of my bed, and the bedside lamp comes on. I shut my eyes against the glare, but not before I glimpse a thin blonde with hair perfectly braided and coiled on the top of her head. I recognize her right away, having just watched *Down for the Count*, a movie about an underdog snowboarder who wins the national championship and goes on to live her best life.

Just what I need. Emilie Abellard is wearing the outfit I wore to Castaway's Volcano and threw at the foot of the bed before passing out in my underwear. The skirt fits her perfectly, which is absurd since I'm nearly eight inches taller than her and not nearly as waiflike. And she's dead.

She tilts her head at me, sympathy oozing out of her cornflower-blue eyes.

"How you doin'?" She sounds the same as she did in an Oscar-nominated role about a woman who goes on a vigilante spree to avenge the death of her mother. *A Daughter's Mission*, it was called. Somehow, the director had made a multifaceted story about a vulnerable woman who goes on a killing spree without crumbling into schmaltz. Emilie looked natural holding a gun.

She hadn't quite been able to lose her drawl when some movie exec had the idiotic idea of redoing *Casablanca* as a miniseries, with Emilie as Ilsa. Critics panned her performance and made unflattering comparisons to Ingrid Bergman. I read that Emilie checked into rehab a few weeks after the show ran. Fans from her home state of Georgia held a vigil for her. Fans all over the country held a second vigil when she died "unexpectedly," alone in her apartment. Overdose. It was front-page news when I was almost finished with college. America's sweetheart, gone at age twenty-six.

"Good night? You smell like a distillery." She looks wistful.

I'd gone out. I'd sat. In a bar. With other people, including an extremely attractive man with a real job. And a girlfriend. I press a palm against my chest. None of that had gotten my heart going. Attempts at normalcy don't seem to be a factor in correcting my dysfunction.

"Until you showed up."

"Mean." Emilie sticks her tongue out at me.

"I don't want to hallucinate beautiful people anymore. I just want to sleep through the night."

Emilie looks thoughtful and eases onto my bed, tucking her legs up underneath her like a preschooler during story time. "My agent forced me to go to rehab after I told him I was being followed around by Ingrid Bergman. He thought I was on hallucinogens."

"Were you?"

She smiles coquettishly and picks at some lint on my skirt.

"Maybe. But she really was following me. No one believed me, but I saw her." Emilie looks up earnestly.

Great. Even my hallucinations are hallucinating.

"Why was she…" I grope for the right word. "Appearing?"

"She didn't like my performance. Said it was her role. People speculated about why I acted so badly, said I was on drugs, but seriously, who could perform well with Ingrid Bergman castigating them every day?" Emilie shrugs expansively, her shoulder and chin artfully coming together. Damn these actors. They make shrugging look good.

"That would make it hard," I agree caustically, and sensing an incoming hangover headache. "I bet I'm underperforming because I keep getting woken up."

"I doubt we're the reason," Emilie says. "You probably sleep too much. I did, after the miniseries bombed. It was a great avoidance tactic. The reviews were scathing. My mom would call me and read them to me."

"That's extreme."

"She said it would force me to perform better next time. I begged her to stop. Then I ended up in rehab and wasn't allowed phone contact. It was probably a good thing. Gave me some perspective. When I got out, I started blocking her calls."

"Ingrid's?" I ask, sleepy, still drunk, and wondering if it's that easy and I can just block Emilie. And Emily. And Emaleigh. And Emmalee.

"No. My mother's." Emilie looks at me askance.

"Right. Of course. Moms are tough," I say after a long pause, during which Emilie keeps her bright eyes trained on my face.

"What's yours like?

"I guess that depends on who you ask. Penny thinks she's a super mom, because she hooked Penny up with some internships at the hospital. Spencer thinks she's a pushover." He'd mentioned it once, in a pleased sort of way that implied it made his life easier.

"What about you? What do you think?" Emilie lays on her side and props herself up with an elbow.

"It's complicated. Mothers. Daughters." I try to shrug as beautifully as Emilie, but only succeed in cracking my neck.

She rolls her eyes. "You're avoiding my question."

"You're a hallucination. I don't have to tell you anything."

"If I'm a hallucination, who cares what you tell me? I told you about Ingrid and how embarrassing is that?"

Penny never understood why my mom and I weren't close. She adored my mother, who wasn't aloof like Lane. But my mom's skill at the practicalities of mothering wasn't enough to break down the wall her affection for my brother put between us. I love my mother. Trust her, not so much.

"You know how people go on and on about how their moms are their best friend?" I ask.

Emilie snorts, an unexpectedly guttural sound from someone so elegant. "It seems like an urban myth. Or denial."

Is it comforting that even dead actors have mom issues?

"Mine doesn't hear me when I talk," I say. "Anything I say bounces off her. Unless it's what she wants to hear. Then she's all ears."

"What are you trying to tell her?"

My brain takes a sharp left, veering away from the name on the edges of it. *Spencer.*

"Just…things," I say, staring over Emilie's shoulder. "Anyway. She wouldn't believe me, even if I told her."

"How do you know?"

"She didn't." Once. Years ago. I prop myself up on my elbows. I'm still drunk, and something in my diet could be causing the hallucinations. All the sugar. I'm going to write this particular episode off as a tiki-induced nightmare.

"People change," Emilie says. "I used to get wasted every night and have a meltdown every time someone said something negative about me. Went into rehab, started drinking kombucha and going to therapy three times a week so I wouldn't feel compelled to go on a bender when someone said I gave a 'wooden, scarecrow-like performance.'"

"Ouch," I say, wincing.

She executes another perfect shrug.

"Things got a little better, with my mother, once I started getting some help. Started talking to a professional, instead of bottling up everything. My mom was still a total stage mom, but I could tune her out better."

"So, what happened? After? If you'd sorted it out and were getting help?" I tread carefully, not sure if I should be reminding people they're dead.

"Sometimes things get real hard," Emilie says. "Harder than you're prepared for. You can't see how they'll ever be less hard. Then you make a mistake, one you can't take back."

Her whole face droops. I reach out and take her warm hand. "Emilie. I'm so sorry." The place where my heart sits, useless, aches for her. I'd seen the stories after she died, which read more like eviscerations of her character than recitation of facts. I'd skimmed them, curious, judgmental, and forgotten she was a person, a messed-up, lonely, sad person. Just like me. Like loads of us.

I wrap my arms around her. My second hug tonight. I'm on some sort of weird roll after a long absence of physical contact with anyone.

Emilie's eyes are bright with unshed tears and she hugs me back, hard. We sit for a long time.

Through the open blinds, dawn peeks through in thin bands of light. "Shit. I have to be at work in three hours and I'm still drunk."

"I should let you get some sleep," Emilie says, patting my arm. Her smile is still wobbly, and the mattress barely shifts when she stands.

"And maybe I'll stop seeing things," I say, falling back against my pillow and closing my eyes. "And my heart will start beating and things will go back to normal. And I will be better than I am."

The bedroom door makes a soft click. When my alarm goes off forty minutes later and I wake up, the room is empty and my camisole is neatly hanging in the closet. I'd left it crumpled on the edge of the bed.

CHAPTER 10

A nother day, another doughnut. Saturday mornings start out peacefully. Most early customers are dog walkers who are barely awake and can't keep up with their fur babies. When I'm on shift alone, I let the dogs into the store, even though there's a sign taped to the window that says Service Animals Only. I shovel half a S'more and More doughnut into my mouth to combat my throbbing head and nausea. Clearly, keeping up with Grace is a bad idea. Breakfast tastes like chalk, so I throw most of it away. Even the coffee tastes off—bland and watery.

"This taste weird to you?" I ask Becca, who sips from the mug I offer. How she got stuck with the early morning shift is a mystery. Usually, she snags prime shifts that don't involve any food prep or extensive cleaning duties.

"Tastes like it always does," she says, before turning back to her phone.

The calm is shattered by 10 a.m. Matt calls ahead to let us know he's coming in around lunch, which puts Becca in a tizzy. She scrubs all the tabletops and scours the coffee pots.

"Those have never been cleaned," I say.

"They should have been," she snaps.

"He won't even notice."

Becca glares at me and keeps polishing.

Our boss, if you can call him that, is into himself and girls like Becca. Girls ten years younger than him who are impressed when he stares soulfully into nothing while singing about finding the perfect love. It's downright predatory, the way he exploits young women. I avoid the Wednesday evening shift on open mic nights so I don't have to endure the spectacle. I always want to drag the girls away and give them a lecture about exactly what type of man in his thirties likes women who are technically still teenagers. He's creepy and women his own age have learned to steer clear. The girls—some of them, anyway—don't recognize him for what he is, because they're still girls, barely out of high school. Attention from Matt isn't icky yet. It's flattering.

Not too long ago I might have fallen for Matt's tricks myself. It's the way his hair falls into his eyes and how he thoughtfully pushes it away and grins sheepishly at the object of his attention. The motion says he's sweet and sensitive and that you're the center of his universe. Then he opens his mouth. Illusion destroyed. Unless you're too young to notice.

He doesn't hit on me. He's thirty-three. I'm not interesting, even though I fibbed and said I was twenty-two when I applied for the job. I'd taken one look at the girls working during my interview, dragged out some vestige of chutzpah, and the lie rolled off my tongue. Matt didn't question me. He barely looked at me. He hired me because the night manager, twenty-four years old and nearly finished with her psychology degree, said someone responsible needed to open on Sunday mornings.

Matt said, "Sure Mel, whatever you want."

Her name was Melody, but I heard him call her Melissa once.

"How are my girls?" Matt booms as he walks in the front door hours later.

Becca beelines for him and puts a hand on his arm.

"Not here, babe," he says, and shakes off her hand. Becca's face is stricken, but she recovers quickly and pastes on an ambivalent expression, her mouth flat.

"Brooklyn, right?" he says to me. As if I don't write his press releases every few weeks. As if he didn't hire me himself.

"That's me." I point at myself and feel stupid for doing so.

"Can you take a couple extra shifts over the next few weeks? Some of the girls bailed, quit, whatever, and rumor has it you don't have much going on."

"Well, when you put it like that, I'd love to."

"Great. It's good to know we have someone we can rely on."

He always talks like this: we make doughnuts; we're doing well; we created this great new flavor; we're having a strong quarter financially. I think a consultant told him this would make people feel more engaged and valued. What it really does is enable him to take credit for everything, and allow the lazier among us to avoid responsibility for anything. Credit, acknowledgment, purpose: they've been mixed in a runny glaze of togetherness. We collectively are responsible for the failure of the shop. But when it's successful, it's Matt's genius that is recognized. It's not unlike my marketing job.

"Brooklyn?" Matt's tone implies he's said my name more than once.

"Sorry. Pondering flavor recommendations."

"We want to push the Citrus Honey Spice this week. We've got a backlog of icing prepped, so we need to move those."

"Got it. Citrus Honey Spice."

"Cool. Make sure everyone is posting those on their social channels."

"You bet."

He puts his hand up for a high-five. Inwardly I cringe, but I obediently go for the high-five.

"I'll update the schedule with your new shifts."

"Can't wait."

"Great attitude."

I give him a thumbs-up.

We enthusiastically greet customers during his visit. Left to our own devices, we wait until they get to the counter to acknowledge them because there's no point in working for an elite, pricey doughnut shop if you can't be disdainful, but Matt loves a chipper attitude. Cheerfulness, with a Mocha Dip on the side. He's effusive to everyone, and underfoot. Customers eat it up and go home and tell people they met the founder of Cute Lil' Doughnuterie. Matt set up the shop up with lottery winnings, hired the right people, and now it basically runs itself. His sister, who I met once at a networking event, back when I had a real job, built the shop's website and handles all the search engine optimization. She's the real genius. I like to imagine she demands an outrageous salary and trolls the shop on social media.

"I had a massive idea," he says, before he leaves. "We should partner with one of those one-hundred-flavor ice cream shops. Do a custom flavor cross promotion. Yeah?"

"It's a good idea," I say, bewildered by his sudden ingenuity. Vancouver's food scene is determined to be more like Portland's.

We copied food trucks; we tried to copy cronuts. Food crossovers create headlines and demand.

"Brilliant, right?" he says.

"Super brilliant." Another thumbs-up from me. I stare at my thumbs like I have no idea what they're doing.

"We should let Becca write the press release and do the social media, if it all works out."

"That would be great," I say.

"Fucking cool."

Kailey walks in at that moment, yoga mat slung over her back, hair bouncing.

"No one says 'fucking cool' anymore, Matt," she says, her tone teasing enough to avoid rebuke.

"No?" He looks mildly curious.

"No way, man. Profanity is so three years ago. Use big words. Nod sagely."

He nods, his mouth falling open to say "fucking cool."

He snaps it shut. Nods again, and goes into the back office. Becca scrambles after him.

"He'll do anything to seem fucking cool," Kailey says. "He's worried about losing his relevancy. Becca gives him his best ideas."

"Becca?"

"The ice cream-doughnut combo was her idea," she adds, dropping her mat loudly on the counter. She glares down the hallway after our boss. "You think he came up with that? Of course not."

"Are they together?"

"For now."

"God."

"Yup."

"Is Becca actually smart?" I whisper, mindful of being heard.

"Class valedictorian."

"I didn't see that coming."

"Whoa, biased much?"

"She's so vapid."

"Vapid girls can be smart."

"Sure."

"You are so judgy."

"She's just so flaky. And angry. At everyone. Except him; she fawns over him."

"She's insecure about their relationship and hangry. That doesn't mean she's not smart. You're twenty-nine. You work in a doughnut shop. How smart can you be?" Kailey says, without heat.

"How did you know how old I am?"

"Melody told me before she quit. She did your hiring paperwork."

"Does Matt know?"

"Doubt it. You'd be unemployed. For lying, not for being old." She sticks out her tongue.

"He wouldn't have hired me otherwise."

"Probably not. That might have been for the best though."

"What?"

"Come on, Brooklyn. You know I think you're a grumpy, hilarious riot. But you hate working here. You're super unhappy."

"I'm taking a break."

"From what? The old job you always talk about to remind us how inexperienced, naïve, and silly we are?" Kailey folds her arms across her chest. "What happened there? I know something happened."

What happened at work? It's what my mother asked me when I told her I quit Lawrence Communications back in March. I should have anticipated her question. Of course, that was the first thing she asked, the first thing she needed to know. Not "Are you okay? How do you feel? Would you like a very large glass of wine?"

Those are questions I could have answered: I'm not okay. I'm terrified that I'm worthless and a failure. Yes, pour the wine.

"From my career. To…" I pause. There must be some explanation I can get past Kailey, who's proving to be alarmingly insightful and perceptive. "To find a more fulfilling job. More in line with my core values."

"And what the fuck are your core values, exactly?"

"Money. Internet stardom. Praise. Sex," I say flippantly.

"This is your problem. You obfuscate and hide behind jargon and refuse to deal with anything real."

"I do not."

"I'd be the first to say work isn't everything, Brooklyn, but it seems like you hate working here. So, then I'm like, why doesn't Brooklyn just go get a fancy, schmancy marketing job? What is she so afraid of? Or is she just a liar about her skills and Cute Lil' is the best she can do?"

Kailey has stripped me down to essentials, succinctly peeled back my skull and poked at the part of my brain that asks those questions on a loop. Is Cute Lil' the best I can do? The future stretches out in front of me, a long dark corridor, possibly filled with artificial flavors and colors.

By the time I'd decided to quit Lawrence Communications, it was a more of a biological imperative than a decision. I was sleeping for twelve hours and barely functional the next day. When people talked to me, it sounded like they were speaking through a toilet paper tube. I woke up one morning in late March and realized the idea of having to go back to work, ever, made me physically sick. So, I threw up, put on an outfit I'd already worn that week, and took a cab to the office, praying I'd have a plan by the time I arrived. I typed up a resignation email on my phone and hit send.

"Just tell me the truth," Kailey says. "It can't be that bad."

I clear my throat and she purses her lips, making a hurry-up-spill-it gesture with her index finger.

Can't be that bad for whom? Had I done a bad job? Or had the job been bad? At first, I could write things off as coincidences or my imagination. Excusable signs. Lawrence Senior—who was mostly retired but was trotted out when Lawrence Junior was dealing with someone who wanted the big dog—asked me to bring him a cup of coffee. I'd brought it; I'd wanted to be nice. After that, I overheard him asking a colleague if I was someone's temporary assistant and he never spoke directly to me again. Vague outlines for client reports were dropped on my desk, due in twelve hours. There was the time I crafted a marketing strategy document for a client whose target market was women aged eighteen to twenty-five. I submitted it to my manager for review, and overnight, he and a male intern rewrote it. The client hated their ideas. The VP of sales was furious—at me—that we didn't get the contract. Explanations fell on deaf ears. My manager said the client just didn't understand their ideas.

I said, "I think the show runners know their young, female viewers are not interested in digital leaderboards and sport metaphors regarding their favorite TV show about a female dragon slayer in post-apocalyptic America."

I was told my tone was inappropriate.

"I don't want to talk about it," I say to Kailey.

I don't want to contemplate the day I quit. How I'd stumbled into Lawrence Junior's office, forced to explain my resignation. My skin was clammy, and I caught a whiff of sour sweat when I moved my arms. I'd hoped my boss, and his bosses, would be relieved that I'd taken my pride, eaten it up, spit it out, and returned it via electronic means, never to be spoken about again. But that's not their style. Shame had to be verbal to count and Lawrence Junior weaponized it. I recognized the tactic, but seeing it didn't change the sharpness of the blade. It cut; I bled.

I keep bleeding.

Lawrence Junior fired me, right on the heels of my resignation. It better fit his narrative. The story was reformed, spun, and regurgitated back out through the machine. If the appearance of Kyle in the doughnut shop was any indication, the story continues to twist and exist outside the confines of reality or truth. After all, it was told by a man.

"How's bottling it all up going for you?" Kailey says, an edge in her tone.

"What do you know Kailey?" I spit out tiredly. "You have no idea what it's like."

"Right. Because you're so wise and beyond us."

"I don't want to hear it."

We stare each other down. Kailey's left eye is twitching, which it always does during confrontations. She wants to back down—it's in her people-pleasing nature. There's a ruckus of voices at the front door, and Kailey breaks eye contact.

A cool wash of relief floods my body as a stream of customers in orthopedic sandals and khaki pants make their way in the door. A cruise ship has docked. Saved by the tourists.

CHAPTER 11

'm still avoiding interactions with Kailey during one of my extra Matt-provided shifts a few days later because I don't know what to say. I was rude. She was pushy. We're stuck now. While I count coffee cups and nondairy creamers on the metal storage rack next to the prep area at Cute Lil', my phone buzzes over and over. It's not Henry. It's Todd. My former coworker. Assistant. He couldn't tell the difference.

The universe has thrust him, unwanted, into my text messages. He's sent a time and place to meet for lunch. Today. *No excuses* written in all caps and decked out with a smiley face emoji wearing sunglasses and an angry face. I haven't seen him since I quit. Was fired. I'm out of excuses to avoid him and would need to resort to grief from the death of an imaginary hamster. He wouldn't buy it.

"Shit," I say.

"What's that?" Kailey asks, her voice muffled because she's half inside a ground-level cabinet looking for an unaccounted-for bag of decaf. Matt loves inventory. The ordeal will be followed with a "gentle" reminder to not "appropriate" Cute Lil' stock. Kailey emerges triumphantly holding up a dusty bag of locally roasted decaf.

"I knew no one would steal this. Disgusting." She throws it on the counter and hops up beside it. "What's up?"

"Nothing. Someone wants to have lunch." I don't want to tell Kailey anything. Todd belongs locked in some far, unreachable corner of my mind, with old boyfriends, Lawrence Communications, Penny, and other painful fragments of my existence.

"Henry?" She writhes suggestively.

"No."

"Too bad. Who?"

"You're nosy."

"You want to tell me." She chucks the bag of unwanted beans at me. It falls to the floor and breaks open. "Crap."

"It's just some guy I used to work with."

"Cute?"

"Definitely no."

"Friend?"

I shake my head.

"Then don't go." She picks a Strawberry Crème out of the display cabinet and shoves half in her mouth. "You don't owe him anything," she says, muffled and sloppy from a maw full of pink custard.

But I do.

When Todd was first hired, we'd gotten along. He'd been assigned to provide me with support on big accounts and handle administrative paperwork. He set up meetings, proofread, and wrote reports on how online campaigns were doing. He'd been average at everything, but I was grateful because I was drowning under my workload.

Todd was thin and short and told me he was grateful to have a woman boss because there should be more women bosses.

He was hired because he'd had an internship at a huge New York PR agency, which he did before he graduated from the same university as me, albeit years later. We had the exact same education, but the corporate partners got stars in their eyes based on the four months he'd spent shilling a major shampoo brand in America. Todd had one interview with Lawrence Junior. Hired.

I'd had six interviews for the same entry-level job. Human resources: phone. Human resources: in person. Direct manager: in person. Departmental lead: lunch. Chief operating officer: in person. Founding partner, Lawrence Senior himself: Skype call. The direct manager voiced concerns about my age and experience, but said they were willing to give me a shot thanks to my references.

I'd wanted the job. Craved it. Deserved it. I'd gotten promoted, quickly, because one person after another had retired, or quit, and I took on their work without a word of complaint and without asking for a raise. Naively, I'd thought they'd recognize my talent, skill, and hard work. Turns out, the powers that be were just too lazy to hire a new person when someone was doing the work already for way less money.

As for Todd, I'd wanted the company to hire another woman. There were only five of us out of forty employees, an unlikely ratio in marketing and communications. We walked briskly in the hallways and avoided eye contact. Shared precariousness doesn't necessarily bring people together. We knew we had to align with the men whose office doors were always closed, who barked orders and took clients out for lunch on company credit cards, which we didn't have.

I don't want to have lunch with Todd.

I text back, *Sounds great. See you then.*

Stupid inner voice, telling me lunch will be good for my career. Telling me to prove to Todd I'm thriving and haven't been beaten down by what happened at Lawrence Communications.

"You're an idiot," Kailey says, when I tell her I need to leave early to make lunch.

"I'm networking. For that career you say I'm avoiding."

"I'm sorry," she manages, awkwardly.

"I probably deserved it," I say, just as uncomfortably. But she grins and we're back to normal. Kailey, at least, is normal.

I duck out from work early, but once I ride my bike downtown, I can't remember the exact name of the restaurant. All the new hot spot names are a behavioral convention or ephemeral concept paired with something natural. Kind & Hazelwood. Wild & Oak. Fresh & Berry. There it is. Nourish & Nature. The restaurant only serves salads, and there's a lineup out the door.

I'm baking in my black sundress, which I'd raced home to change into. I can't do anything about the smell of yeast and deep fryer in my hair. It's seeped into the follicles.

Todd is late, so I stare at an accusing menu taped to the inside of the window, carefully positioned so the people who didn't use an app to preorder fifteen dollars' worth of mostly unrecognizable greens can read while they wait. Endive. Tatsoi. Speckled lettuce. Sweet potato leaves. Romaine is nowhere to be found. "You need me," the menu says. "All those carbohydrates you've been eating."

There's a nasally shout, and Todd swoops in and hugs me firmly enough to crush my handbag against my stomach.

"It's so good to see you! It's been ages. You look good. Love the hair. Messy bun. New look for you."

"Thank you." I smile weakly.

We edge forward in the line, and Todd rattles off the names of my old coworkers, asking if I've seen them. He chats interminably about the projects he's working on. It seems stilted, like he's spewing office gossip until he can get to the point. Todd bounces in his leather loafers, barely containing some private excitement.

"My treat," he says, when we finally order our arugula and quinoa with salmon monstrosities. "I can't imagine a doughnut shop pays all that much."

"Minimum wage."

He winces.

I let Todd pay without arguing. I'm paying, in one way or another, for everything that's happened since he started working at Lawrence Communications.

"So." He sits down, opens his arms expansively. "Tell me. What's new?"

"Just the usual. Networking. Had some great meetings. Seen some interesting job postings. Talked to a couple of recruiters in Toronto and Montreal. Looking for the right fit," I lie. "How about you?"

This is the opening he's been waiting for. He takes a deep breath and his thin lips stretch from ear to ear. He angles toward me, both hands gripping the edge of the glossy, black table. This meeting was never a benign catch up between former, almost friendly coworkers. Kailey is right. I'm an idiot.

"You'll never guess," Todd says. He hasn't touched his salad. I eat mine mechanically. Shovelling it in. It's flavorless and slimy in my mouth. Doughnuts dissolve because the sugar content is so high. Masticating barely required.

"I'm sure I won't," I say, around a mouthful of salad. Once I'm done, I'll have the freedom to leave.

"They promoted me! To a senior communications strategist role!"

"Wow. That is amazing. Congratulations." I drag a grin to my face. A "I'm so thrilled for you" curl of lips. I want to be sincere. I think.

"I'm killing it," he blathers. "Everyone is telling me I'm doing great, and I smoothed over that methane gas client who was pissed about the media coverage after those deaths at one of their job sites. Lawrence Junior gave me your old desk. I can see the North Shore mountains if I crane my neck."

"That's so great."

His face radiates pride. "They said next year they'll probably promote me to your old job. We've got some goals outlined and a whole plan in place."

"You're practically me." I grin awkwardly and try to swallow. Quinoa and fennel stick in my throat. Can I die from choking if I don't have a heartbeat?

Todd laughs and smooths his pastel yellow tie against his chest. "They said they really see my potential. I got them to agree to that idea you had about an email newsletter. Presented it and *wham*! I got to hire a designer and developer to get it set up too." He beams at me. "I'm not sure why the bosses were so resistant before. It seems crazy for a marketing agency not to have an e-newsletter."

"I'm sure having a penis helps bring Lawrence Junior around to your point of view."

Todd startles, and his shit-eating grin slips. He blinks his droopy eyelids as if he can't believe what I just said. I can barely believe it, but I'm being fed by a prickle of indignation in my gut.

"Whoa, Brooklyn, that's not fair. I earned the promotion."

"You certainly had one relevant qualification," I say. "You know there were real issues with how the company treated women. You saw it. You *know*." I slam my palm on the shiny table, which rattles the water glasses.

The vice president cornered me at last year's Christmas party. He caught me by the wrists and tried to kiss me. I was thin and frail from stress and anxiety about Penny, who'd been missing for months by then. I didn't have any fight left in me, and I was trapped in a corner behind a pine tree lit with white and red lights. The scent of fresh pine and stale whisky still makes me gag. Todd ran over, grabbed my hand, and invented a noisy, client-related excuse to drag me away. He saved me in a moment when I couldn't save myself.

"You know I care about women being treated as equals," he says, cautiously, as though I may fling my salad at him in a rage. He inches away from the table.

"Not enough to speak up. Not enough to do something besides watch me get railroaded without saying a word."

"I don't think your performance issues were related to gender." He doesn't make eye contact and fidgets with his fork.

"My performance issues. Unbelievable." I shove my salad away, and what's left slops onto the table.

Once Todd had settled into his role as my junior assistant and gotten comfortable, he'd started questioning every decision I made, every email I sent, every idea I came up with. Always softly, as though he was raising a reasonable question or alternate path. His suggestions were so mild, so reasonably spoken, I barely noticed until they came all day, every day. Nothing I did went without his second-guessing. But what was I supposed to do? Tell him to quit it? I would have been labelled defensive and uncooperative. There was no safe way to make him stop telling me how to do my job.

Despite his apparent lack of faith, he'd confided in me, gossiped with me about the staff, and flattered me in front of clients. He brought me lattes on Monday mornings, and picked up lunch on days I'd forgotten to eat. He made jam with his mother, for God's sake, and brought me a jar. His behavior in front of others was impeccable. I quashed sparks of irritation when he said things like, "I think what Brooklyn is saying is…" during meetings.

Then he started questioning me publicly and presenting my ideas as his own. Management started checking up on me, started leaving me out of strategy meetings, moved my clients to other team members under the guise of finding a more advantageous fit. I'd sensed stirrings of discontent, but I'd assumed the rumblings were about me personally, not about my work. I'd figured the unrest had been about the fact that I didn't offer to bring senior staff coffee during long meetings and refused to take a turn cleaning out the fridge since no one else with a director title did.

They pushed me out of my job by preventing me from doing it and then finding grounds to dismiss me. I'd been deep-sixed. I'd thought it couldn't happen. I could turn a bad campaign around overnight, or talk a client out of a stupid idea. Then, suddenly, I couldn't. Or at least, my bosses thought I couldn't.

"There was nothing wrong with my performance, Todd. My desk was littered with awards and thank-you cards."

"You weren't always a team player. You had that aloof tone. You skipped some office events. People weren't sure they could trust you," Todd says.

"Is that you talking? Or Lawrence Junior?"

"I advocated for you," he says. "I said you were a great manager when they asked me for feedback. And, because I still believe that, I wanted to let you know I put in a good word for you where my buddy works. They're looking for a junior marketing strategist. They're really interested in you. You'd kill it."

He grins wolfishly.

"That's a demotion," I say, managing a calm, nonoffensive tone. I'm quaking with rage but not willing to lash out. Anger hasn't won any battles. Todd, skinny, well-dressed Todd, is not the same physical threat Spencer is. Spencer fills a space like a balloon expanding. Todd is a fly. One good flick and he'll be gone.

Emmalee's voice pipes up in my head: "Tell him to fuck off." She would swing a sword, throw a grenade, and the dragon would be slain, lives saved. At the very least, her detractors would be muzzled in the face of her defiant victory.

Fuck off rolls around in my mouth, tripping over itself to be spat out all over Todd's H&M, navy-blue suit.

"I think it would be a great way to rebuild some bridges and get back in the door," Todd says. "Working at a doughnut shop, Brooklyn? Really? This would be so much more impactful for your career." He tuts.

"You wouldn't consider a junior position."

"Gotta start somewhere."

"I started years ago. I don't need to start at the bottom." My hands curl into fists.

Todd stiffens. "I'm trying to help you. You're not making it easy."

"Helping me? Is that what you're doing?"

"Whatever, Brooklyn." He flags a server for a to-go box for his half-eaten salad. "Trying to support you was a mistake. No wonder Lawrence Junior fired you. You couldn't handle the workload anyway."

"Is that what he's saying? That he fired me? That I couldn't hack it?"

Violence uncoils in my stomach, urging me to hit him, to throw something, to scream until I'm hoarse and worn out. It's ugly and dark. I breathe deeply and stand.

"There were complaints," Todd says, his eyes not meeting mine.

"You got them too," I say, evenly. "It's not a business where everyone is happy all the time." We had one client who didn't like to deal with women, so Todd always accompanied me to meetings and repeated everything I said so the client could hear it. Of course, this caused the project to go over budget—which pissed the client off even more.

Todd looks uncertain and fidgets with the edges of his to-go salad container.

"Do you know that Lawrence Junior refused to give me references?" I spit. "That they walked me out, with security, on the day I resigned? That they fired me after I had already quit?"

I had stood in Lawrence Junior's office as rivulets of water streamed down the window behind him. Clouds obscured the mountainous vista across the water. I loved the view from his office. It said I had made it somewhere important enough to have a multimillion-dollar view. I stood there, while Lawrence Junior told me I had been useless, and that he'd been planning to fire me anyway. I had been a splinter in his palm, one he'd planned to rip out as soon as he found time in his busy schedule.

"I have to get going. Thanks for lunch." I spin on my heel and walk out.

Conflict has sapped my strength. I can barely move my legs fast enough to keep my bike upright and headed away from Todd and the stupid restaurant. I want to collapse in the bike lane and lay there until someone comes and scrapes me off the asphalt. The headline would read: "Cyclist Dies in Bike Lane and Is Run Over by Other Cyclists Until She's Unrecognizable Pulp." Or something punchier.

At home, I drag the bike through the back door and collapse onto the kitchen's cold laminate floor. The bike topples onto me, and the handlebar digs into my shoulder. I don't move. Physical discomfort is easy to ignore. I've practiced pretending it doesn't exist for years.

"Why did Todd even want to have fucking lunch?" I complain out loud. "Can't he just leave it alone? Leave me alone?"

Exhaustion creeps over me, and although I should get off the grungy kitchen floor, I drift off.

"Bad day?" The question pulls me from my sleep.

Emily Porter lifts the bike away from me and relaxes against the fridge. Her lipstick is as hot pink as ever, and she's wearing a replica of my work skirt and T-shirt, which she's knotted into a crop top to expose her flat abs. I roll onto my back and sigh.

"Bad lunch," I say. "With a former coworker. He wanted to tell me how great he's doing and how I'm a loser who should work an entry-level job."

"You do work at a doughnut shop," Emily says.

"An entry-level communications job," I clarify.

"Todd is the kind of guy who needs to lord things over people," she says. "He wants everyone to know how awesome he is, because he's super insecure."

"How do you know so much about Todd?"

"Everybody knows a Todd," Emily says, nonchalantly. "They're everywhere. Why did you agree to have lunch with him?"

"Obligation? I don't know. He's not all bad. He's done a couple of good things. Once or twice."

"Why are you making excuses for him? Just admit he's an asshole. Say it out loud. What's going to happen if you call him out?"

"It wasn't a big deal."

"*It wasn't a big deal,*" Emily parrots, rather snidely considering she's perpetually bubbly. "Is that why you're passed out on the floor and super upset about this?"

"I should have just said my hamster died and avoided lunch," I said.

"Why won't you call him an asshole?" She stamps her foot.

"Because maybe he's right! Maybe what happened at work was my fault," I burst out. "Todd's doing an amazing job. Got promoted. Maybe I deserved everything that happened to me because I couldn't handle it. The conflict, the demands, the stress. I could have pushed through, if I was a little tougher, or smarter. Or maybe I wasn't any good in the first place. I just thought I was and I was wrong." Fear. Forced to the surface. I could choke on it.

"That's bullshit."

Emily kneels and lays a hand on my shoulder, as if she's reaching toward a skittish animal. I feel warm where our skin meets. The warmth draws attention to the fact I'm freezing cold again. My skin is blue under my fingernails.

"Your career was steamrolled and you were harassed," Emily says. "Don't swallow the lie that Todd and your old bosses are trying to feed you. You don't have to. Just because people say something is true doesn't mean it is."

"Ella wouldn't have tolerated it," I say, referring to her *This High-School Life* character.

"Neither should you," Emily says.

"I should have told Todd there was no way in the whole world I was going to take that shit job."

Emily nods. "Exactly."

"Penny was so good at calling people out. She would have smote him." I dredge up a thin smile. It feels more like a scowl. "I can't believe he thought I should be grateful for an entry-level opportunity."

"What's worth standing up for, if not yourself?"

I scrub my face with my palms. My eyes sting, but there are no tears. A new bodily glitch. Now, my sad cerebrum isn't even doing what it's supposed to, which is let me cry.

"I didn't fight for my job. I gave up instead. I let them ruin me." My voice fades to nothing. I clear my throat and try again. Emily cocks her head at me, one ear turned toward my mouth. Her eyebrows raise questioningly.

"I couldn't take it anymore," I mouth.

She shakes her head, as though my words made it through the silence.

"You didn't have to take it anymore," she says. "It wasn't worth it. You *shouldn't have to take it.*"

A response fails in my throat. I must look wild-eyed and terrified, because she keeps touching my arm soothingly, the way someone pets a dog shivering in a corner because of a loud noise.

"Something's wrong. With me." I say the words, but there's no sound. And then pain blossoms with a wrenching cramp in my heart. I clutch my chest and try to breathe through the pain, which ratchets upwards.

"No." She's stern. "There has never been anything wrong with you."

The pain builds and builds, each moment more excruciating. My body convulses into the fetal position and my hands jerk toward her.

"Brooklyn," Emily says, worry finally in her voice. I make a wet, gulping noise.

Then I black out.

When I come to, I'm on my side. "I need to see a doctor," I say, clear and bright.

But Emily is gone.

CHAPTER 12

Evidence is mounting that I'm seriously ill. My doctor, the same one who looked at my ankle and couldn't find my heartbeat, has an opening, so I drag myself to the clinic and sit in the still-blistering waiting room. At least one child is red-faced and crying—her mother is nearly on the verge of tears too. No one makes eye contact. Everyone looks droopy and run ragged. A wobbling, elderly man sits in the chair next to me and knocks my elbow off the arm rest between us. He settles in with a loud exhalation and his eyes glide over me as if I'm not there. I try to catch my reflection in the security mirror in the corner near the ceiling. There's no one sitting next to the man.

"Not again." I jump to my feet, the back of my damp thighs ripping off the cheap vinyl seat. No one reacts as I frantically pace. Panic is trapped in my chest and slowly expanding downwards through my stomach to press on my bladder. Someone calls my name and I rush toward the sound.

"I didn't see you there," the doctor says as I stumble to stop in front of her. "Come on in."

We enter the small treatment room.

"You can see me?"

"You have an appointment, so yes." She wears a look of doctorly concern, but her eyes are drifting to the clock above the door.

I get one question, preferably one that can be answered in less than eight minutes, as per the sign on the door. I don't know what to ask that won't sound deranged.

"Is there a test to see if someone is hallucinating?" It's the only thing I can think of.

"Are you on drugs?" Her fingers are poised above her keyboard. Judgement flickers on her face.

"No," I say, affronted, curious. Would drugs work?

"What makes you think you're hallucinating?" She lowers her hands to the desk, next to the containers of cotton swabs, tongue depressors, and a display rack containing pamphlets about HPV, measles vaccines, and depression.

"Sometimes when I wake up, there's someone there. A person. Different people each time."

"Are you sure you're awake?"

"I'm awake."

"But you could be asleep." Her hands return to the keyboard, ready to write off my visions as nothing but a dream.

"I feel awake." My certainty fades in her dismissal.

She sighs, and starts running through what must be a checklist of questions designed to assess if someone is on drugs, or suffering from something else.

"Are you afraid of whomever you think you're seeing?"

"Not after the first time."

"Do you hear sounds, voices, bells? Those are common auditory hallucinations."

"Voices."

"The person talks to you."

"Yes."

"You talk back?"

"Yes."

"Interacting?"

"Yes."

"Seeing bright colors or patterns across your vision?"

"No."

Her forehead scrunches and she types harder. Then she whips her wheeled stool around to look at me.

"Your symptoms are uncommon, even among benign perceived hallucinations. Most people can't interact with what they're experiencing. Auditory or visual, not both, is more likely among patients who present with hallucinations. It's best if you're honest about your drug use."

She stares at me. I stare back and shake my head.

I hesitate. Then: "I read somewhere that people on their deathbed sometimes see people who have already died?"

Now she looks worried, rather than resigned about my apparent dishonesty about my drug use. "Are the people you're seeing telling you to hurt yourself?"

"Definitely no." If anything, they seem concerned about me.

"Well, you're very much alive. Google is not a doctor. You have neither the skills nor the expertise to diagnose yourself. Understand?"

She's glowering at me so that I truly understand the sin I've committed by believing the internet.

"Do you know what a hypnagogic or hypnagogic hallucination is?"

I shake my head no.

"They occur between sleeping and waking. They can be hard to distinguish from reality. Some more extreme cases involve hearing voices, and it can even feel like someone is touching you, or is in your bed."

"It feels real," I say. "They're tangible. I can smell them."

The doctor turns back to her computer and types a few words. She's not much older than me. She's thin with dainty features, not at all like the gruff elderly man who took care of me when I was a kid. He retired years ago. Does she have his files? Did she read them? What did they say about my past injuries? The concussion, the cracked rib, the burn on my calf. Two broken arms in one summer.

"Weren't you just in here for a sprained ankle?" she asks.

I point at my foot, which is no longer swollen although it still aches at night. "That's me."

"Otherwise healthy?"

No.

"Yeah. Sure. I eat too much sugar. Don't we all?" I make an encompassing gesture with my hand. The doctor raises an eyebrow.

"Cut out the sugar. You getting any exercise?"

"Sure." I had a sprained ankle. Of course not.

"Feeling depressed?"

"I don't think so."

She scribbles on a notepad, hammers away at her keyboard, and hits print. She hands me all the papers it spits out.

"Requisitions for blood test, urine test. That last sheet is an evaluation checklist for depression. I'd say that's more important. Get it all done, and we'll look at the results and talk about an MRI for your brain if you still think you're seeing people. Hypnagogic hallucinations can present in people experiencing insomnia or anxiety. Stress. Depression, et cetera. Come back in two weeks."

She stands, opens the door, and ushers me out.

I dump the papers on the passenger seat of the car, get into the driver's seat, and beat my forehead lightly on the steering wheel. I can't even hallucinate properly. Hypnagogic hallucinations would make perfect sense if that's all there was. I'd love for that to be the answer, to have something knowable. Vanishing from reflective surfaces, being unable to speak, no heartbeat—those can't be explained away so easily.

I gather up the paperwork and shove it into the glove compartment. At best, the tests will be inconclusive or befuddle the technicians. I visited clinics and doctors so often as a child I'd do almost anything to avoid them now. The two visits I've made recently used up what tolerance I've built up in the years since I moved out of my parents' house and away from Spencer.

Later that evening, my phone rings. I upend my laptop, where Emily's face sits on screen, as I scramble to the bedside table where the phone sits out of reach. *Penny, Penny, Penny.* Please be Penny. Who else could it be? Adrenaline and optimism bolt through my body as I lunge and hit accept for the unfamiliar number.

"Yes?" I exclaim breathlessly. All will be right with the world.

"Brooklyn? It's Henry."

His rumbly voice fills my ear.

"Henry. Hi." I fail to muster up enough warm in my voice. "I didn't recognize your number."

"I'm at the office. Working late. This a bad time?" He sounds cautious.

"Not at all." I force enthusiasm into my tone while I steady myself against the wall and swallow. Henry is great, but I'd rather hear from Penny.

"Would you be up for a quick trip?" Henry is saying. "There's an exhibit at the Victoria Museum about the development of North American cities, and every single person I've asked to go with me said it sounds like the most boring day ever. No one wants to go."

I laugh and almost jump at the sound, it's so unexpected. Fingers crossed Henry can't hear the death rattle as it trails off. *Penny.* Hope crashes back to my toes.

"I thought you might. Want to go. On the weekend," he spits out in a rush. "Unless you're working."

Not working. Maybe that's the only miracle I get today. I do the math in my head. The museum is on Vancouver Island off the coast of the mainland and requires a ferry ride plus driving time to the ferry and back. It's a day trip, twelve hours at least. With Henry.

"You probably already have plans." He's hedging against my long pause.

"You're really selling it. Telling me it'll be a drag and that I'm your last resort for company."

"Shoot." He sounds chagrined. "That's not, I mean, I want you to come. Obviously. It's just. I'll try to explain later. You're my first choice," he spits out in a rush. "It's just complicated."

"I don't have plans," I say. "And I do love museums. Even the boring exhibits."

When was the last time I went to a museum and wandered through the past? Some people find peace at church, or by mediating, but a museum does it for me.

"Really?" he says.

"Really."

"Awesome. I'll pick you up."

A woman says something to Henry in the background. He muffles the phone. Kashvi? No, he's at work. Still, this is a mistake. Henry has Kashvi. I am a hot mess with hallucinations that don't seem to fit any medically approved format.

He comes back and I feel like I should resist. One of us has to be smart. I don't want to turn his life as upside down as mine is.

"We should leave early," Henry says. "Beat the rush?"

"Yes," I say.

CHAPTER 13

Saturday morning at 6 a.m., I stare at my closet. At summer dresses, half of them sliding partially off their hangers and wrinkled from disuse. Summery pink, melon orange, neon blue. A mint-green sheath with a lace back. A lilac dress, flared from the waist. A black peplum I only wore once and doubt fits now. An empire-waist maxi in a blinding pattern of lemon, raspberry, and violet. I need a dress that won't embarrass me.

"It's ridiculous to count on a dress to not embarrass me when I can do that all by myself," I say to the closet.

I flick through hangers. So many hangers. I pull out a few outfits, and then give up and toss them on the bed into a growing pile of cotton and polyester. I pull out a loose-fitting gingham romper and tug it on. Critically, I turn from side to side in the mirror. It fits. It's not flirtatious. This is not a date outfit. It's not a misinterpretation waiting to happen. Good talk, I tell myself.

I scrub my teeth, find a pair of sparkly flip-flops under my bed, leave my usual message on the Parkers' voicemail, and manage to make it outside before Henry pulls up in his four-door Toyota. Gray. Plain. There's a bike rack on the back and roof racks on top. It's quintessentially West Coast. The same roof racks are on my parents' car; the same bike rack on Penny's car, which still sits in her parents' driveway. Robert starts it once a week and drives it around the block. When the Parkers went on vacation in the spring, the task was left to me.

"Morning," Henry says as I climb into the passenger seat. "You're looking less pale and sweaty than the last time I saw you in a car."

"I can still sprain my other ankle. There are stairs in the museum. Or maybe I'll break an arm falling down the escalator."

"We'll take the elevator," he says, merging onto a main road.

I pay for the ferry over. I insist, since he's driving, paying for gas, and he drove across town to pick me up.

"When was the last time you were on a ferry?" he asks, after he parks the car on a lower deck. His voice is muffled by the ocean breeze and the din of other car doors slamming shut and dogs barking. The air reeks of salt and of sour, decaying seaweed. We wander onto a passenger level and find a place sheltered from the wind to sit.

I shrug. "High school. I played a lot of soccer and volleyball, and the teams travelled."

"Star athlete?" He grins. "MVP? Won the big game?"

"I was okay. I sat out more often than I wanted to because of injuries. But it was fun." Spencer liked to mete out an accident right before a big game, just to remind me that he could. I'd nearly missed the provincial volleyball championship because he'd caught my wrist in a car door. I'd seen it coming and leaned into the door enough with my shoulder that I'd gotten off with some light bruising down my entire left side.

"I thought about going to the university on the island," Henry says. "Before my outdoor adventure fiasco."

"I checked out the University of Victoria too. The cultural, social and political thought program, in the department of history."

"But you didn't study history? Marketing, communications, right?"

"Right."

"Did you travel first, or go right to school?"

"No gap year for me."

Penny and I had talked about going to New Zealand for three months the summer before university. When we got back, we were going to start classes at whatever university took both of us, followed by the usual: date inappropriate boys, live in a grimy basement suite and get jobs at a bar in a borderline part of town. Penny had been noncommittal and waved a hand airily when I tried to get her to sit down and buy plane tickets. I hadn't noticed that, for months, it had mostly been me talking about our plans. I was too relieved to have a foot out the door of my parents' house to notice her disinterest. When she finally worked up the nerve to bail, we fought spectacularly.

Henry props his back on the flaking white railing, framed by water and sky behind him. Small, spiny-treed islands dot the expanse of water. The rumbling ferry passes so close to the hardy lumps of land, I could jump off the boat and swim to shore, vanish onto some rarely visited, desolate patch. Of course, the ship's turbines would get me first. Or hypothermia. I root myself more firmly to the metal deck so my imagination doesn't carry me away.

"Aren't history and marketing opposites of each other?" Henry asks. "History is about exploring the past. Marketing is about presenting a future or idea and getting people to buy it."

I flinch at his distillation. Marketing teaches you to spin, and I've made myself dizzy with rationalizations about how I ended up in career I didn't want. I've spent every day since university pursuing current events, the best story, the freshest research, the biggest trends. I've lived in the moment and ignored the past. Mine. The universe's.

"I thought it would be easier to get a job in the museum industry so I could have it both ways," I admit, trying not to bristle. "That I'd somehow make time for my own projects, do history studies on the side. Go back to school and take some classes I cared about while working full time. Before I knew it, five years were gone and I'd done nothing but bust my ass off at Lawrence Communications."

He blows out a commiserating breath. "What was it about history?"

"At first, I loved memorizing all the events and dates," I say. "But then I kept reading and started learning about the buried voices and the people who've been silenced by accepted interpretations of history. You find a thread to pull, and you keep pulling. History is full of unsolvable mysteries, but when you uncover something or learn something people have forgotten or ignored, it's fulfilling."

Henry watches me intently, and I flush. The last time I flushed under the scrutiny of a handsome man, my heart pounded. One without the other is half a feeling.

"We think the past is fixed," I say. "It's not. Most of what we learn about in school or have come to accept as the "truth" is from the perspective of white men. So many voices are omitted or missing. Women, people of color. The past belongs to them too. Those are the bits I love—the missing stories, the ones we need to create an accurate context and frame. History is more than the version we accept as fact because we learned about it a specific way in school. There's so much more we could learn if we heard from forgotten or erased voices."

I try to hold onto the excitement I feel as I talk, but it flickers and dims. My books, research, and old ambitions are buried in the same closet as the '90s women magazines. The newsletters I get via email from the Smithsonian and other museums around the world are deleted without being opened. I can't quite bring myself to unsubscribe or to donate the books to a thrift store. It would feel too permanent. Like giving up. Although, haven't I, already? Look where I am. Look at what I'm doing.

Henry turns to face the dark, choppy water. I join him at the railing and look outward. His shoulder is against mine, a warm spot in the cool morning. The wind whips some of my hair across his cheek and I pull it back and wrap it around my ponytail. He doesn't move away.

"I can hear your heart, when you talk about history," Henry says.

His words are sweet and perfect, like a line. They should sound insincere. But I can hear his heart too.

When the ship's horn goes, rattling my teeth and announcing our arrival at the dock in Victoria, we head back to the car. We disembark the ferry and drive past farmlands and woods into the city. At the museum, we wander. Sometimes together, sometimes apart. Henry is not immersed in the details of who and when. He's interested in how. He stares intently at images and explanations of how buildings, landmarks, and infrastructures were built. He does what he wants at his own pace and lets me be. I used to visit art galleries and museums with Penny, who'd agree to come and then stick to me like glue, bored the minute she set foot in the door. She lives in the moment and compartmentalizes everything. She's not hungry until she is; she's not tired until she's suddenly sound asleep. She's not angry until she explodes; she's not happy until she's laughing. It's why she's so good at her work. She only sees what is right in front of her. There's no space for anything else.

Henry lets me think—his mind occupies itself. For all I know, he could be dwelling on how hungry he is.

Henry beats me through the museum and waits patiently at the exit. I'd nearly forgotten he was there while I was lost in a travelling exhibit about European fashion throughout the ages. Some of the fabrics are hundreds of years old.

"Elevator," he says, steering me away from the stairs with one hand on my shoulder. "Food?"

We find a restaurant a few blocks away and sit on the patio, which is surrounded by high fences and glossy green foliage to block the street traffic roar. We order salads, falafels, and chicken skewers.

"I haven't been to a museum in ages," I gush. "It's been the worst year ever, and it was nice to do something that got my brain thinking again."

"Why has it been the worst year ever?" Henry's eyes are hidden behind his sunglasses.

I hadn't meant to say anything. Half my brain was stuck in a bygone civilization, and the words fell out of my mouth. Penny is a wound better left alone. Do I say anything? Do I keep my mouth shut? Penny takes up space in a corner of my mind and it might be a relief to talk about her, to say her name out loud, to someone who won't compare me to her and find me lacking. Unlike my mother. If I drag Penny into this moment with us, maybe she won't feel so far away.

"Last summer," I say, while I turn the stem of my sweating wineglass between my fingers, "my best friend, Penny, went missing in Syria. She's a disaster-aid worker. We haven't heard from her, and we don't know what happened." I say the bare minimum. Too much will rip me open and spill my insides all over the tastefully decorated table and shiny flatware. I can't give that much away to Henry. To anyone.

"I'm so sorry." He reaches across the table, past the centerpiece of flowering herbs in a clay pot, and clasps my free hand. Then he's quiet, and his silence allows me keep going.

"Sometimes I forget for a few minutes. Then I remember, and it feels like I'm being smothered by a pillow. No matter how hard I try to breathe, all I inhale are feathers."

A perky server places our food on the table. The interruption gives me a few seconds to pull myself together. I pick at my lunch. It smells amazing, but tastes like sawdust the minute the falafel hits my tongue. I try the chicken instead, and under the salty, cumin flavor, there's something rank. I put down my fork.

"Unlike you and I"—I manage a laugh—"Penny decided in high school to do relief work and stuck with it. She didn't mess around. I didn't see it coming."

One day, while I was still babbling about booking our pre-university trip, Penny sat me down and steepled her fingers together, like she always did when she was about to say something no one wanted to hear.

She said, "I need to tell you something."

I said, "You slept with Deacon from your Mandarin class?"

She said, "Brooklyn. I'm trying to be serious."

She told me about her career plans, and I made the requisite effusive noises. "You'll be amazing at that." Girl squeal. Friend duty done. I half believed she'd end up like my mom, patching people up in the ER. Home in time for dinner, or breakfast, depending on the shift.

Then she'd dropped the real bomb: she wouldn't be travelling. We wouldn't be going to the same university, or sharing a dingy basement suite near campus. She had to live at home to save money, because instead of working part-time, she would be volunteering at my mom's hospital. That was when I lost it. I needed to get out of my house. She hadn't understood, and I hadn't been able to tell her why.

"When I didn't recognize your number yesterday, I thought, maybe, just maybe, it was Penny," I say. "Stupid me, really because was a local number. I just so badly wanted to hear her on the other end. Not that you're not great company."

"I wish it had been her too," Henry says. He squeezes my hand, which is still in his, and runs his thumb across my knuckles. He seems reluctant to let go.

"I see her everywhere. I turn a corner on a street and she's a few steps away, or someone comes into the store and for a millisecond I think it's her and every time it's not. It's like losing her all over again, every time."

Henry pulls his sunglasses off and looks at me for a long moment. His gaze feels like it's pulling apart my skin and taking in whatever is underneath. It's the type of look that says "I see you." Neither of us looks away and a heat that has nothing to do with the blazing sun overhead builds.

"I don't know what to say, except that I'm here if you need me," Henry says. "I can't even begin to imagine how worried and stressed and heartbroken you are. I can't." There is pain on his face, and knowing it's for me loosens something in my shoulders, which had crept up to my ears while I spoke about Penny. I'd been guarding myself against some performative platitude, or worse, a minimization of the raging sense of loss and panic that is eating away at me. But there is nothing but compassion in Henry's expression. No judgement, just one human looking at another and accepting what's there.

I nod and he nods and it's as solemn as a vow made in a church. Then, Henry slides on his sunglasses and picks up his fork, and proceeds to demolish his lunch. The strange spell dissipates and I drink my wine, which still tastes sharp and crisp like it should.

Henry notices me pushing bits of salad around on my plate.

"Don't like the food?"

"Not hungry, I guess."

I push the plate toward him, and he scoops my share of lunch onto his plate.

"I could eat this all day. It's amazing." He pats his stomach. "These are the best falafels I've ever had."

So, the food is a me problem. Food tasting like garbage was on someone's listicle for "symptoms you're already dead."

After our late lunch, we wander around the city. Henry tries to keep the conversation light, as if he knows I can't think too hard about Penny.

When it gets too hot to be outside, we duck into a bookstore and point out our favorite titles. His: *Dune*. Maybe *1984*. *Harry Potter*. Mine: all of them.

"I love everything. Except stories where everyone dies at the end." I push my fingers into the base of my neck as I say it and feel for a reassuring thump-thump. Nope.

"Every woman I've ever dated has loved *Wuthering Heights*. I can't tell if they're just saying that, or if they actually love it."

I grin. "Not a fan. Toxic love isn't a real love story."

He makes a *whew* motion with his hand. We both ignore the inference in his slip of the tongue, but two high spots of color appear on Henry's cheekbones. I turn away and realize that I'm incapable of blushing. Must be the missing blood flow.

Penny doesn't come up again, but Henry doesn't act any more careful with me than he did before. He heckles me for being a dangerous pedestrian when I trip over the edge of the sidewalk, even while he steadies me so I don't end up headfirst into a planter teeming with begonias and daylilies. He keeps away the gnawing worry I feel whenever I think about Penny. At the same time, a tiny voice runs in parallel to Henry's—this one scolding me for being out in the sun, enjoying the brilliant July sunshine while Penny is somewhere else. Lost. I let Henry's voice drown my internal one.

We catch a late ferry back. As the sun lowers, the sky turns purple, then black. We wrap ourselves in a blanket from the trunk of Henry's car and share a coffee on the deck. We talk about little things—his friends, doughnuts that malformed in the deep fryer and came out too inappropriately shaped to sell to children, work, and our favorite television shows. Kashvi doesn't come up, but she hovers in the background like an apparition. Her name forms on my tongue as a question: what about Kashvi? I don't let it form in the air, because I was wrong. This is a date. Between two people who can't be dating. Who most definitely are not dating.

CHAPTER 14

As we turned onto my street, Emmalee waves at me from under a street lamp. I nearly wave back before I realize Henry doesn't see her. When I glance back, she's gone.

Henry stops the car and turns off the engine.

"So," he says.

"So," I echo back, awkwardly.

"Museum wasn't boring?"

I shake my head, and my hair gets stuck in my sticky lip gloss. Graceful, as always.

"It was probably the best day I've had in a while," I say, and try to pick out the hair without Henry noticing.

He exhales deeply and stares out the windshield. "Me too," he says, so softly I'm sure I've misheard. I'm hardly great company, what with my sad story and general sorry state.

I reach out and pat his arm, part thank you, and partly because I've wanted to touch it all day.

"Brooklyn!" Henry yelps. "Your hands are freezing. You should have said something. I would have turned off the air conditioning."

"I didn't notice," I say. He's right, though. My hands are so cold that my dexterity is limited, which is probably why I'm struggling so much to pull the hair off my mouth.

"You'd better go inside and warm up."

It's a dismissal, albeit a sensible one. Who knows what sort of spell would be woven if we continued to sit here, breathing in and out in the dark with barely any space between us? The drive home had been bad enough. I'd practically had to sit on my hands to stop myself from grabbing the one Henry kept casually on the shifter between us. The air had been heavy with tension, and we'd both studiously avoided looking at each other. I might be a hermit, but I'm not totally oblivious to interest, even if it mystifies me that it exists.

"Goodnight, Henry," I say, and open the car door. I swing my legs out the side, but before I entirely escape, Henry's hand wraps around my wrist. For the first time since we exited the ferry, I flick my gaze to his. A zap of electricity shoots up my arm from where his fingers form a bracelet.

"I'm so glad you came," he says. "You were my first choice." He looks marginally ashamed of himself, and Kashvi looms larger than she has all day. We're both walking a fine line of appropriateness. I don't want to be this person, hurting another person, even if she doesn't know. I hurt enough people when I dated Kyle. I said horrible things to classmates. I even said horrible things to Kyle because of the spurt of power I'd felt when I cut him down.

The silence thickens. It would be easy. I could lean toward him. He's already leaning toward me because he had to reach for my wrist. But I've worked very hard to not be unnecessarily cruel. My family has Spencer for that.

"I'm glad," I blurt. Then I flee.

I head upstairs to where my parents are instead of into the basement, in case Emmalee is waiting for me. I want to enjoy being normal for a few more moments. In the calm of my mother's kitchen, I blast the hot water and stick my hands under the faucet. Then I fill a glass with water and drain it. As the hot water fills my stomach, exhaustion settles in and Penny threatens to rise up, along with the knowledge Henry is going home to Kashvi. The day has been filled with emotions I usually avoid. Happiness. Sadness. Grief. Joy. I try to maintain an even keel of nothing at all, but it's getting harder. There's too much pressing against my skin from the inside.

There are no listicles that tell you how to stop dying, aside from those that suggest eating more kale and doing high-intensity workouts three days a week. Those are about prevention. I already don't have a heartbeat. All the antioxidants in the world aren't going do a damn thing.

"Brookie?" Mom calls.

The door leading onto the upstairs deck is open, so I peer outside. My mother is seated in an Adirondack chair next to round metal table with a bottle of wine on top.

"White?" she asks.

"Sure." I duck back into the kitchen for a glass and plunk myself down in a faux-wicker patio chair next to her. The overhead lamp in the kitchen above the table glows through the window and gives us enough light to see each other.

"What are you doing out here in the dark?" I ask.

"Too many bugs with the lights on. It's too hot in the living room, and your dad is snoring. I couldn't sleep. It's too hot everywhere. Last summer all it did was rain. This summer we've got nothing but forest fires and water shortages. When was the last time it rained?"

"May?"

Mom's teeth flash. "Sounds right."

We sit listening to the night—the burble of the fountain in the backyard, tipsy laughter from two doors down, crickets chirping, and the crackle of a firepit from a few homes away. Banned, of course. Mom is relaxed enough from the wine that she's not ranting about calling the city's bylaw line. Next door, the kitchen lights flick on and the shadow of a teenage boy paws in a fridge.

"How's work?"

"The usual," I say. "Someone dropped a Glazed Blueberry Compote on the floor the other day. Becca stepped on it and slid a couple of feet before wiping out. It made a beautiful blue streak on the floor and up her butt when she fell on it. It was hilarious."

"Did she think it was funny?"

"Of course not," I say. Kailey and I had howled, and Kailey had thrown Becca a damp dish towel to clean herself up, but we made Becca clean up the mess on the floor.

"You should be supportive of your coworkers," my mom says. "A healthy team is an effective one."

What inspirational poster she did she read that on?

"Mom. It's not like this job is going to become awesome because I wipe up someone else's mess."

"You don't know for sure," she says. "Maybe they'll make you head of PR or marketing or something."

"They won't."

"Why not?"

"Because I don't tell Matt how amazing and smart he is every day," I say. "Becca does. Becca will be head of marketing, should such a job ever be necessary for the doughnut shop. She's dating him, so she's the best candidate."

I can feel my mother frowning in the dark. It comes across in the sudden drop in her tone.

"Is Becca as good at marketing as you are?"

"No. Maybe. I don't know." Becca wants to be good at marketing. She's already finished the required reading for her first semester. I loaned her my old textbooks months ago, and she asked to keep them. Becca might be better at marketing because it matters to her.

"Skill is more important than telling the boss how amazing he is," my mother says.

"Not most places."

"You could have a better job than the doughnut shop—really, Brooklyn."

"I don't want a better job," I say.

"Why not? You're such a smart, talented girl."

"Because I'm tired. Because *women* like Becca"—*men like Todd*—"get promoted. They want it badly enough that they'll do what's necessary, and sometimes what's necessary has nothing to do with skill or talent."

"If you work hard—"

"That's not how it is," I interrupt. "Work ethic sometimes has nothing to do with it. You can work your ass off and your boss will overlook you because you're not his buddy's kid, or because you have boobs, or because he didn't like your tone in a meeting, or because someone else has better boobs. Or because he's threatened by your competence. Or because he has a different favorite lackey. Or because someone else licked his ass better. It's reductive and stupid and wrong, but it happens."

This is why I don't tell her what happened at Lawrence Communications. She'll make it my fault: I didn't work industriously. I didn't perform. I *misunderstood*.

"Brooklyn, that's a vile thing to say. 'Licked their ass.' Really."

I can tell she's smiling though. She does enjoy creative profanity on occasion.

"Sexism is real," I grumble. "Hierarchy is real. Ass licking is real."

"Honey, maybe it's your attitude?" She sounds hopeful. I guess my attitude seems like an easier fix than institutionalized sexism or toxic workplaces.

"Mom. Seriously. How many times must we fight about this? Sexism is real. God."

"I've never noticed."

"You've never had someone give you the evil eye because you said something contrary to a doctor? Been told how to smile at patients, or how to do your job? Had a patient request a 'real medical professional'? Been asked to pick up cake for some male surgeon's birthday?"

My mother shakes her head. I don't believe for two seconds she's never been discriminated against at work. For once, I wish she'd agree with me. It might make it easier to bring up more difficult subjects—also known as Spencer.

"Will you help me with the Labour Day barbecue?" she asks after a long, itchy silence during which I struggle for the magic words that might convince her I'm right. I've never found the perfect alchemy of nouns, verbs, and adjectives.

"Don't I always?" I sigh.

"Usually Penny is around, which makes it more fun for you."

My fingers clench convulsively around my glass.

"It doesn't seem right to cancel, even with Penny's situation," Mom says, sounding apologetic.

"What are you serving this year?" I ask, masking my sudden fury. How can we have this party without Penny? How can the days keep passing? The world should pause on its axis, waiting for her. No more sunrises or sunsets until Penny is home. That would make more sense, not this inexorable movement forward. Another Labour Day party. Life, time—everything—is rushing past me. I'm a rock in the current, waiting, as water whooshes by.

"I was thinking do-it-yourself tacos."

"What?" I say, sounding strangled.

"Tacos," Mom repeats.

She has a one-track mind about this party.

"We should do margaritas too, instead of just beer and wine," I say.

"Good idea," my mother says, sounding appeased both by my suggestion and assistance. Every year, my parents throw a Labour Day barbecue for friends, family, and neighbors. The party is a big deal. Last year, Mom forgot to invite the Carlsons from across the street, and Tara Carlson refused to speak to her when they bumped into each other at the organic bakery. My mother had to send flowers and profuse apologies when she realized why. It took Tara three more weeks before she caved and popped by with a pitcher of sangria and a serving of neighborhood gossip.

My mother should've been an event planner. She probably would have more fun than she does cleaning up other people's bodily waste and God knows what else an emergency room nurse gets stuck doing. I like picturing her behind a large desk covered in party invitations, food menus, and decoration samples. Would I have been different, if that person had been my mother instead of this unflappable, practical woman?

"Did you send out invitations already?" I ask. A few years ago, I convinced her to send e-vites. She thinks they're tacky, but likes that it's cheaper than mailing dozens of invites. She gets nearly instant RSVPs too, which she loves.

"At the end of June."

"Wow," I drawl. "You'll need to send reminders out soon. It's the end of July. No one is going to remember they got a party invite in June."

Her eyebrows raise. "They will. People like getting invited."

"Did you invite the Parkers?"

"Of course. They declined."

"Of course."

Same thing, every year. Only Penny comes. The two of us make off with a bottle of rosé and sit hidden by the curtain of wisteria trailing over the deck. We snicker every time my mother calls for us and drink straight from the bottle. We don't come out until everyone is gone and our feet are wet and clammy from the dewy grass. There will be no one to hide with again this year. Penny's presence kept Spencer away. Alarm swirls in my stomach, and there's a lump in my throat when I swallow.

"Would you mind if I invited a couple of people?" I ask, before I lose my nerve.

"Friends?" Even in the darkness, my mother's skeptically raised brow is prominent. It's been a while since friends other than Penny have been mentioned.

"Kailey, from Cute Lil'. Grace and Alisha. Henry." I grimace. "And his girlfriend."

My mother perks up at this. "That would be lovely," she says. "Of course. Invite whoever you like. Make sure they reply to the invite directly though, not to you. I need to stay on top of numbers, and you never tell me anything."

"Yes, Mom."

"I'll see if Spencer wants to bring anyone. Is he still dating that girl, from a few months ago?"

"Doubt it." I wouldn't know, and she knows it. The question is my mother's way of reminding me that Spencer has been dating and that I have not been dating. His name makes my arms goose bump.

"He's usually good about doing setup. I hate to ask him though, when I know he'd rather be studying."

"We don't need him," I say. "He probably doesn't want to come. Why don't you just not invite him?"

"Brooklyn." Her tone is a warning, a flashing red light. One that's always stopped me before.

"I just don't understand why you're so preoccupied with him. You baby him, and he's kind of a jerk most of the time. He..."

Tell her, tell her, tell her beats in my chest like a drum. Like a heartbeat.

I inhale and open my mouth.

My nerve fails me. It always fails me. I growl in frustration and sink back into my chair.

"He's your brother. And he's my son, and I love him. I love you too, even though I don't understand why you're working in that shop when you have a university degree, or why you're living with your old, cranky parents. I don't know what you're doing. Spencer is so driven and organized. You've always seemed lost." She clucks at me. Clucks. She's the worst sitcom parent ever.

She stands up and grabs the empty bottle off the table. She pauses at the door.

"Coming in?"

"I think I'll stay out here," I say.

"Suit yourself." With her free hand, she pats my shoulder and disappears into the kitchen. The tap runs, and there's a clank as she puts the bottle in the recycling bin under the sink. She switches off the overhead light, and I'm left in complete darkness with my half-finished wine.

"Chickenshit," I whisper.

AUGUST

CHAPTER 15

In August, the morning light goes from yellow to orange as fall peeks its head up over the North Shore mountains and stares down at the city. The breeze carries a whiff of desperation instead of sunblock as everyone tries to cram as much summer as they can into the remaining four weeks. Panic is most obvious in the mothers. In July, they wandered into Cute Lil' around 10 a.m. wearing sundresses and jangly earrings. Now, they're pounding through the door at 8 a.m. to pick up treats for day trips with a wild look in their eyes, their T-shirts untucked and covered in someone else's breakfast. People who haven't made it to a beach yet look just as frenzied. The only way people feel they've gotten their money's worth out of summer is if they've told someone how awesome one of the city's beaches was.

When I arrive for an early morning shift a few days after my outing with Henry, the front door is unlocked and Kailey is already working. Being on time is a first for her. She must be stressing. I'm buoyant about the texts Henry's been sending:

pictures of book covers; jokes about places I shouldn't go hiking; a request for a lunch recommendation by my old office. I haven't seen anyone named Emily in days, and I haven't done any disappearing acts in the mirror while I put makeup on in the morning. Aside from my heart, feeling cold all the time, and food tasting of garbage, I seem stable. I can't afford to be too fussy. Good enough is something.

Kailey rushes around the counter and hugs me. "You invited me to a party," she crows, her hair bouncing in my face. "Your mom's party, but still."

"You don't have to come. But all the food and booze are free. And you're a starving student." I make the hair-flip emoji with my hand.

"I already RSVP'd. Look at you, socializing. Inviting me to hang." She eyes my neon-blue jelly shoes. "Wearing color."

"Don't get too excited. I'm going to regret wearing these once they start digging holes into my feet." The shoes are cuter than my grubby black sneakers, but don't jibe with my bland work outfit.

Kailey hands me a stack of printed online orders—printed because even though the orders come electronically, Matt refuses to buy an extra iPad for the shop.

"Those came in. I need you to fill them before the afternoon rush. Matt decided to start selling doughnut sandwiches between noon and 2 p.m. and it's ruining everything. I'm spending the next forty minutes putting ham and cheese on doughnuts. Super gross." Kailey looks nauseated.

"When did he decide this? Overnight? What happened to the ice cream–doughnut match-up?"

"That's happening too," she says as she yanks a knife out of a drawer and brandishes it. "Two flavors in the fall, four in the winter. They want to hit twelve by next summer. Matt's talking about putting ice cream in at the Gastown location. We don't have space here."

"Why doesn't he just do a pop-up with the ice cream producer around Stanley Park next summer? Food truck style?" I pick up a pile of newspapers from the floor, where they landed after being shoved them through the mail slot, and start organizing them. Kailey looks dangerous with that knife.

"That's an awesome idea. You should tell him. He'll take credit for it."

"I'll leave a note," I whisper, barely able to hear Kailey over the buzzing in my ears.

Penny's face is plastered in full color on front page of the *Globe and Mail*. It's an old picture. Her hair falls in heavy waves to her shoulders and she's wearing burgundy lipstick and a smirk. The headline reads "One Year Later: Canadian Nurse Still Missing in Syria."

I scan the article but keep blinking because giant black spots are blurring my vision. The reporter talked to the PR person at the NGO Penny works for, one of her old bosses, our high school principal, and a handful of people whose names I don't recognize. It says her parents declined to comment. The quotes describe a robot, someone serious, focused, and devoid of personality beyond a passion for serving in dangerous situations.

"Crazy, hey?" Kailey says as she peers over my shoulder. "She's, like, your age."

"I know her," I whisper.

"What? Really? Like, from college?"

"Elementary school," I wheeze. The paper rustles in my hands.

I sit heavily and gasp for air. I put my face down on a cold tabletop, and rest my hand on Penny's face. Kailey's voice is distant, like an echo. Penny is still missing. *Missing, missing, missing. Gone, gone, gone.*

I haven't seen Penny since last July. She'd come home and stayed a week. I picked her up at the airport because her parents love her, but not enough to miss a day's billable hours. Penny came out of the arrival gate looking like a shadow of herself, stretched long and thin, with crisp edges created by the angle of the sun. We hugged, but neither of us mustered the energy to squeal and jump up and down like we did when she came home the previous Christmas. Instead, we stood there, embraced, and let go.

She said, "You look terrible."

I said, "I missed you too. That's a horrible thing to say."

She said, "I spend all day with people who are starving or destitute, and you look worse than them."

I'd grabbed her bag and marched over to where I'd paid fifteen dollars to park so I could wait inside for her plane to land.

"Sorry," Penny said, nearly sprinting to keep up with me. "It was a long flight. I'm super cranky. I shouldn't have said any of that. I forget how to be polite. Too long in the field."

We drove home in uneasy silence. The Vancouver airport is across the lumbering, brown Fraser River. We hit rush-hour traffic on our way back into the city and were stuck on a bridge named after a dead politician. When I was a teen, I'd imagine our family car going over the railing and plunging from the deck into the grubby, rushing water below. Somehow, the whole family, except Spencer, would live. The fantasy was so real that sometimes my fingers would jerk compulsively on the door handle.

"I met someone," she said abruptly. It was an apology, a secret, to make up for her snarky attitude. Intimacy to make up for coldness.

"You never said in your emails."

"I wasn't sure if he was someone, or just you know, something that happens. He works for one of the agencies." She paused. "He's married. I didn't know at first."

"Penny," I said, worry creeping into my voice.

"That's why I didn't tell you," she said. "I could hear you going 'Penny...' Anyway. You don't know what it's like. Sometimes you need a break. Something to let you forget where you are. There's not a lot of options."

Before, Penny had always been so scornful of men who cheated on their wives. She was contemptuous of their wives too.

She'd always said, "How do you not know that your husband is cheating on you?"

I said, "Some people hide from the things that hurt them."

She wasn't as observant as she liked to think, given the secret I'd kept from her.

"What are you going to do now?" I asked.

"I don't know," she said. She laughed, a scattered, tinny noise, like rocks being thrown down the metal slide in elementary school, and rested her head against the car window. Her lips were dry and cracked, and her short hair stuck up.

There was a time when she wouldn't leave her bedroom without her face perfectly coated in a custom-blended foundation and the right shade of plum lipstick. It's how she looks on the front page of the newspaper. The paper doesn't show how she'd discarded everything she didn't need. Makeup, clothing, frivolity, insecurities, remnants of whimsy and childhood. Me.

My head weighs one thousand pounds and I'll never be able to lift it off this table. I'll never move again. My body will be swallowed by the floor, and I won't do anything to stop it. I'll just wait here. However long it takes.

Muffled voices reach me.

"Shhhh," I mumble. "Loud."

A glass of cold water is pressed into my hand and warm hands lift me into a sitting position.

"I've got you," Henry says, as I try to focus on his face.

I sway. The sensations flooding my body remind me of being nearly black-out drunk.

"I saw the paper this morning. I wanted to check on you before I went to work." Over my head, he exchanges a look with Kailey and then he glances down at the newspaper under my hand.

"It says..." I rasp, "It says she's not the first who disappeared. The others haven't come back. Still gone. Presumed dead." Vomit rises in my throat. I push Henry away and careen to the sink, barely fast enough to heave my guts into it. I haven't eaten, so it's all water and bile.

"Thank God there's no customers in the store," Kailey says, as she rips off a length of paper towel and wipes the table where my face was plastered.

Henry whispers to her, and she inhales sharply. He must be explaining exactly how well I know Penny. I use one hand to wipe my mouth with a napkin. The other hand is curled into a claw around the edge of the stainless-steel sink. My shaking body rattles my teeth. I can't imagine being without Penny, even if I don't quite recognize the version of her who came home to visit last summer, or know a single one of these friends and colleagues described in print. How could I not feel the cosmic, shattering shift of Penny's status every moment? Her poorly reprinted face has brought back everything about her in a landslide. The idea that I may need to find a way to live without Penny worms through my turmoil. I shove the thought into a corner of my brain and let it wither like the plant in my bedroom.

Henry comes to my side. "Kailey says you should go home. She'll ask Becca to come in."

I nod.

"Let go of the sink."

"I can't."

Henry wraps an arm around my waist and puts a hand over mine. He coaxes my freezing fingers away from the edge, and my hand relaxes into his. He supports most of my weight as we walk toward the door. Emaleigh Taylor jogs by the shop's window and waves vigorously before rounding the corner.

Kailey stares me with wide eyes, her cheeks pale and expression wobbly.

"I didn't know," she says.

"Not your fault," I mumble.

Henry's heart beats against my side, where his ribs are pressed to mine. I flatten my hand against his chest and peer upwards. He looks down, his face filled with concern.

"Henry?" I whisper.

"Yeah, Brookie?" he says, as he reaches down to brush my hair off my cheeks. His fingers are feather light.

"She left me."

"She didn't mean to."

He doesn't understand. She left me, long before she went missing in Syria. She left me in my house, with Spencer. Moving out after high school hadn't been a superficial whim. I had spent years dreaming of being somewhere safe, somewhere away from Spencer. The concept of living with strangers or even my peripheral friends was terrifying—they could be like Spencer, or worse. Penny was the only person I trusted. And once university started, she slipped away even further: homework, volunteer work, new friends, new responsibilities. She'd kept going, and I'd stayed stuck.

We shuffle to his car, and he lowers me into the passenger seat. Before he starts the car, he makes a call.

"Grace, I'm not going to make it in. Can you let people know?" He pauses. Grace's concerned voice filters through, but it's unintelligible. "It's Brooklyn," Henry continues. "I'll tell you later. No, it's nothing like that."

"Don't worry about me," I say woozily when he disconnects. "You should go back to your regularly scheduled activities." The world is dull and flat, as though the colors have been stripped away and only left a faint stain behind. I shiver, disturbing a stack of papers on the dashboard.

"I'll take a sick day. You shouldn't be alone. You've had a bad shock."

"I should have expected it," I say. "I know how the news cycle works. I always thought that she'd be back, safe and sound, by now. I *believed* it. But a whole year has gone by. I didn't even realize what day it was this morning."

I hiccup. I've lost Penny all over again. My body is hollow and turned inside out, the soft meat of my organs and muscle exposed. It wouldn't take much—a cruel whisper, a bruise, a bump—to obliterate whatever is left of me. Who am I, without Penny? A lump of guts and flesh? A heartless zombie wandering the city? I'd imagined our identities were only separate because of the physical distance between us. That one day she'd come back, and the solidity of her presence would align my place in the world. I wouldn't be *alone*, once she returned. However unrealistic my expectation, I'd clung to it. There hadn't been anything else to hold on to.

Henry takes my hand like he's been doing it for years. I cling to it, ashamed I need the warmth of it so badly. On the way to my parents' house, he stops at a liquor store.

"Don't move," he admonishes, and jogs inside. He comes back with a bottle of bourbon.

"Just in case," he says, handing it to me.

At home, I brush my teeth, change into a tank top and running tights, and collapse on the couch. Henry sits in a chair, his feet up on a small bench. I nestle into the couch, cold despite the midsummer heat. My eyes keep sliding to Henry, soothed by the way his hair dips onto his forehead and the serious way his eyes look at me. I wish I could cry. There's a torrent of tears behind my eyes struggling to be released.

"It's not too early for bourbon, is it?" he says, finally breaking the silence that had been punctuated by my heavy breaths.

I shake my head.

He searches the cupboards in my kitchen. He's wearing navy dress pants and a crisp white shirt with the sleeves rolled up, and his hair is slightly messy. I should've borrowed an outfit idea from one of the Emily incarnations instead of picking something off the floor. Then again, I've looked worse in front of Henry and he hasn't seemed to notice.

"Glasses?"

"Tumblers. Second cabinet to your left."

He finds them and fills both halfway before handing me one. I sip, and it burns down my throat but doesn't leave any residual warmth in my stomach.

Henry sits beside me, hip to hip. He exhales deeply, and seems to brace himself. "My dad died when I was ten."

"Oh my God. Henry." I put my hand over his and his fingers lace through mine. It's hard to know who's squeezing harder.

"It was the worst day of my life," he says. "Or, the second worst. The first worst was learning how sick he was. When we found out, my mom was a trooper. She kept saying that things were going to be fine. She forced my dad to sit in the yard for fresh air and made him eat. She kept working because she wouldn't accept what was happening. Eventually, my dad told her that there was no point in pretending things were okay because they weren't. He said we could be scared and sad. He said he loved us, and that would have to be enough. He didn't mean to leave either." His voice cracks.

Penny *meant* to leave. She meant to leave me. She didn't mean to go missing.

"We fought," I say. "The last time she was home. She'd come for a visit. She was aloof, almost mean, and it felt like she hadn't left wherever she'd been."

After I picked her up at the airport, we'd gone for dinner at a restaurant overlooking the ocean. We'd watched women jogging with strollers and cyclists as they went by on the paved seawall along the coastline. Everyone seemed effervescent, thrilled to be soaking up the sun.

"Must be nice," Penny commented, when a group of twenty-somethings went by in flip-flops carrying their beach towels and coolers.

"Which part?" I asked, as I stared enviously at the laughing faces of the people in the crowds. I couldn't remember being as happy as they looked.

"To not understand that there are horrifying things in the world."

"Just because people look carefree doesn't mean they are," I said.

Penny raised a skeptical brow. "I'm just saying."

"I know what you're saying," I snapped. "We all lack perspective. You've mentioned it once or twice."

I felt judged about my silly little life and problems. I knew she'd tell me to suck it up, that my problems were nothing in the scheme of things. I couldn't talk about my job and how badly it seemed to be going. It—I—felt superficial and commercial after hearing Penny's stories about people's struggles for necessities in war-ravaged countries, or how she went everywhere in Kevlar.

"What did you fight about?" Henry asks.

"Her plans to go to Syria," I say. "Things were still uneasy between us when she left. And then she was…Well. You know." I swallow hard.

Penny and I had driven to Spanish Banks, where the beaches offered views of the city, the gray-green mountains across the water, or the open Pacific Ocean, depending on the direction you looked. The sun was descending and casting a pink-orange glow over everything, which blackened the lapping waves. On the water, freighters with their cargos stacked in containers colored like Lego blocks floated far enough away to look thumb-sized.

We'd sat on a blanket and stared outward as the sun set.

"The work is harder than I expected," she said, out of nowhere. "And I expected it to be hard."

"So, do something different. Work for a safe injection site here, or a local nonprofit. Or the hospital." I tried not to sound too excited even as plans unspooled in my mind. We could rent an apartment together. She'd force me to go running and talk me into quitting my job, where the toxicity was climbing the walls like ivy. Things could go back to how they were. And, most of all, I wouldn't be lonely.

"Just like that? Ditch my career? Come home?" Penny said, skepticism ringing in her voice.

"Why not? You have options. You're trained to handle crises, and you've worked in the most challenging places in the entire world. You're hardy. Imperturbable. Any organization here would be thrilled to have you."

Penny had propped her chin on her folded knees and stared past the horizon, her face pensive. Above us, the sky purpled and darkened. The city glittered in the distance. When I was teenager, I would stare at the lit-up city, sure that any moment it would open its promise of adventure. That out of it, I would carve a less ordinary self. Later, I realized the bright lights cover up an awful lot of ugliness. The glimmer wasn't tangible. It was an idea. A marketing trick.

I'd willed Penny to say she'd stay. Instead, she'd changed everything.

"I'm going to Syria."

I swear I felt my heart contract and shrivel when she said it.

"I want to go," she said, hurriedly. "But it feels like this will be my last field assignment. For a while anyway." A shiver went through her.

To Henry, I say, "She said she was going to come home for a while, after Syria. Maybe try something new." Pressure builds and builds in my eyes. My voice is thick and reedy with unshed tears.

"I told her she was being selfish by putting herself into such a precarious situation. I yelled at her, told her it was a bad idea and to stop trying to be some sort of hero. I was an asshole. She didn't do that work to be a hero."

I cover my face, and feel Henry shift beside me. He scoops me into his lap, and I curl against him and rest my forehead in his neck. I try to breathe around the memories. I'd driven her back to the airport. The sun came up during the drive, casting a watery, pale sheen over everything. Penny's expression immobilized, tightened into polite interest. I imagined her stripping off little bits of the past ten days and leaving them like litter in the passenger seat. The distance yawned between us, even though I could reach out and touch her.

Despite her objections, I walked her into the airport and hugged her goodbye. She was a skeleton against me and smelled like dry air and roses. She used to smell like grape chewing gum and nose-burning chemical drugstore perfume.

A shudder runs through my body, and Henry's arms tighten around me. One of his hands strokes my hair.

"I should have begged her to stay," I say, my voice muffled against him.

"Would it have made a difference?" he says, and the rumble of his voice shoots straight through to my bones.

"I don't know." I could have told her about Spencer. Told her I needed her to keep Spencer away. Would it have been enough to keep her here? Or would she have failed to keep me safe, like my mother had? Would she have abandoned me? Would she have accused me of just being overwrought Brooklyn?

I didn't say anything to her in case the answer wasn't what I wanted. How could I expect her to put me before the rest of the world?

"Listen, Brooklyn. I can't know what you're thinking. But, just in case no one has ever said it, it's okay to feel how you feel."

Screwing my eyes shut and burrowing myself as close as I can against Henry, giving myself a moment of just him, I whisper, "The truth is I'm furious at her. For going on dangerous assignments. For going away at all! I want to throw things and yell and tell her she's an idiot. And I know I'm immature and selfish, and I don't want to be this person who hates her sometimes for hurting all of us this way, for letting this happen. I blame her, and it's not fair, but that's how I feel, under all of it."

As the words pour out, pressure builds in my chest. Pressure turns to pain and I gasp, muffling the sound against Henry's collarbone. The pain grows and grows and bursts into a white-hot blade right where my heart silently sits. For a moment, I see black and white pinwheels in my vision, and am sure I'm going to puke from the pain centered in my body.

Beat, I scream internally.

But as soon as the pain bursts, it leaves only remnants of fire in my heart, like a comet tail burning out across the sky. The spasm defuses and is gone. I'm left exhausted and sagging. Henry's body adjusts to accommodate my sudden floppiness.

"I hated my dad for getting sick," Henry says. "One day, I didn't hate him anymore. That was worse, because then I had to be sad. Heartbroken."

I force myself to pull back so I can look at him. He has a faraway look in his eye that says he still is heartbroken.

"I wish things were different. For both of us."

Mostly, I wish the spasm in my chest would come back. Pain is better than nothing. I want to suffer physically—it's less excruciating than wanting. Wanting for the world to be different is like a black hole, and I'm being dragged further into it. I want to press my mouth against Henry's. I want his father's fate to have been different. I want to kick away the terror licking at my ankles like a small, pesky dog. I want Penny to come home. I want Spencer to be kind. I want my mother to believe me. I want to cut down every boss who's made me feel worthless. So much want I could drown in it, and nothing has come from wanting.

Henry runs a thumb across my cheek like he can't stop himself. I lean into his hand. If I could stay curled in his lap, I would.

"I keep thinking about you," he blurts. He can't make eye contact now. "I didn't mean … shit. Now isn't the time. You're upset and I'm not being fair. To any of us."

He's right. I'm wrecked with grief, exhaustion, and bourbon, and there are more issues between us than my missing heartbeat.

"You care about her." I can't say the word "love." Or Kashvi's name.

He looks ashamed. "Yes."

He spares me by not saying he loves her, although the look on his face says he does. Or did. Maybe not loving her is new enough his face hasn't caught up. I clumsily extricate myself from his lap.

"I thought we were happy enough," he says. "Our relationship felt normal. I was used to it, didn't question it. Then I met you, and now I feel the enormous distance between Kashvi and me. She's studying all the time. We barely see each other, but I don't know if what I'm feeling is real, or the result of our present, temporary circumstances."

"You don't need to explain," I say.

"I feel like I do."

"I didn't ask you to."

"Seems like you don't ask much of anyone. Maybe you should."

Both of us have been through an emotional ringer, and it's brought us right to the edge. Anger floats on the surface, but it doesn't feel like it's directed at each other. I don't have any room in my body to be angry at Henry, not when there have been so many worse offenders, and he looks like he regrets snapping at me.

A car roars into the driveway and falls silent. I stand up. "My mom's home."

"I should go." He pulls on his shoes and stands to face me. "Brooklyn." He lifts a hand like he's going to touch my cheek, and I flinch away. His face falls.

"Today has been a lot. But thank you for being there." I clear my throat and go for broke. "I needed you."

He hesitates. "I can stay."

"No. It's fine," I say. "We're fine." Fine should be a four-letter word parents never teach their daughters.

"For what it's worth, I'm sorry," he says. "For more than just Penny."

I nod and manage to keep my expression from shattering into a million pieces. He lets himself out, and I teeter back against the couch feeling as though I've been shaken by a giant. My bones are unstacked. Henry dug what's left of my heart out and left a raw, bloody wound behind. Before Henry, my heart may not have been beating, but it was still in my body. Now, it feels like he's taken it with him.

There are soft footfalls on the stairs, and my mother enters the basement suite.

"Kailey emailed me," she says, her face pinched. There are new lines around her mouth. "She told me what happened."

"The newspaper."

My mother winces. "I had your dad put ours in the recycling bin this morning. I was hoping you wouldn't see it." She sits and puts her arms around me.

"Tell me she's going to come home." I beg for reassurance from my mother who, despite her job as a nurse, has never quite managed to be soothing. There's too much uncertainty about what she knows, or chooses not to know.

"Penny is a smart, strong girl. She's a survivor."

"But what if?" I feel like the crying emoji—nothing but a stream of water pouring down my face. It remains dry, though.

She doesn't answer. She cries for both of us instead. This is how my father finds us, nestled together on the couch, mom bawling, me shaking with unshed tears.

He sits and wraps his arms around our shoulders. "My girls," he murmurs. "My girls."

CHAPTER 16

In the morning my face is puffy, and cold water does nothing to lessen the swelling brought on by a sleepless night.

"Today would be a great day to not see my reflection," I say to myself in the mirror. My features are thin and wan, and the purple moons under my eyes are full and plump rather than their usual sharp crescents.

I hesitate over the phone. Habit dictates I call the Parkers, but considering yesterday's news, what's the point? It summarized the status of the world. I sigh and hit redial on the Parkers' number. Why change now?

"Hello?" Lane's voice, not the voicemail, rings in my ear.

"It's Brooklyn." I falter.

"Brooklyn." Her voice is thick and swollen.

"I wanted to check in."

"Thank you," she says. Always courteous.

"I saw the paper," I whisper. "Who were all those people the reporter interviewed?" One of them could have been the man Penny was sleeping with. She never told me his name.

Lane clears her throat and says something muffled.

"I'm sorry?" I say.

"I think it might be best if you stop calling," Lane says.

"What?"

"Please, don't call anymore. It's too much. Robert will let you know if we hear anything."

"If that's what you want," I whisper, nausea rising.

The only response is a soft click. I stare at the phone, stunned. My last physical connection to Penny has been severed by Lane's low voice.

I haven't seen the adult Parkers since they were in my mother's living room to tell us about Penny's disappearance. They'd come from work and were still wearing their somber court black. Lane had hugged me. Her arms were too tight, like two sticks squeezing my body. Exactly like Penny's arms.

"We got a call, a few hours ago, from Penny's team lead," Lane said, releasing me.

"Gently," warned Robert. He wasn't concerned about my feelings. He was worried about a scene. He'd heard Penny and I together, loud with anger or hilarity, everything performed at maximum volume.

My mother's perfume, something soft and floral, was overwhelming in the hot living room and tinged with rot. It was her summer perfume, which she hasn't worn since that day. I'd pressed a palm against my mouth to hold back an unholy mess as the Parkers spoke. Lane didn't approve of vomit.

"Penny's supervisor didn't have a lot of information, because the whole situation is very chaotic, but Penny didn't show up at a clinic. They don't think she took off on her own. He wanted to know if she'd been in touch." Lane looked at me hopefully, as though I could tell her Penny was on plane home.

"I haven't... She hasn't," I said, stumbling through whatever I was trying to say. I crushed everything I felt under an imaginary shoe. I pictured my feet as large as a house and stamped downwards with all the force I could muster.

Robert kept clenching and unclenching his hands. It frightened me more than what Lane said. Robert was a scary criminal lawyer, not a man who fidgeted.

"Brooklyn, we need you to contact us immediately if you hear from Penny. Find out where she is, what she's doing. Tell her to call us." Lane was a wisp of a woman. There was no room for grief in her pencil skirt and fitted sky-blue blouse.

"Is there anything we can do?" my mother asked. She looked worse than Lane.

"We can't do anything right now. We have limited information," Lane said, her voice grim and practical.

My mother had reached out to grip my hand, and I was overwhelmed with gratitude. Her own sins were, in that moment, less grievous than Lane's. Mom would at least make a good show of hysterics if I was unaccounted for.

Lane and Robert stood at the same time, as though they'd rehearsed it. They left us with a Penny-sized crater.

"It was good of them to come," my father said. "They didn't have to tell us."

"Yes, they did," my mother snapped. "I practically raised that girl."

"You're exaggerating," my father said.

"I'm not."

"She's not," I said, tiredly. "Everyone is overreacting. Penny is going to be fine."

Wrong, wrong, wrong.

And now the Parker's have cut me off entirely.

I stare stupidly at my phone. Now what? I half-heartedly move my heavy, clumsy limbs. Work is a nagging responsibility no matter how I feel. Compulsion to obey the shop's shift schedule forces me to get dressed. I excel at obedience. When we were kids, Spencer would lose his shit if I didn't play games his preferred way, or if I didn't follow his instructions. It was easier—safer—to do what he wanted. I've applied that lesson wholesale. It's made me easy to walk all over. I'm letting a sociopathic bro named Matt force me to serve overpriced doughnuts to people. I'm polluting the world, one body at a time. Including mine. I resolve to give up sugar, and since I haven't been able to eat in days, it's an easy thing to quit.

I mechanically put on a pink dress that is sticking out of the closet and pull on a pair of Lycra shorts underneath. I wheel my bike through the backyard and onto the street, barely registering the traffic around me. The ride to work is interminable. I could just turn around and go home. Lie on the floor and stay there until an Emily shows up for a pep talk or my mother forces me upstairs for another dinner. And then what? What happens the day after that, and the day after that? In a week? A month? Another year? How do I keep going? How long can I keep going? Listlessness chases me down the road, no matter how strenuously I pedal.

"He's here," Kailey says as she gestures to my bike. "Outside with that."

I gape at her dumbly, and she rushes over, pulls the bike from my limp hands, and wheels it outside. She swears under her breath as she wrestles with the lock. My body trembles with fatigue and emotion.

"Brooklyn. Good, you're here," Matt says.

"Where else would I be? I'm scheduled to be here," I say, sharply. I'm tired of Matt's swagger. I'm tired, period. I've barely slept in days thanks to Emily, Emmalee, Emaleigh, and Emilie. Thanks to Penny and Henry. Thanks to the terror that Spencer will let himself in my parents' front door and suffocate me while I sleep, or cut me into pieces. Paranoia and fear keep me awake, follow me into my dreams.

"Right," Matt says. "Listen. I need you to take the night shift at the Gastown location on Saturday."

"Can't do it."

"I'm in a bind. Couple girls quit."

"I'm not working down there at night. It's sketchy."

Matt runs his hands over his greasy hair. It's not that his hair isn't washed; it's his hair product. He keeps it in the top desk drawer at both locations. The smell precedes him everywhere. Oily lavender. He pastes on a chagrined, hangdog expression, sure it will work. It always works, even on me, thanks to my inability to refuse authority. *Not this time*, I tell myself.

"Come on," Matt wheedles. "Becca says you have plenty of free time."

I was just starting to like Becca.

"Back off, Matt," Kailey interrupts. "Brooklyn's dealing with stuff. Her best friend is missing." She shoots me an apologetic sideways glance.

"Man, that's rough," Matt says, faux sympathy oozing. "Another shift will keep your mind off things."

"Not cool," Kailey says.

They start to squabble, and I'm mercifully forgotten. It's nice to have Kailey look out for me. It's not like I've done it for myself lately. Ever. Instead, I avoid my mother and harbor unspoken feelings for a man who loves someone else. I hold corresponding resentment for a woman I don't know, but feel confident doesn't deserve him. Not that I do. I'm a barely functional twenty-nine-year-old working in a doughnut shop with most of my past locked away in a mental file that says "Do Not Read." None of this is healthy.

Matt and Kailey turn and look at me expectantly.

"Take the shift," Matt says, crossing his arms. Kailey makes a slashing motion across her throat.

I don't have anything else happening, and Matt, everything, has worn me down.

"I'll do it," I say.

Behind him, Kailey makes an appalled face. She mimes strangulation before marching off to the brand-new sandwich station. Containers crash onto the metal counter and a slab of ham rolls precariously to the edge.

"I don't know why either of you made such a big stink if you were just going to say yes," Matt says, throwing his hands in the air.

"It's a bad location and I'm sick of taking everyone's unwanted shifts," I spew, barely aware of what I'm saying. My calves and thighs are wobbling and my eyelids drop, impossibly heavy. I shake my head, trying to regain a semblance of attentiveness.

"I don't want any more attitude," Matt says. "Everyone is pumped to take extra shifts, except you."

"I take every spare shift. I do your marketing." I'm crankier and more verbal than usual.

"You girls don't work that much. You spend most of the day chatting among yourselves or with customers."

Making nice with a rotating cohort of randoms is difficult. Jerk.

I straighten up and force myself to look him in the eye, fueled by a tiny lick of resentment up my spine.

"We work hard. We clean everything because you won't hire a professional with real disinfectant, and we put up with your friends who come in and demand things for free. We say no to them because you don't have the balls to. Kailey orders all the supplies—she even comes in on her days off to do it, because you won't train anyone else," I say.

"I trust Kailey," Matt says, appearing unruffled by my sudden backbone. "We go way back."

Noticeably, he ignores the comments about his friends. He's told us not to give them anything for free. They tell us Matt is their bro, and how he totally said they could get free doughnuts whenever they were in. Becca makes it worse: she gives them the doughnut and then writes it down as a staff comp. How Matt believes that girl is putting away any doughnuts at all is a mystery. She looks deader than I do, nothing but skin stretched over bone.

"That's great that you trust Kailey," I say. "But it's not fair for her to come in on her own time twice a week to check stock."

Matt rolls his eyes. "This is a great place to work. I'm super flexible with all of you. You get whatever shifts you want; I comp your meals and I throw great parties a couple times a year. The least you can do is help me out now and then."

Doughnuts are meals?

"My best friend's mother is an employment lawyer. That's why I know what's legal and what's not. If I take the Gastown shift, you're going to have to pay me overtime. I've already worked forty hours this week. Kailey has too."

Matt smirks at me. "I'll talk to my accountant," he says.

"You should."

Stalemate. He's not going to talk to his accountant, and I've used up all the fight in me. I deflate. This is not the first time he's had this conversation with someone. The difference is I'm not seventeen, and I know what he's doing is illegal.

Penny would know what to do. She would organize a protest, a boycott, and possibly commit a felony by stealing doughnut ingredients from delivery trucks until Matt was out of business.

Henry might be right. I should demand more from people. Including myself.

"Gotta run, girls," Matt says. He points at me. "Behave. Or we'll be having another discussion about your attitude."

"Can't wait," I say, waving at his back as he leaves. Then I reach behind the cutting boards for an apron. I'm chilled and want an extra layer.

"I tried to get you out of it," Kailey exclaims once Matt is gone.

"It's easier to do what he wants." In the short term, anyway. Doing what other people want hasn't worked out particularly well for me.

"I understand." Kailey hugs me. Her arms are strong, and she smells like icing sugar. "I got your back anyway."

"I know you do," I say, perplexed. "Why?"

"Because, even though you always seem like you're a million miles away and hate talking to people, I can see a funny, smart person under your 'bad attitude,'" Kailey says, putting Matt's comments in air quotes. "I get that you're going through a difficult time. But you don't need to be so prickly. I'm your friend."

I've made no effort to befriend Kailey, or to get to know her, and she still gave our boss shit for me. She thinks we're friends. Or that she's mine, anyway.

"It's like I tell the kids at the summer camp where I volunteer," she says. "Most people are nice when you get to know them. And if someone isn't, maybe there's a reason and we need to show them extra patience."

"I didn't know you did that," I said.

"Provided sage wisdom to minors?"

"Volunteered."

"You never asked."

Some person I am. All I do is talk about myself. With Kailey, Henry, the Emilys.

"I'm the one who needs your extra patience, in this scenario?" I ask.

"Yep."

"I'm an asshole," I say.

"That's true too," she says, nodding.

I perch on a stool and make a go on motion with my hands. "Tell me about the camp."

When Kailey's finished gushing about her volunteer work, she becomes contemplative and stares at the floor, which is smeared with raspberry jelly and desperately needs a mop.

"You know why Matt trusts me?" she asks, not looking up. "Because one of his buddies hit one of my girlfriends. They were dating, kind of. I didn't tell anyone, and I didn't make her report the guy. She didn't want to, but I should have encouraged her. And I should have quit working here. But I really need the money for tuition." A few tears track down her cheek, and she brushes at them angrily, her bright orange nails stark against her skin.

"Matt says I can work here as long as I want. He even pays me more than the rest of you." She looks like a forlorn teenager instead of the confident young woman she is. "I'm sort of an asshole too."

Jesus. I'm tired and old and wrong about everything and everyone. I'd written Kailey off as a shiny, clueless optimist, busily bouncing along. I'd believed she wouldn't understand a damn thing.

I get off my stool and wrap my arms around her. She's had to live with the weight of her silence, just like I have. I tell her the one thing no one has ever said to me: "It's not your fault."

CHAPTER 17

You know what? There've been too many emotions in the past couple of days. I decide to ghost my feelings. I'm cold—again—tired—again—and my whole body aches. Turns out, emotional revelation after emotional revelation is hard physically.

"Television on, everything else off," I say, waking up my laptop after work. I'd grabbed a sleeve of saltines from upstairs and hacked off part of a block of cheese for dinner, but by the time I'm curled up in bed, neither is appetizing. "I don't want to hear it," I say, out loud, when my brain starts cycling through anything upsetting it can come up with.

The only thing I feel like watching is *Dragonslayer*, so I put it on—and pass out.

I wake up to someone aggressively shaking me.

"Finally," Emmalee exclaims. "I've been trying to wake you up forever. You were sleeping like the dead."

"What time is it?" I say, floundering to look at the digital clock buried under the clothes the Emilys have removed from my closet.

Emmalee fiddles with a blue stone bracelet around her wrist. Penny gave it to me for Christmas in high school, when I'd spent the holiday with the Parkers in Mexico. It hasn't been out of the jewelry box in years.

"It's late. I've been waiting for you get up."

"What do you want?" I sigh, resigned to being awake, or hallucinating. I'd blame the cheese, but I didn't eat any before passing out.

"I'm glad you took my advice."

"What advice? Is it the middle of the night?" It's dark outside the window.

Emmalee tugs the elastic off the end of her French braid and starts unwinding it. "You went on a date!"

"It wasn't a date," I say automatically.

"It looked like a date. More than one. There was booze and food and he seemed into it. Both times."

"How do you know? Actually, never mind." I'm not sure it's a point in my favor that my brain thinks Emmalee is omniscient, or possibly stalking me.

"He seems decent. Unlike Marshall. Or Kyle. Has anything good ever come from a guy named Marshall?" She mock shudders.

"You woke me up to talk about the shitty men I've dated?"

"You need to loosen up. Chat with people. Make connections. Maybe with Henry." She writhes her hips. "I like him. You're not all squirrelly and twitchy with him, like you are with pretty much everyone else."

"Twitchy?"

"You basically duck and cover with every other dude you talk to. Especially that asshole boss of yours. And that Todd guy."

"I don't know what you mean," I say as I reach for my quilt and pull it up to my chin.

"Right," she says, dragging the word out. "So, you don't make yourself as small as possible in their presence before doing whatever they want, whenever they want?"

"I can see your point." I wish I could unsee it. The thought had been hovering unformed somewhere in my body, and Emmalee forced it to coalesce with one blasé statement.

"You don't do it, as much, with Henry. You're bigger. More yourself. Seventy-five percent yourself," she qualifies. "Why?"

"He's a good person. He doesn't set off alarm bells in my head. He doesn't think I'm lazy, or irresponsible, or a liar."

"He's not that good," Emmalee says. "He's super into you, and he's got a girlfriend."

"Fair point." I gnaw a hangnail. Moral gray area. I hate it. Here's something Penny and I have in common—infatuation with inappropriate, taken men. I've already established that I'm obsessed with talking about myself. I might as well continue. "Is he? Into me?"

"Please," Emmalee says, as she starts rebraiding her hair. She tucks a platinum hair comb, also from my jewelry box, into the side of her braid. Then she props her right leg up on my desk chair and starts stretching over it, her arms extended above her head like a ballerina.

I should start going to yoga with Kailey before my entire body seizes up.

"Definitely into you. But. Girlfriend."

Kashvi. It's hard to reconcile. I'm not so puritanical that I can fully judge him for inching closer to me. I haven't stopped him and have no moral ground to stand on. In his own way, he's lonely, which is one emotion I fully understand. I get that it goes away when we're together. He has options though. No one is making him stay put, feeling alone with the person who he shouldn't feel that way with.

"He doesn't judge me," I say. "It's like all the messy parts don't faze him."

"Even Penny is critical of you, isn't she?" Emmalee asks. She drops to the floor and starts doing crunches. Every few seconds, her face appears over her knees. "Your mom too? Your bosses? And yourself?"

"Penny is none of your business." Nonetheless, a little voice in my head concedes. Penny held both of us to an unattainable standard. There wasn't room for me to be broken or weak.

After our high-school protest, Penny had insisted it wouldn't be the last time.

"I don't want to get in trouble," I'd said. I avoided getting in trouble if I thought Spencer would find out. He always spun stories with me as the instigator for our mother.

"Are you serious right now? Who cares?" Penny said. "We can't let old white dudes spread racist and sexist propaganda." She bounced with enthusiasm. "We have it easy, the least we can do is stick up for what's right."

"Things aren't easy for me," I yelled, snapping unexpectedly. Penny reared back as if slapped.

"What do you mean? Seriously, Brookie. What are you talking about? We barely even got in trouble." She was shouting too. "Why are you so afraid to step out of your comfort zone for once?"

Then she paused. "Is there something you're not telling me? You've been spacier than usual. You ran into the bathroom yesterday when Spencer brought you your lunch you forgot at home. You never miss a meal. You pregnant?"

I stood there with my chest heaving and pins and needles starting in my fingers and toes. I gasped for air, Spencer's name on my lips but refusing to be spit out. I couldn't tell her. What if she stopped coming over after school? Spencer left me alone when she was in the house. If she knew she might confront Spencer, and he'd take it out on me later. Or on her immediately. I had no idea what he'd do if challenged. He might hurt her. By keeping my mouth shut, I could protect her and myself.

"Panic attack," I wheezed, as tingling spread up my arms and legs. She dragged me to the nurse. It was the closest I ever came to telling her about Spencer.

"Maybe that's why you like Henry," Emmalee says. "He's the only person who doesn't find you wanting."

"Unlike you. You're judgy," I say, as snidely as I can.

"I think you should get some exercise. Start running again. For your mental health, not because I want you to be a different person." Emmalee pants between sentences, still busy doing her sit-ups. She'd even cleared a space on my clothes-covered floor.

"Henry is dependable. Not sleazy."

"What a high bar." She pauses her crunches to look at me like I'm an idiot. "His girlfriend probably doesn't share your perspective."

"What do you want me to say?" I snap. Then I groan and flop back on my bed, splaying my arms open. "I need to forget him. He's with Kashvi."

"If their relationship is so great, why does he keep showing up for you?" Emmalee says. "People break up. He can make a clean break. Start over."

She keeps making valid points.

"It would never work."

"*This* is what you choose to be confident about," Emmalee grumbles.

"It's not like I can love someone. No heartbeat, remember?"

"Love is all chemicals and choices and shit. Your heart, functionally, has nothing to do with it." Emmalee finishes her exercise and folds herself into a cross-legged seat. Her face is expectant.

Of course I know this. Not having heartbeat is a convenient excuse to brush off what I could feel, if I let myself. The people I've loved have hurt me. By accident, like Penny. On purpose, like Spencer. By obtuseness, like my mother. I'd rather pretend my heart controls love—I've got the perfect excuse to avoid the whole thing.

"It's time to sever things, whatever they are. Before they go further." As if they haven't gone far enough.

"So that's it? No more Henry?" Emmalee asks.

"No more Henry." I jut my chin resolutely.

"Good for you," Emmalee says, her doubt clear in the purse of her lips.

"Besides."

"Besides?"

"I'm getting worse," I say, hesitant to admit it out loud. "I'm exhausted all the time. Can't eat. My body keeps poofing from mirrors. I heard clucking chickens yesterday, which, by the way, was mentioned in the list of symptoms about being dead. Unless the neighbors got backyard chickens?" I should check.

"You really should stop self-diagnosing on the internet," Emmalee says.

An alarm goes off on her watch, shredding the air. We both jump. "I'm late for my dead-lift class. I gotta go. Later, Brookie," Emmalee yells, as she sprints for the door.

How does she have the energy? I pick up my bracelet off the bedspread and put it around my wrist. The blue stone glows against my pale skin. I pound on my chest like some sort of deranged Tarzan giving himself chest compressions. My stupid, useless heart.

CHAPTER 18

"**L**unch!" Grace's voice booms through my cellphone while I'm lying on the couch with my laptop balanced on my stomach watching old episodes of *Cop on Campus*. My hand dangles in a bowl of popcorn, which I decided to make but can't stomach eating. The short-lived series stars Emilie Abellard as the titular cop. She goes undercover at a university and is tasked with finding a dangerous drug ring alleged to be operating on college grounds. The students she meets make her question her life choices, and her internal struggle consists of montages of her staring longingly at piles of textbooks in the school library.

I'd forgotten how much I loved it. It's schlocky, pro-cop, pro-American, pro war-on-drugs propaganda, but addictive. Probably because Emilie's love interest, a fast-talking drug dealer with a backstory involving a dying mother, is smoldering. I'm trying to displace Henry in my affections. What's one unavailable man in exchange for another?

"I'm starving and bored and haven't left the office for lunch in three months," Grace yells through the phone. "Get your butt off the couch and come eat with me."

I hit the spacebar to pause the show right as the drug dealer is about to confess to Emilie's character that he wants to be a good person, but sometimes life detours and you run out of options.

"How do you know I'm on the couch?"

"That's where I'd be if I wasn't at work," Grace says. "Get moving. I'll see you in thirty minutes. Make that forty-five." She texts me an address to an unfamiliar restaurant.

I'm flattered and anxious that Grace has asked me to lunch.

I struggle to get up and out the door. My quads burn with fatigue from the simple act of wandering around my bedroom, and my hands shake when I reach for my lip gloss. Today's symptoms are worse. I call a cab to take me downtown, not sure I can make it on my bike and not trusting myself to drive.

Grace picked a restaurant with floor-to-ceiling front windows and exposed brick walls covered in textiles—fabrics in frames, tapestries, and elaborate woven concoctions hanging off pieces of driftwood as thick as my arm. None of the chairs or tables match, and the overall effect is cozy, like a living room in a magazine spread about cottages in lake country.

Grace is in the back of the restaurant, seated next to a potted pine tree. I paste on a smile. Being forced off the couch is probably a good thing. The couch, however, is easier than sitting up in a chair pretending to be human and alive. The server scurries over and we order.

"Give me the biggest sandwich you've got," Grace says. "With fries. And gravy. Actually, make it a poutine." She rubs her palms together, practically wriggling with excitement. She pats her tummy. "Starving."

"Grilled cheese. Tomato soup," I murmur, sure I won't be able to eat it.

"I meant to call sooner," Grace says once the waitress leaves. "Been busy. You know. Life."

"Life," I echo, my voice thin and reedy. I clear my throat.

"Henry told me about your friend. Penny. I'm so sorry. I wanted to say that earlier, but I wasn't sure how to. It didn't seem like an appropriate text message."

"Sorry about your best friend? Frowny face emoji? I guess not." The bitterness in my tone startles me.

Grace seems unperturbed by my mini outburst. She drinks her water and keeps her gaze trained on me.

"Sorry," I mumble.

"Don't be. It's brutal. Want to talk about it?"

"Absolutely not." I don't want anything getting back to Henry, and Grace is chatty. There's no reason to provide him supporting evidence to any theories he might have about my mental state. Even if I'd sworn him off earlier.

"Are you sure?" Grace asks. She lowers her glass. "There have been times when I would have killed for someone to talk to."

"I'm fine."

Grace raises both her eyebrows. She sighs. "Look. It's none of my business." The "but" is implied in her body language.

I look at my wrist and push my fingers against the blue veins under my translucent skin. No pulse. The stone in my bracelet is cold against my skin.

"Say whatever you want," I say, waving my hands at her in a go-ahead motion. "Everyone else has been." Everyone named Emily. Or Kailey.

"I was really struggling to keep my mouth shut." She grins and leans across the table. "What are you doing? Working in a doughnut shop? Pining after a man who's too clueless to realize he's pining back? Dragging yourself around with that vague expression on your face? I can tell that you're a smart, talented, sassy girl."

This is how women talk. We call each other girls, because we're not comfortable with the word "woman." Woman has been so ripped from our collective lexicon that it's hard to spit it out. She's not wrong. I'm a girl. A lonely, miserable girl with a shit career and a friend who might be dead. A yawning pit of despair opens in my mind, and I sidle closer to its edge. It might be easier to dive into it and see how quickly it swallows me, rather than sit here in this world and be ripped open over and over.

Grace has worked herself up. "I meant to be less blurty and nicer," she says, looking chagrined.

"That's not you though, is it?"

"Not so much," she says. "Alisha gives me crap for it. Love that woman, but she's cool as a cucumber. Can't relate."

I open my mouth to tell Grace I'm doing awesome—that the doughnut shop is temporary, that Henry and I are just friends, and that my life is a sparking adventure temporarily on pause while I regain my equilibrium. That's not what comes out.

"I'm dead," I wheeze, moisture clogging my ducts. If someone pricked me with a pin, I'd explode in a cascade of hot, salty water, because the tears are trapped in my body.

It's easier, and almost a relief, to talk to someone that my senses trust is really there, unlike my litany of famous friends.

"You're not dead," Grace says. "You're a mess. Been there, done that."

"You don't understand," I wail.

As I talk, my wrist fades in and out, the skin decomposing around my bones. Skin, meat, fat, gone. There's nothing left but a thin white radial styloid process.

I lift the bones from my lap to the table to show her. She misunderstands and grabs my hand, squeezing it before letting it go. My bones are invisible to her. We say nothing while a girl—another "girl"—puts our meals in front of us. Grace's sandwich is piled six inches high. Mine looks pathetic in comparison. Oily cheese between two burned pieces of bread. Grace exhales in satisfaction and uses two hands to pick up half her lunch. My stomach heaves at the rich smell coming off her poutine.

"Anything else?" the server asks, sounding bored. She's probably in university, thinking the whole world and every option is before her. So many choices. I'm too tired to make choices. I'm buried by the ones I made. Or didn't. The choices I didn't make are suffocating me.

"I do understand," Grace says, after devouring several mouthfuls of her sandwich. "I had a meltdown when I was thirty. I was miserable. I was living in Ottawa, and I'd just come out to my parents. It didn't go over well. My mom is Vietnamese Baptist, and she thought I was punishing her. She wouldn't let me come home for Christmas because I'd shame the family, not to mention God. I ended things with the man I was dating. He was my boyfriend *and* my best friend, but when we broke up, he said he never wanted to see me again. I spent Christmas Day alone in a basement suite—it had mice, by the way—crying, sure I'd be alone forever." She takes a deep breath.

"What happened?" I ask. My arms reappear: fat, meat, skin. Nothing like your own flesh to put you off lunch.

"After the holidays, I went back to work. My boss refused to promote me, even though I met all the requirements. I stood outside the building and realized I never wanted to go back to my desk. Turned around, slipped in the snow, ripped my coat on the sidewalk, and scraped my knees. I sat there, soaking wet and bawling my eyes out. In two weeks, I'd thrown away my family, partner, and job, and I had no clue how to become who I thought I wanted to be."

Grace looks at me intently. "My friends were having kids, or had great jobs, or were getting married, and I was sitting in a slushy puddle looking like I was coming down from a bad high. I felt like I was the only person in the universe who had no idea what I was doing."

"No," I object, unable to believe that this confident force of nature had ever been anything but. "You're friendly, successful. Lovely to people you barely know." I point at myself.

"You bet I am," Grace says, nodding in self satisfaction, as she picks cheese curds out of her poutine and puts them in her mouth. "But I wouldn't be this person if I hadn't blown up my old life. I would still be completely miserable."

"What did you do?"

"Started over. Moved out here. I felt like shit ninety percent of the time, could barely find the energy to order takeout. I wanted someone to fix everything for me. Instant new life." She wipes her fingers on her napkin and tackles her sandwich again. Her eyes nearly roll back in her head. "This is so good," she says.

"I wish someone could fix me," I say.

"Someone can. You." She gestures with her sandwich. "I'm not saying you need to do it alone. Therapy is your friend. I'm your friend, even though we just met."

"What if I keep making things worse?"

"Life hurts, baby."

"Thanks for the platitude."

"What can I say? Instagram is making me stupid. Most of my advice is limited to a few words that can be written in a hipster font and displayed on a pastel background. Likes, please."

Despite everything, I laugh.

"Things can always get worse," Grace says. "But face it: Things aren't that great for you anyway."

"Ouch." And Grace doesn't even know about Spencer, or my absent heartbeat, or my degrading body. "What do I do?"

"Something! Anything. I started with things I wanted to do, not the things I thought I should do. I went out with a girl for the first time. It was a disaster, but it was honest. It felt good. As good as a bad date can feel." She snickers at her memories.

"I don't know what I want. Everything feels too hard."

"I know," Grace says.

I nibble at my grilled cheese, but it tastes like greasy sawdust, so I spit into my napkin and drop the sandwich on my plate.

"What do I do about Henry?" I whisper, in case Kashvi is lurking behind a potted fern or Spencer is behind the fake fence separating our table from a row of booths. Vancouver isn't *that* big of a city.

Grace takes a huge chomp out of her sandwich and chews for ages.

"I love Henry, but he's got his own issues. Kashvi being the biggest. He's moved on and can't admit it. Sort yourself out, then worry about him. He's not going anywhere. And if he does, he's just another thing you need to get through. That's life. You have to survive it over and over."

"That's only slightly better than an Instagram post," I mutter.

She flicks a piece of lettuce in my direction. "Eat your soup."

When we get up to leave, Grace crushes me against her.

"You're strong for such a tiny person," I gasp as she squeezes. Her heart pounds against my breastbone, a steady, solid reminder of what I don't have. It echoes through my body and darts its way into the crevices between my bones.

"You're strong too," Grace whispers in my ear. "You've made it this far."

At home, I look in the mirror and face a watery outline of a person. I could be anyone. Once I've checked to make sure my parents aren't around, I crank the baseboard heaters, even though my mother's voice is in my head telling me not to waste electricity. It's seventy-nine degrees outside, but my hands feel like they've been gripping ice cubes. I crawl into bed with my laptop. I can only fix myself, Grace says. Where to even start?

I click through pages of classes available at local colleges and universities. It's not the first time I've done this; I read course summaries like other people watch porn: furtively, and with a growing shame and worry that someone will catch me. I scan history classes with long syllabi; economic studies for developing nations; textile workshops; language programs for French, Japanese, Welsh, and Greek; and charcoal drawing classes.

I imagine being on the Greek islands and conversing with the locals, living in the whitewashed buildings, jumping into perfect blue seas, or taking off with a Greek guy to some little village no one here has ever heard of. I fantasize about being front of a classroom in London, teaching art history classes and living in a knick-knack-filled flat above a tea shop. There, I'm grading papers with a long-legged man who is wearing a tweed jacket. I could be hiking across Wales, wandering through little towns and discovering crumbling ruins of castles with no one for company except sheep. I see myself in a little shop selling handmade woven scarves. I smile at my customers, and pat the cat on the countertop, feeling content and at ease.

I've never signed up for a class. I just read about them and spin elaborate stories about who I'd be if I'd chosen differently, or been less subjugated by cowardice, expectations, and fear. Running away is a pleasant fantasy that won't bring Penny back, or provide the right career, or undo any of the damage Spencer wrought on my body. I won't magically become a new person overnight. I'm still me, and I'm stuck. The knowledge required to unstick myself is out of reach.

Grace's exhortation to take back my life offers a slippery hope. Control over your own destiny and all that. I buy it. Bought it, at least. But Grace's ability to bounce back included one important addition. She had a heartbeat.

I cover my face with my hands, and exhaustion pulls my eyelids closed.

"What's the worst that could happen if you took a class?" Emilie says, sitting cross-legged at the foot of my bed. She's wearing black nylons and a silk top my mother gave me that made me look like a tall pumpkin. Orange might not be her color either, but she's wearing it like a sexy mini dress. Her hair is braided in a thick coil on the crown of her head.

"Did I fall asleep?"

"Are you ever awake?" she drawls.

"What?"

"Just pick a class. Any class. Go for it," she says. "What are you afraid of?"

"I don't feel like it."

"Your search history says otherwise," she says.

"I have an education. I have a career. I'm going to look for a job, and I won't have time for classes." The words are sour in my mouth.

Emilie unfolds her legs, rolls onto her stomach, and props herself up on her elbows.

"I loved school. I would have stayed in school forever, even after I got my degree in classical literature," she says.

"That sounds…"

"Useful?" She laughs with a dainty, musical tinkle. "Like acting? God. My mother was furious. Two career paths, both destined for poverty and debt. That's what she always said."

"You won an Oscar."

"I know, right? And I read so many books while I was in rehab. Kept me sane, so the degree wasn't a complete waste. It meant I could teach too, if my acting career continued its downward spiral."

"Downward spiral?"

"My most recent movie, *Last Moments*, tanked at the box office. Horror is not my genre."

"I didn't see it."

"No one did," she grumbles. "Critics said my fake screams sounded totally fake. I had back-to-back flops. Oscar winner to box office pariah."

She shakes her head contemplatively. "It sucks when everything is going your way, and then suddenly, it's not. Feels like you're free falling into a giant pile of steaming shit and it's everywhere and everything stinks." Her crude statement is at odds with her genteel drawl.

I giggle. I'm so far into the shit I can't envision how to drag myself out. I look at Emilie again and I see the fatigue on her face. She's been through it and somehow, for as long as she could, built a life up around her anyway. She won an Oscar, got a university degree, went to rehab, and tried over and over until she couldn't anymore. She fought for her life, while I've let mine drift away from me.

"I'll take a class," I say, because there's nothing else I can do for her.

"Excellent." She plucks some lint off the tangerine blouse. "One more thing. You need to get rid of this shirt. It's grotesque."

"You can have it. I was only hanging onto it because I didn't want my mom to know I hated it."

"You're setting a dangerous precedent by not being honest with your mother about her fashion choices. Who knows how many more hideous shirts are in your future?" She mock shudders.

"Burn it."

"My mom would despise this," she says, a devious look flitting across her face. "I'll send it to her. I'll say I thought of her when I saw it."

She stands up and smooths her hands over her braided crown. While she preens in front of the mirror, I wake up my computer and type in some local universities.

When I glance up, Emilie is gone. No big production or dramatic exit, just gone. It's creepy.

"It's really annoying how you all keep popping in and out," I call. "It's rude. You show up, make a mess with my clothes, and lecture me." Hello? What am I doing? Stop talking to no one.

Fuck it. If I was to take a class, what would it be?

My mother hadn't been the only one to steer my career. My high school guidance counsellor didn't help much either. When I said I loved history and research, he, like my mother, steered me toward marketing and public relations. At sixteen, I'd assumed he had secret grown-up knowledge about the world, and by that time I'd been subjected to plenty of stories about university graduates working at restaurants for minimum wage. It was a cautionary tale teachers provided students who were considering art or creative writing majors.

Now that I'm adult-ish, I realize I probably shouldn't have taken the advice of someone puffy eyed from lack of sleep, divorced, wearing a shirt two decades out of style, with three molding cups of coffee on his desk and breath like an ashtray. This is not a person who knows what's up.

I'd asked him, "What did you want to do?"

He'd said, "Work with people. Advise them. Enable them to discover their passions."

"How'd that go for you?" I said. "Teenagers really are so malleable, aren't they?"

He'd sighed. "Brooklyn. Your grades aren't bad. You could probably bring them up with some extra credit before the end of the semester. But you've got some marks on your record because of the antics you and Penny got into during the last four years."

I made a scoffing noise.

"You cut classes, and you got caught with beer on the senior volleyball trip. There was the protesting. You and Penny hid all the school's hockey sticks on the roof. You're a good student, but not a stellar one on paper. You'll be lucky to get into a technical college."

"Penny always says post secondary schools are a business and they'll take anyone who can cough up the money," I said.

"It's a bit more complicated than that, and Penny's grades are better than yours so she can say whatever she wants," the guidance counsellor said. He gave me three university and technical school pamphlets with communication programs. "It's this or nursing. Your mom worked with Penny on her prerequisites. Get her assistance."

"This is bullshit," I said. "I'm smart. I play on three sports teams. I have top marks in history and English classes. I'd be great in an academic field."

"Communications. It's your best bet," the counsellor said. He added a "Say No to Drugs" booklet to the pile in my lap, along with an "Options for Sexual Health" brochure. I handed them back.

"I don't need these."

"Take them. The principal counts them every week to make sure I'm giving them out." His bloodshot eyes were forlorn.

I don't have to listen to the echo in my head of that counsellor telling me what I can't do.

Before I can talk myself out of it, I add a standalone nonfiction writing course to my online cart, yank my credit card from my wallet, pay, and find myself signed up for a class on Saturday afternoons in September.

I want to call Henry and tell him, but I've stuffed him into the increasingly crowded corner of my brain containing things I don't acknowledge. We haven't spoken since he left the basement suite. Not a single text. I can't work out how I feel about it. Irritated, because I haven't heard from him, or relieved because I don't need to deal with him and whatever confusing mess we've gotten ourselves into.

Right now, I'd be grateful if Emilie came back. She'd be proud that I took her advice. Instead, I text Grace: *I signed up for a writing class.*

She sends back balloons and celebrating hands emoji.

I poke my chest, my neck, my wrist. No *thump thump*. Taking a class hasn't fundamentally altered me. But it's something.

CHAPTER 19

The dreaded Saturday late-night Gastown shift arrives. I wear my usual work skirt, but in a spurt of enthusiasm borne of registering for a class, I root a pair of silver flats and a hot-pink T-shirt from the dark recesses of my closet.

"Not too bad," I say to my blurry reflection as I apply a thin coat of makeup. I can't quite make out the details of my face in the mirror, so I have to pray my eyeliner isn't overly winged.

I've done one other shift at the main Cute Lil' location, because someone had skipped out and I'd been the dummy who'd answered my phone when the night manager called. The shop is right in the middle of the club scene and does a lukewarm business between midnight and 2 a.m. Girls teeter into the shop in bunches, their makeup melting, their hair flattening, their feet blistering in their high heels. Their dresses, which looked good when they left the house, droop. By 1 a.m., feathers, sequins, and cleavage are a mistake. The men—boys—aren't much better. They're just as drunk, louder than the women, and some of them sing. "Wonderwall" is a popular pick, for reasons I, in a sober state, don't understand. Everybody is drunk and messy and the whole shift is an absolute drag.

I'm filling in for Hilary, a powerlifter hoping to make it to the next Summer Olympics. Matt hired her on the spot, the story goes, because during her interview she'd easily hoisted five ten-pound flour bags at once. The rest of us complain about lifting one bag. I haven't picked up anything heavier than a coffee pot since I sprained my ankle. Matt had made it clear, via a Post-it, that he doesn't want a workers' compensation claim.

At 8:30 p.m., I walk into the Gastown shop to serve dough-nuts to drunk club kids who can't find the late-night pizza place around the corner.

"You look familiar," I say to the other sucker behind the counter.

"I live two doors down from you," he says.

"Raj?"

"Yeah."

I babysat Raj once—my first and only experience as a baby-sitter. I'd spent the entire night on the phone with Penny and hadn't been asked back. Raj probably knows how old I really am. Hopefully he won't do the math and divulge said fact to Matt.

"You always work this shift?" I ask.

"When I'm not clearing tables at Station Club."

"You're our only male employee."

"No competition for college girls," he deadpans.

Raj is not talkative the way all eighteen-year-old guys are not talkative with women they have no interest in. He sits with his phone, his thumbs moving rapidly. I pull a novel from my over-sized purse and check the doughnut stock in the display case.

"We need to do some stuff for the bake team," Raj says without looking up. "Mix some flour. Feed the starters. Make sure the icing doesn't dry out."

"Great," I say. Another reason to hate working the Gastown shop. At the other location, the doughnuts arrive fully formed. There's barely a kitchen. There is no prep, aside from filling up the coffee machines with beans and occasionally icing some plains if we sell out of a basic like Honey Lemon. Or slicing cheese for Matt's newfangled doughnut sandwiches.

"Is it usually busy?" Raj's lack of communication motivates me to prod and poke him with questions.

"Mostly shift workers and restaurant staff at midnight. A little rush around 2 a.m., when the bars close."

"Super."

Bored, I wipe down the long counter and benches along the window at the front of the store and stare at the street. This is one of the oldest parts of the city, which makes parking a nightmare because the streets are narrow and cobbled. A pair of girls in their club dresses walk past and trip on the uneven ground. I wince as an ankle rolls, but the legs belonging to the foot recover. My sore ankle twinges lightly in response, as if it empathizes. It's nearly dark, and the old-fashioned cast-iron streetlights throw warm circles every few meters. As I gaze out the window, a hunched-over man with a clattering grocery cart containing his possessions rolls by. Gentrification hasn't completely driven out people who are struggling with addiction or who are unhoused, but it has pushed them further from the places they used to call home, and made their situations more desperate. Gotta make room for those high-end furniture shops and stores selling BeaverTails to tourists, I guess.

I finish cleaning the tables and plunk myself down on a stool behind the counter, relieved to not be craving anything sugary. My waning appetite means I'm not putting away two or three doughnuts a shift anymore, and my skirt's waistband is beginning to loosen. But I'm starting to miss wanting to eat. It used to be fun.

"We're out of Lemon Lavender," I say.

"Doesn't matter," Raj says, still texting.

"What do we do with the day-olds?"

"Put 'em in tinfoil and then drop them in the back alley by the door. Somebody will pick them up."

Quiet descends, aside from the perky music coming out of the speakers. Matt picks the music. The only time he ever yelled at Kailey was when she put on her playlist.

He said, "This music is an affront to the vibe I've created."

Kailey said, "Fuck off."

He didn't fire her. Now I know why. I want to throw a doughnut at his head and see what bounces off what.

Between trying to read a novel and serving the occasional customer, I examine my hands. They're translucent, pale, and blue. When I hold them up to the pendant lighting above my head, I can see right through them. Raj doesn't ask what I'm doing, although I probably look touched. Maybe he thinks everyone on the dark side of twenty-five is daft anyway.

"Gotta pee," Raj says, hopping off the counter around 11:30 p.m. "Lock the door until I'm back. Matt's rule. Nobody by themselves with the door unlocked. Mel had a bad scare a couple months ago. Probably why she quit."

I start to ask what the scare was, but he slips into the gloom at the back of the store, beyond the kitchen and prep station. This location is triple the size of the Strathcona one because it has a large storage area along with the bakery itself. As I head to the front door to lock it, it swings open and two men walk in. I'm forced to take three steps back as they stand there, filling up the doorway, their feet covering the small welcome mat printed with a maneki-neko—a lucky cat. There's a second ceramic maneki-neko on the doughnut case. I can tell in an instant that neither lucky cat is going to do me a damn bit of good.

There's a sour smell coming off both men, and their clothes are ill-fitting and stained with house paint splatters. They look strong and wiry, like they spend their days doing physical labor. I scurry behind the counter as they prowl into the store.

"Raj," I call over my shoulder, suddenly nervous. I should have gotten to the door faster and then I wouldn't be alone with two strangers late at night.

The men haven't done anything. Chances are, they're just going to order. They're hungry; they want a snack, they'll leave, goodbye. That's what my head says. My body doesn't agree— their physicality, their stances, triggers something dark and ugly and afraid. They move deliberately, like Spencer before he strikes.

My hands start to shake, and a tingling sensation spreads from my fingers, up my arms, and back down through my chest to my knees.

"We'll take four doughnuts," the slighter, shorter man says, putting his hands on the counter in front of our till. His nails are ragged.

I clench my hands into fists and try to speak.

"What flavor?" I rasp. There's a boa constrictor wrapped around my windpipe.

"Orange Creamsicle. Two Chocolate Banana. One of those Vanilla Swirls. You got any apple fritters?"

"No. We don't do fritters," I squeak.

"She doesn't do fritters." The bigger man spits a glutinous blob on the floor. His pupils are dilated. His hair is tied in a ponytail with a piece of string, and his T-shirt has a rip in the collar. Both men's jeans are torn and grimy with oil and dirt. I can't guess their age—they have that worn appearance people get when they spend too long outdoors, using substances, without regular access to healthy food.

Where's Raj?

Calm, stay calm, I chant to myself. They're probably from a few blocks over, where the gentrified streets quit and give up, giving way to tenements, single-room occupancy buildings, and homelessness, drug use, and poverty. Once, I was followed down the street only two blocks from here by a man looking for a hit. He looked like these guys and screamed profanities at me as I ran away. Nothing happened. I know that most of the people living on the street are too concerned with survival and immediate needs to interact with people who have the luxury of passing through the neighborhood.

There's nothing to fear. They're hungry. I can feed them. This shouldn't be a big deal. They're people, like me, and there's nothing to get worked up over. My body doesn't get the message, and the panic attack spreads down my legs into my toes, which start to contract and curl in my shoes.

"We want a box," the small guy says. "Put them in a box." They've edged closer.

Matt has rules about boxes not going to anyone with fewer than six doughnuts, but I'm not about to argue. If he complains, Kailey can tell him to fuck off.

"No problem," I say, getting a box from the pile behind me.

"Add one of them bright green doughnuts," the big man says, gesturing to the display case.

I add it and nearly drop the hot-pink box as I hand it over. They're too close to me. Right against the counter. My eyes water from their smell—body odor long settled into the skin. *Back up,* my body screams. *Get out of here.*

"I don't like the pink. You got something else?"

"No. Sorry. That's the only box." I tuck my vibrating hands under my armpits. Their presence is overwhelming. Familiar and menacing. He has stood over me, just like this. Spencer. Moments from the dark places in my memory start to burst open. Fists, feet, teeth, elbows, contact, torment. Every moment of shame, embarrassment, and pain I've spent years suppressing is welling up, and I'm drowning. I'm losing my hard-fought-for mental control and now is not the time, situation, or place. Flashes of light crest across my vision. Fear creeps through my body.

"You got any drugs? Weed?"

I shake my head, the room around me starting to pulse. If I could've, I'd have given Spencer whatever he'd asked for. If I'd only known what he wanted, I could have made it stop. There's nothing I can do here now, either. I know these men are not the threat Spencer is, but my body has started the long drop down and there's nothing I can do to stop it mid fall.

"Cigarettes?" the bigger one says.

"Don't smoke," I gasp. Where is all the oxygen?

"Beer? You got some beer here?"

"No beer."

The bigger guy is looking over his shoulder out the window. There are few people on the street. It won't be busy until the bars start to close. My bladder contracts, and I shrink away from the men, curling in on myself.

"Raj," I call again, my voice tremulous and small.

"Why you keep saying Raj?" the little guy says.

"My coworker," I gasp out. My throat is starting to close. I'm not sure I'll be able to yell if it comes to that.

"Coworker?"

"Look. You've got your doughnuts. On the house. Please go."

"You want us to go?" The smaller man's watery, red eyes focus on my face.

"Yes. Please." The world sways. I've lost control of my body and memories. Terror and the past are coalescing into these two men and this moment, as the small guy crowds the counter. My knees are starting to wobble. I suck in big gulps of air, trying to breathe despite their smell. Where the fuck is Raj? Smoking? Outside on the phone, talking to whoever he's been texting all night? No one walks by the store's front window. The overhead lights are blinding and I force my eyes to stay wide and focused on the men in front of me. It's no good. Black spots crowd my vision, and the room is dissolving around me. Time's blurring and Spencer's face is taking the place of theirs.

"We don't have to leave. This is a public place."

Where the fuck is my phone? My hands scuttle under the counter. I'm not sure what I can do with a phone because my fingers aren't working—they've curled into claws.

The retro cuckoo clock on the wall has never been as loud as it is now. The ticktock clanging in my ear. Tick. Tock.

"Maybe you'd like a seat." My arm jerks in the direction of a table furthest from where I'm standing. I can't move my legs and I need space, distance, to regain control.

"You know what I'd like?" the big guy says. His voice is Spencer's—the same lazy vowels.

"What?" It comes out as a whisper from my pinched throat.

"The cash."

They've clocked me and know I'm vulnerable.

"Right," I wheeze, punching blindly at the iPad we use to control the till. I can't remember the password. Shit. I keep pushing buttons. "There's barely any cash. Most people pay with cards."

The smaller man leans in and puts his face inches from mine.

"Hurry," he says.

The big man looks impatient. His hands are dinner plates. His very fingers threaten. I start to sway as the black spots in my vision take over. I've never been so fucking alone. I'm going to die on the floor of an artisanal doughnut shop.

The world goes dark.

There's nothing, except Penny. She's fuzzy around the edges, but her short hair and heart-shaped face are unmistakable.

"You shouldn't be here," she says. "You need to get up. I mean it." She sounds desperate. "Brookie. Come on. Wake up." She shakes my shoulder, hard.

CHAPTER 20

"Penny?" I say groggily.

Raj is right above me, his face where Penny's had been, and he's talking on the phone. His dark brown eyes are huge and his mouth is moving quickly. His fingers are around my wrist, searching for a pulse. I crawl backwards on my elbows, out of his reach.

"Oh my God! Brooklyn. Don't move. Who's Penny? One sec."

He goes back to the phone.

"Her eyes are open. She's breathing. Talking."

He looks at me.

"You breathing?"

I nod.

He hangs up on whoever he was talking to.

"Police and ambulance are on their way," he says.

Shit. "How long was I out?" I move gingerly into a sitting position.

"Four minutes."

"Four minutes? I didn't even hit my head."

Raj hands me a paper napkin and points to my forehead. "Think again."

I press the napkin against the side of my head, next to my hairline. It comes away red.

"Shit. Where did the two men go?" The tingling in my limbs dissipated while I was on the floor. Now I'm just cold and clammy and have a dull ache in my head.

"They ran when you collapsed."

From my proximity to the floor, which is filthy, I can see a baseball bat propped on the soda fridge a few feet away.

"What's that for?"

"I heard you call my name. It was in the back. I grabbed it and ran out here."

"Where were you?" I demand.

"Bathroom. Why didn't you lock the door?" There's a flicker of guilt and apology on Raj's face.

"I was about to when they walked in! I called for you a bunch of times!"

The shop fills with red and blue lights. Paramedics bustle through the door and around the counter. They mop the blood from my face and they ask how long I was on the floor. When Raj says four minutes, they frown and check me over again. They apply white tape and anti-infection cream to my forehead. Apparently, I don't need stitches. I want to think about Penny, about what she'd said, but there's too much going on around me to focus—and my head does hurt.

"I'm okay," I keep saying. I bat the paramedic's hand away when he tries to find my pulse. The last thing I need is for anyone to find out what a freak I am. I'll have to go to the hospital if the paramedic can't find a pulse. My mother will find out, and she'll get Spencer involved. That's all a big nope.

Eventually, the emergency responders let me stand. I wobble and sink into a chair. Raj talks to two burly police officers, who'd followed the paramedics in. The officers fill up the front area of the store; the female officer, who's shorter than me, is imposing and serious in her uniform and gear. She looks like she could lift as many bags of flour as Hilary. The male officer comes into my usual store.

"I'm fine," I say, as heads swivel to look at me. The woman frowns, and recognition dawns on the male officer's face.

"They should have warned you it can get sketchy around here," he says. "Not as quiet as Strathcona. Usually, it's just bros blowing off steam, but sometimes we get residents popping in. Hilary takes care of them—they like her. They're harmless most of the time. Just after something to eat and some change. But there have been a couple thefts on this street the past few weeks. Different crew. Not people from the neighborhood."

"Didn't feel safe," I whisper, remnants of terror still coursing through my body. The cop is right, though. I did all the damage to myself. The head wound, the fainting, all of it. All me. I'd scared the men enough that they ran away the second I went down like a Douglas Fir at a Christmas tree farm in December.

"What happened?" he asks.

I describe the two men. In the retelling, fainting seems like an overreaction—a hysterical response to a minor threat. The panic and revulsion are already being shuffled to the back of my mind. Trying to explain why I fainted is tricky. I try to downplay how badly I was spooked and blame low blood sugar. Raj picks up where I left off, explaining how he'd only seen the men from the back as he exited the hallway brandishing the baseball bat.

"They grabbed the tip jar and maybe fifty dollars from the till," Raj volunteers.

"Matt's still gonna freak," I say.

The male officer looks sympathetic, but the woman watches me thoughtfully, as though she can see old wounds on my skin and she's tallying them up.

"You sure there's nothing else?" she asks in a low voice as she crouches beside me.

I shake my head; the cut on my forehead pulls. "Nope. Of course not." The words tumble out, and whatever attempt at a smile I paste on my face doesn't seem to convince her.

She passes me a business card with her name and office number on it. "You call me if it turns out there is something else." Her fingers lightly squeeze my shoulder as she stands.

Raj hovers anxiously over me, asking if I'm okay, and Matt topples in.

"You called Matt?" I yelp. "Raj!"

Matt is drunk and trying to not appear drunk in front of the cops.

"We're closed," the male cop says. He moves carefully toward Matt, his hand lingering above his Taser.

Matt flips the sign to closed and shuffles forward. He rubs his eyes.

"Who are you?" the female police officer asks as she moves in the direction of her partner.

"His name's Matt. It's his doughnut shop," Raj says. He heads to the espresso machine, makes a shot, and gives it to Matt along with a large glass of water. "Get it together, man," he whispers.

"Officers, can I get you anything?" Raj asks in his regular voice.

Raj is handling this pretty well. I want to be the one standing calmly at the coffee machine, not the one bleeding and shivering. I need to get my shit together before it kills me.

"Do you have any security footage?" the male officer asks.

"Never needed it," Matt slurs. He keeps blinking, and the female officer glares at him with disgust. Too bad he's not sober enough to feel the brunt of her scorn. He starts to nod off.

Before they leave, one of the paramedics suggests I have someone keep an eye on me tonight.

"I'll wake up my mother when I get home." That's a hard pass. I'll watch *Dragonslayer* and Emilie's career-ending horror movie.

"Can I drive?" I'd been planning to take a car share home.

"Probably not," the paramedic says.

Before I can object, another man whips through the door. Henry.

"This is a crime scene," the male cop says, half-heartedly. "Who are you?"

Henry ignores him as he scans the room and rushes over to me.

"What are you doing here?" Once again, I'm falling apart in front of Henry. At least he's a familiar face. Aside from Penny. I *saw* Penny. Then again, I might have a head injury.

"Some guy named Raj called me," Henry says as he kneels next to me.

"Raj!" I crane my neck to yell at him. "Why?"

"His number was the most used in your phone," Raj calls over the noise from the coffee machine. "You were out cold. I didn't know who else to call. Figured he was your boyfriend or something."

"You need to start locking your phone," Henry says. His hair sticks up in every direction.

"It was locked," Raj says. "I pushed her thumb against it while she was passed out on the floor."

"Raj," I shout, again. The shouting makes my head pain more acute.

"Did he wake you?" I say, turning to Henry, taking in his scruffy face and rumpled T-shirt.

"I was up." Henry stands and pulls a chair up next to me. Our shoulders brush when he sits, and I lean into him. I point at my forehead with a tiny pout. Henry runs his thumb underneath the injury. "Aw, Brooklyn."

The cops look impatient. "We need to finish up," the female cop says. "And this store needs video security. When your boss sobers up, or wakes up, tell him the police department recommends he get a security camera. I'll drop by later in the week and tell him myself. And you." She points at Raj. "Next time you lock the door before you go to the bathroom. I don't understand why a doughnut shop needs to be open late." She's almost grumbling by this point. "We're here every other week dealing with something."

"I'm so sorry, officers. And Brooklyn." Raj's eyes snap to mine.

"It happened really fast," I say. "Wasn't your fault."

"I'll make it up to you," he says. "I can take some crappy shifts, or whatever."

"What happens now?" I ask the officers, curling closer to Henry. I've had a shock and he's toasty. I'll swear him off for good tomorrow.

"We'll look for anyone matching your description. It's not the easiest thing, in this neighborhood," the male officer says. "Call 911 if they come back."

The officers leave, taking with them their reassuring red-and-blue lights.

"What do we do now?" Raj asks.

"We close," I say.

"I'll do it," he says, quickly. "You sit."

He rips through the closing checklist and makes Henry a latte before he cleans the espresso machine. While he wipes tables, Raj tells Henry the paramedics said someone needs to keep an eye on me.

"They want to make sure she doesn't have a concussion. She's supposed to go to a hospital if she starts puking or feels confused or has a seizure. Or loses consciousness."

"You can stay at my place," Henry says as he reassuringly strokes the top of my hand with his thumb.

I look at him like he's lost his mind. Going to Henry's is not part of the "avoid Henry" game plan.

"Kashvi went to her parents' to study," he says, quietly so that Raj doesn't hear. "Said she'll be back Sunday afternoon."

Danger, danger. How can I resist?

Henry doesn't let go of my hand. He lifts me to my feet and holds me against him as I sway. His heartbeat bumps against my fingertips.

"What do we do about Matt?" Raj asks as he unlocks the door for our exit. Matt is slumped over a baby-blue tabletop, his face propped up on his bicep. His mouth is open and he's drooling.

"Leave him," I say.

We turn on the motion-activated alarm and lock the door behind us. Matt is in for a rude awakening.

"I don't want to burden you. You keep rescuing me like I'm a pathetic loser." I wrinkle my nose. "Or a damsel in distress. That's even worse," I say, trying to give Henry an out once we're in his car, which is illegally parked across the street. The neighborhood's frenetic bylaw officers have offered him a boon: Henry is miraculously without a parking ticket. His car is immaculate, except for six to-go coffee cups stacked in the cup holder on the driver's side. Most of them are the hot-pink cups from Cute Lil'.

"First, you're not a damsel in distress. You're a person who's dealing with some pretty horrible things and doing her best, and everybody needs somebody. And, second, you're not a burden. I rushed over here to see what was happening." He grips the steering wheel and stares out the windshield. "Raj wasn't super clear on the phone. He said you were out cold. I jumped in my car. I didn't even think. I ran a red light."

"I'm sorry."

"Don't be sorry. I'm the one who should be sorry, because I'm glad I could rush over here and see you because Kashvi is at her parents', and because I fell asleep in front of the TV instead of going for drinks." He hesitates. "I would have come no matter what."

"If you'd been out drinking?" I ask.

"If Kashvi had been home," Henry says, like a confession.

"Oh." What does it mean? What does he mean? What does any of it mean?

Uncertainty flickers on his face. "I've been trying to give you space, to give me space, to see if whatever I was feeling would wear off, and instead I just kept wondering what you were doing, and how you were doing, and when I could see you again. And it's only been a couple of days."

Want. We both want impossible things. Or at least, hard things.

I *want* to say, "Let's go. Let's pretend you don't have a girl-friend and that I'm not dead-ish. Let's pretend we're happy and in love like characters in those made-for-TV Hallmark movies starring Emaleigh Taylor, before she got super famous."

What I say is, "I don't want to cause trouble."

"You won't," Henry says. He sounds resigned. "I'm doing it all by myself." He looks so despondent that I drag out my best marketing lingo.

"Let's shelve this snackable content, and instead focus on a hard pivot with a targeted, scalable audience and low-hanging fruit within an intuitive context."

"What?" Henry asks, but there's a grin attempting to break out of the corners of his mouth.

"I mean, let's go see your fancy apartment," I say, and attempt to saucily lift my chin. It stings my forehead. "It is fancy, right? And clean? Your car is so clean." I reach out to pet the dash in front of me.

He starts the car.

"Henry."

"Yeah?"

"You can change your mind. About all of it. Drive me home. It's not too late."

"Sure it's not," he says.

CHAPTER 21

We drive past clumps of club-goers and night owls and, as much as I don't want to see them again, I search for the men who came into the store. It's too dark to see faces standing in alleys or between streetlamps and already the details are fading. The evening air is cool and smells of ammonia and sewage until Henry turns onto a side street off a main road.

I let my mind wander in the silence. I saw Penny. My imagination conjured her when I needed her most. She forced me to wake up.

Henry lives in an older part of the city, where towers went up in the '60s. They have basement laundry and dim, carpeted hallways. He lives in a coveted corner unit on the fifteenth floor with two bedrooms and picture windows in the living room.

"You have a view?" I ask.

"A sliver of Pacific Ocean that way. Lots of buildings in the way." He flicks an arm in a westerly direction.

The apartment has light-gray furniture and yellow throw pillows. Across from the large windows, a bookshelf runs along an entire wall. There's a Henry-sized bike in the hallway. Kashvi's shoes are mixed in with his. Aside from that, there's little evidence of her. There must be more hidden spots where she's made her presence known, medical texts next to studies of subway systems and battered George Orwells.

I gaze out the window as a cat winds himself around my ankles. He's not a posh cat; he has a scar on his head and only one eye. Most of the other apartment buildings leering in the distance are dark. But the odd light is on, and I get glimpses of televisions, people, coatracks, kitchens, and houseplants. I'm seized with longing—the longing to have whatever it is that these people have. Their apartments look full and complete. They've figured out how to be happy and whole, while I keep stumbling around my small and shrinking life.

"I used to wander around the city at night and sneak peeks into people's windows," I say to Henry, who hands me a glass of water when he joins me. "I would imagine what their lives were like, based on their dogs, or their artwork, or their sports equipment."

I'd stopped because the risk of bumping into Spencer on my way back into the house while my parents slept was too high. It was safer to hide in my room and lock the door than to slip in and out. When I moved out and started working full time, I was too tired for whimsy.

"You were a creepy stalker? A peeping Tom?" Henry asks.

"A voyeur. Creepy, for sure."

He points to a neighboring building where a living room light is still on. "They fight all the time. I've seen her throw things at him. They were eating dinner on the deck and she stood up, grabbed her plate, and threw it at his head. He ducked and it went over the edge. They're on the eighteenth floor or something. She could have killed someone below."

So much for happy.

"Sounds dangerous," I say.

"I had a girlfriend who was a thrower. Threw a shoe at my head once. One of those insane shoes with metal studs on it. I dodged. It knocked over a plant. She told me to clean it up and stormed out."

"What did you do?"

"I swept up the dirt and dumped it in her bed. Then I left and never saw her again. That kind of behavior is bullshit."

"I had a boyfriend who could verbally annihilate people without raising his voice. Before him, I didn't understand that verbal abuse was a type of violence." Because I'd only known one kind— the kind Spencer meted out.

"Why do people do that to people they're supposed to love?" Henry asks.

If I knew the answer, I could fix it. My family could be normal. At Christmas, the worst thing that could happen would be someone puking from too much hot buttered rum instead of ending up in the hospital with a deep thigh gash from an "accidently" dropped carving knife.

"My stepdad hit my mom and she blamed herself," Henry says, after drinking from his water glass. "She left him, but it took years of therapy before she stopped making excuses for him."

"Did he hit you too?" I ask, carefully. It's none of my business; it's too close to home.

Henry shakes his head, his face tight with anger. "If it meant he wouldn't hit my mom, I would have let him."

It's an opening, a moment to be honest about why I'd reacted so badly to those men in the doughnut shop. I can explain how they reminded me of Spencer; how their body language promised violence and injury, how anyone can seem like a threat when people who were supposed to be safe never were. I can pluck my past out of my body and share the burden. Stop suppressing it, stop putting it aside like it doesn't matter. Henry would understand. But it's unfair. We're already too intertwined emotionally, and he still has a girlfriend that we're both sidestepping and it's not right. Henry could slip away tomorrow and be nothing but a number in my phone history holding my biggest secret. If I'm being honest, telling him on top of what has been the Brooklyn shit show since the moment he rescued me from the Chief feels abhorrent. ‘

Besides. Henry is not the person who needs to hear about Spencer.

I bury my admission, swallow it, even though it shreds the lining of my throat all the way down. There's an excruciating lurch in my gut that dissipates quickly. My stomach is used to digesting the past. It's reinforced and girded with secrets.

"I'm sorry your stepfather was an asshole," I say. "The only person whose fault it was is his. You know that, right?" Easy to say. Hard to accept. On some level, I blame myself for what's happened to me. I've allowed it by remaining silent. My brain knows this isn't the whole story, that relationships with the people you love are complicated, but chooses it anyway.

"Sometimes, I think Kashvi and I have stayed together because of her dad. He's the best. Kind and funny. I needed to see that there are great dads, since mine was gone and my stepfather was an asshole."

"I wish that families were like the ones in the movies," I say. "They fight, but by the end everyone loves and understands each other."

Henry laughs. "Right? Whose family is like that?"

"Mine's okay. Except Spencer." Spencer is too close to the surface. He's slipping out. "I'm a horrible letdown to him, and my mom."

"I can't imagine why." Henry flushes high up on his cheekbones.

"Really?" I swat at him. "Every time we see each other, I'm in the middle of a disaster. Crying, throwing up, falling, fainting. You're always cleaning me up and taking me home."

"True," Henry admits. "But I've never seen you lose your temper, or blame anyone else, or freak out. You keep your sense of humor, which is easy to do when things are awesome. You do it when things are falling apart."

His words warm tiny places deep in my chest. Did I ever notice that about myself? Did I appreciate it? I'm being forced to see myself, lately. At least, I'm being forced to see someone I could be.

"I've had a bad year," I say. "Or two. Or three. But I'm trying. I signed up for a writing class at my old university." I want to appear stronger than I have been. Fake it till you make it. Too bad I can't fake a heartbeat.

"A writing class?" Henry gestures me over to the couch and we settle at opposite ends. I fixate on the blanket folded on the foot stool, and Henry grabs it and tosses it to me. Our eyes skip over each other and focus on the darkness outside. "No more marketing?"

I don't want to go back to my old job, or one like it, but admitting it, accepting it, is terrifying. I busted my ass at Lawrence Communications, poured myself into my job to prove I could do it and do it well. I didn't connect with people. I didn't keep in touch with college friends, and barely kept in touch with Penny. Long days meant I didn't have the time to run or play sports much.

I didn't pick up a book on ancient Egypt or the American civil rights movement or famous centuries-old shipwrecks. I barely ate. And for what? I didn't make a life for myself.

"I liked being good at it. I hated doing it."

Henry smiles from his end of the couch and silent applauds.

"What?" I chuck a yellow throw pillow at him, embarrassed.

"You had this dazzled look on your face, like you couldn't quite believe what you were saying."

"I dread starting over again. Having to fetch coffee as an intern. More school, or retraining, if I can decide what I want to do." I feign a shudder.

"It's that, or spend the rest of your life doing work you hate," Henry says. "Remember, I was going to be an adventure tour leader. But the bugs. The dirt. The tourists." He mimics *The Scream*.

Do I have time to start over, or one day will I fade away completely and not reappear? How long can my body last? I don't know what I'd even do, given a chance to do something new. I used to want to study history more than anything, but too much has changed. I'm not the Brooklyn who was obsessed with the past. Her needs and dreams are smudged with time and experience. History feels like a burden. At least, mine does, and it's one I don't know how to put down.

"I'm not sure what I want to do," I say.

"You'll figure it out," Henry says.

His belief is fuel.

"I've been thinking about Penny," I say, because she's close to the surface too, and for the moment, I'm being brave. What I told Henry before was true: I am angry at her. But that's not the whole story. "I was mad at her. But I'm also afraid of life without her. Even though sometimes I feel like she abandoned me, she made me live and do the things I was afraid of. Some of the best moments in my whole life only happened because Penny made them happen. What if..."

That's as far as I can go. The rest of the words won't take shape outside my body because if they do, I can't take them back. But they rattle and form in my head anyway. What if I can't find a way to live without Penny? What sort of life is left for me?

I wouldn't have gone to Europe in high school if Penny hadn't convinced me to ask my parents to let me. I wouldn't have snuck out of our hotel room in the middle of the night to see Athens. I wouldn't have jumped off a cliff into the ocean in Mexico. I might not have dumped Kyle if Penny hadn't pointed out how horrible and stupid I was being, and how bad for me, for everyone, he was. I wouldn't have had much fun—goofy, childhood fun. There are so many tiny moments I wouldn't have had if Penny hadn't dragged me along with her. I learned to ride a bike with her, how to swipe cookies from the school cafeteria, how to put on lipstick, how to drive. Tiny things. Big things. She tricked me into talking to my first crush; she made sure I never had to eat lunch alone in high school. She lived her life and thought I should live mine.

And I've been waiting, with everything on pause, for her to come back because I don't know how to move forward without her. So, I take one step.

I reach out and place my hand on Henry's. He shifts, and suddenly we're close together. It doesn't feel like before, when we casually collided, boundaries intact, our hands clutching our drinks instead of each other. Somewhere, in the car on our way here, or while I was lying on the floor unconscious, the barriers around us were knocked over. Or maybe the boundaries were fences. Permeable. Suggestions instead of firm lines. Henry's nose grazes mine. My breath hitches. Stops.

My heart should be thundering, and my pulse racing. Both are entirely still while my brain pushes me toward something, tripping over itself in its hurry to get there. How can love merely be chemicals, mixed up with personal preferences, choices, and how someone looks at you at the right moment?

"Brooklyn," Henry whispers.

My eyes close and his mouth is on mine. His lips are soft, and his stubble scrapes against my chin. We shift, and I'm in his lap, one hand wrapped in his beautiful hair, the other trapped flat against his chest. One of his arms tightens around my waist and tugs me closer to him. My brain stops working as he deepens the kiss. There is only the lemony scent of his hair product and the warmth radiating from his body. He holds me firmly against him.

Henry pulls away first, enough so he can gasp for breath. He runs a thumb across my bottom lip. "You taste like sugar," he says. His heartbeat is erratic under my fingertips, and I pray he won't notice the stillness of mine. I lower my lips to graze his and his hand captures the back my head, holding my mouth in place. The kiss goes from exploring to desperate. His hands are hot against the skin of my back.

Then I remember.

"Kashvi," I breathe. Henry obliterated her hovering presence when he kissed me. Saying her name now sends a twist through my gut.

"Fuck," Henry says.

A fraction of space opens between us. I run my fingertips across his collarbone and up the line of his neck, knowing I need to pull away entirely. His lips brush mine again. We could forget her. I see the idea reflected in his eyes. It would be easy, like tumbling down the Chief. There's guilt there though, the same guilt I've been trying to ignore by telling myself that nothing has happened. Something has happened now. No more excuses. I don't need to hurt Kashvi any more than I already have, even if she doesn't know.

"Grace is right," he says, almost to himself. He buries his face in my neck, with his arms still tight around me. "I'm a liar. I've lied to myself, to you, and to Kashvi."

"What did you lie about?" I ask, stroking his hair.

"About being a good guy. That I'm not going to hurt anyone."

I awkwardly extricate myself from his lap. It's hard to let him go, but I manage to get away without kissing him again, and catapult myself to the opposite end of the couch.

"It didn't happen," I say. I'm nothing if not the queen of denial.

Henry cocks an eyebrow at me. "Pretty sure it did." He touches his mouth with his index finger and goosebumps appear on his arm.

I brandish a pillow between us.

"That's your side of the couch. This is mine."

"I don't want to forget," he says, softly.

Now I understand why Penny fell for her married coworker. She wanted something too: something beautiful, something good in the midst of something terrible. I shouldn't have been so hard on her for that. Not when I want the same thing.

The anguish on Henry's face is genuine. He didn't set out to lose Kashvi, or to be lost by her. At some point, the very idea of losing her would have been crushing. Impossible. Suddenly, there's a different future, a different outcome—one he maybe wants. But it's still a shock. It still hurts him, to realize how quickly there may be a world for him that doesn't include a woman he loves. Loved. He and I were an abstraction, a tantalizing idea he could resist. Now he has to look himself in the face and address the truth: he cheated on his girlfriend. He's not exactly who he thought he was.

"I'm a mess," Henry says. "Clearly."

"We all are," I say, glad to have something I can say honestly. I've been mute about so much for so long.

"I let this happen, instead of dealing with what I was feeling. I had plenty of opportunities to make a decision, to not let things get so messed up. Instead, I just floated along, thinking it would all magically work out. I should have made a clean break."

With who? I press my fingers against my mouth so the question doesn't slip out. The answer won't make me happy, either way. I don't want Henry to be unhappy, and even if he picked me—well. There's no guarantees I'll be around to enjoy it. Besides my very serious risk factors, I don't want to be an available rebound, an accident. I don't want Henry to be with me just because he doesn't want to be with Kashvi anymore. I want to be a choice.

"You deserve more," Henry says.

That's my line, I think. Underneath that, though, there's a whisper in my head that says Henry's right.

"It's kind of nice to know you're not perfect," I say. "Those damn dimples were pretty misleading. Instead, you're a confused human with problems." Like me. Kailey. Penny.

Henry winces.

"For what it's worth, I like that about you. At least you're being up front about your shortcomings." I add.

"I'm kind of a dick human."

"Totally," I agree. "For right now. You can do better."

"I want to do better. Why aren't you furious at me?"

"We're all just doing our best. Sometimes it's not good enough." It sounds true, coming out of my mouth. Maybe I should offer myself the same understanding.

He sighs raggedly. "What now?"

"Now, we follow the paramedic's orders and watch television until we're sure I don't have a concussion. I get to pick."

CHAPTER 22

"Isn't this adorable."

I open my eyes and am nearly blinded by sunlight. A woman, presumably Kashvi, stands at Henry's end of the couch. She's holding a backpack, which she drops to the floor with a thud. The noise startles Henry and he scurries off the couch, away from me. He's not quite awake and his movements are clumsy. He almost goes over the shiny white coffee table before he pulls himself upright. I lurch into a seated position and blink sleep from my eyes.

"What is going on?" Kashvi asks, her tone surprisingly moderate. Perhaps she'll be reasonable and not jump to the very worst of conclusions. Henry and I are both fully dressed, right down to our socks, and I have an ugly bandage on my forehead.

"There was an incident at Brooklyn's work and I picked her up," Henry says. "I wasn't expecting you until later."

This is the exact wrong thing to say. Kashvi's dark eyes narrow and she whirls toward him. I barely exist. I won't get away scot-free, but it's clear she's just not sure who to erupt at first.

"I realized I haven't been home much, and I thought it might be nice to go to breakfast with my boyfriend." She jabs him in the chest with her index finger. "You thought it would be okay to sleep with another woman because I wasn't here?"

"No. Of course not. It's a misunderstanding. Hang on a minute." Henry can't think on his feet.

"Cute Lil' was robbed and I was unconscious," I say, going for an assist. "My coworker didn't know who to call and saw Henry's number in my phone. The paramedics said someone needed to keep an eye on me in case I had a concussion."

"Why didn't he take you home?" Kashvi demands, going from angry to furious in a flash.

"My parents are out of town." It's the best I can come up with. Kashvi's hostility is sucking all the oxygen from the room.

"Brooklyn," Henry finally splutters, sounding bone-weary.

"Brooklyn? Spencer's sister Brooklyn?" She circles, judging. "You look like you've been hit by a truck. No friends you could have gone to?"

I hesitate, flustered, then shake my head. Even at eight in the morning, Kashvi is poised and perfectly made up. Her eyeshadow is blended perfectly into her creases, and her lipstick is glossy and looks like it was applied with a pencil and a ruler. She's shorter than me by half a foot, and I feel rumpled, grungy, and oversized. There's dirt on my T-shirt from the floor at Cute Lil'. Kashvi's perfect skin glows with righteous fury.

She smirks. "Of course not. Spencer mentioned your only friend is dead."

I gasp, involuntarily, and the word "dead" rings around the room. The word "dead" is so big. So loud. My hand reflexively bats it away, and Kashvi's eyes follow the movement.

I get that she wants to hurt me, that she's furious at me, us, and she's cutting where it counts. It's cruel, to hear Spencer's word for Penny in Kashvi's mouth. I gasp for air and try to block out sound so that word stops tearing through my body.

"Not quite all there, are you?" she asks. "Spencer says you're a ghost. Barely hanging on. Hang on somewhere else."

Of course, Spencer sees what I am. Hasn't he always? Knowledge is how he's been able to break me into nothing.

"Kashvi, don't talk to her like that," Henry says, his voice tight with anger. "It's a misunderstanding."

Whose? Mine? Hers? His? I knew better, and I let this happen. I can't even come to my own defense.

"God, Henry. Who cares what I'm being like? I'm not the problem here. You're both so out of line. Spencer told me she's obsessed with you, and here she is." Kashvi waves dismissively at me. There's no question in her mind that I'm the guilty party and that Henry is the hapless idiot who fell for my poor little broken girl routine.

Henry stares at me uselessly. Whatever he feels about me is mixed up with whatever he still loves about her. Henry never made me any promises; he didn't say he was going to break up with her. Anything euphoric or real from the night before fades. He wants to be nice, to be kind, and it's way too late for him to be who he wants to be.

"I'm going to go," I say, as I pick my purse up off the floor.

Henry starts toward me like he's going to walk me to the door, and Kashvi shoots him a look so poisonous that he stops dead in his tracks. "I'm sorry," he mouths instead.

I'm sorry too. Sorry I don't have the guts to tell him to come with me, and that he doesn't have the guts to decide, for himself, who he wants to be with. He's stuck in a rut of his own making. We have that in common.

I barely escape the apartment before Kashvi lays into him. She's loud enough that the neighbors will be able to file a noise complaint with the strata.

I walk until I find a coffee shop, where I buy a lemon tart and a black coffee. The sugar is restorative, even though it tastes like shit. I sit on a rickety metal chair next to an equally rickety table on the sidewalk and let the sun seep into my shoulders. The heat doesn't reach my bones, and I shiver despite the warmth.

I hail a passing cab, and it drops me off at my parents' house, which, for the first time in a long time, feels like home. It's the only one I've got. I fumble with the lock on the front door, exhaustion catching up to me. Before I can insert the key, my father swings it open. He's pale-faced and thin-lipped.

"Where have you been?" he says.

"Out." I hadn't expected they'd notice I wasn't home.

"Your mother is worried sick. She went down to check on you early this morning and you weren't there. And you're not answering your phone."

I pull my phone out of my purse. Dead battery. "Since when does she check on me?"

"Since Penny. Every night."

I close my eyes and exhale. "Sorry."

"Your boss called. He said there was an attack, or an accident at work? I couldn't hear him that well because an alarm was going off in the background. He said to call him right away. What happened, Brookie?"

My mother appears on the landing, Spencer right behind her.

"Whole gang I see," I say, and look longingly in the direction of the basement and my bed, even though I won't be able to sleep with Spencer in the house.

Spencer has a look on his face—one of knowing superiority.

"Busted," he mouths. He holds up his phone, and I make out a stream of texts from Kashvi. It seems that in the time it took me to get home, Kashvi provided my brother with a story about his shitty sister trying to steal her boyfriend. I'm mostly indefensible. If I thought I could steal him, I would, if only because Kashvi said Penny was dead, even though Spencer said it first.

A flash of rage burns though my body. It builds, and I can see it perfectly: how I'll launch myself at Spencer, tackle him to the ground, and pour every ounce of my fear, hurt, and fury—yes, fury—out onto him. I will pull and gouge and rip and claw and kick and bite and hit until there is nothing left of him.

Years of cruelty—and nothing is worse than him giving up on Penny. To tell a stranger she's dead. I can imagine him saying it, how his face grew concerned and his eyes even more blue with compassion for the dead woman, and most of all, for his sister, who can't cope and can't accept it. He probably dredged up a glimmer of tears for the two girls he grew up with. Maybe he shared a warm moment from our combined childhood. Kashvi probably would have hugged him and murmured sounds of comfort. She would have admired his care for his lost sister. She could've understood why someone like me would turn to someone like Henry, someone dependable and generous with help. Someone solid.

Whatever's on my face causes a grin to break out on Spencer's. His teeth gleam, and his eyes hold a challenge. Will I tell our mother that he said her favorite faux daughter is dead? Will I tell her the rest?

He tilts his head and raises an eyebrow. "Do it," he mouths. Then he laughs and turns his back, because I won't.

My mother won't believe any of it. Worse, she might agree with Spencer: that Penny is gone. She's never contrary where his opinions are concerned. He's her smart, precious, brilliant baby boy.

"Coffee," my dad calls from the kitchen.

I trudge upstairs. The four of us gather around the kitchen table, and I try to summarize what happened at the doughnut shop. My father wears a thundercloud on his face, and my mother keeps pursing her lips and wringing her hands.

"The men in the store weren't dangerous, but I slipped and fell during the incident. I hit my head and passed out," I say, trying to explain why I'd fallen while saying nothing about the fear that had tackled me like a linebacker when those two men entered the shop. The reason for it sits across from me, drinking his coffee out of a blue stoneware mug.

"When I was passed out, Raj from down the street—who works at Cute Lil'—called my friend Henry," I carry on. "Henry offered to keep an eye on me in case I had a concussion. It's not a big deal. I didn't want to wake you guys."

"I'm a nurse," my mother objects. "You should have come right home."

"I wasn't thinking clearly," I say. "Since I hit my head."

"What did the paramedics say?" Spencer inserts himself. He rattles off a bunch of information about concussions and infections. He takes a quick glance at my mother, as if to make sure she's noting his concern and knowledge.

"It's going to be wonderful having a doctor in the family," my mother says before leaving the table.

My father and I share a wry look over our mugs. He, at least, can acknowledge that Spencer is a know-it-all.

Mom comes back with a first aid kit. Moving efficiently, she pulls off the paramedic's dressing and does it again, more neatly.

"You should quit that job," my father says. "Not worth it."

"I might get fired anyway," I say. "Since I allowed the shop to get robbed and I closed it a couple of hours early."

"Firing you for that would be illegal," my father says.

"Your father's right. You should quit," Mom says.

"And do what? Another mind-numbing marketing job? I don't want one."

The birds outside stop chirping. Based on the flattening of her lips, my mother is working up to something stinging that communicates exactly what she thinks of my ongoing nonsense. I could tell her I was sexually harassed at work, which is a fair reason to be soured on the whole thing, but it's another thing she won't believe. It's too far outside the realm of her experience.

"Finding a job, with Penny's situation, is a lot to deal with," I say instead.

It's not the first time I've used Penny as a shield, and while it might be manipulative to use Penny to stave off my mother's judgements, I'm so tired I can barely see straight.

"I think we should talk about this," my mother says as she packs up her medical supplies. "You're ignoring your education and scraping by. This is the time to be building your career. We didn't pay for you to go to university so you could mope around here."

"Helen," my father says in a warning voice.

"This has gone on for far too long," my mother snaps. "I'm sick of it. You're a grown woman, and you should be working full time and not living in the basement. It's not normal."

"It's pretty normal," I say. "Everybody I know my age or younger lives with their parents. Rent in this city is bananas."

"Spencer doesn't," my mother says.

"Spencer lives on campus. Which you pay for." I put my cup down and coffee sloshes over the side.

"Because he's still in school."

"I had to live at home while I was in school," I point out. "You didn't want me to live by myself. You thought I would get murdered."

The real danger was under her roof.

"That's enough," Dad says, before things can deteriorate further. "Helen, I know you're upset because Brooklyn didn't come home last night. She'll call next time. She's twenty-nine years old and can have some leeway. And for the last time, Brookie can stay in the basement until she's ready to leave."

"That'll be never," Spencer mutters.

I whip my head around. The second our eyes meet, goose-bumps sprout on my skin. How can my parents not see that there's no light in Spencer's eyes, no ember of human emotion? He clenches a fist, looks at it, then looks back at me. I blink, and the alien look in his eyes is gone. They're blue, just like my dad's. Just like mine.

"I'm going to go to bed, now that it's clear I don't have a concussion," I say, and stand up.

"Are you going to call your boss?" my father asks. "I think he said something about a press release about the robbery."

"He came in drunk after we were robbed. I'll wait until he's not hungover."

My father nods. "That seems reasonable."

I escape downstairs and make sure my bedroom door is locked before I fall asleep. Despite multiple cups of coffee, I'm groggy.

I wake up jam-side down, my face smooshed in a pile of fresh laundry my mother must have done in her distress.

"Your mom is a piece of work."

Emaleigh Taylor's presence, alongside her honeysuckle perfume, fills the room. She's dressed in my pastel-mint cropped sweatshirt and high-waisted black skinny jeans. She found some thick gold bangles from the back of my dresser drawer to pull the whole thing together. She looks like a badass, bald supermodel—albeit a very short supermodel. I'm still wearing yesterday's clothes and some of Cute Lil's floor juice.

I groan and move, as though I'm wading through partially dry cement to sit upright.

"She's just preoccupied with the marvel that is Spencer," I say, panting lightly at the effort to sit.

"Tell her."

"Tell her what?" I say, as blasé as I can manage.

"About your brother."

"I don't know what you mean."

"You can't even look me in the eye when you say that." Emaleigh scoffs. "I get it. My mom did her own thing. We moved around a lot. I missed so much school I had to redo two grade levels. She didn't believe in doctors or dentists. Once, I ended up in the hospital with a fever because a neighbor noticed I looked sick. Mom refused to consider her parenting style might not be good for me. She wasn't up for a reality check."

"My mom's not like that," I say. "She's a nurse."

Emaleigh rolls her eyes. "Way to be purposefully obtuse. What I'm saying is, I love my mom, but it's complicated."

"It's not complicated. She loves Spencer more than me. They have shared interests. I confuse her and piss her off because I'll never be a doctor."

"Your mom is in denial. That guy has fewer human responses than a reptile. You straight-up flinch when I say his name."

"I do not," I shoot back. "And it's not anybody's fault that she loves him more."

"It's a little bit her fault," Emaleigh says. She folds her arms across her chest. "She's partly to blame. You know that. You should talk to her. Clear the air. What do you think will happen if you say what you mean?"

"It's not that easy."

"Did I say it was easy?"

I sigh. "Talking about Spencer makes me feel like my chest is being crushed by an elephant. Like my entire body is going to explode and shatter into tiny pieces and nothing will be left."

Admitting this to Emaleigh is easier than thinking about talking to real people, but even skirting the Spencer issue causes my limbs to tingle with the not-subtle promise of an incoming panic attack. Left unchecked, I'll be on the ground, just like last night, gasping for air, hands involuntarily curled into claws, limbs quaking, and uncontrolled tears streaming down my face. Assuming I'm able to cry. I suck in several deep breaths and force my hands flat on the mattress.

"I can't lose what's left," I say. "Haven't I lost enough? My career. Penny. Henry. My heartbeat. My reflection. Bodily fluids?" I clear my throat, trying to make my words less rough and scratchy. "At least by keeping my mouth shut I have a place to live and parents who care about me. For the most part."

"There's always more to lose," Emaleigh says, quietly. She's staring at the carpet, an uncharacteristic scowl on her face. She lifts her face, her gaze fierce. "You want to talk about loss? Reputation. Friends. Life. *Everybody* loses. Sometimes you bounce back. You recover. But not you. You just keep giving up."

"I'm not like you," I shout. "I'm not brave. I don't know how to stand there and admit what happened to me while the entire world judges me, while the people I *love* judge me. Or worse, don't believe me."

Emaleigh's face falls.

"You have no right to come in here and tell me everything I'm doing wrong. You're a hallucination. You're not here, you're just in my head. You're not even alive." I'm breathing hard from my outburst. "You're not real." These last words come out as a wail.

She grabs me and shakes me so hard my teeth rattle. "I'm here because you need me."

"I don't. I just need Penny. Once she's back, everything will be normal. Better."

"I think that your normal isn't very good, Brooklyn. And hasn't been for a while." Emaleigh feels sorry for me. It's written all over her face. "Don't you want more?"

Emaleigh places her hand on my shoulder. Even though I see her do it, there's no physical sensation.

"Shit. Pinch me."

"What?"

"Just do it," I snap.

Her sharp nails squeeze my left shoulder. I don't feel anything at all. I try to raise my right hand to touch her wrist, and my arm doesn't move.

"What are you staring at?" Emaleigh asks while I look down in horror at my arm. I will it to lift above my head, but it stays stubbornly at my side like a slack climbing rope.

"My arm won't move."

"That can't be right," Emaleigh says, her voice going up in pitch. "Try it again." She shakes me even more vigorously than before and I tip over, my body frozen in a seated position.

"Oohmph," she groans, as I fall into her. She gingerly pushes me upright.

"I think I'm turning into a corpse."

We stare at each other in panic.

"Well, that's just, I can't, it's just," Emaleigh splutters and waves her arms. "Maybe you're just cold? Do you want me to shake you again? Or hit you?"

"What's hitting me going to do?" I glare at her, relieved that my facial muscles at least are working.

"I'm just trying to help," she snaps.

It's nearly comical. Emaleigh jumps to her feet and starts to pace. "Doctor?"

"How will we get there? What do we tell them? I'll sound hysterical."

We stare at each other and a wave of despair crashes into me. There's no one I can turn to. No scientific reason for anything that's happening to me. I can't stop it or control it and I don't know what any of it means. There's no way out and the signs aren't good.

"What do we do?" Emaleigh's face is contorted with worry.

"I'm the wrong person to ask. I have no clue," I say, as a burning sensation spills down my arm and through the left side of my body. It's worse than falling asleep on a limb and letting the blood flow restart. Carefully, I lift my arm. Then I stand.

"Back to regularly scheduled programming I guess." I flop down on my bed and wait for the tingling to stop.

"How are you so chill?" Emaleigh asks.

"Because none of this is real. Nothing is real."

"If it isn't, you should have way better hallucinations. Road trips and shopping blitzes in New York. A sexy man fawning over you. Wild parties. Not hanging out in your disgusting bedroom. Throw out that dead plant already."

"It can't be real," I say. "This isn't my life."

I didn't sign up for a violent sibling, a missing best friend, a negligent mother, and career burnout by age twenty-nine. I didn't select loneliness, doubt, isolation, failure, and an inexplicable feeling of otherness from a drop-down menu. I certainly didn't want to work in a doughnut shop, or be half in love with a man who's just…not half in love with me. I thought I'd belong in my life.

I can't put my finger on what I want, but it's not this. There's only one thing I have any control over right now, since I can't even control my body and the impossible things it's doing.

"Go. I want you to go," I tell Emaleigh. "Leave."

I refuse to look at her. I don't want Emily or Emaleigh or Emmalee or Emilie showing up and taking over even though they're ingrained in the good parts of my life and they matter to me. Or, at least, the characters they play do. They've been there when I had no one and I've always been able to turn on the TV or a streaming service and see their faces, making them reliable like no one else has been. But right now? They're part of the problem, along with my missing heartbeat and general corpselikeness.

She sighs. "You need me. Being alone isn't a good solution."

"Leave." My voice is strangled.

When I look up, Emaleigh is gone.

I scoop my dead phone off the floor and plug it in. It beeps when it turns back on. There are dozens of missed calls and text messages from Matt and my mother. I call Matt. Best to get it over with. Maybe he'll fire me, and I'll never need to leave this basement suite again. It's not like I'm ever hungry and need to surface for food, or have anyone I need to see.

"Way to take your time. I need a press release right away," he says without saying "hello."

"About the robbery?" I ask. "It won't make the news. Barely anything was taken."

"No, about the ice cream partnership," he says, eye roll implied. He rattles off what he wants in the news release.

"Fine," I snap. "But I'm never going back to the Gastown location."

"You'll go where you're scheduled. Cute Lil' is not a democracy. I'm the boss. I decide where you go. You're lucky you have a job after what happened." He hangs up.

I grab a pillow and scream into it. It would have been better if he just fired me.

CHAPTER 23

The remnants of August are sweltering, even while trees drop their leaves and hint at September. Late-August sunlight is buttery and languid, distinctive enough to know what month it is without looking at a calendar. In July, the light suggests summer will stretch forever. July is a liar.

My first shift after the robbery, back in Strathcona, Kailey hugs me so hard my ribs crack and they stay stuck, not quite sitting right under my skin. "Remind me never to take a shift at the Gastown location. So scary," she says as she squeezes and I gasp.

Kailey wilts inside Cute Lil' and drags her feet to serve customers, who blanch at the temperature inside the air-conditionerless shop. For two days, doughnuts mold in the humidity and we throw out more than we sell. I wear a sweater, which does nothing to keep my icy hands from fumbling cutlery or stop my teeth from chattering. Hot coffee, layers, standing in the bars of sunshine cast by the windows—nothing thaws me. Kailey grabs my hand to press it against her sticky neck and groans lustfully at my frigidity. I move sluggishly and awkwardly because it's as though my arteries have solidified and shortened, giving me T. rex arms. My skin feels crunchy, and no amount of moisturizer is making a difference.

For the first time, Kailey notices I'm not quite right.

"Did you fight?" she asks, after Henry fails to appear for three days in row. "You look like you're not sleeping."

Wordlessly, I unlock my phone and slide it down the counter to her. Her eyes skim text after text from Henry, all delivered in the two days after the blow out with Kashvi at his apartment. I've memorized each message.

> *Can we talk?*
> *How are you doing?*
> *I really need to talk to you. It's important.*
> *I don't think text is the right way to talk about things. Please, pick up.*
> *I'm sorry I was an asshole.*
> *I need to apologize.*
> *Please answer.*
> *I miss you.*
> *Brooklyn.*
> *I know I made a mess. I can fix it.*
> *Let me fix it.*
> *Okay, I can take a hint. I'm sorry. This is my fault.*
> *Please don't blame yourself.*

I can't absolve Henry. I'm busy carrying my own guilt.

"Why haven't you answered him?" Kailey demands. "There are like, a bunch of messages here, and five missed calls."

"I know what he's going to say."

"Do you? What?"

"That he's staying with Kashvi, because he's been with her for years, and he loves her, and I'm not worth it."

Kailey looks dumbfounded.

"She's beautiful, and talented, and is going to be a doctor and I'm just ... no one. A distraction, maybe, for a little bit, and I made it easy for him to see what he's got."

"You're delusional."

Sure. Just not the way she thinks. I shrug and slice the dough-nuts for sandwiches, which, despite their nitrate-loaded ham slices, have developed an avid following.

"What if you're wrong?" she pushes. "I think you're wrong. There's something real between the two of you."

Dying, I remind myself. Doesn't matter.

"You weren't there. You didn't see what I saw." A sleepy, stunned Henry who'd suddenly been confronted with two women. One of whom didn't belong.

He should stay with Kashvi. I'm worse every day. A little less real, a little more gone. If I start to vanish and stay that way, it's better for him to pick Kashvi.

The phone buzzes, and we both whip our heads to look at it. Kailey picks it up and hands it to me.

"It's not him," she says.

God, I miss Henry. How he smells, how he feels pressed against me on a couch, how he lets me be. How he sees my poten-tial, not my failures.

The text is from Grace, inviting me to come to lunch again.

Can't, I text back. *Busy.*

I don't want to give her a chance to make excuses for Henry. Worse, she might tell me to let him go, which, let's face it, is a skill I don't have. Nothing gets let go. Everything gets hoarded under a trapdoor in my brain. I know Grace heard about Kashvi finding

Henry and I together, because the day after that mess she sent me a series of messages that only included wide-eyed emojis, followed by heart-eyed emojis, followed by angry-faced emojis. Given how Grace feels about Kashvi, at least I know I'm not the one she's angry at.

Besides, with Labour Day just over a week away, for the first time in months I'm swamped. My mother is all in on party execution. Until the day of the party, her consternation and micromanaging will increase incrementally until she explodes into a crying fit about how none of us are doing enough and how the party is going to be a disaster. Same pattern every year. The party is always an incredible success.

My father rejected do-it-yourself tacos in favor of do-it-yourself burgers, sausages, and something with chicken thighs or some other meat on a stick—the same food we serve every year.

Dad said, "Tacos are too messy and not what people are expecting."

Mom said, "You never cared about the food before."

Dad said, "Helen, I get to cook this much meat once a year."

The matter was dropped. We decided to keep the margaritas, though.

Behind me, Kailey sighs heavily. "Matt just pulled up."

"Of course. Because we were already having such a wonderful time," I say.

"Can you whip up some content for social media and the website about the fall flavors?" Matt asks me as he breezes in. "The one on the collab with Silvia's Ice Cream was decent. We're doing a cranberry-rum-apple, and smoked walnut maple glaze. And candied bubble gum on vanilla bourbon. I'm thinking we call it Sugar High. It's going to be epic."

"No Pumpkin Spice for Life?" Kailey asks, dismay sending her voice to the stratosphere.

"No. We're trendsetters. We're going to blow pumpkin spice away. These doughnuts are going to annihilate every other flavor." He goes in for a fist bump, but Kailey locks her arms beside her.

"We're already getting inquiries from customers about when pumpkin spice is coming," Kailey says. "We sold out before 10 a.m. every day last fall. Every day, Matt."

"People will get over it." He turns away from her.

"People are not going to get over it," Kailey insists. "Customers screamed at us when we ran out. Lines started at 6 a.m. Two girls quit from the abuse, remember? A woman threw a box of dough-nuts at me. We should at least do a limited run of pumpkin." She shoots me a distraught look.

The service industry. No one warns you about all the custom-ers who can't handle small disappointments.

"We need the press release tomorrow," Matt says, ignoring Kailey. "After I review it, share it and email it around. Make sure you do something for our newsletter and put together a list of influencers who need free samples. Bloggers, whatever you think is best. The first shift after Labour Day can box up and ship the new flavors. We'll get some bike couriers to deliver. Those ones who wear bow ties and dress pants. Keep it classy."

"When am I supposed to write the release and do the market research?" I ask.

"Tonight?"

I nod, as if I'm considering it. What I'm really thinking about is how upset Kailey is and how stupid Matt's hair looks, curled and greasy around his face. I hate his pastel cargo shorts, and his casually untucked linen shirt, through which I can see his abs. I'm thinking of all the shit employees are going to take in mid-September because Pumpkin Spice for Life, the top-selling doughnut last year, isn't going to be on the menu.

It's my fault I've ended up here, letting this man-child take me for granted and talk to me like I'm property. Most of the other employees, who are young and inexperienced, think Matt is someone because he learned how to sell doughnuts for four dollars a pop. I see him. And I see myself clearly for a blinding, shining moment. I'm not disintegrating in the morning sun today.

"Sure," I say, as I try to straighten and put down the last of the magazines I'd been tidying. I overshoot the counter and they cascade to the ground, flapping noisily. "I can write content and make you a media list. I charge ninety-five dollars an hour. Minimum four hours of work. I can get it to you before the weekend. Not tomorrow."

"What?" Matt had been leaving, walking toward the back door and the parking lot where his new Jeep is parked. It has leather seats, according to Becca. He whirls to face me.

Behind him, Kailey's pink lips form a perfect circle and her eyes widen. I wink. Her eyes get bigger.

"I charge ninety-five dollars an hour for professional communications work. It's a competitive rate."

Matt's mouth opens and closes. "You've done them before."

"I shouldn't have. If you don't want me to do it, I can refer another contractor."

Matt's face reddens. Kailey makes a high-fiving motion. His back is to her, and I cross my fingers he doesn't turn around. No point in us both getting in trouble.

"I pay you to work."

"You pay me fifteen dollars and twenty cents an hour to serve people doughnuts and coffee, and to greet them with a smile. That's it."

"Did I catch you at a bad time of the month?"

"That's inappropriate to say in the workplace," I say. I clench my hands behind my back to keep them from shaking. "Or anywhere else."

Kailey snorts. Matt stands there gaping at me, a dark flush sitting high on his cheekbones. I look right back at him, forcing my face to be open and patient. *Serene*, I think to myself. *Be serene.* Channel Penny, channel her daring. The front door chimes behind me. Matt struggles to regain control of his temper while Kailey pulls it together enough to bounce up the display counter and cheerfully greet whoever has come in behind me.

"We'll talk about this later," Matt says, spinning on his heel. I stand frozen as the customer leaves. All I see of her is a familiar flash of blonde hair.

"I think we should talk about it now," I call. I'm this far in. Might as well go all the way. It's time to be the thing that moves rather than the thing that gets moved.

"You want to talk? Let's talk about your attitude and your tone," Matt says, walking toward me aggressively. I refuse to cower, or to back down in front of this man. He is not a threat. He's powerless. No one. I've faced worse.

He holds up his hand and uses his fingers to count. "Customers don't like you. You don't smile enough. Becca says your press releases are shit. You lied about your age—some guy named Todd came in and told me you were twenty-nine."

"I want to talk about some things too. You're sleeping with Becca. You're her boss. She's eighteen. You're what, thirty-one?"

"It's not illegal."

"It's borderline, and it's unethical. You *employ* her."

"My store got robbed because of you."

"It got robbed because of you. Because you keep it open, unnecessarily, until the bars close. I looked at the receipts for the last six months. You're not moving that much product. It costs more to staff it. Do some math."

"I want it open for brand awareness," Matt splutters. "It's important to saturate the market for maximum name recognition. Like Starbucks."

"Oh boy," I exhale. I'd forgotten that Matt believes he's the Steve Jobs of doughnuts. "Besides that," I add, loudly, for the benefit of the customer I sense loitering in the doorway behind me, "I think the Labour Relations Board may be interested in your hiring practices. Except for Raj, who only works here because he'll take the Gastown late shift, you don't hire male staff. Also, asking people's age, and then discriminating against them, is illegal. And guess what? This is a shitty place to work."

"You're fired," Matt shouts. Kailey jumps and claps her hands over her mouth. Her eyes can't get any wider.

"You know what? That's fine. I'm just fine with that." I untie my apron and drop it on the floor. Then I pick it up, so Kailey won't have to.

"You'll never work in the food industry again," Matt says, his face purple and tight with anger. My knees knock together, but I will myself not to be petrified. To use my voice.

"Oh, so you think it's my dream to work for someone like you serving average-tasting doughnuts?"

"You're fired."

"You already said that."

Matt stomps out the front door. He's shouting into his phone before he's out of sight around the corner. Kailey runs around the counter and throws her arms around me, her long red hair tickling my face and sticking in my lip gloss. I let her hold me up because my legs want to collapse.

"That was best thing I've heard anyone say to him. Ever." She crushes me with her yoga-strong arms.

Becca strolls in, beanie-less and wearing a white tank top tucked into her hipster black denim skirt.

"What did you do to Matt, Brooklyn?" she says. "He's rage-kicking an abandoned sofa in the alley." She pins me with a glare.

Then her face cracks into a grin. "Which is awesome. He's a douche. He totally forgot my birthday, and he was hitting on some blonde girl the other day, right in front of me."

In Kailey's retelling of my standoff with Matt, I'm heroic. Becca and Kailey giggle and gossip and Becca divulges more personal information about Matt than I ever wanted to know. Kailey squeals in disgust. I'm caught in the eye of their storm, a willing, quiet center.

"How much do you think I can charge him when he asks me to write all his shit because you're not going to do it?" Becca asks, her face eager and bright. "I could use some extra cash."

"As much as you freaking want," Kailey says. "Make him pay for it, girl."

My hoarded resentment toward Becca and any lingering splinters for Kailey dissipate into the heat.

Make him pay for it. It's a teasing, throwaway comment. It's piercing. I've been paying for my past with a steep currency: shards of myself. The cost—my deteriorating body—is too high. It's time to find a way to make someone else pay.

My heart contracts and expands creakily in my chest, leaving me gasping from the shock of it. The muscle, rusty from disuse, stretches and expels blood. A pumping sensation floods my body, filling me with warmth and its more elusive companion: hope.

Once. Twice.

My heart stills again, as if out of batteries. It's enough to feel the blood slosh through my arteries, to feel the veins come unstuck like crumpled old rubber gloves as you force your hand into them. I imagine a suctioning noise as they pop open. In the waning summer sunlight and effervescent camaraderie, the world becomes luminous and zoetic, like a promise kept seconds after you lost faith it would be.

CHAPTER 24

I wander home through neighborhoods verdant with foliage and redolent with nostalgia: snatches of laughter, wafts of charring hamburgers, a summer anthem booming from a passing car. The air is hazy with smoke from a forest fire up north, and the way the smoke blocks the sun turns the light and everything it touches golden orange. It's a drowsy color, and I walk home dreamily, occasionally pressing a palm against my chest, searching for the elusive beat. Two beats weren't much reprieve, and my body is already seizing up and obliging me to walk haltingly.

At home, I leave a note on the whiteboard on the upstairs fridge: *Quit. More like fired. Still living in basement.* I add a smiley face because it will irritate my mother. Unemployment is liberating this time around. I'd made a choice, and I'd done it by standing up for myself, and for Kailey. Even Becca. It feels better. I'd been beaten down by Matt's sexist bullshit and recovery had taken longer than it should have. But I got there.

In my room, I eyeball the dead plant. "I think it's time, buddy. You had a good run."

I carry it to the compost pile in the far corner of the yard. The plant has calcified in its pot, and I wrestle it out before disposing of it on top of the pile like a crown

Back inside, I survey the piles of clothing and junk in my bedroom. All my friendly neighborhood Emilys managed to make a huge mess of my closet. I model some of the outfits they put together when I locate the pieces on the floor, or under the bed, or hanging out of my desk drawer, or off the back of a chair. The outfits don't look half bad, and startlingly, my clothes mostly fit again. Not having an appetite for weeks has undone several months of solid doughnut consumption. I'm somewhere between where I started—too thin—and where I ended up. Middle ground suits me. The weight doesn't matter anyway. It was just another way I let the expectations of others control me.

I clean for hours, the whole time feeling like an excavator. Unearthed items include pairs of shoes I haven't worn since before I'd moved back in with my parents and photographs of Penny and I from when we were kids, still wearing pastel pink sweatshirts unironically. We both wear serious faces in most of the images, but for the life of me, I can't remember why. Did we think we looked older wearing stoicism? Or did we know, in our tiny, childish bodies, how much we'd own those sadder, contemplative looks later?

I rehang the clothes and stack boxes of shoes in the closet. I put all the bracelets and necklaces Emilie and Emaleigh pulled from a shoebox back into the top drawer of my vanity. Except Penny's bracelet. That I leave on. Emmalee's exercise equipment gets dragged back to the garage, and I set my runners by the door to remind myself to use them. Then, I scrub every surface with disinfectant and stretch new sheets on the bed. The room sparkles and smells like lavender instead of stale deep-fryer oil.

"Good job," I say, then groan. Still talking to myself.

"Brooklyn," my mom yells from upstairs. "Dinner. Now! Move your butt."

Right. I'd forgotten about the party-dinner dry run. While it's possible to avoid Spencer on Labour Day, participation at the dinner is not optional. Which means while I've been cleaning, unaware, he's been nearby.

I take my seat and avoid eye contact with everyone, except Dad, who I manage a thin-lipped smile for. My father loads the table with meat to taste test. Chicken thighs doused in Thai rub or smoked chili powder, bratwursts, chipotle turkey sausages, lamb and pork sausage with fennel, marinated beef and lamb skewers, hamburgers with barbecue sauce right in the meat patties—there are no veggies. We eat until we've tasted everything. Meat and seasoning are voted on by a show of hands. My father implemented a no-talking rule when I was in the sixth grade because our preference selection got out of hand. There was yelling, and I threw a link of sausages at Spencer's chest. He punched me in the boobs later to make up for it.

And every year, Penny joins us and says we should serve lookalike soy products because free food means no one cares what it tastes like. People are vultures.

"We should serve veggie dogs," my mother says, as if she's pulled the memory right out of my brain. She wipes her eyes with a paper towel and leaves a smear of honey mustard on her cheek.

"Still no sign of Penny, huh?" Spencer says, as he drops an empty wooden skewer on his plate.

"No, she's back safe and sound and we just didn't tell you," I say, weary from all the tiptoeing on eggshells I've done around him.

"You don't need to be so snarky," Spencer says. His foot smacks against my calf. A warning shot.

I stuff chicken seasoned with my father's ranch-flavored not-so-secret secret sauce into my mouth so I don't verbally retaliate. The chicken is bland but familiar, so I make appreciative sounds and spit most of my dinner into my napkin. Dad makes notes, then my mother pulls out the dreaded party planner, which lives in a thick, yellow, legal-sized notepad decorated with Post-its.

Without Penny, who has only missed two planning sessions over the years, there are more to-dos for everyone except my father, who only buys and cooks the meat, puts out chairs, and mows the lawn.

Mom hands Spencer a prepaid liquor store card and me a grocery list and a corresponding preloaded card. I'm also stuck with the job of running out for any last minute or forgotten purchases the day of the party, which guarantees heading right back to a store the moment I leave it. For hours. For someone this organized, my mother forgets a lot of necessary items.

"How come Spencer doesn't have to clean anything?" I ask as I stare in horror at my endless list of chores.

"He doesn't live here, and you're not working. I saw your note," Mom says. "Penny normally helps with kitchen prep, so I'll need you for that too."

"Who knows. Maybe Penny will show up in time," Spencer says. He's not smiling, and there's a calculating look in his eyes that suggests he wants to get a rise out of me.

I don't bite. Open mouth, insert more chicken. I can barely choke it down, but it's better than triggering Spencer.

"I've got final numbers for the guests," Mother says. "Brooklyn, everyone on your list RSVP'd except Henry. I've got Alisha, Grace, Kailey, and Raj. Becca can't make it."

I'd invited Raj, via text message, so he'd know there were no hard feelings about what happened in the shop. Becca I'd invited to be polite. Henry's lack of response sends a stab of disappointment through me, but it's not anything I didn't expect. Kailey is so, so wrong about him.

"Is Kashvi invited?" Spencer asks.

"Henry's invite included a plus one," my mother says.

I can see what's coming a mile away. Spencer is glowing with victory. Since I went to university and moved out, access to my body has been limited, but he still has verbal and psychological weapons loaded and ready.

"I understand why neither of them want to come," Spencer says. "Since Kashvi found Brooklyn trying to sleep with Henry." He's been waiting to drop that bomb. I'd wondered why he hadn't mentioned it when we'd all been gathered around the kitchen table the morning I'd come home.

"Brooklyn?" my mother says, with a wounded tone that confuses me.

"I was at Henry's, after the store robbery," I say. "You know this. I told all of you. And I slept on the couch."

Spencer snorts. "So did Henry."

My mother looks appalled.

"Kashvi was so upset," Spencer adds. "She found them together before summer school finals, and she couldn't focus on studying. Her grades suffered. She told me you gave Henry an ultimatum: Kashvi or you. He picked her." Spencer's lip curls up gleefully.

I never issued an ultimatum, but it's crushing to hear his choice confirmed, even if I was expecting it. Kashvi. Why wouldn't he pick her? Why shouldn't he?

"Brooklyn!" my mother shouts. "How could you? That poor girl."

"Are you kidding me?" I snap back. "Even if anything Spencer just said was true, it takes two people to cheat. I wouldn't have done it by myself."

"You're such a liar," Spencer says.

"We can never just eat dinner, can we?" my father asks. "There always has to be an explosion."

"Dad, she's super out of control," Spencer says. "She needs help. Meds. A therapist. Maybe time in professional care. I'm worried. She's not behaving normally."

Spencer has been cruel, but careful, so my parents remained oblivious. His ability to walk the tightrope is remarkable.

On the other hand, I always go for blunt force, which is probably why I'm the one who comes across as the instigator. Like now. Consequences be damned.

"I never want to see your ugly, stupid face again," I say, resorting to childish, petty insults. I stand on quivering legs and head straight for the basement, where I fling myself on the couch and yank a throw over my head. I try to inhale calming breaths, but it doesn't work. I end up gulping nosily.

Quiet footsteps alert me to my mother's presence. She sits on the bench across from the couch. Her body is a shadowy outline through the loose weave of the blanket.

"Spencer started it," I preempt as I emerge.

A muscle jumps in her jaw and she squeezes her hands, turning her knuckles white. Her wedding ring sits loosely on her finger, held in place by the small engagement ring.

"I'd like for you to be honest. Are you having an affair with this man?" Her formal tone says she's uncomfortable with the question, and a little ashamed. Ashamed of me, for making her ask it.

I'm way too old for this conversation.

"Mom. No. Was I friends with Henry? Yes. Did we hang out? Yes. Is it any of your business? No."

"There was a woman once, years ago, at your father's office. She was quite taken with him. I thought that maybe they…" She trails off, and humiliation chomps through my intestines, like teeth chewing overcooked meat.

"What, so you think because on the off chance your husband is a cheat, your daughter is too? As if it's genetic?" I angle my body away from her, unable to look at her. No one assumes the worst as well as my mother does.

"David knew she was interested. That was when he asked for the transfer to the Burnaby office. He thought—well, I thought— we should remove temptation. Your father said he never acted on her invitation, and I believe him."

I have vague recollections of that time. I was around eight years old, and Mom cried a lot. Spencer slept in my room, at the foot of my bed, like a cat. It was before he changed. Or before his behavior manifested. There was a lot of whispering behind closed doors and my parents stopped talking every time Spencer or I walked into a room. I'd felt the tension in the air, but couldn't recognize the source. How could I? I was a child. I'm still a fucking child.

"It was a painful time for me," my mother continues. "I only bring it up because you need to think about how your actions impact other people, Brooklyn."

Imagine if she knew about Penny and her married man. Penny might get some compassion, but Spencer has already woven his spell where I'm concerned. I stare at my mother and imagine that my gaze turns her to granite. I'll Medusa her. Problem solved. The fantasy doesn't work any better than the one about the family car flying off the bridge and into the water below. I open my mouth with no idea what's going to come out.

"All I do is think about other people!" I scream. She jumps.

"How they'll feel. What's best for them. What they'll think. Spencer twisted what happened with Henry," I say, spewing the words like bullets. "You think I'm the dishonest one? You're so quick to believe every piece of bullshit Spencer feeds you."

"You and Penny always made a such a game out of telling white lies," she says, holding up her hands defensively. "Always whispering, telling fibs, covering for each other. The two of you were so wild when you were together. Spencer was so obedient."

"We were children. What happened then doesn't make me a liar now, or mean I'm lying about everything. It doesn't mean Spencer is always honest."

I'm trying not to rip her throat out. She's making it hard.

She exhales, long and slow.

"Why does he hate me?" The words come out strangled. This is the question that plagued my childhood. It still does.

"He doesn't hate you," she says on perfectly timed autopilot.

I snort. "We both know that's not true. What I don't know, what I've never known, is why." It's just me. Something uniquely me that he hates enough to hurt. If I knew, maybe I could fix it. Fix me, and everything would be different. I would be different. Someone who could really live. Find a job I love, and a person like Henry. My best friend wouldn't be missing a world away because I'd be worth sticking around for.

My thoughts are spiralling, and I frantically try to catch them and put them back where they belong—unthought.

"Spencer is a very smart boy. He's not the best at relating to some people," my mother says, in a tiny admission that her son isn't perfect. "He's sensitive about his looks. You shouldn't have called him ugly."

"Why not? He called me fat earlier this summer."

"This is what I mean. You're so defensive around him, and quick to lash out. If you could be a little nicer, you'd get along. I'm sure of it."

"Oh, you want me to be nicer?" I get up and start pacing in the confines of the tiny downstairs living room. "Of course. I'm the one who isn't nice, and as the girl, that's my job, isn't it?"

She doesn't say a word.

"It's more complicated than that," I say. Complicated in the form of bruises, scratches, broken bones, and the time it looked like I'd tried to cut my own hair but had been Spencer's work, executed while he held me down on the floor.

Despite what she says after a few glasses of sangria about loving us equally, Spencer wedged himself in her heart and snatched some of the space that should have belonged to me.

"You're both my babies," she says. "Your father says I have to learn I can't control either of you. You're going to fight. Or make decisions that I don't understand, and I have to accept them."

She looks so woebegone that she's not allowed to make decisions for us, or bully Spencer and I into being besties, that I laugh. A faint smile crosses her face.

"I haven't heard you laugh in a long time, Brookie." She stands and pulls me in for a hug. "I do wish you'd get a real job though, honey," she whispers in my ear. "Especially now that you're not working at the doughnut shop."

"You're unbelievable," I whisper back, wanting her to love me.

I rest against her and breathe in jasmine perfume, generic shampoo, clean laundry. Her skin is not as firm as it used to be, and her hair is not as dark. She's letting it gray, willing to accept it. Willing to accept that time passes. I wonder how she'll accept it if I can't get my heart beating and I shrivel away to nothing. I wonder if she'll be as sad as she would be if it happened to Spencer instead.

SEPTEMBER

CHAPTER 25

The day before my mother's party, I run a handful of errands between bouts of listlessness and naps. I'm cold, stiff, and can't get enough rest.

While I'm out, Emmalee waves from inside a spin studio. Emaleigh pops up while I wait in line to purchase plastic margarita pitchers. Emily bikes past me while I sit on a park bench and stare at the ocean without seeing it. Emilie calls my name from a storefront as I brush past to pick up cleaning supplies. They reach for me and I keep moving, pretending not to see them, because somehow my brain has surfaced one unalterable fact and forced it to stick: Emily, Emmalee, Emaleigh, and Emilie are my loved ones, who have passed on first. They're the ones I'm seeing. At the end.

When the idea crystalized and formed, no amount of pushing would shove it away. I had to vomit. Nothing came up but bile. This is the road I've been on and I saw the end coming. Those little blips of heartbeat were never going to be enough to save me.

After my mother's errands, I lie prone on my bed with my head turned toward my computer, doing my utmost to let nothing but television take root in my brain until the party, which feels like insult added to injury. A good chunk of what remains of my life is going to be spent at a party I'm going to hate.

Sleep is a relief. I wake up minutes, hours, later as the mattress shifts underneath me. I blink groggily, but my foggy brain clears the instant I see who has plunked herself in the middle of my bed.

"Penny!"

She's clutching a pillow and sitting cross-legged next to me. I lunge and fling my arms around her. The scent of dust, smoke, and dried roses fills my nose as her ribs dig into mine.

"When did you get back? Why didn't you call? Why didn't your parents call?" Then I remember my uncharged phone sitting in my purse by the bedroom door.

Joy rips through my body. Wild, unfettered joy. It's as though scattered pieces of me have snapped back together and given me whiplash with the force of their arrival.

"Oh my God. You're here." I keep squeezing her.

"Brookie. You're crushing me."

I release her, out of breath with gratefulness and relief. The world is brighter than it ever has been, because she was gone, and now she isn't. Euphoria, gratitude—all magnified by her return. The yawning black pit in my mind is already shrinking.

Penny gazes at me, her dark brown eyes wet in the corners. She can't quite make eye contact, but her face is expectant. "Brookie," she says.

"How did you even get in here? You still have a spare key?" I burble, giddily. "What happened? Or is it too traumatic? You don't have to tell me. I'm just glad you're here. Those were the worst twelve months of my life. Probably yours too. I'm just glad…" I trail off, startled to see so much grief etched on her face. I reach for her hand, which is dry and cool. Her skin is rough under my fingers, as though the moisture has been sucked out of it.

"Penny?" Something is setting off my "caution, danger ahead" alarm bells. Whatever happened to her must be worse than anything I've spent twelve months imagining, or more accurately, trying not to imagine. We'll deal with it. We'll get her whatever she needs. I'll be there for her.

I go to hug her again, but she holds an arm up to block me.

"You can see me."

"Of course, I see you. You're right here." Elation spins like a whirlwind in my core.

She shakes her head and wraps her arms around me. "I shouldn't be here. Or you shouldn't?"

"What do you mean?" I demand, shifting away so I can look at her.

She gazes past me, her expression suggesting she's halfway around the world and a year away. "The last thing I remember was being hot, and so tired. I could barely lift my arms to move supplies. A vehicle pulled up. Not one I recognized. Someone shouted at me. I got in. Maybe I was pulled in. I can't picture the driver's face, or exactly what happened. I think they…"

She seems to drift and waver around the edges. When I reach out and touch her, she feels insubstantial. A familiar knot grows in my stomach and shoves out exhilaration.

"We drove," she continues, still wearing a vacant mien. "It was dark for ages. Later, there were bangs, explosions, screaming. Time passed. Now I'm here. You can see me."

"You're scaring me." After being unable to sweat for weeks, there's a thick sheen of perspiration coating my forehead and chest. Penny must have injured her brain. Or she's blocking painful memories, which I'm unable to fault her for. Same.

"I don't think you shouldn't be able to see me," Penny says, chagrined.

"I don't understand." Nothing she's saying makes any sense. My brain slams on the brakes.

"I've heard children, in the refugee centers, talking to their mothers, who have already passed on. The children aren't far behind. It's like a veil lifts between life and death and they see the impossible. But this…" She trails off. "You shouldn't be able to see me. Not now. In decades, maybe. When you're old and wrinkled. Very old." She says it more firmly, and gives me a stern look. "I mean it. So old, Brookie. As old as possible."

The barricades holding everything back are breaking down. Cracks are forming where I keep all the things I don't want to acknowledge. What Penny is saying is the thing I want to deny most of all.

"No," I say. "No." I grind my fist into the pillow.

Penny is wispy around the edges. "I think you've known for a while that I wasn't coming home."

A wretched sound escapes my throat.

"I'd spare you the news, if I could." Sorrow rises off her. I nearly rock with the impact. "But I need to know? Are you sick? Is it serious?" Panic sits on her face, and she chews a fingernail, a habit she broke in the seventh grade.

"I don't know." I press my cold hand to my chest. "My heart isn't beating. I'm always cold. I vanish from mirrors, and sometimes my voice goes away. Food tastes like crap, and I keep seeing actresses from all our favorite shows. And they're chatty and perky, and they're dead." My voice cracks.

Penny lays two fingers against my neck and wraps her other hand around my wrist. She tilts her head quizzically and releases me. "Huh. No heartbeat."

"You're just going to accept this? I thought you were a nurse! People without heartbeats are *already* dead."

"I've seen plenty I can't explain: beautiful, harrowing, amazing things. What's a missing heartbeat if it means I can say goodbye?" Penny's soft voice is filled with affection.

I shake my head so vigorously my hair whips me in the face and stings my cheeks.

"I don't accept that. I won't," I say. Dread unfurls and wraps up my spine, like the ivy on my mother's garden trellis.

"You have to."

"Why are you giving up?" I demand. "That's not who you are. Fight. Come home."

"It's too late," she says. "Otherwise, we wouldn't be having this conversation. This outcome was always a possibility. I made peace with it years ago. Doesn't mean it was my first choice." She wrinkles her nose. "You're the one who needs to fight, Brooklyn."

"I don't know how," I whisper. "Not without you. You were the strong one. I just followed along behind you."

"I've gotta say, I think my leadership qualities were overrated. I think that maybe I wasn't always who I should have been."

"You are amazing. Always have been. You make hard things look so easy. You always take action. You don't take shit from anyone, and you step up to make a difference in the world. I don't do anything. I never have."

"That's the stupidest thing I've ever heard you say." Penny glowers at me, then sighs deeply. "I don't know how much time we have."

I bite back a howl.

"One last secret?" she asks, as she elbows me. "For old times' sake?"

"You first." Mine is clawing its way up my throat, attempting to burst out. I close my mouth, not ready, afraid she'll leave the second the words form in the world.

"The man I was seeing?" she says. "His wife found out. He told her, then called it off. It broke my heart, and I didn't see it coming. I thought that I'd move on from him like I move on from everything. Nope. I didn't even know I could get my heart broken by one measly person. I thought I was tougher than that. I guess I didn't know myself as well as I thought."

"I'm sorry he broke your heart," I say. "I'm sorry I couldn't be there for you."

"You were," Penny said. "I channeled my best inner Brooklyn and gave him the cut, just like you did to that asshole Kyle when it was clear he wasn't good for you. Now, your turn."

I cover my face with my hands. She pulls them away and forces me to look at her.

"I know something is wrong. Keeping quiet will kill you. Spill it."

I shake my head and clutch my arms around my stomach. She pries my arms loose and grabs my hands.

"There were times in school, even back in high school, when you looked like a ghost. I was caught up in saving the world and thought you were just being basic. A drama queen. I should've asked some questions then, and last summer, about how you were doing. You looked terrible. Not as bad as you look now, though. I wasn't nearly as smart and insightful as I thought I was when it came to you."

"Spencer." I clear my throat and try again. Nausea builds, and sweat blooms all over my body, behind my knees, across my forehead, down my back. The world sways and tilts, but Penny remains constant.

I pull my knees into my chest and wrap my arms around them while I gasp for air. Habit holds the words in my body. The truth, once released, can't be taken back. It shouldn't be. It should fill the air, swell, take shape. I let the words go.

"Spencer physically abused me. Hit me, kicked me, punched me, pushed me. Bit me, once. He's hurt me since we were children. I wasn't as klutzy and good at hurting myself as I pretended to be. It was him. Always him." The monster bursts from my lips in one exhale. My throat is raw and bloody from the force of it leaving my body.

Penny's hand convulses on my arm. "No!"

"You don't believe me?" I swallow. Penny's denial is worse than my mother's.

"All those times you got injured at school, or got a bloody nose, had bruises from soccer—that was all Spencer? Your broken arms? That cut on your leg at the ice rink? The concussion at the waterslides?"

I manage to nod, still not sure what side of the fence Penny is on.

"I want to ruin him," she says. She's vibrating with rage, not disbelief. "How come you never told me?"

"I could barely admit it to myself. I couldn't prove that any of it was on purpose. He would say it was an accident."

"They weren't accidents though, were they?"

"No." Inside my chest, it feels like a spring has unwound and is ricocheting around.

"You should have told me."

"You were so outspoken, and I didn't want you to tell anyone. It was embarrassing, and Spencer said no one would believe me, or you, since we were always getting caught lying." I throw her a slanted glance.

"I would have believed you," Penny says, fervently.

"I was afraid you'd think I was pathetic," I whisper. "What kind of person lets someone treat her like that? I thought you'd see how weak I was, and you'd realize you didn't need me."

Penny makes a mewl of pain and buries her face into the bedspread. "I was too hard on people. I was so self-important, busy trying to save the world. You were my best friend, even though I treated you like shit. I wanted to be right all the time. Infallible."

"You didn't," I object.

"I never listened to you, and I made you do everything I wanted to do," Penny says.

"But you were also brave and fun and forced me to try things and go places when I would have just stayed home, afraid and locked in my room."

Penny snorts, then laughs—her real laugh, in all its braying glory. The joy I'd felt at her appearance rekindles at the familiar sound. Everything good I remember about my childhood and teenage years is connected to that laugh.

"I only could be brave because you always supported whatever crazy idea I had, like that time I organized a sit-in at the zoo and you were the only person who showed up," she says. "I knew you'd be there for me. You were always the better of us. Kind. Resourceful. Supportive to a fault, really. You were a better friend than I deserved. I took advantage of your big heart, because I knew you'd let me, and you'd still love me.

"You know," she continues, "you're the only person who never told me not to go. I never told you how much that meant to me."

"Should I have told you to stay?"

"No. I got to do what mattered to me because you never asked me not to, or told me to take the safer path. That meant something to me. It meant something that you let me be the truest version of myself."

She glares at me. "And I swear, Brooklyn, if you blame yourself, I'll haunt you forever, and not cute little hauntings like taking your socks or hiding your favorite shoes. I'll write frightening messages with your expensive lipstick on the bathroom mirror and break shit until you slowly go mad from the torment."

I wipe my snotty nose on my blanket and exhale shakily. "Okay. I won't."

"Stop blaming yourself for Spencer too. You don't deserve what he's done."

"I'm not—" I start.

"Don't even," Penny interrupts. "I know you. You internalize everything." She grabs my face between her cold palms. "Tell someone." Her eyes burn into mine, and in them I see the fury and righteousness that has always been there, banked and waiting. She's saved the last of it for me.

"I told Mom once," I say. "Spencer trashed my room and shoved me into the bedpost. Cut my cheekbone. Black eye. Mom said that I misinterpreted what happened. That he was just roughhousing and it was an accident. After that, he didn't stop."

"Your mom." Penny sighs as if she's expelling years' worth of frustration. "Is an idiot. Tell someone else."

I shake my head.

"Yes," she says, simply. "You have to. And I don't want to see you again until you've lived your life. All of it. Fully."

"I've never known how to do that," I say. A black hole of sadness is coming for me, threatening to absorb my whole body.

"Time to learn," Penny says. She casts an anxious look at the window. Outside, dawn hesitates on the horizon. "I have to go."

"Stay." I'm desperate to hold onto her. For the first time in years, our friendship feels solid and real. I am not alone, because of Penny.

"You know I can't. Accept it."

"No."

"You want to waste time arguing? Or do you want to say goodbye?"

I thrust my chin out and cross my arms.

"Say it," she demands.

"No."

"Say it," she repeats, taking another concerned look toward the window.

"I'll miss you, Penny Parker." I hug her hard. "Every day."

"Not every day," she says. "Fuck. Give yourself a break. That's exhausting."

"Fine," I snap.

"I'll miss you too, Brooklyn Thomas. You *are* brave. Capable. Strong. I love you. Don't forget."

"I won't," I whisper. "You were my best friend. Always."

"It's not a bad thing," she says, with a wobbly grin. "Talking about me in the past tense."

Tears—mine, finally free—are falling, fat and heavy. They splatter onto my bedsheets, leaving behind growing wet circles.

Sleep tugs at my eyelids preternaturally. I link my arm through Penny's to keep her next to me and grounded to the world as I battle to hold my eyes open.

"Let go," she murmurs. "Let go."

When I wake up, the sun is diffused through the blinds and Penny is gone. There are short black hairs on the pillow next to mine. Grief drowns me. I drown and I drown. And then I get up. Because it's Labour Day, and my mother's party cannot be stopped.

"You were dreaming," I say, firmly. "Asleep. One of those hypnopompic dreams the doctor told you about."

I almost believe it.

CHAPTER 26

Rain threatens. My mother keeps looking out the kitchen window and scowling.

"Your face is darker than the clouds," my unfazed father says. He presses a kiss against her head. "Stop worrying. The weather app says this too shall pass."

He escapes the storm brewing inside by heading to the butcher to buy hamburger, sausage, and boneless chicken thighs for sixty people.

"Spencer is coming in a couple of hours. Try to be nice," my mother says, once my father is gone.

"Did you tell him to be nice?" I snap, politeness impossible as I try to rub some feeling into my stiff fingers. They've been curled into claws every afternoon for the past week.

"Just get along for a couple hours. It shouldn't be too much to ask. You got along just fine as children." She's peaked and spoiling for a fight. Party stress is her excuse.

"Until he gave me a black eye and destroyed most of my toys when I was ten," I spit out, the words hanging in the air before I'd realized they were coming. I nearly clap a hand over my mouth, but my arm seems stuck, extended at my side. Rigor mortis?

"You're exaggerating," Mom objects. "It wasn't that bad."

"I wish you could admit that it was. You sent him to therapy, for God's sake."

"That woman said Spencer was a typical boy. Boys being boys. He played too rough, got carried away."

"She was a bad therapist," I say, suddenly eager for a fight too. "And he only went once."

"Brooklyn."

"Mom."

We stare at each other. I should be able to tell my mother what kind of person Spencer is. How Spencer is the kind of person who hits his sister, not just the time she was ten. How all those childhood and teenage injuries she'd bandaged up or taken me to the doctor for weren't me being clumsy or too enthusiastic on the sports field.

How Spencer should be in jail, not med school. How I'd been afraid to move home after I left Lawrence Communications because he'd be able walk in the door at any second, with no warning. How, because of sky-high rent costs, I'd had no choice. How Spencer's violence and my mother's deliberate ignorance have destroyed my ability to speak for myself. How I am so afraid, every day, of being in the world, alone.

"We have a lot of prep to do," my mother says, as she turns away from me.

"Mom," I say, my voice tremulous and wavering. I try to gather up courage around me. I try to be brave, because Penny asked me to.

She holds up a hand. The purple veins on the back of her hands are swollen under the dry skin. Her nails are pastel pink. They're strong hands, the hands of a middle-aged woman used to knitting people back together. Fixing them. Except me. Her shoulders rise and fall with several deep breaths. They square, and her hand lowers.

"I need you to pick up a few last-minute things," she says, her back still to me. "There's cash in my purse."

"You knew. Didn't you? About Spencer. About what he did. Not just that one time."

"Stop by the party supply place and get extra plastic cups. I'm not sure how many we'll need, since we haven't done margaritas before."

"Did you know?" The words burst out, fast and hot. They taste bitter.

"Brooklyn," she sighs my name. "We need mixed salad, two watermelons, cups, and napkins. Get going. We're on a schedule." She strides toward the kitchen.

"Why didn't you do something?"

She looks over her shoulder and clears her throat. "This discussion is over. We have lots of work to do."

Her face gives her away. She wore the exact same expression when she spent more money on Christmas gifts for Spencer one year than she did on me. She denied it, but the shape of her mouth, the tension on her forehead, the way she fiddled with her hair said it was true.

My mother, who claims to have eyes in the back of her head. Of course, she knew something, if not everything.

It was easier to love her when I could believe she didn't.

Blindly, I go through her purse on the hall table, pull out two hundred dollars in twenty-dollar bills, and flee to my car. I unlock the driver's side and collapse in. I sit there long enough for the clouds outside to start to clear.

At the grocery store, I buy the items on my mother's list. I dawdle through the rest of my errands. Plastic cups. Napkins. I head straight for the back of the party supply store and find a dozen packages of snowman napkins in the clearance section.

When I finally pull into the driveway, my father has mowed the lawn and strung up white fairy lights on the downstairs patio and upstairs deck. My mother has used potted plants to block the back entrance to the basement suite, so I'm forced to enter the front door.

"Home," I yell.

"What took you so long?" my mother shouts back.

I lug the bag from the party supply store up the stairs and drop my burdens at her feet.

"What are these?" She holds up one of my purchases.

"Napkins," I say.

"These are Christmas napkins."

"That's all they had." I've earned this moment of passive-aggressive bullshit.

"I'll get Spencer to pick some up," she says, as she pulls her phone from a pocket. I head downstairs before he can answer. The slight exertion leaves me breathless, as though my body is functioning like that of a seventy-five-year-old.

"Dad?"

He's on the couch.

"What are you doing down here?" I ask as I grab the blanket off the couch and wrap it around me. He never comes downstairs anymore. My old bedroom upstairs was converted into a TV room/office, and he usually shelters there when my mother is running amok.

"Hiding."

"Me too." My body creaks into a seat on the piano bench.

"You're a good kid."

"Tell that to Mom. Sometimes I think she'd rather it was me instead of Penny who went missing."

"That's not true."

"Penny is saving the world, or at least trying to. I've been promoting consumerism, tooth decay, and diabetes by serving sugar to minors."

"She just wants what's best for you. She doesn't think living in the basement and making doughnuts is best for you."

"Frying doughnuts requires skills I don't have," I say. "Besides, she doesn't want what's best for me. She's made that clear since I was a kid."

My father makes a humming noise and places his hands on his knees. He shifts uncomfortably on the couch and peers around the room, his eyes never settling.

"Helen was very upset when I got home. She said you blew up at her about something that happened when you and Spencer were kids. She thinks you're trying to stir up trouble before the party."

My father watches me for a moment. "The thing is, Brookie, I know you wouldn't do that. What's going on?"

The words crowding my body are clamoring to be heard, to be recognized. They've been watered by Penny's belief in me, given oxygen, and are bursting out of my body. I can let them grow, or I can cut them off at the root. Go back to being quiet and safe. Wither back into myself. Or try something different—try to live the way Penny did. Does. By being my truest self.

"Remember that camping trip when I tripped and accidently ran headfirst into a tree, then burned myself by the fire?" I say baldly, praying to whatever gods exist that my father will believe me. "Or when I was sixteen and came home from a hike with a cracked rib and a huge bruise? That time in elementary school when I got a gash on my leg at the ice rink? All the times I went to the hospital, or fell, or tripped, or got cut up?"

My father nods. "I wanted to wrap you in bubble wrap."

"It was Spencer. He did all of it. I pretended to be clumsy, and always wore long sleeves or pants to cover up my injuries. I said I was cold, or feeling bloated, which should have been so transparent to you adults. I wore a sweatshirt whenever we went to the beach! Instead, you all believed my absurd excuses. Spencer said if I told anyone, he'd drown me. Or stab me with a kitchen knife. I've been terrified of him my whole life."

Rage unfurls on my father's face. The lines on his features deepen as I watch.

"Did you know?" My voice wobbles.

My father's breath hitches and his eyes redden. He's playing out a nightmare in his mind. I know, because I've done it for years.

"I didn't know, Brookie. You never said, and I was a damn fool who didn't see what was going on in his own house."

My father, who has loved me the best way he knew how to, despite my stubbornness, or the times as a teen I told him I hated him for one of the bazillion reasons teenage girls hate their fathers, is quivering—from rage and sorrow.

I sit next to him on the couch, and after a moment's hesitation, I lean my shoulder against his. Lightly, but enough that we can feel each other.

"He still does it? Now?" my father asks hoarsely.

"Less opportunity," I say. "But he's the same person he's always been, if that's what you're asking."

Tremors come off my father's body. He clears his throat, several times. I wait, because whatever he's building up to say is going to hurt him, and we both need time to ready for it.

"Your mother knew?"

He's braver than me. He isn't going to spend the next twenty years hiding from the truth.

"She knew something. I told her, the first time it happened. She said I misunderstood."

"You were always so banged up. You played so many damn sports. I just thought…"

"I like sports, but they also explained away a lot of injuries." What would Spencer have done if I'd been bookish or into video games?

"Why didn't you say anything?"

"Daddy, I thought if Mom knew, you did too. You did everything together. I thought you were complicit, before I knew what that word meant."

I swear I see my father's heart break in two.

"I was a child. I thought, 'How can none of you see what happening?'" Tears spill over. "I thought, 'Why don't you care about me? Why doesn't anybody love me enough to see what's going on?' I was invisible, and I just wanted someone, anyone, to see who Spencer really is."

There's a violent twist in my chest, like a stubborn lid being wrenched off a glass jar. My heart pounds furiously, frantically, and snaps to a stop. I press both my hands against my chest.

My father looks like someone has smashed his universe to pieces. He's rewriting our history to a version closer to the truth. His face flashes and contorts as each moment aligns into something new, something messy and ugly and heartbreaking.

We both have some rewriting to do. But for me, the past is not as painful, knowing my father didn't abandon me to my brother's abuse.

Today isn't done with us yet.

My cell, which I'd plugged in earlier on the side table next to the couch, rings, and we simultaneously glance at it. Robert Parker's name is emblazoned on the screen. I feel the color rush from my face, and my father places a hand on my shoulder. We brace ourselves.

I reach for the phone, my hand shaking so badly I fumble the device.

"I'm ready," I whisper. I inhale sharply, and hit the answer button.

"It's Robert," Penny's father says, when I answer. "It's about Penny."

He starts to talk, but I can't hear him over the thunder rolling through my ears.

"I'm so sorry, Brooklyn," he's saying, when I can finally make out words. "She was lucky, to have such a good friend."

"We both were," I whisper.

He hangs up.

"She's gone," I say to my father. "Penny is gone."

CHAPTER 27

In the wreckage of our illusions, in the midst of our grief, we throw a party for our friends and neighbors and carry on. My father's pride won't allow us to become a point of gossip among our neighbors, and he won't humiliate Mom by cancelling the party, even if he's so angry he refuses to look at her. She's so distracted she doesn't notice.

My father and I can endure one night carrying Spencer and what he's done, although I'm starting to realize endurance is not necessarily a positive quality. It's a state of being that hasn't done me any favors. I endured far more than I should have so I could convince myself I was doing the right thing for everyone around me, except myself.

My burden is lighter, but my father stoops as he stacks food by the barbecue. We've agreed not to tell Mom about Penny until tomorrow. This is my father's gift of love to my mother, whose grief will be too vibrant in its freshness. Grief isn't done with me, but mine is dull and worn. I've carried it since the Parkers were in our living room over a year ago. I've grieved for her absence, for what it meant for me. Penny is right—I did know, somehow, that she might not come home, even if I denied it.

We finish our party preparations. I dump an uncalled-for amount of tequila into the margarita pitchers. What does it matter if the neighbors get drunk and messy? I've felt drunk and messy for months.

My father stands in front of the barbecue with a lighter in one hand, staring into space. Our barbecue is gas-powered, and the lighter is built in. When I walk past him to put chips and popcorn on the deck, I remove the lighter from his hand.

"Dad. The barbecue is already on."

"You stick close to me tonight," he says, his eyes glazed and fixated on the snack bowl. "You stay close by."

"You got it," I say, relieved. Dad will watch out for Spencer. I'll be able to look in one direction instead of every which way, unsure of where he'll come from.

"Don't drink the margaritas," I warn. "I may have put too much tequila in them."

"Maybe I should drink them," he says, grimly.

We stand on the deck long enough that my mother comes looking for us.

"What are you two doing out here?" she asks, dragging a cooler loaded with beer and ice behind her. She arranges it in the corner of the deck, across from the barbecue. "Brooklyn, I need you to make sure your dad's office is locked and that there are enough lawn chairs set up on the grass downstairs. David, move the cars closer together so there's more room to park on the driveway."

"People will just need to park on the street," Dad says.

"Spencer is going to be here soon, and he needs a spot."

My father whirls around to look at my mother. His face is pinched, and there's a muscle jumping in his jaw.

"I don't care, Helen!" he roars. "The little shit can park down the block like the rest of these freeloaders you've invited."

My mother and I jump. My father doesn't shout; he's the walking cliché of a man who speaks in a soft voice or doesn't speak at all. Dad storms off and slams the kitchen door so hard the windows overlooking the deck rattle.

"What did you do?" my mother asks, smoothing a hand across her hair to hide how shocked she is.

"I didn't do anything."

She raises an eyebrow at me.

"I'm not responsible for every crappy thing that happens in this house," I say, trying to speak quietly and with weight, like my father, whom I love more than I have ever loved another person because he called Spencer a little shit and meant it.

"And look, sun!" I say, pointing upwards. Her eyes follow my hand, and I make my escape.

Emily Porter is waiting for me downstairs. She's wearing sparkly pink lip gloss and my makeup is spread all over the vanity behind her. The lipstick looks cute with her outfit, which is made up of my cream high-waisted slacks and a navy-blue crop top.

"You again," I pant, fatigued from my labored journey down the stairs.

"I wanted to check in. How are you?"

"It's been a good and bad day," I say. Good, because my father believed me. I'm having to reframe my childhood around the idea that my mother knew, but he didn't. He *didn't*. Bad because of all the rest.

"Most days are like that," she says. "Still no heartbeat?"

"Once or twice."

"Not enough," she says.

"What's going to happen to me if it doesn't come back?" My body is slipping away more quickly than it was at the beginning of summer. Immobile joints, lack of appetite, and general despondency suggest I'm in big trouble.

"How should I know?" Emily says. "I only *played* a nurse once. Guest starred on three episodes of *The Surgery*."

"You're basically useless," I say.

"Was I?"

I yank my hair into a ponytail. Death hallucination or not, I needed her. She was a friend when I had none. She made me talk and let me feel less alone, if only for a few moments.

"No. You weren't useless. I needed you. I was alone and you were there. You all were."

"I think you're running out of time," she says.

"I know. But I don't know how to fix it. If I should fix it. If I can." That's the terrifying truth. My body is shrinking and slowing around me. "I had to pull my eyelids open this morning." I haven't peed in days, but that's too much to share, even with Emily. Boundaries are a good thing.

"Remember that movie I told you about?" she asks. "Straight to DVD?"

"About the woman who wanted to live for her man?"

"The important part is that she had things to say and business to finish," Emily says. "I think you do too."

"I'm trying." I nudge Emily with an elbow and meet the warm resistance of her body.

"Try harder."

"Do you have any useful advice?" I yank a sundress over my head. It's nude fabric with a blush-pink lace overlay. It's way over the top for a block party, but I feel like looking pretty. Like I deserve to, for once.

She hands me a tube of lipstick and points at her mouth. "It's your color. 'Honesty, Honestly.'"

I snort. "Such a ridiculous name."

"You should try it."

"Penny bought it for me last summer. I never wore it. I'm more of a natural-lip kind of girl."

"Maybe she was trying to tell you something. 'Honesty, Honestly.'"

I apply a coat of sparkling neon pink and make kissy lips in Emily's direction. "Satisfied?"

"Pretty satisfied. Not about everything. I got the lead in a new Netflix movie. The bigwigs said I was too short, too blonde, too cute, and too old, and then I knocked their socks off. I was going to be a secret agent instead of the sweet little thing next door. Didn't get a chance to finish my business though."

"I would've watched that. You would've been great."

"I really would have been," she says wistfully.

I hold out my arms, and she launches herself at me. We hug hard. I catch a whiff of dry roses and dust before she pulls away.

"Go all out," Emily says in my ear. "Risk everything. It won't kill you. You've taken care of that all on your own."

"Gee, thanks," I say.

"Brookie!" my dad hollers from upstairs.

"I'll see you around," Emily says. She waves and bounces out. The front door slams.

"I kind of hope not," I say to my empty room. Emily, Emaleigh, Emmalee, and Emilie, harbingers of doom. They were more important to me than I realized.

Today seems to be picking up speed. I feel like I'm tripping and tipping toward a looming finish line and I can barely keep up with what's already happened.

I grab a sweater for later and head upstairs, using the railing to haul myself up as my quads burn, then take up a spot by the grill, where my father makes stilted conversation with neighbors and his former coworkers as they trickle in.

"Hey, Brooklyn!" Raj shouts from the downstairs patch of lawn. He's carrying a case of beer with a box of twenty-four doughnuts balanced on top. "Come on down. Kailey is around here somewhere."

"She's hot," he mouths at me, and grins.

"In a few," I yell back.

"That kid," Dad mutters as he glowers in Raj's direction, "does a lot of drugs."

"Not that many. Weed, mostly."

He scowls at the marinated chicken thighs on the grill. "Hand me a couple of patties, will you?" I dutifully pass them over. The burgers sizzle with the delicious smell of summer, but I'm still not hungry. The voices from the crowd in the yard and on the deck blend together to create a homogenous rumble, and it feels like I'm drifting away, tethered to the scene by an unspooling thread.

Behind me, someone clears their throat. I snap back to myself and turn around. Henry is holding a bottle of wine and a bouquet of peonies and daisies. By the way he's shifting on his feet and trying to rub the back of his neck, despite the bottle of wine clenched in his fist, it's clear he's nervous.

"It's you," I say, stupidly. My father looks up from where he's brooding over grilled pineapple and pins Henry with a dad-esque stare.

Henry flushes. "Is it okay? I know you didn't answer my calls, but Grace said I should come with them. Her and Alisha. Last-ditch effort to clear the air. I can leave, if you'd rather." He gestures to the sliding kitchen door with the hand holding the flowers.

"Just you?" I ask.

He nods.

"Stay."

Relief floods his eyes. "For your mom," Henry says, gesturing with the bouquet. "Wine is for you."

"Brooklyn should get both," my dad says, right before he jabs me in the back with the barbecue tongs. I hope he used the clean end.

"Henry, this is my dad, David." They shake hands firmly. My father appears to be calculating Henry's propensity for violence now that he knows it can come with handsome, intelligent faces. He raises an eyebrow at me as if to ask, "He's good?" I nod, and my father releases Henry's hand, which had been turning white.

"You keep an eye on her this evening," Dad says. "Don't let her out of your sight." He's gone from oblivious to mama bear in the span of an afternoon.

"No problem." Henry shoots me confused look.

I don't argue that I can take care of myself. I haven't been. Instead, I tuck my arm through Henry's to drag him away.

"Serious guy. What's going on?" he says, as I pull him through the empty kitchen.

"That is a long story for another day," I say. I have enough to process emotionally without reliving the day in the few minutes we have before we join the party.

As soon as we're in the upstairs hallway, Henry sets the flowers and wine on a narrow table that usually holds keys and the contents of my mother's emptied purse. Awkwardness floats in the air between us.

Well, what the heck. I'm wearing Honesty, Honestly lipstick and I've been spewing my feelings all day. My heart's not beating. My best friend is never coming home. Secrets are worming their way into the world. I may as well go all in. Risk it.

"Kashvi?" I ask. Whatever I tell him next depends on what he says about Kashvi and how I feel about that. How I feel about him.

Henry exhales and squares his shoulders. "I took a long, ruthless look at my future and who is in it and why. I asked her to move out. Or said I would. We're still deciding. She's been staying at her parents. I guess I had to learn, again, that sometimes I need to reevaluate my life and make new choices."

"It's hard to lose people, even for the right reasons," I say.

"I lost her a long time ago," Henry says. "I hung onto her out of habit. I couldn't admit that she changed, and what I needed, wanted, wasn't her anymore. She didn't need or want me anymore either. Not as much as she wants to be a doctor, anyway."

Our eyes meet nervously and then skid away. I stuff my face in my hands and stifle a giggle. The bad, always mixed up with the good.

"I wanted to tell you in person," Henry says. "I thought you were furious at me and never wanted to see me again, which I deserved. I was hoping you'd give me one more chance. Either way, it was time to let Kashvi go."

"Do you still love her?" I ask, peering up at him.

I want to be with someone who is free to love me.

"Not anymore," Henry says, after he takes the time to think. "I'll miss her sometimes. And who we were, when we first got together. I'll miss the good old days, I guess. The idea of what they were."

"I miss Penny, and she's gone. For good." My eyes fill up. "I lost her a long time ago too, but I couldn't admit it either."

"I'm so sorry, Brookie. So sorry."

Henry opens his arms, and I step into them. He holds me up while I take several deep, shuddering breaths. Hurt swims in my body, but Penny was right. I've been grieving since she stepped on that airplane last summer, before I knew she wasn't coming back. Longer, even. Since the Penny from my childhood and teenage years turned into an unfamiliar adult.

"Let's find Grace and Alisha, drink margaritas, and make fun of the guests," I say. I wipe my face with my palms and pull away.

"And complain about our bosses," Henry says, and he runs his fingers down my arm to find my hand.

"Deal. But I don't have a boss. I got fired."

Henry slings an arm around my shoulders. "I didn't like the doughnuts anyway. I never ate them."

"What?"

"I brought them to work and left them in the lunchroom. I liked *you*."

I giggle at the absurdity of a man who hates doughnuts, a woman from a doughnut shop who doesn't have a heartbeat, and the impossibility of life. How do any of us survive it?

Henry pulls me closer, and this time when his lips brush mine it's just the two of us. We take our time heading outside.

"There you are," Grace shouts as we step into the backyard, which is teeming with people and the heavy scent of coconut-banana sunblock. I wave at a few familiar faces, and Kailey, who waves back with her red Solo cup and laughs at something Raj says. I'm glad to see her—Kailey and I *are* friends, even if it doesn't look like what Penny and I had. It's something new.

Grace rushes over and herds Henry and I to a corner of the backyard where Alisha is sitting on a blanket.

"I don't know what's in those margaritas, but they're strong." Grace is at her most gregarious.

"She's already had two," Alisha says. She looks relaxed with her legs sprawled out in front of her and her back propped up on the tree that used to have a tire swing dangling from its branches. I join both women on the picnic blanket, which is partially out of view of the rest of the party.

"She's a little drunk," I say.

"It's summer," Alisha responds. "She quits drinking when the rain starts. Did your mom invite the whole neighborhood?" More people are pouring in the back gate and onto the deck where the barbecue is. Trees cast shadows on the lawn, and people congregate in the sunny spots. It's obvious who's been at the beach earlier—they're lobster colored and look drained.

"No, but it usually shows up. We end up with leftovers no one admits to bringing and more alcohol than we bought. My mom pretends it annoys her, but she lives for it."

"Maybe you should eat something," Henry says to Grace, as he looks pointedly at her brimming cup.

"Off you go then. I want a burger. Beef. Not chicken. The works."

Henry shoots me a worried glance. "David said…"

I look around. Spencer isn't around, and Dad is visible from where we're sitting. The food table, covered in a blue Hawaiian print cloth, is only a few feet away.

"It'll be fine," I say. He nods and leans down to press his lips against my temple.

"He dumped her," Grace announces in a stage whisper once Henry is at the buffet.

"He mentioned it."

"Now what?"

A thrill rushes through me. Now what? As much as I'd love to jump up and down squealing, I still have serious problems. Out of the corner of my eye, I catch Emaleigh darting by. In my bedroom window, Emilie is wearing my favorite shift dress and texting on her phone. Emmalee pulls a beer from the cooler and waves at me. Emily is sprawled in a lawn chair. When she catches my eye, she taps on her watch with a worried look. I blink, and they're gone.

I shrug at Grace as if to say "Who knows?"

Deader is my general direction. Is it fair to get involved with Henry when I could keel over any moment? Should I be making plans? Doubt creeps in.

A voice cuts through the boisterous conversations and party chaos. It slices through the pouring of drinks, the sizzle of food, the laughter. Spencer's voice. I've lost sight of Henry, who was cornered by Raj and the other vultures around the food, and look up at the upper sundeck. I catch my dad's eye, and he slams down his beer and the plate of meat he's holding and races into the house. Spencer saunters over.

"Mom says you two had a little fight today," he says. "You shouldn't upset her before the party. You know how she gets."

"I know," I say, cautiously. I inch away from Grace and Alisha, trying to put some distance between them and my brother.

Grace manages to straighten up. "Who's this?"

"Spencer," I say. "Brother." There's a glint in his eye, the one that promises trouble.

"Who are they?" he says to me. I hurry through their names, still searching the crowd for my father and for Henry. From the ground, all I can see are unfamiliar legs and feet.

"Henry's friends," Spencer states.

Spencer is well-informed. I spare a second of worry for Kashvi. Someone, maybe Henry, needs to encourage her to stay away from Spencer. I'll warn her myself, given the chance.

Spencer scopes the partygoers. "Henry here?"

"Yes," I say, weakly.

"I invited Kashvi, along with some friends from school," Spencer says. "She might pop by later." He stands over us and casts a shadow across our laps. He's coiled tightly, ready to strike, and his eyes don't leave mine. He doesn't blink.

Alisha seems to realize the atmosphere has darkened and tugs Grace and me closer to her.

"Might be awkward for you if Kashvi shows up," Spencer says, his gaze still trained on me. "You should take off early. Wouldn't want you to get in the way."

Alisha mouths, "What the fuck?"

Spencer crouches and puts his hand on my upper neck. I don't make a peep as he twists the skin of my nape between his thumb and index finger. Alisha pales.

"Why would you invite Kashvi? Henry broke up with her," Grace says, alcohol making her slow to catch on to the ratcheting panic on Alisha's face and the fear I'm sure is plastered on mine.

"For my stupid sister?"

"Okay, man, this isn't acceptable," Alisha says. She stands up. She's only had one beer and is considerably more sober than Grace—and I've been drinking Grace's margarita, under the guise of slowing her down.

Spencer leers closer. "I'll say whatever the fuck I want." He's openly disdainful because Alisha and Grace mean nothing to him. They don't warrant behaving. He'll say, and do, whatever he wants. He only performs for authority—parents, teachers.

Humiliation breaks over me, but from the expressions on Alisha and Grace's faces, Spencer is the one they're judging. They look like they want to rip his face off his skull.

"You should leave," Alisha says. "Right now."

"No, bitch. This is my house. You can head out, though." Spencer smiles his Jokeresque grin, and I shudder.

"She can stay." My dad has joined us, and his expression is bleak. Henry comes up behind him.

Spencer straightens up and brushes off his T-shirt. "Hey, Dad. How's the meat? Need to me to check it?"

"No, son." His voice cracks on the word. "I need you to leave. Right now."

"What do you mean? I just got here. I need to make the rounds." Spencer grins, genuinely, and claps my father on the shoulder.

My father closes his eyes. "Spencer. It's time for you to go. We'll talk later."

My father is trying to spare my mother a scene. He doesn't know that Spencer thrives on the edge of almost. *Almost* getting caught, leaving a mark that *almost* can't be explained. Spencer believes he can escape unscathed, that my mother will fish him out of trouble, make excuses for him, and smooth things over so that he can rinse and repeat later.

"He called Brooklyn stupid. I think he's threatening us," Alisha pipes up. I make a slashing motion across my throat with my hand, but she just shakes her head.

"It has to come out," she says, her voice brimming with compassion and the message that she knew what Spencer was in an instant.

"Sorry, who are you again?" Spencer asks, mildly, charm fully restored. He turns to face our father. "Dad. Come on. I would never say that about Brookie."

My father deflates at the lie. "I wish I could believe you. It would be easier than believing I raised a man who would call his sister stupid. It would be easier than believing you abuse her. I'd much rather believe Brooklyn's the liar. She's not, though. Is she?"

Henry slips past my father and wraps an arm around me. We're all on our feet now, standing in a tense tableau. Even Grace, who's swaying despite the firm grip Alisha has on her.

"Right," Spencer says, dragging out the vowel and casting a glance over his shoulder. "Where's Mom?"

"She's not going to be able to help you this time," my father says. "If you leave now, we can all talk later. When there are no guests."

Spencer starts to fidget. He spots our mother at the same time I do and hollers at her to come over.

"Sweetie," she says, rushing over and giving him a hug. "I didn't see you come in."

She turns and looks at the rest of us, her smile deteriorating as she takes in our strained faces. Henry's mouth is a thin line, and there's a muscle jumping in his jaw. The arm around my waist shakes as his past collides with my present. I shoot a pleading look at Grace, who grabs his other hand. She must know about his stepfather.

"What's going on?" Mom asks.

"I've asked Spencer to leave," my father says in a measured voice. "We'll discuss what's going on in a few days, when I've calmed down and am less likely to beat the crap out of him."

"David!"

"Helen, he hurts our daughter. Our baby girl. He's been doing it for years."

"One time, he accidently hit her one time, years ago, and he's never done it since." She turns to Spencer for validation. He's smirking, pleased Mom has sided with him. He wipes it off as soon as she looks at him and nods seriously.

"I learned my lesson," he says. "Never did it again."

"Brookie?" my father rasps.

I breathe in. Exhale. Take in Grace and Alisha's faces, the support written there. I absorb the strength from Henry's arm around me, and wrap myself in Penny belief. In my father's. I find my courage, remembering Emaleigh's. I am not alone.

"Every injury I've ever had, except the sprained ankle this summer, was from Spencer," I say. Out loud. In front of witnesses. Who knows what will be devoured and what will withstand it? "It was him. Always him."

Spencer's blasé expression falters. My father's breath catches. The momentary blip in Spencer's façade forces my father to abandon any fragment of hope that maybe Spencer can be redeemed, that maybe I had misunderstood after all. Love, family, fear—these things are no longer in the right places. Then again, they never really were.

My mother purses her lips and bobs her head between me, Spencer, and my father, trying to decide where her loyalties lie. Who to believe. Uncertainty sits on her face.

Spencer decides for all of us. He lunges, like a cornered animal does, at the threat. Which is me. He grabs a fistful of hair. My scalp is on fire, searing like the untended barbecue upstairs. I yelp and try to yank free, automatically slipping into flight mode.

It's Grace, despite her drunkenness, who unfreezes first. She knees Spencer in the dick and he goes down.

My mother finds her voice, but Dad doesn't let her use it. She had her chance—chances—to speak up for me and didn't.

"Helen, get him out of here. I don't want to hear any excuses for him. Or you. Not now, not ever."

Then he staggers over to the food table. My mother bundles Spencer off before my father returns, her face tight and worried. Spencer projects vulnerability and confusion and he murmurs, "I have no idea what Brookie is talking about," as they walk past me, nearly grazing my shoulder in their hurry to get away. He should have taken drama instead of biology in school.

My father comes back to our little group with a full pitcher of margaritas and a stack of red cups, which he fills and passes out to the group. He shakes Grace's hand vigorously during introductions. He pats me on the shoulder or arm whenever I'm within reach.

The party ebbs and flows around us, but guests give us a wide berth. We must look wild-eyed and overwrought.

I feel as though a clamp has been removed from an organ or a limb and I can suddenly stand tall and breathe again. People believed me. Penny, my father, Henry, Grace, and Alisha. Without hesitation, without asking me to explain. Their trust curls around me protectively. My mother doesn't try to talk to us, although I see her from time to time, flitting among the friends, wiping up spills, and refilling empty chip bowls and coolers. My father, who's getting drunker every round thanks to generous beverage serving sizes, keeps his back to her, as if he always knows where she is.

Henry presses a kiss into my hair. "You could have told me."

"I didn't know how to let the words out," I whisper. "They spent years buried inside me."

The party dissolves as the sky darkens—purple, then blue, then black velvet. Neighbors offer goodbyes and walk home.

Alisha calls a cab and hauls Grace to her feet. Henry stumbles into the vehicle with them, all of them cackling and teasing. I wave until I can't see the car anymore.

I stare at the house I grew up in. Its lines are as familiar as my limbs. The front steps, where Penny and I once ate an entire pie crust, avoiding the sludgy filling. The downstairs picture window, which I broke with an out-of-control baseball. The lawn, where my mother set up the sprinkler that Spencer and I ran through on hot summer days, until he pushed me and I fell face-first on it and broke a tooth. Home. The place where I dreamed about my future, and lived in terror of the present, and hid from the past. Some of the stories I've carried need a rewrite. A rewrite means there can be a different ending.

I feel pressure on my shoulder, a hand that belongs to someone no one else can see. It could be any of the Emilys. It could be Penny. I don't turn around, and after a few moments and a light, encouraging squeeze, the weight is gone.

A light goes out in my parents' bedroom. Another goes out in my dad's office. Tipped folding chairs are scattered on the lawn, and a few garbage bags sit half full. People will drop by over the next few days to pick up forgotten blankets and dishes. They'll tell my mother what a great party it was.

It was a great party.

CHAPTER 28

I t's stuffy in the basement, which was closed tight during the party. I shed my shoes and socks and yank the bedspread off the mattress. Back outside, I place the blanket on the patch of grass next to the fountain and lie down, then roll myself up burrito style. Moisture from the lawn seeps into my back. I stare at the handful of stars I can make out—the brightest ones in the sky that manage to make it past the light pollution. Their brilliance starts light years away and travels long after they've gone supernova. I'm staring at the past. It's possible to put distance between now and then, to travel beyond one's beginnings.

"It's time," Emmalee says.

"In or out," Emilie says.

"Face the music," Emily says.

"I wouldn't have made it this far without you," I say. They got me talking, thinking, and up and out the door. They were there when no one was. They reminded me that everyone is a mess, and it's okay to be a mess. As long as you're honest about it.

"We're going to go. You don't need us anymore," Emaleigh says, firmly. "You know what to do."

The clues have been there all along.

Penny's voice in my head: "Be brave."

Bravery has a price. Letting go. Accepting what has been. What is. Being honest about my feelings, about myself and what I want out of my life, instead of shoving everything into the trapdoor in my brain and doing my best to forget. Feeling is the worst.

Being honest is hard. Necessary. But not feeling? That's a death sentence. My poor heart and deteriorating body.

There's a raw wound in my heart, and it aches instead of beats.

On a breath, the barriers crumble and I release everything I've shut away. My heart bleeds; it pours out grief, hurt, pain, laughter, joy, regret, love, reverence, and every moment since birth into my veins, organs, and cells, which creak and stretch. I've hidden my sadness, suffering, and want so deeply that it wakes like an animal from winter hibernation, blinking sleepily before bursting from its secret spot and into the sunlight with a roar and bared teeth. Hungry.

I grieve the loss of my childhood friend, and the woman I will never truly get to know.

I mourn the relationship I will never have with my brother, who's a violent stranger bound to me only by blood and fear.

I unbury the rage I have toward my mother, who failed me so completely and didn't do the one thing she should have: kept me safe.

I rail at the bosses who quashed me.

I mourn the time spent pursuing careers and interests that weren't mine.

I wallow in regret about contorting myself to fit the expectations of people like Kyle, Marshall, Lawrence Junior, and Todd.

I shriek from the desperation of it all. I howl to the heavens. The night around me remains still and silent while I thrash and rage. There's nothing but my anguish and my body and soul, bloody and pulped under the inky black heavens.

The stars whirl above my head at dizzying speeds, and my life flashes before me: my mother in her work clothes, tying my shoes; my father's beaming face when I graduated university; Penny heaving a fist into the air, her mouth open in a battle cry; Kailey chucking a doughnut at Matt's retreating back and squeezing me hard; Grace and Alisha holding each other up; Henry smiling at me like I matter. And me, moving like a ghost through every moment.

Given a second chance, I will stand up. Speak up. Figure out who I am under everyone else's expectations, demands, and limits. I'll live. Even when it's hard. I've survived this much.

Is it enough?

My chest carves in two as my heart expands and retracts, ripping and shredding, as agonizing as shattering a leg bone or breaking a wrist. I would know. Heartbeats stumble and trip and try to align. My heart thunders faster and faster, like a panic attack on steroids and bulletproof coffee. I can't breathe as white-hot fire spreads through my body, wrenching through my arteries, bringing feeling and warmth to my limbs, bringing sensation to every atrophied inch.

I scream as my heart bursts open.

— — —

"Brookie. Why are you sleeping on the lawn?"

I blink up at my father, who's backlit by morning sun and standing over me with two coffee mugs. My clothes and the blanket are soaked through, but my skin is warm. My hand drifts to my heart. It thumps under my fingertips.

"It worked," I whisper. My skin's warm and blood is moving through my veins. It's glorious. Perfect. Everything is brighter than it's been in months.

"Brookie?"

I lurch to my feet. I suck in deep breaths of the cool, damp air. It tastes like honeysuckle and coffee and everything good. My body hums with energy. I could run a couple miles. I *want* to run a couple miles.

"Henry's not here, is he?" my father says, frowning and looking around as though Henry might pop out from behind the boxwoods.

"No. He went home with Grace and Alisha. You waved goodbye." I squint at my dad, whose face is tinged green. "You all right?"

My father shrugs. "I haven't had that much tequila in a long time," he says, and hands me one of the coffee mugs. He rights a few folding chairs, and I lower myself into a seat across from him.

The whole world seems to sparkle and gleam—maybe because I'm really looking around me for the first time in years.

"I like that Grace girl. Woman, I mean," my dad says as he settles into his spot. "She's got spunk. She's like you and Penny that way."

Spunk. Dad thinks I've got spunk. Penny's name causes a stab of misery. I let it linger. No more pretending the things that hurt don't exist. Penny's loss will sit with me, and I'll let it.

"Just us this morning?" I ask.

"I asked Helen to go stay with her sister for a few weeks. I need some time, and you need a break. After that, I don't know." Dad shakes his head. "I used to think I understood how things worked. Bridges. Buildings. Structures. The basic tenants of society and the world. Not everything, mind you. I'll never understand how people can watch so many cat videos, and you kids were mystifying when you were teenagers. But I thought, no matter how crazy the world was, that I understood our family." He sighs. "I thought I knew your mother."

His face is wreathed in sorrow. I muzzle the impulse to apologize. His suffering isn't mine to atone for. We never had the family he thought existed. It was a fantasy, bought with my silence.

I take a cautious sip of the coffee. It tastes bitter, rich, and delicious. I sigh contentedly. Then my stomach rumbles so loudly it can be heard over the lawnmower starting up next door.

"I guess that's my cue," Henry says from behind me. My heart lurches and speeds up. As it should, when he appears. How totally normal. My mouth tugs upwards in a smile.

He holds out a bag, which I eye warily.

"Those had better not be doughnuts," I say. "I never want to see another doughnut as long as I live."

"That's a long time to give up doughnuts," Henry says.

I hope so. I promised Penny, and myself, as much time as I can get.

"Give it," I say, and reach for the bag. I pull out an almond croissant and pass the rest of the baked goodies back. "Find a chair."

The three of us sip our drinks as the neighborhood wakes up. Car doors slam, and the trampoline two doors down squeaks, and someone calls for their dog. Comforting sounds. Sounds that make a life. Henry makes my dad laugh while he holds my hand, fingers intertwined tight. The morning air is cool and fragrant with fresh cut grass. There have been losses—my mother, Penny, a career—and gains—my father, Henry, friends. A more honest life—one that's really mine. Good, endlessly mixed up with the bad. All of it is more than I could have imagined in the hopeless-ness of June.

It's clear from the way the watery morning light falls across the backyard that summer is fading. Fall, more change, is around the corner. Everything needs to die to come back. I press a fin-ger to my neck. There's a steady thrum under my skin. Solid, pur-poseful. Alive. I'm here.

ACKNOWLEDGMENTS

Surprisingly few doughnuts were harmed in the writing of this book.

I used to write acknowledgments in my head so I wouldn't forget anyone, but now that I'm writing them down for real, the stakes seem very high.

Nothing truly happens in a vacuum, not even writing a book, even though it feels like you are alone in the universe and your book will never be more than a jumble of words only you've read.

Thank you Haley Casey from Creative Media Agency who believed in *Brooklyn Thomas Isn't Here* from the outset and had such great ideas and feedback. Your plot and character problem solving and instincts are spot on and always made it better. Paige Wheeler, also from CMA, thank you for your early encouraging words. They kept me going.

Working with my kind and thoughtful editor Adriana Senior and the team at Post Hill Press has made the publishing process feel easy. I bet it will never feel easy again, but it has been a treat.

My incredible writing partners—Lindsay Foran and Steffany Marynovska. I regularly think about how you'd each do something and then do my best to write like that. Your voices are in my head. Jen Sookfong Lee from the SFU Writer's Studio, thank you for bringing us together, and mentoring our projects.

I also had some patient beta readers: Colby Spencer, Elizabeth Jarrard, and Stephanie Braconnier who all suffered through a draft riddled with nonsense. Thank you for your time—I know how valuable it is and I didn't take it for granted.

Crystal Purvis—knowing that out there is someone who has the same childhood memories and experiences I do is a relief. I can write about friendship because of you.

I'm lucky to have friends who have been there for me for decades (yikes) and who always supported my dream to write a book (books). Joscelyne Yu and Jessica Zuk, I feel like I grew up with you and I'm so grateful to have two such smart, hardworking, and talented women in my life. Thank you for listening to me go on, and on and on.

The Whistler Writers Festival's incredible team, especially Rebecca Wood Barrett and Stella Harvey, have been an inspiration. The festival is one of the most welcoming spaces I've ever stepped foot in. Thanks for letting me be such a part of it.

My parents Beulah and Gary Vail decided early on that our house would be mostly TV free. Thank you for ensuring I'd turn into a little bookworm and that I'd find the things I love to do most in life: read and write books.

All the women I've worked with—there are less of you than there should be (thanks patriarchy!) Your stories are important and I remember them when I sit down to write about workplaces and the things that happen in them. I sometimes joke that no one can hear me when I talk in meetings, but I don't mean you. Extra high-fives (no touching) to Rosalyn Bowen, Justine Yu, Melissa Taylor, June Liu, Shahad Rashid, and Heather Stoutenburg for demonstrating every day how to be a badass at work.

I'm going to be the person who thanks the dog, Shermy, because he's a very good boy and gives excellent hugs, and we spend a lot of time together while I stare blankly at my computer.

There's one more. Byron Theriault. I can't tell you how much it meant to hear you say that I should bet on myself and that you believed in me. I wouldn't have made it this far without your endless faith and support. You can say I told you so now.

ABOUT THE AUTHOR

credit: Rob Trendiak

A lli Vail is a former journalist for national and provincial award-winning community newspapers. She is a content writer and marketer for literary festivals and nonprofits, and has worked in tech, video games, and politics. She's happy she's no longer the only woman in work meetings. She studied creative writing at Simon Fraser University.

Alli lives in Vancouver, Canada, with her anxious dog (who she wrote about for *The Globe and Mail*) and her partner.